Praise for

Barbara Metzger

"One of the freshest voices in the Regency genre."
—*Rave Reviews*

"Barbara Metzger deliciously mixes love and laughter."
—*Romantic Times*

"Metzger's prose absolutely tickles the funny bone."
—*L.A. Life Daily News*

A Suspicious Affair

and

An Angel for the Earl

Barbara Metzger

SIGNET
Published by New American Library, a division of
Penguin Putnam Inc., 375 Hudson Street,
New York, New York 10014, U.S.A.
Penguin Books Ltd, 80 Strand,
London WC2R 0RL, England
Penguin Books Australia Ltd, Ringwood,
Victoria, Australia
Penguin Books Canada Ltd, 10 Alcorn Avenue,
Toronto, Ontario, Canada M4V 3B2
Penguin Books (N.Z.) Ltd, 182–190 Wairau Road,
Auckland 10, New Zealand

Penguin Books Ltd, Registered Offices:
Harmondsworth, Middlesex, England

Published by Signet, an imprint of New American Library, a division of Penguin Putnam Inc. *A Suspicious Affair* and *An Angel for the Earl* were each orginally published by Fawcett Crest, a division of Ballantine Books.

First Signet Printing, December 2002
10 9 8 7 6 5 4 3 2 1

Printed in the United States of America

A Suspicious Affair

To Elaine Noel Edel, Madame Journet.
I wish I had known better, earlier.

Chapter One

"Facts is facts," quoth the Bow Street Runner. "They don't change for nobody, not even a duke." Mr. Jeremiah Dimm ("That's my name, not my brain") unbuttoned his red vest and leaned back in his stuffed chair, official ledger, pads, and pencil on the table next to him. He sighed once in contentment when his son poured another bucket of hot water into the basin in which the officer's aching feet were splayed. Then he sighed again and took his good luck piece out of the vest's pocket. The lad had to be taught right, if he was ever to be a successful thief-taker like his da.

"Now listen, Gabriel, facts is like this here rock." He dangled the stone from its string so Gabriel could see the streak of gold through it. "You can turn it this way and that, look at it from every side and every angle, and it's allus the same. You, me, everybody, we all see the same rock. That's a fact."

He held the stone in one beefy fist and let the string trail down. "Now, suspicions, they is like this string. Sneaky, snaky bastards a man can get to take on any shape. See, they can wrap theyselves around your facts a hundred different ways." He illustrated his point by twining the cord one way, then another around the rock, finally ending the lesson with the string tied in a square knot around the stone, like a package. "You got to make sure the supposition fits the facts."

Young Mr. Dimm hung on his father's words, even though he'd seen the demonstration countless times out of mind. Anxious to follow in his father's illustrious if aching footsteps, Gabe nodded eagerly. "Like the Denning case."

His father agreed. "Like the Denning case. It would be easy as pie to pin the thing on the duchess. Witness saw her at the scene, she admits having words with Denning, and lud knows there was motive. But."

Gabe leaned forward. "But it doesn't fit?"

The older Dimm reached out for his occurrence book. "It fits too neat, if you was to ask me. And there be a dozen different theories that fit just as well. Problem is, there just ain't enough facts to make any quick resolution to the case. His nibs ain't going to be happy."

"His nibs" being Mr. Dimm's boss at Bow Street, the officer consulted his notes again, looking for insight. What he had was deuced little to look at.

Late that November afternoon, Duchess Denning had received a note, directing Her Grace to the carriageway between Denning House, Portman Square, and its neighbor, Armbruster House. There Lady Denning had come upon her husband's closed carriage, whose door she opened to find the duke *in flagrante delicto*, as it were, with Lady Armbruster. The duchess declared her intention of retiring to the country to have her child, with the duke or without, and damn his eyes, while Lady Armbruster fled out the other side of the carriage. Both women's testimony agreed to that point. Then the duchess made her cumbersome way back to the ducal property, let herself in the side library door while the servants were at their supper, and retired to her bedchamber to start packing. Which was where her maid found her when the Watch banged on the door, after the driver returned, as ordered, to restore His Grace's carriage to the coach house in the mews.

So facts were as thin on the ground as hen's teeth. Mr. Dimm had the note, which had been delivered by an urchin, the Denning butler reported. He had Lady Armbruster's pantalettes from the closed carriage. He had a recently fired pistol, the mate of which was still in Lord Denning's desk, and he had one very dead duke.

Both of the women involved were unavailable for interviews by the time Officer Dimm was assigned the case. Lady Denning's physician had prescribed a heavy sedative immediately after the local constable took her deposition, and Lady Armbruster had dosed herself into laudanum-laced sleep after telling the constable what little she knew, between hysterical bouts of "I'm ruined, I'm ruined."

She sure as Hades wouldn't be getting any invites to Almack's, if Mr. Dimm knew the ways of the ton, which he did, as much as any working man could, which was why his nibs had given Dimm the case.

If he could not question two of the people most directly involved in the crime, Mr. Dimm could at least spend profitable hours querying the employees, the neighbors, and the residents of both houses, and both Their Graces' associates and relations. Which he did, traipsing across the raw London landscape from servants' halls to gentlemen's clubs, from ladies' parlors to taverns, gathering blisters and gossip. He didn't find any witnesses to the crime or any more pertinent evidence, but he did get enough information to compile a list of suspects three pages long in his daybook, with every motive that ever existed for murder, and nary an alibi that could hold water. The only surprising thing he found from his investigations was that Lord Arvid Pendenning, Duke of Denning, had lived this long without someone killing the dastard ages ago.

If Jeremiah Dimm had the handling of the thing, all those suspects would be gathered up and hauled off to little cells in Bow Street and held there until one of them sweated out a confession or a valid accusation. But his nibs had vetoed that idea. Bow Street's funding would be slashed if the nobility found themselves treated like common criminals. Handle the toffs like lambkins, he'd ordered Jeremiah Dimm. Don't make the scandal any worse than it is, he'd commanded. Don't offend the innocent or the influential. But solve the bloody case, and do it quick!

So Jeremiah Dimm tracked down all his other likely prospects, besides the sleeping ladies, that is, taking notes well into the night. That was how, for once, he found his crowded little house on Hill Street in Kensington blessedly quiet of chatter and squabbles and cooking clatter. He lit a clay pipe and sighed again. A man could enjoy peaceful times by the fireside like this, if he didn't have so much else on his mind, and swollen ankles.

With smoke rising from the pipe, the Runner read through his notes. He had started with the servants at Denning House, interrupting their celebrations at the duke's demise. If ever there was a loose screw, His Grace was it. Extravagant in his own pleasures, Denning was a cheeseparing tyrant with his household. He was vicious and abusive to the men and not above taking liberties with the women. He was often in his cups, frequently violent, and capricious both in dismissals and paying earned wages. Of course, they had all claimed, conditions were much better since Her Grace had arrived three years ago. Half of the staff refused to believe such a kind, courteous female could commit ruthless murder; the other half thought she was justified, especially in her condition.

Dimm had no real suspicions of the servants. For one thing, there had not been a dismissal in a year, and the most disgruntled had left voluntarily for other positions, not the nubbing cheat. Life was bearable under the duchess, and good jobs were hard to find. Besides, they were all accounted for at the approximate hour of the crime, having early supper in the belowstairs dining room. The only ones missing were the chef and his two assistants, who were starting preparations for the family's dinner, and Her Grace's woman and the duke's man. Having helped her mistress from her bath and onto her couch for a rest, the maid, Eleanor Tyson, was in the ironing room, pressing the gown the duchess would wear to dinner. As Tyson noted, Her Grace's condition required a great deal of fabric to be ironed. Tyson usually ate later, while the family sat to dinner. Purvis, the valet, was laying out the duke's evening clothes while waiting his turn to smooth out any creases in the duke's neckcloths. But one of the footmen had placed his finger alongside his nose. Purvis, it seemed, was sweet on Tyson, and took any excuse to share her company. Good for them. Dimm shrugged and turned the page.

The servants, even those who staunchly maintained their mistress's innocence, admitted that the ducal marriage was less than ideal. Miss Marisol Laughton had accepted the dissolute duke in her come-out Season because her family was at *point non plus*, and he promised relief. Arvid, Lord Denning, had taken a bride almost twenty years his junior because she was a Diamond and he needed an heir. He hadn't come through with the commission for her brother or the annuity for her aunt; she hadn't conceived for nearly three years. Neither got what they expected, and the servants agreed Lady Denning got the worst of the deal. Her Grace's maid reluctantly revealed the use of the hare's foot to cover up bruises on Her Grace's fair skin, although those occasions were blessedly less numerous once Lady Denning was known to be awaiting a blessed event. Arguments between husband and wife grew more frequent, however, as the duchess's time grew near.

From the lofty butler to the lowest scullery maid, every member of the Portman Square staff knew Her Grace wished to leave for the family seat in Berkshire, to ready the nursery, to breathe healthy country air. And everyone in the house had heard the duke bellow that he wasn't about to give up any part of the Season for some puling female. Women gave birth in the streets of London's slums, he'd roared once from the sidewalk; his wife could damn well spawn in the luxury of Denning House. No one in all of Portman Square, and therefore in all of London, could think this was a love match. But would a lady, a lady moreover who was in an interesting condition, seven-and-a-half-months interesting to be exact, commit cold-blooded murder? Or even warm-blooded, finding him in the arms of another woman?

Your typical crime of passion? The jealous spouse? Inspector Dimm sucked on his pipe stem. He doubted it. The jury'd be like to suspend sentence in the case anyway, if Her Grace's undoubtedly expensive barristers earned their fees by claiming temporary insanity. The duchess's mind was obviously disordered by the pregnancy. Everyone knew breeding women came over queer sometimes. Jeremiah Dimm had seen his own calm and quiet Cherry grow attics-to-let when her time got near. He added a big question mark next to Duchess Denning's name and turned the page.

Now Lady Armbruster could have committed any number of emotional acts, judging from the constable's report and the servants' grapevine. She was nigh unintelligible with hysteria—and that was before she was informed that her lover was dead. What if she'd gone back to the carriage after the duchess left and discovered that Denning was indeed leaving her to follow his wife into Berkshire? Her reputation, what there was of it, was ruined, and all for nothing. Hell hath no fury like a you-know-what, Dimm muttered to himself, Gabriel having fallen asleep on the sofa.

Lady Nerissa Armbruster could only be a suspect if the murder weapon were already in the coach. Not even a gentry mort in the throes of unrequited love could be expected to creep into her lover's house, steal his pistol, and shoot him with it, not when her own husband's dueling Mantons were close at hand. Dimm made a note to check with the coachman in the morning. If they'd been driving out of London near Hampstead or through the City and its stews, the nob was like to have his barker with him. This meant that anyone could have come, argued with the duke, struggled with him for possession of the weapon, and run off after the shot was fired. But his rings, purse, and diamond stickpin were all found with the duke, so Dimm was ready to discount the casual robber.

Not so Lord Armbruster. The jealous husband arrives at Portman Square to see his raving wife running through the hedges with her slippers in her hand, shrieking of her fall from grace. On the other side of the hedges, His Grace is buttoning his trousers. Lord Armbruster grabs up the pistol and shoots his rival in the heart.

Dimm nodded. He liked the scenario. But what about the note to Lady Denning? And what about Lord Armbruster's claim that if he shot every man Lady Armbruster slept with, the House of Lords would be an echo chamber for octogenarians? Then again, Lord Armbruster hadn't offered a convincing explanation for his own whereabouts at the time, only that he was visiting with a friend. Dimm bribed his lordship's butler to find the location of Armbruster's love nest, rather than threatening the peer. The Runner made a notation in his expense book, hoping his nibs was happy. No one was at Armbruster's hideaway in Half Moon Street, not even a servant to bribe with the governor's money. Dimm made another entry on tomorrow's list, under *Lady A.* and *the widow* and *the pistol.*

If Lady Armbruster's husband hadn't flown into a jealous rage and defended his lady's honor with a bullet, perhaps someone had sought to avenge the duchess's disgrace, someone like Lady Denning's hotheaded scapegrace of a younger brother. At age twenty, Foster Laughton still hadn't mastered his adolescent humors nor found a channel for his energies. The army would have settled him nicely, Dimm reflected, but the boy hadn't been given the chance to make a man. Left destitute and landless by his father's ill-advised investments, the young marquis lived on a pittance and at his brother-in-law's sufferance. It was no secret belowstairs at Denning House that the duke had kept the youth dangling in London without the wherewithal to amuse himself like other sprigs of the nobility. So Foster got into trouble, associated with riffraff, and chafed at his sister's scrimping on her dress allowance to pay his bills. Denied his patrimony, cheated of his army career when he came of age, and forced to watch his sister's degradation, how much abuse could a young man's pride take? Not much, it seemed, as Dimm had found for himself that very evening.

"How dare you?" the youngster had blustered, threatening the older man with his riding crop. His handsome face an angry red, Foster had raged on: "I might have an empty title, but I still have my honor. I'll have you know I wanted to call the blackguard out any time these past three years for what he's done to my sister. I even did once, but he only laughed at me. Marisol forbade me to challenge him again."

"Dueling's illegal," the peace officer had felt obliged to point out.

Foster made a rude noise. "Yes, and I'd be forced to flee the country if I managed to kill the maw-worm. Marisol reminded me of that, too, and how distraught she'd be without me. And then she reminded me that Denning's a crack shot who killed two men before she met him. She'd be even more distraught over that, so she had my word of honor." He looked away in disgust, beating the crop against his pant leg. "Word of a gentleman."

"So if you couldn't fight an honorable duel . . . ?" Dimm had prompted.

"I prayed some other poor bastard would do it for me. I did *not* shoot an unarmed man in a closed carriage, no matter how much I hated him."

Dimm tended to believe the young toff's high-minded attitude toward honor. But the volatile marquis could have argued with the duke, Dimm reasoned, threatened him with that whip until Denning pulled his own weapon. Another struggle over the hair-triggered pistol, the same dead duke. The young fool's own words even put him riding back to the mews from the park at just the right time. Alone.

"So you think your sister did him in?" Dimm had asked just to see the young man's reaction, after wisely taking a step out of range.

"Damn you to hell!" Foster snapped the whip in half in his hands and tossed both parts to the ground at the Runner's feet. "My sister is a lady, besides being one of the kindest, most generous females in all of London, and I don't care if you're the Lord High Magistrate himself, you shan't say otherwise in my presence. Why, she married that villain just to save me from debtors' prison."

"And he reneged on his promises."

"And that's enough to convict her? I promise you this, you put my sister on trial—you even charge her with such a crime—and I'll confess to killing the bastard. I followed him and Lady Armbruster home from the park, ran inside where I knew he kept his pistols, waited for my sister to leave, then shot him. You cannot charge two people with the same crime. I'll be more convincing."

Dimm underlined his notation about finding if Denning had the pistol with him in the carriage. Then he tapped out his pipe, got up, and toweled off his feet. He padded over and threw a blanket over Gabriel, hoping his own boy never felt such a need to prove his manhood, hoping, too, that Gabe would have such a brave, loyal heart if he did.

As he placed another log on the fire, Mr. Dimm wondered if the new widow could really be such a saint. According to her aunt, who was next on his list, Marisol Pendenning, *née* Laughton, was ready to be canonized. His Cherry, bless her soul, would never have stood for him raising his hand to her, much less him smiling at another woman. Not that Jeremiah ever would have done either, of course. But what kind of woman tolerated such abuse? Poor downtrodden wretches he saw every day, broken-spirited wraiths whose husbands considered them chattel. But ladies of the ton? Leading hostesses of the *beau monde* who held intellectual soirees? He shook his head. Perhaps Duchess Denning swallowed her own pride for the sake of a dependent younger brother and an impoverished old auntie. On the other hand, perhaps one day, this day, she happened to choke on that swallowed pride.

Chapter Two

Another log on the fire, another page in Officer Dimm's book, another suspect. Miss Theresa Laughton, spinster aunt to Foster and Marisol, was a lady of a certain age and a definite refinement. She even offered Dimm tea during their uncomfortable interview. Miss Laughton was also ready to confess to murder rather than see either of her chicks face charges. Of course, her hand was shaking so badly she could hardly hold her cup, and she frequently had to dab at her eyes with a tiny scrap of linen and lace.

"Not that I am crying for Denning, I hope you know," she'd confided to the Runner. "The man was a . . . a dirty dish. There, I've said it, even though one should not speak ill of the dead. Poor, poor Marisol."

"On account of Denning's being dead, or on account of her being one of the suspects in his murder?"

She rummaged through a work basket next to her and began stitching on a tiny knitted sweater. "What's that?"

"You said 'poor Marisol.' I wanted to know why."

"Because that awful man made her life such a hell, with his temper and his women and his nipfarthing ways. And now this awful scandal, just when the baby is coming, and the uncertainty of it all."

"What uncertainty might that be, ma'am?" Dimm wanted to know.

Aunt Tess waved a plump little hand around, trailing a skein of wool. "Oh, the settlements and things. Such a mess."

"Surely the widow is provided for?" He hadn't been to see Denning's man of business yet.

"What's that?"

"I said, Denning was known to be deep in the pocket. There cannot be any financial worries, can there?"

"Who's to say? The scoundrel had the terms of the marriage contract worded so that he agreed to 'provide' for us all, after paying Laughton's debts. Dear Foster was too young to understand, and Marisol was already making such a sacrifice for the rest of us, and I . . . well, I confess I have no head for business. The solicitor said there was so much money, not to worry. None of us ever saw a farthing of Denning's fortune. If dear Marisol ever complained that I was to have an annuity, Denning threatened to send me to a cottage in Wales. Provision enough, he said. And he withdrew Foster from university because the boy was a dunderhead anyway, he swore. I pray the Lord will provide for us now, for that sad excuse of a nobleman cannot be trusted to do so even from the grave."

"So you were entirely dependent on him?"

"What's that? Oh, the money. Yes, I cashed in my consols to give Marisol her Season. It was our only chance, you see." Miss Laughton set aside the knitting to wipe her eyes again. Then she squared her shoulders and raised her chin. "No matter if we are thrown on the parish, I am glad the duke is dead.

So you can put the manacles on me now, Mr. Dimm."

"Uh, Miss Laughton, do you know how to fire a pistol?"

"Of course I do. You aim the round part away from you and pull the little metal thing where your finger goes."

Dimm rubbed his chin. "And where did you say you were that hour or two before dinner?"

"Why, right here, in this little back parlor. Denning never comes near it, don't you know, but it has the prettiest view of the gardens."

Dimm opened the drapes, which were pulled for the night. He could see the roof of the stable complex, but not the alleyway. "Did you see anyone running through the gardens? Anyone suspicious loitering about or acting oddly?"

"Oh no, I was working on my knitting. The baby is coming soon, you know."

"Then did you hear anything? Quarrels, carriage doors slamming, gunshots?"

"What's that?"

So much for Lady Denning's family. Dimm relighted his pipe from a spill at the hearth, thinking of Gabe's brothers and sisters sleeping upstairs, all the nieces and nephews in nooks, cousins and inlaws nigh to bursting the rafters of this little house in Kensington. There was that huge Denning mansion, the ballroom bigger than Dimm's whole place, yard and all, for just four people. And one of them was dead. Dimm puffed and sighed, and went back to his notes.

The duke wasn't much for family either, it seemed. His mother was fixed in Berkshire, two married sisters lived in Wales and Scotland, and the only brother had rooms at the Albany.

Dimm had found Lord Boynton Pendenning there, trying out gray waistcoats, black arm bands, mourning boutonnieres.

"Such a decision, don't you know?" the pale, thin man had drawled, gesturing the Bow Street officer into his dressing room. "I mean, one wouldn't wish to appear the hypocrite, would one, with sackcloth and ashes? On the other hand, one must consider the proper degree of respect before paying a call on the grieving widow. Such a dilemma." He tied a black stock under the white cravat at his thin neck, then turned to ask his valet's opinion. "I tell you, I've been fretting over it ever since I heard the news."

Dimm blinked when the valet clapped his hands together in approval, but proceeded with his questions: "Where might that have been, milord—where you got the word of your brother's death?"

Pendenning waved a long-fingered, beringed hand. "Murder, you mean. The news is everywhere, don't you know. I suppose I was in some gaming hall or other; that's where I spend the afternoons. Before coming home to dress for the evening, of course."

"Mightn't you be a tad more specific, milord? Like, do you start dressing at four? Five? Six?"

"That depends entirely on the cards, my man. Let me think. Ah yes, the dice were cold at Pimstoke's, so I went on to the Pitpat." Dimm noted that Lord Boynton named less reputable gaming parlors, where the stakes were often higher than at the gentlemen's clubs, the company less select, and the games often rigged.

"The cards were against me at Danver's place," his lordship continued.

"But you got lucky in the carriageway at Portman Square?"

Pendenning turned from the mirror. "What, pray, can you be insinuating? That *I* shot old Arvid?"

"Begging your pardon, milord, for being blunt, but word is you're pockets to let."

His lordship nodded without disturbing his carefully arranged curls. "Dressing properly is not an inexpensive hobby. Ask Prinny. Then again, gaming is not a steady income. I make no secret of either pastime."

"And greed do be a powerful motive in these here circumstances. Jealousy, too."

"What, jealous of Arvid's title? I never thought to step into m'father's shoes. Heavy old things, no sense of fashion, don't you know. I do admit the fortune is more tempting. But think, my good man. Why would I wait this long to do in old Arvid? Everyone knew we were at loggerheads since childhood. He never shared his toys, not even back then. It was no shock that he could never see his way clear to increasing my allowance now. Or make the occasional loan, not old Arvid."

"Then you two brothers were not close?"

"About as close as two gamecocks in a pit. He was a bastard, may my dear mother forgive me for the slur to her virtue. Still, I could have arranged for highwaymen, you know, or thugs to follow him home one night any time these past ten, fifteen years that I've been on the town and up River Tick. There are any number of ways to succeed to a title."

"Without getting your own hands dirty."

"*Naturellement non*, my dear sir. But again, I ask, why would I do the thing now?"

"Pressing debts he wouldn't honor?"

"But my so-charming sister-in-law has a pressing date with the *accoucheur*, as my loving brother delighted in reminding me. M'brother's heir is even now supplanting me from the womb."

"The babe could be a girl."

"With my luck? Not even I am laying money on that bet."

Next Dimm had trekked up and down St. James's to the men's clubs. His big toe started throbbing again just at the thought. He'd been going from White's to Brooks's to Boodle's, chatting up the various doormen and majordomos, trying to locate any of the recently deceased's friends. He'd have found the lost continent of Atlantis sooner.

Arvid Pendenning was one unpopular bloke. If he wasn't a shade too lucky at the tables, he was a mite too familiar with wives and daughters. He was arrogant, rude, or downright cruel to anyone below his rank, anyone less deadly with a pistol, or anyone unfortunate enough to play cards with him. Most club members seemed amazed the killer had managed to get a pistol ball into his heart, so small and shriveled that organ must have been.

Wagering in the betting books was heavily in the duchess's favor, if you could call it a favor to be the one considered most likely to hang for the crime. The bucks were already calling her the Coach Widow, drinking toasts to her aim. There was even, in one club, talk of taking up a collection to hire Her Grace the finest lawyer in the land in return for the favor she'd done them all. Boynton Pendenning ran a distant second in the race to the gibbet in the betting book, with young Foster Laughton trailing badly. It was the long shot, however, who caught the Runner's attention.

One gambler had put his money, a considerable sum, too, on Carlinn Kimberly, Earl Kimbrough. Dimm whistled. The Elusive Earl, they called Kimbrough, because he rarely came to Town, never took part in ton gatherings when he did, and refused to be feted as one of the past heroes of the Peninsular campaign. He'd sold out, what? Three, four years ago, Dimm recollected, when he came into the title. Then Kimbrough seemed to disappear from the gossip columns as well as the dispatches. Now, it seemed, the earl had traveled to London for the express purpose of confronting the Duke of Denning about a parcel of land that separated their Berkshire properties. By all reports this confrontation was acrimonious, *ad hominem*, and an education in the high art of name-calling without issuing a challenge.

"Absentee landlord" degenerated into "leech," "lecher," and "boil on the butt of humanity." "Bumpkin" became "manuremind" and "mold spore that should crawl back under its rock."

Kimbrough outright refused to duel, not when men were dying for better causes in Spain. He announced this right there at White's, looking down from his greater height into the duke's empurpled face. And Denning, according to the waiter on duty two nights ago, was fully mindful of the earl's reputation as being one of the cavalry's finest swordsmen. He was not about to throw down the gauntlet and let Kimbrough have choice of weapon. With footmen hovering, the proprietor wringing his hands, and wagers being entered in the book as fast as ink could flow, the two men nearly came to cuffs. Then Kimbrough stormed off, muttering curses that would have made his troopers proud.

He was still cursing when Officer Dimm had tracked him down at Pulteney's Hotel, just a few hours ago.

"Of course I heard about the bastard getting caught with his pants down. I'm sure everyone in London has heard by now. That's all the people here do anyway, isn't it—snicker and snort like pigs at the trough, then go repeat their filth to the next hog on line?"

The army lost a good officer when Kimbrough resigned, Dimm reflected, and society had gained an Original. Loud, forceful, a man of action, he was impatient with the claptrap of the polite world. As Dimm's dear Cherry would have said, may the angels bear her company, the earl was also a fine broth of a man. Big, broad, well muscled, and with a healthy tan, he had hands that were callused with honest labor. His eyes were a dark brown that looked through pretension, piercing eyes that, by force of will alone, would not miss their mark.

"Well, happen I'm here, milord, mind if I asks a few questions?"

"Of course not. You are only doing your job." Kimbrough stopped his pacing and took a seat, indicating his caller should do likewise. He lit a cheroot, after Dimm refused one. "But I'm afraid I cannot be of much help. I never even met the jade."

"The, ah, jade?"

"The duchess. The Coach Widow. Black widow, more like."

"Then you are convinced Her Grace was the perpetrator?" Dimm took out his pad and licked the point of his pencil. "My sore feet bless you for whatever evidence you have."

"Evidence? I have no evidence. I told you, I never had two words with the woman."

"You mean you didn't see her bring the gun out of Denning House, or hear the gunshot? I thought you must of called there to continue your argle-bargle with Denning and seen something."

Kimbrough stubbed out his cheroot onto a saucer. "Why would I call on Denning when he flat out refused to sell me the land the night before? The man's as hardheaded as a jackass and as useless to have an intelligent discussion with."

Dimm closed his notebook. "Then why, begging your pardon, milord, if you weren't there and you don't know the woman, are you so sure she killed the duke?"

"Because I know her kind. Spoiled, feted by the ton, society's darling has to give up her own empty pleasures to bear the son of a bitch an heir. Then she goes off her looks and the duke strays. So she blows a hole through him, figuring that if she cries incompetence or some thing, she'll have all the money, all the power, and none of the inconvenience of a husband."

Dimm scratched his head. "A mite hard on her, don't you think? A' course, I ain't met Her Grace yet myself. How does it happen that you don't know her, being neighbors and all?"

"I was in the Peninsula during her come-out Season and in mourning at the time of the marriage. I chose not to accept Denning's invitations the first time they spent Christmas at Denning Castle, so I suppose she dropped me from her list. I doubt she spent a month of her marriage in the country altogether. When I am in London on business, you can be assured I do not frequent the routs and revels where the likes of Duchess Denning will be found."

"Hmm. Well, can you tell me about that piece of land that Denning wouldn't sell?"

"What do you want to know? How Denning rechanneled a stream through the property line, changing the boundaries? How the new stream overflows its banks every hard rain and destroys my tenants' crops, or how their old wells go dry in the summer? Or perhaps you want to hear how I offered to buy the blasted land that should be mine by rights, and the limb of Satan refused. I came to London to try again, so work could be done over the winter before the spring rains. I have men with no income, and jobs that need doing, such as getting that deuced stream back to its proper flow, damn him. May he rot in Hell."

"He most likely will, from all I hear. Ah, one more question, milord, then I'll let you get back to your pacing. Uh, packing. The clerk downstairs didn't happen to notice your comings and goings this afternoon. Could you tell me where you might of been a few hours before dinner?"

"A few hours before—Devil take you, too, you long-nosed snoop!" Kimbrough rose and stomped to the door, flinging it back on its hinges with a loud slam. "Get out before I boot you out. I'm a bloody magistrate, you clunch, an ex-officer of the King's army, for heaven's sake, and a peer of the realm, for what that's worth. I wouldn't kill even that misbegotten maggot over a soggy acre or two!"

Jeremiah stood and shuffled toward the door. "I ain't the only one with a suspicious mind, so to speak. They have a bet on you at White's."

"You mean I'm part of this bumblebroth? Hell and tarnation!" The earl smashed his fist against the door, making a substantial dent in the heavy wood. "Blast! That's just what I despise most about this town. They've nothing else to do but ruin reputations and stir up scandals. Scandal's just what I wanted to avoid, with a young sister to fire off soon."

"Denning never made advances to that sister, did he?"

"I wouldn't have let that rotter within a mile of Bettina. And no, I never dallied with Lady Armbruster either. Damn your eyes, I didn't kill Denning, but I sure as hell might rearrange your nose for you if you're not out of my sight at the count of five!"

Jeremiah was gone by the earl's barked "Three." Alone in his little parlor except for the soft sounds of his son's breathing, it occurred to Dimm that his lordship never had explained where he was at the time of the murder. The devil was in it now. He'd have to go back and ask that question tomorrow, too. Dimm wrote *Kimbrough* at the bottom of his list. Maybe the earl would be gone by the time he got to it.

Jeremiah yawned. He should go up to bed, with tomorrow like to be another long day. But his bed was cold and lonely since Cherry had passed on, may she rest in peace, and his thoughts were all of her up there. Snugged in his chair downstairs he could keep mulling the Denning case. Gor'blimey, all those suspects, motives, and theories, and not a one of them feeling like a good fit. Something was missing, if he could just put his finger on it. He picked up his charm and dangled the rock on its string until the stone fell to the floor with a clatter that startled him awake. “Old fool,” he muttered, “putting yourself to sleep like that German quack.”

He sat up, wide awake. That was it: putting himself to sleep. The duke could have killed his own self! His nibs would love it!

Chapter Three

"Suicide? That's the most ridiculous idea yet," the grieving widow declared. "Arvid was too mean to do us all such a great favor."

Duchess Denning had agreed to meet with the representative of Bow Street at eleven that morning. She was reclining on a couch in a parlor done in the Oriental motif. Jeremiah felt an unaccustomed stab of envy—not for the vast reaches of the gilded chamber, nor the thick carpets, priceless vases and lacquer-work cabinets, but that the lady had her feet up on dragon-crested cushions, a blanket tossed over.

"Doctor's orders," she'd apologized for not rising to greet him at the door. "Swelling, don't you know."

He did indeed, and not just from his Cherry's five pregnancies, God keep her soul.

The duchess was going on: "Besides, what possible reason could Arvid have for taking his own life?"

Dimm looked around again at the opulence of the room, the pretty young wife big with child, and wondered himself. Her Grace was understandably haggard, her face drained of color by the black shawl over her shoulders, and her pale hair pulled back in a loose, untidy knot, but he could see the fine cheekbones beneath the added weight, the fine blue eyes. Yes, she must have been a Diamond of the first water, but there was something even more attractive about a woman in her condition. To his way of thinking, at any rate. That duke was more of a fool than he thought. Dimm cleared his throat and consulted his notes.

The coachman had earlier given his considered opinion that the duke habitually took a pistol along when he was involved in dalliance, which was to say most times he called for the closed carriage. Suchamany angry husbands and irate fathers had been scared off by the sight of that very same pistol, the driver swore. The butler confirmed the coachman's testimony. So the weapon was likely in the deceased's possession, not brought to the scene by someone else. "It's only a possibility, Your Grace. Another avenue what needs to be explored, that the deceased ended his own life because of the scandal over his discovered affair."

"You cannot have done your homework, Mr. Dimm, if you honestly believe my late husband gave a thought to public censure, before or after he acted."

Dimm nodded. That was what everyone said. "Still, there be reasons what are less obvious sometimes. Like His Grace's health might have been failing. Or mayhaps he suffered financial losses no one knew about yet."

The duchess merely raised an expressive eyebrow. Dimm had to admit his brilliant notion was not quite so convincing by the light of day. The duke's secretary refused to hand over his late employer's books and bank statements, not without a writ of investigation, but the figure he gave, just a rough estimate, the cully claimed, was more than

Jeremiah Dimm would see if he snabbled every crook on every reward poster from here to kingdom come. By about a hundred times. And the mortician who was laying out the body upstairs found nothing amiss with the duke's physical remains, except a great gaping hole in the chest, of course.

" 'E was tuppin' 'is ladybird, wasn't 'e? An' 'is own wife's breedin'. Can't say that sounds like a fellow about to stick 'is spoon in the wall."

Dimm couldn't say it either. He did have to make one last, feeble effort at solving the case with the minimum of inconvenience to any of the other highborn suspects. "Maybe he got remorse."

"And maybe pigs will fly," the duchess replied. "Besides, suicides cannot be buried in consecrated ground. What would you have me do, lay the Duke of Denning in a corner hay field? Arvid *is* going to Berkshire to be placed in his family's crypt alongside his father. My aunt is already having palpitations of the heart over spending another night with Arvid there upstairs, so we are leaving tomorrow to get on with the thing, unless you either come up with a suicide note or a warrant for my arrest."

"Now, there be no call to—"

Marisol held up a hand. "No, I have heard all the rumors flying around. I even know the odds being wagered on my guilt or innocence. The servants are very good about that kind of thing, you know. I did order the newspapers burned so my aunt and brother need not read the scurrilous attacks in the gossip columns nor see the outrageous cartoons. But I do know I am your likeliest prospect." She tossed back her head in a haughty gesture that only served to disorder her hair more. "And I do not care. Do you understand, Mr. Dimm? I do not care what anyone says. I am going home to have this child. That's all I ever wanted."

"Home being . . . ?"

"Oh, not my home. That's been sold off ages ago, if you are afraid I'll escape your clutches in the wilds of Lancashire. I'm going to Denning Castle, in Berkshire, where Pendenning children have been born for centuries."

"I understood you hardly ever visited there."

"That was Arvid's choice. He hated the country, disliked having to give up the pleasures of Town life, the high-stakes gambling and the high-flyers."

"And you, ma'am? You like the country? Begging your pardon for asking so many questions, Your Grace. It's me job, you ken."

Marisol nodded her understanding. "Berkshire is beautiful. All rolling hills and trees, flowers and farms. I loved it at first sight. I never lived in a city until my presentation and my marriage, you see."

"Yet you adapted something wondrous," Dimm noted, recalling what he'd heard about her triumphal Season, her standing among the hostesses of the *haut monde*.

"I was raised in the country, Mr. Dimm, not in a stable. My father might have been improvident; he was still every inch a gentleman. My mother's family could trace their ancestors to William the Conqueror."

So could Dimm's. His forebears were the chaps carrying all the gear and picking up after the horses. "I meant no offense, Your Grace. Just wondered why, if you liked the country so much, you made your home here in Town."

"You didn't know Arvid. I told you, he found the country dull. And he liked having me near him, he said, so he refused to let me live apart. He forbade the servants to help me, and they would have suffered terribly if I had disobeyed."

"Jealous type, was he?"

"Of me?" She looked down at her ungainly figure. "I am not quite the goddess to inspire passion, am I?" Marisol stopped to think a moment. "No, Arvid was more possessive than jealous. At first I believed he saw me as an ornament, part of his collection of *objets d'art*. Then I became an asset to the smooth running of his household. Recently . . . ?" She shrugged. "Recently he was just more perverse. He knew I wanted to be gone from London. That was enough to make him decide to stay."

"So you argued." That was a statement, not a question.

"So we argued," she acknowledged.

"And were you jealous of him?"

"Of his affairs, you mean? Of his birds of paradise and his opera dancers and Lady Armbruster? Why don't you simply come out and ask if I killed him, Mr. Dimm?"

"Because his nibs at Bow Street says that ain't the way to handle duchesses, Your Grace. But since you was the one what mentioned it, did you shoot the duke when you discovered him in the carriage with your next-door neighbor?"

"No, Mr. Dimm. I did not. I was no more jealous of Nessie Armbruster than I was of Harriet Wilson. My husband was a known womanizer when I married him, and a constant philanderer later. It never mattered before. It certainly never mattered after. In fact, I was more than happy when he took his attentions elsewhere."

"I see," said Jeremiah Dimm, wishing he'd never embarked on this line of questioning. For that matter, he wished he'd been given the Carstair case instead. What was a simple ax-murder or two compared to this mare's nest? No wonder all those newspaper chaps were camping in Portman Square. He wiped his suddenly damp forehead and took up a new line of inquiry. "Do you have any idea who sent that note, Your Grace? Might be that whoever wanted you to find your husband in the carriage meant to throw suspicion your way."

"No, I have no notion whatsoever. The butler said an urchin brought it, and no one had any reason to detain him at the time."

"And you don't recognize the hand?" Dimm held out the folded sheet.

Marisol took the letter reluctantly, as one might take a worm meant for fishing bait. She dutifully reread the message and studied the writing. "No, I'm sorry, it's unfamiliar to me. The script does look feminine, though a bit crude, as if disguised."

"You think it could of been one of your friends, passing on unpleasant news?"

"My so-called friends have never hesitated before about keeping me informed of Arvid's little peccadillos. They usually gave me the news to my face over tea, mixing a little spite with the sugar."

"But it must have been someone as knew you'd be home."

She shrugged. "That wouldn't be hard to surmise. A woman in my condition hardly goes for curricle rides in the park at the fashionable hour."

Dimm took back the note, folded it carefully, and placed it securely in the inner pocket of his waistcoat. "Notice anything unusual about the message?" he asked.

"You mean how the person misspelled *lying*? *Your husband is lieing, with a lady in the carriage alley*," she quoted from memory. "I remember wondering if he was lying there injured, telling a falsehood, or carrying on some liaison. Knowing Arvid, I guessed correctly, it turned out. Either my correspondent is a poor speller or undecided which crime was worse."

"As in some other woman altogether he might have promised the moon?"

Marisol shook her head. "I'm sure I do not know the latest *on dits* concerning Arvid's affairs. He could have had any number of mistresses. What he might have promised them besides money is beyond my imagination." She removed a ring from the chain around her neck. "I already had this, for all the joy it brought me. Even if my fingers were too swollen to wear it."

The duchess looked about to weep. Dimm hurried on: "So you went outside, even though it was a biting raw day and you had to go down that fiercesome tall stairwell in the hallway, then out and acrost the lawns. How come, Your Grace, if you didn't care?"

"I didn't go down for the confirmation. I went because I wanted something. I didn't think even Arvid could deny my request to leave for the country when he himself was found so much at fault."

"Were you surprised that the female was Lady Armbruster?"

"A bit, since I had thought we were by way of being friends, but her reputation was none too steady."

"Neither were her nerves, it seems, shrieking and carrying on like a banshee."

"Yes, I wondered why she was so distraught, once I had time to think. Surely she must have known I'd never have bandied her name around, but dallying with a married man in his own driveway had to be a chancy thing at best."

"Do you think she came back to the carriage after you left, and shot Arvid? The duke, that is. No disrespect, ma'am."

"I wouldn't have thought she could hold the pistol steady enough, the way she was carrying on when she ran away. But why would she have shot her own lover? Even as high-strung as Nessie is, she must have known that couldn't stop the gossip. I'm afraid I cannot explain her actions. You'll just have to ask her yourself."

Dimm scratched his head with the pencil. "Now that'd be a fancy piece of investigation, even for Bow Street's finest. I suppose you didn't hear all the news making the servants' grapevine after all. Lady Armbruster got up last night and took herself another dose of laudanum, then another, and another. She'll be pleading her case at the pearly gates, not Old Bailey."

Marisol gasped and clutched at her chest. Dimm leaped to his feet, ready to race for the bell pull.

"No, no," she said, halting him in mid-wince, "I am all right. Just let me catch my breath a moment."

Dimm was all apologies for breaking the news to her that way. "Deuce take it, I should of known better. Are you sure I can't call for your woman or your aunt?"

"Aunt Tess is prostrate with the vapors already. I'd not have her disturbed with more ill-tidings. And Tyson is busy with the packing. Heavens, I cannot decide which is harder to comprehend: Nerissa Armbruster taking her own life . . . or killing herself over Arvid, of all things."

"If you don't mind, Your Grace, could you answer a few more questions?"

"Certainly, Mr. Dimm, if you think it will help. Be sure I'd like to find my husband's murderer as much as you."

The Runner consulted his book. "What do you think of Lord Armbruster?"

"As a dance partner or as a killer? No, please forgive my levity, sir. I am just a trifle addled right now. Perhaps a sip of Madeira, if you'd be so kind to pour." She indicated a decanter and glasses on the Chinese fan table. "And please join me."

When Dimm was reseated, thin-stemmed crystal goblet gingerly in hand, the young duchess gave her opinion of her next-door neighbor. He'd always seemed a courteous, soft-spoken gentleman when they'd met socially, she said. Of an age with Arvid, he had a much more refined air about him, making Nessie's preference for Arvid even harder to believe. Marisol had an even harder time picturing Lord Armbruster in a rage, shooting a fellow nobleman. "Doesn't he have an alibi? That's what you look for, isn't it?"

Dimm consulted his pages again. "Well, he does and he doesn't. He says he was visiting a friend, but he ain't giving up the friend's name. We located his pied-á-terre—that's a love nest, don't you know—but no one in the neighborhood seems to recall who meets him there."

"Obviously a lady whose husband is less tolerant than Lord Armbruster. But there, if he was meeting his own light-of-love, what complaint could he have with Nessie? Not enough, surely, to murder her paramour. If he feared a cuckoo bird in his nest, he'd have done better to shoot his wife, if divorce was too distasteful."

Dimm drew circles with his pencil. "Stap me if I'll ever understand the gentry and their ways. Don't none of them keep to their vows?"

"I did, sir," Marisol answered with that touch of arrogance he was coming to recognize as the duchess on her uppers. She might be of an age with his daughter Sarah and friendly-like to a nobody like Jeremiah Dimm, but she was a lady through and through, right down to that steel in her backbone and that slightly long, straight nose in the air.

"Begging your pardon, Your Grace. You just seem powerful casual about Denning's lapses, and Armbruster's, too."

"And why not? It's the way of the world."

"That's what I mean, Your Grace. It's not the way of *my* world, not by half."

"Are you married, Mr. Dimm?"

"I was for twenty-two blessed years, until the good Lord saw fit to take my Cherry, and I never strayed onct."

"What, never?" she asked in disbelief.

"Never even thought on it, or my name isn't Jeremiah Dimm. I loved her too much to want any other woman."

"Then your Cherry was a very lucky woman, sir, to have you, and you were a lucky man to have the luxury of marrying where your heart desired. I suppose we are different, those of us considered more fortunate, for we have to wed for title and property, wealth and position. I would it were otherwise," she said with a new bitterness in her voice. "I do envy you your good fortune."

"I don't know how fortunate I am after all. Don't suppose I'd miss her so now, iffen I'd loved her the less."

"I am sorry. I did not mean to bring up sad memories. Who else is on your list of suspects? Besides my brother and myself, of course. I know Foster's name is being broadcast, but he is a right one, as the gentlemen say, although regrettably hot-to-hand. We needn't even discuss him."

The Prince Regent couldn't of done it better, Dimm decided to himself. Only thing was, the more pride she showed, the less likely he was to believe she put up with that blighter's behavior. He'd have to think on it later. "If not *your* brother, Your Grace, what about the duke's?"

"What, Boynton Pendenning? The man is a fribble. An expensive fribble, granted, who was constantly arguing with Arvid over money, but to murder his own brother? I cannot believe it."

"Neither could Adam and Eve, most likely, but it happens. Jealousy, greed, ambition. One brother has the world on a string; the other brother has a rope necklace."

"But if Boynton was so eager to step into his brother's titles and vaults, why wait to murder Arvid now, when I could be carrying the heir?"

"That's just what he said. A' course, babies has been known to die in infancy."

Dimm almost bit his own tongue off when the duchess clutched her stomach. "My baby! Do you think my baby could be in danger? Please, I pray you, tell me no."

Dimm prayed he could, too, but no use lying to the poor thing. "Well, a girl will be safe enough," he reassured her, "and a boy will be, too, if you can think of anyone else besides the heir presumptive what might of ventilated the duke. Sorry, Your Grace," he said yet again when she turned a bit green at his choice of words. Lud, his nibs'd have Dimm's liver and lights for this day's work. "Anyone at all."

"Why couldn't it just have been a passing thief seeing easy pickings in an empty coach until he saw Arvid still inside? Or someone he cheated at cards? He did, you know, even when we played piquet. He couldn't stand to lose. I just want it to be a stranger, someone I don't know and won't have to fear is hiding behind every bush. Not a neighbor or an in-law."

"Speaking of neighbors, how well do you know the Earl of Kimbrough?"

"The Elusive Earl? Not at all. Goodness, never say he is a suspect? When I said a stranger, I meant a nameless footpad, a faceless cardsharp, not someone whose name is a byword both here and in Berkshire."

"He had an argument at White's with the duke the night before the murder. A real loud brouhaha, they say."

"All of Arvid's arguments were loud. I daresay it was over that piece of property again?" At Dimm's grunted assent, Marisol explained: "I knew there was some bone of contention over the land, but Arvid never consulted me about business matters or anything of that nature. He simply forbade me to invite the earl to any of our parties the few times we were in Berkshire, so I never even got to meet the man. But the people in Berkshire think highly of him, and he was some kind of hero, wasn't he? And I understand he only comes to London to speak in Parliament on reform issues. That doesn't sound like a murderer to me."

"You never can tell. If there's one thing I've found in my years on the force, it's that every criminal is somebody's son or lover or mother or brother. There's a berserker in every one of us. One time or another."

Chapter Four

A berserker? Boynton Pendenning? Arvid's brother certainly did not look like some blood-crazed fiend, not in his cheek-high shirt collars, nipped-in waist, and padded-out shoulders. He looked like a middle-aged dandy, laughable or ludicrous—not dangerous. Then Marisol looked more closely, at the lines of dissipation around her brother-in-law's thin mouth, the pouchy gathers under his deep-set eyes, the unhealthy pallor to his indoor skin. Suddenly Boynton wasn't just an amusing rattle. He was also a hardened gamester, always a short jump ahead of his creditors, like his friend the Prince, a man who lived—or died—by his wits. He could have been desperate enough for fratricide, gambling on not being caught, gambling on coming into Arvid's legacy by hook or by crook.

Marisol's hand shook when Boynton brought it to his mouth in greeting. She'd had to permit him to call, of course, since she had been unable to receive him last night. They had to discuss arrangements for the funeral, the makeup of a cortege to transport Arvid back to Berkshire, the provisions that might be needed for the reception following interment, and a score of other details Marisol felt Boynton should decide, since he might well be the next duke. She clutched her shawl more closely to her at the thought, and wished she hadn't sent Inspector Dimm away with Arvid's secretary, Mr. Stallard, to inspect the contents of the safe. Dimm, she knew, was holding out a last hope of finding a suicide note. Marisol thought his chances were much better of finding a fistful of vouchers. Some unfortunate cardplayer whose chits Arvid held could have come to ask for an extension in payment. Arvid would never grant the poor soul more time, of course. There could have been an argument; the pistol might have gone off accidentally. And Boynton Pendenning could go back to being an amiable here-and-thereian.

Meanwhile, she was alone with him except for her aunt's little terrier. At least Max could be counted on to yap at any loud noise. Or soft noise, clatter of dishes, passing lorry. "How do you do, Boynton?" she asked, motioning him to the chair recently occupied by the man from Bow Street.

"Well enough under the circumstances, my dear," he answered. "Surviving m'great loss as bravely as can be expected." She could see his lip twitching and had to smile in return. At least Boynton wasn't going to offer her any fustian about being grief-stricken or shed crocodile tears for the brother he loathed.

"Yes, I can see you are bearing up well," she noted, while he preened for her inspection.

"You don't think the trailing black ribbons are too much, do you?" he asked in mock anxiety.

Marisol pretended to consider the matter carefully. "Why no, they add a certain flippancy to your otherwise somber elegance. Arvid would have hated them."

"I thought so, too," he said in self-congratulation, then he took out a jewel-handled quizzing glass and surveyed her in turn through the horridly enlarged eyeball he presented. "And you are looking as lovely as ever, my dear, despite that abysmal black thing around your shoulders, the slight puffiness I detect around your chins—ah, chin—and the windblown look to your hair. Oh, did I neglect to offer my condolences?"

"I believe you did, Boynton, but let's consider them said, shall we? And give over, do, Boynton. I don't need your Spanish coin. We both know I am looking sadly pulled."

"And who's to blame you, under the circumstances? But you still have that Madonna-like quality to you, the glow those painterly types try so hard to capture. I always knew m'brother had all the luck in the family. Then to find himself a beautiful, tolerant, fertile bride." He gave an exaggerated sigh, polishing his looking glass with a handkerchief edged in black lace. "Too bad Arvid never appreciated what he had."

"I never did understand why you never married, Boynton, especially if you hold such tender feelings about women. A wealthy young bride could have solved your financial difficulties and added comfort to your life."

"Ah, but I could never have tolerated a female more beautiful than myself, and looking at the phiz of an ugly wife every morning would only turn me off my kippers. There's no hope for it. I should just scoop you up right now and carry you off to Gretna Green."

"You and how many footmen?" she teased.

"Oh, at least three, I shouldn't wonder. Wouldn't want to strain the seams of my coat, don't you know. But just think, I could marry you out of hand, get the fortune, the title, the heir, and a charming life's companion, all in one throw of the dice! Ah, those wretched laws of consanguinity."

Marisol nodded in sympathy, if not in agreement. As if she'd ever give her life—and that of her child—

into the keeping of this jackanapes! She put her hands protectively over her swollen middle. "You might have it all soon enough anyway, mightn't you? The fortune and title, at any rate."

"If there is a god in heaven, ma'am, my niece will be as exquisite as her mother. That's what I pray every night."

"Before or after gaming, wenching, drinking to excess, and taking the name of the Lord in vain?"

"During, my dear, during. But seriously, Marisol, it's the devil of a coil, isn't it? The timing does leave all of us hanging."

Her Grace wished he'd chosen a more felicitous turn of phrase, but she had to sympathize with Boynton's quandary. "What do the solicitors say?"

"They won't say beans over there at Stenross, Stenross, and Dinkerly. Quiet as clams, those chaps. They say I'll have to wait for the reading of the will next week, like everyone else. Oh, they did mention all funeral costs and household expenses were to be covered until then, on your signature. Believe they were to meet with Arvid's secretary over the matter earlier this morning. I don't suppose proper mourning attire counts as a legitimate outlay, does it?" He picked a dog hair off his black superfine coat.

"I don't see why not," Marisol told him. "The Pendennings do have an image to maintain, to counter this awful, ah, embarrassment. Send your tailor's bill over; I'll sign it today before we leave. In fact, I think you might need two sets of mourning, since you'll be greeting all the neighbors at the church in my stead, and then again at the Castle."

He raised her hands and kissed the right, then the left, then the right again. "And I'll say a special prayer that my precious niece has her mother's generous heart. I'll just be toddling off, shall I, so I can have something ready by the funeral. I'll return later to settle any of those tiresome details you seem eager to thrust onto my shoulders, and I'll be sure to bring Weston's accounting."

"Why don't you come for luncheon? I have invited Mr. Dimm from Bow Street to take the meal with us when he is finished with Mr. Stallard. You might be able to help him decipher some of the names of Arvid's debtors."

Boynton raised his plucked brows. "A redbreast at the ducal table? My, my, how standards have flown in just a day. I'd be delighted to come, my dear, just to listen for Arvid gnashing his teeth upstairs. He does lie in the duke's chamber, doesn't he?"

"Yes, would you like to—"

Boynton held up a manicured hand. "No thank you, Your Grace, not before a meal." He took his leave then, but paused at the door and held up his quizzing glass again. "You really should do something with your hair before luncheon, especially if there will be strangers present. Image of the Pendennings, don't you know."

"Yes, I shall. But my head ached so this morning I couldn't let Tyson fuss with the curling irons. The hairpins seemed to be as heavy as horseshoes, but Arvid never did like me to leave my hair down. He thought it immature and undignified for a noblewoman of my position. He forbade me to wear it down my back, in fact," she concluded with a grin, tossing those diabolical hairpins this way and that until heavy blonde curls lay against her shoulders. She shook her head, sending the curls into luxurious, wanton disarray and causing the little terrier to set up a shrill yapping. "He really is gone, isn't he?"

Boynton just winked and went out the door.

Marisol sat back against the cushions. This was the first moment she'd had alone to think, without the numbing effects of the physician's possets, her brother's restless diatribes on Arvid's moral turpitude, or her aunt's fretting over what was to become of them if the child Marisol carried was a girl. The duchess laughed to find herself wondering whose prayers were more fervent, Aunt Tess's or Boynton's.

She didn't care which, boy or girl, just that this baby be healthy—and safe. No one could wish ill of a daughter, now that Arvid himself was gone. He'd have been furious, of course, to be cheated of his heir. He'd threatened often enough those first years of their marriage to cut her off without a farthing if she proved to be barren. But they would manage, Marisol swore. She, Aunt Tess, and the little girl could live in a cottage somewhere on the sale of Marisol's jewels, those that were not entailed, of course. Arvid had been intent on his duchess presenting the right impression to the ton; she had no say in their selection or when he took which piece from the vault for her to wear, but the gems were hers. If the income was not enough to purchase a pair of colors for Foster, she'd have to let him enlist as a common soldier. That was what he'd begged for this past year, when they both realized Arvid was not going to fulfill his promise. Serving on the line was more dangerous, and beneath the dignity of the Marquis of Laughton, but Foster was brave enough and dedicated enough to rise through the ranks on his own merits. Others had made their own successful careers this harder way. Foster would have to; Marisol vowed that she would not sell herself again.

Arvid was dead. She tried not to think of what he looked like when they carried him in, all the blood and gore. She recalled instead how he appeared when she first met him, an older, sophisticated man-about-town to her wide-eyed debutante naiveté. He offered a fortune, one of the highest positions in the land outside of royalty, and security—everything people told her she wanted in a husband. That wasn't quite all Marisol had wanted in a husband, in fact, but those same people told

Marisol she'd be a fool to look any further than the polished and poised duke.

He was patient, he was gratifyingly attentive, and she had no choice.

Why hadn't *they* told her he was arrogant and cruel, petty and dishonorable? Likely because she had no choice.

Arvid planned the wedding; Arvid selected her gown, her attendants, and her lady's maid. Marisol had not been permitted to make an important decision on her own since her "I do" in church three years ago, until her "I am going home" speech yesterday. And deciding to wear her hair loose today. No man would ever have that power over her again, she vowed. No man would demean her, abuse her, or threaten her family. Arvid really was dead.

Luncheon was a strained affair, and not just because of the empty chair at the head of the table. Arvid's brother took a step toward it, and Marisol's brother growled. Boynton inspected Foster's thrown-together ensemble and carelessly tied neckcloth through his quizzing glass and offered to recommend a tailor. At which Foster offered to rearrange Boynton's nose. At which Aunt Tess kicked her nephew under the table and hissed: "You gossoon, he might just be the next duke."

At which Marisol asked Mr. Dimm if he had any luck with the papers in the safe.

Jeremiah put down his spoon. Turtle soup, by George! Wait till he told his sister Cora. "You was right about them gaming slips, Your Grace. His Grace held vouchers from half the gentlemen in London, looks like. Thing is, most times a swell can't pay his bets he puts a hole through his own brain, not someone else's."

"That's called honor, my dear sir," Boynton drawled.

"How would you know?" Foster demanded from across the table.

"But you are going to investigate the names, aren't you?" Marisol wanted to know, *and* wanted to distract her two other male guests. Aunt Tess had recovered sufficiently from her nervous indisposition to join them for the meal, but she was too busy feeding Max tidbits under the table to be of much help, if she even heard.

Dimm swallowed a mouthful of something that looked like a tadpole swimming upstream through a sea of white paste. Not bad. He thought of the miles he'd have to cover to interview half the names on his list. Not good. "Yes, Your Grace, me or my associates will go have a chat with all of them. Except the prime minister, I reckon."

"Good grief, never tell me he owed Arvid money!"

Jeremiah nodded, scraping some thick sauce off the next dish so he could see what was beneath. Beef? Bedamned if the toffs didn't buy such cheap cuts of beef they had to hide it!

Meanwhile Foster was asking what was to become of those outstanding debts.

"If Arvid had owed anyone, the estate would be expected to pay," Boynton stated. "So the estate should collect," he added hopefully.

Remembering his own father's burgeoning obligations, passed down to him, Foster sneered. Before he could make a cutting remark, Marisol intervened again. "I'm sure the solicitors will tell us what is correct. I, for one, would be more than willing to forgive any debts."

"Might be for the best," Dimm commented, looking askance at the smallest little chicken he'd ever seen, set in a ring of peas and beans on the plate in front of him. He was supposed to get the meat off those tiny bones without picking the blasted thing up in his hands? Not in this lifetime! He pushed it aside and took up a forkful of vegetables, then noticed that they were all waiting for him to explain.

The Runner slid a deck of cards out of his pocket onto the table. "These was in the wall safe along with the jewels. Fuzzed."

"What's that?" Miss Laughton asked.

"Shaved, ma'am. It's a crooked deck. I ain't saying yes, and I ain't saying no, but those gambling wins might of been dishonorably come by."

Foster and Boynton were both eagerly reaching out for the deck. Marisol won, picking up the cards and handing them to the butler with instructions to see the things burned before they brought more dishonor to the house of Pendenning or Laughton. The butler handed the pack to the footman outside the door, who was the real winner, until he was caught out and stabbed by a very sore loser. But that was another story.

Marisol was discussing the coming journey, leaving Dimm in peace to enjoy the next course, until the footman whispered in his ear that he was supposed to dip his fingers, not drink the stuff.

"When you make the arrangements with the stables, Foster, figure on one less passenger. My maid Tyson has decided she'd rather stay on in London."

Dimm came to attention, missing the pastry tray altogether. "Kind of sudden like, ain't her decision?"

"Well, the whole move is rather sudden," said the duchess. "I admit to being a trifle discomfited by her timing, but I do understand Tyson's position. Her family is here in London, for one thing, and I really do not need a fancy dresser in my condition, for another. Tyson feels her talents would be wasted, what with the baby, and mourning, and country entertainments."

"Deuced disloyal, if you ask me," Foster grumbled.

"I do believe she has a *tendre* for Purvis, Arvid's man, and that's the real reason she wants to stay behind. There's no purpose for him to travel to

Berkshire, naturally. I said I would write them both recommendations."

"I still say it's dashed inconvenient and inconsiderate. I mean, there's no time to find a suitable replacement, and you should have a maid with you for the journey at least, in case you need anything."

"The trip to Berkshire cannot take long, even at the pace the physician insists I keep. And you forget, dearest, that Aunt Tess and I were used to doing for ourselves. We'll manage."

"Especially if you wear your hair in that charming new style," Boynton put in, drawing attention to the simple black ribbon keeping Marisol's long hair off her face. Foster looked thunderous, seeking the insult in the fop's words, but Marisol just smiled and went back to peeling an apple.

Gor'blimey, Dimm thought, it's a wonder they don't starve!

"I have the answer to the problem, dear," Miss Laughton addressed her niece, after feeding the terrier half a pork chop. A pork chop! Dimm griped to himself. Now where in hell did she come by an ordinary, unembellished pork chop? He felt like challenging the rugrat for it.

"Really, it's the perfect solution. You send a note next door and hire Lady Armbruster's abigail. Obviously she is looking for a position."

Marisol almost choked on a thin slice of cheese. "Really, Aunt Tess, I do not think I could be comfortable with my dead husband's dead mistress's maid bringing my chocolate in the mornings."

"Happens I have a daughter looking for work, Your Grace," Dimm offered, shoveling cheese and fruit onto his plate before the footman could remove the serving dish. "She used to be an apprentice seamstress but her eyes were going bad and her husband didn't want her working none. But he's off with the army now and she's lonely and bored. Might answer both problems."

"And it might get you an informant in the household," Marisol congratulated, raising her glass to him. "But since I have nothing to hide, it might serve. Send your daughter to me this afternoon and we'll see if we suit." She stood to leave the table. The men, perforce, stood. And the footmen cleared away the plates. Dimm sighed.

Chapter Five

A tart had fallen to the floor. Jeremiah beat the little dog to it and was munching the thing on his way out of Denning House. It was coming on to rain, naturally, so he paused in the doorway to raise the collar of his overcoat. He'd learned a lot this noontime, but not much of it having to do with the case.

He was trying to decide whether to go to Lincoln's Inn Fields to try to winkle the terms of the will out of Stenross, Stenross, and Dinkerly—as in who would have benefited most from the duke's passing—or to return to the gentlemen's clubs and start raising the hackles of half the nobs in town by discussing their gaming debts. Debts of honor, the nodcocks called them, and the toffs didn't usually pay them off with a ball of lead. Still, an investigator's job was to turn over every rock and see what crawled out. Jeremiah nodded. Had to remember to tell young Gabriel that one.

Then a horseman galloped up on a tall bay horse all flecked with mud, and drew to a halt in a splash of water. Likewise spattered, the rider dismounted, tossed the reins to a groom who ran out, and strode two at a time up the stairs to the covered entrance to Denning House, where Dimm was still standing.

"Have you found the killer?" the Earl of Kimbrough demanded when he saw the Runner in the doorway.

"No, milord, but I'm working on it."

"No, you are not, by Jupiter," his lordship snapped back. "You are standing around wasting time, eating sweets and trying to keep your toes dry. You would not last long in the army, mister, nor in my employ."

"No, sir," Dimm found himself murmuring, almost tempted to salute, except the rest of the tart was in his saluting hand, and he wasn't in the army anymore.

"Blast, then it's even more important I see the female. Here," he said, turning to the butler who had come to the door. The earl handed over a card, one corner carefully turned down to show he had called in person. "Tell Her Grace it is important that I see her."

"I am sorry, my lord, Her Grace is not receiving." The butler looked up, subtly trying to draw attention to the hatchments over the door, as if Kimbrough were unaware this was a house of mourning.

"Dash it, she has to see me! Tell her it's crucial. Tell her it's about her husband."

"Her Grace is resting, my lord. Perhaps you'd do better to discuss your information with Mr. Dimm here, who is handling the investigation."

The earl's curled lip spoke eloquently of his opinion of the Runner's investigation. "Just tell her I absolutely must see her."

When the butler moved off, shaking his head, Kimbrough paced the narrow hallway. "Blister it," he muttered, "she'll send back a polite refusal. A slight indisposition, dash it, or a headache. Yes, I'd wager on the headache. By Jupiter, the baggage is not going to put me off." He stormed down the hallway after the butler, dripping raindrops onto the Turkey runner.

Now Jeremiah Dimm would have given his eyeteeth to hear the conversation between these two folks what swore they never set their peepers on each other. He did the next best thing, giving some of his nibs's silver to the footman on duty in the hall. In exchange he was led to the room adjoining Her Grace's Chinese parlor. The connecting door wasn't too thick, the keyhole wasn't too low, and the bonbons in a little dish weren't too filling.

One day her husband was murdered, almost in his lover's arms. The next day her maid gave notice. What else could go wrong?

"Carlinn, Lord Kimbrough, requests an audience, Your Grace. Pardon me for disturbing your rest, Your Grace, but he insists it is—"

"He insists it is a matter of life and death," an angry voice bellowed from directly behind the very upper servant.

The stately butler's face took on a pained expression, to be caught so derelict in his duty as to permit an unwanted guest to intrude on his mistress's privacy. Then he noted again the height and breadth of his lordship's imposing physique and the thunderous scowl on his dark visage. The butler beat a hasty, not-so-dignified retreat. His mistress's privacy be damned. She was leaving for the country tomorrow anyway. She'd find plenty of privacy among the cabbages and turnips.

Marisol looked up from her reclining position, and up some more. So this was Kimbrough. Indeed he was larger than life, just like the tales of his heroics. She thought he might have been attractive, had his thick brows not been furrowed and his mouth not been turned down in a frown of disapproval. He did not have Arvid's classic features or Boynton's elegance, of course, and certainly not Foster's boyish good looks, but, yes, he was handsome. Marisol was sure many a young girl would be sighing over that cleft chin, those intense brown eyes and weathered cheeks, did he show his phiz in Town. No wonder they called him the Elusive Earl. Debutantes and their mamas would be falling all over themselves to get to him if he participated in the Season.

Of course, Marisol herself did not appreciate such rugged features, such oversized virility. Nor did she appreciate mud on her Oriental carpet, nor being stared at so rudely. She struggled to a sitting position and cleared her throat.

Kimbrough jerked back to attention. Gads, for the first time in his life he wished he carried one of those foppish quizzing glasses to give the jade a set-down for her inspection of his person. He hadn't missed the curled lip at his muddied boots or the haughty lift to her eyebrow at his buckskins. Then she'd raised her nose—not the dainty little turned-up affair he admired in a female—as if he'd brought the smell of the stable in with him. Even if he had, she was an arrogant piece of goods with the bold look of a strumpet. Why, she was not the Diamond he'd been expecting at all. Her dress was less than elegant, and her blonde hair was loose like a wanton's. Of course, circumstances were such that lapses could be excused, and those sky blue eyes, he noted objectively, were undoubtedly her best feature.

What Carlinn couldn't tear his eyes from, however, what Marisol caught him guiltily absorbed in, was the sheer bulk of the duchess. Zounds, he'd seen dead cows in the hot Spanish sun less bloated. He hadn't realized she was this close to term or he might have reconsidered his approach. As it was, he was forced to apologize. "Forgive me for staring, Your Grace. I, ah . . ."

"Yes," she interrupted with a slight lift to the corners of her mouth. "I have never understood why they call it a delicate condition myself. As you can see, there is nothing whatsoever delicate about it."

Instead of smiling in return, Kimbrough frowned even more. He took a step closer, and Marisol reached for the bell on the table at her side. At his step, however, Max the terrier started barking and tearing around, snapping at the earl's scuffed boots.

"Hell and tarnation," Carlinn swore. He bent down, grabbed the dog, and lifted Max to eye level. All four feet paddling in the air as if one of the dragons from the Chinese tapestry had come to life and was breathing fire at his nubby little tail, Max whined. Marisol was about to demand the dog's release when Lord Kimbrough declared, "You, sir, are an embarrassment to the entire canine family. Now behave yourself or I shall lock you in one of those lacquered cabinets."

He lowered the dog and Max ran to hide under Marisol's skirts, trembling. "How dare you frighten my dog!" she exclaimed, forgetting for the moment that Max was actually Aunt Tess's pet and a nuisance to boot.

"A real dog wouldn't need to be frightened," he snapped back, "but it's all of a piece." He waved his arm around at the exotic furnishings, as if they met his standards as poorly as Max or Marisol herself. Well, she'd had enough. Enough of some angry gentleman forcing himself into her presence and then doing his best to intimidate her. By heaven, she was not going to permit this . . . this ruffian to frighten her.

"Get out, sirrah! I did not invite you, and I do not wish to see you. I demand you leave at once!"

"Not until I've had my say, I won't, so don't you get on your high horse with me, Duchess. It won't wash."

"How dare you! You barge into a lady's drawing room without permission—into a house of mourning, I might add—wearing mud and buckskins like some . . . some—"

"Country rustic? Gentleman farmer? Honest Berkshire landowner? I'm not surprised you cannot recognize the breed, ma'am."

"And I am not surprised you stay away from Town if these are your manners! How dare you come to my own house and insult me!"

"And how dare you involve me in your sordid little scandals? My family has never been tainted with such filth before and wouldn't be now, if not for you and the London rumor mills. Thank heaven my parents are not alive to see how low you and your kind have brought our good name. But what about my sister, Duchess? Have you considered anyone else in this? My sister will make her come-out next year, if her reputation is not already so besmirched by your scandal that no hostess will invite her anywhere and no man will offer for her."

Outraged, Marisol sputtered. "My? My scandal? I involved you? My husband was murdered, and you were the last person known to have words with him! You threatened him. Scores of witnesses heard you."

"Denning was a bounder."

"He was my husband!"

"My regrets, ma'am."

Marisol gasped. "Why, you— Here you are, spouting some fustian about finding your name in the muck, when you thrust yourself uninvited into the presence of an unchaperoned female. A recently unmarried female, I might add! For all I know you killed Arvid and you've come to continue your bloody path."

"Don't be absurd, Duchess. Not even gapeseeds from the hinterlands go around seducing or strangling pregnant women."

He looked as though he might wish to do the latter, though, so Marisol demanded, "Then why in the name of all that's holy *have* you come?"

Kimbrough drew a folded sheet of newsprint out of his inner pocket and tossed it down on the table beside Marisol. "I have come because of this," he said with a snarl, "and a demand that you insist they print a retraction."

The man was mad, Marisol decided, as she unfolded the paper. That was all there was for it; he was a Bedlamite. That he thought she could get a journal to issue an apology for a scandalous cartoon proved it. The drawing showed the interior of a coach where an *enceinte* woman and a large gentleman both held pistols on an entwined couple on the opposite seat. The caption read: "After you, my dear."

"This?" Marisol asked in disbelief. "This is what has you so up in the boughs? It's not even a good likeness."

"Devil take the likeness! I don't even know you, ma'am, and I resent being pictured with you in this filthy thing. You must go— No, you can write the newspaper at once, demanding they recant."

"What, after you walked past that platoon of journalists on the street outside? Or were you so burning with righteous indignation that you did not notice the ragtag group out there with sharpened pencils? Shall I parade down to Fleet Street and sob to an editor that I don't count any large gentlemen among my associates, or did you mean the one I had tea with this afternoon?"

Kimbrough ran his hand through his hair. "Blast!"

Marisol felt no sympathy for his chagrin. "Indeed. Not only would I be made to look more a fool than any cartoon could ever do, but I would destroy whatever credibility I possess at this moment. I cannot begin to imagine what Mr. Dimm would be thinking, after I told him we had never met. I thank you for casting doubts upon my honor, sirrah!"

"Honor? What would a Pendenning know about honor?"

The duchess was very much afraid that if she did have a pistol right then, she would use it. Eyes narrowed to slits, voice low and harsh, she told him again to get out. "For you are the rudest man of my acquaintance, and having been intimately acquainted with Arvid Pendenning, that is saying a great deal."

"I suppose that last was uncalled for," he conceded, pointedly eyeing the chair she had not offered. She still did not, so he paced to the mantel and examined a Ming dog there, while Marisol held her breath that the clumsy oaf would not drop the priceless porcelain. "So what are you doing about this bumblebroth?" he finally turned and asked.

"I am not confessing to Arvid's murder, if that is your aim, no matter how it might suit you, my lord earl. Instead I am assisting Mr. Dimm to the best of my ability and opening my house to him both here and in Berkshire, so he might follow *all* his leads."

Her emphasis on the *all* left Carlinn in no doubt that the duchess considered him the prime suspect in Berkshire. He swore under his breath as he stomped back and forth in front of Marisol's couch until she was growing seasick. 'Twould be useless to ask him to desist, she felt. If he wouldn't obey a direct order to leave, he wasn't likely to care about her queasiness. Either the lunatic would exhaust himself with that furious pacing—Lord knew she was growing tired watching—or he'd wear a hole in her lovely Oriental carpet, or she'd cast up her accounts. Marisol was wondering which was likely to come first when he muttered, "Botheration. This is getting me nowhere." He came to a stop across from her and impatiently asked, "Duchess, who controls the Pendenning lands now? Is it you? That caper-merchant Boynton? The solicitors?"

With great satisfaction at his frustration, Marisol was able to reply that she honestly did not know how things were left. "But knowing Arvid, they will be as awkward as possible. You shall just have to wait on the reading of the will with the rest of us, and on the birth of my child, I should suppose. You might join your prayers for a girl to Boynton's, for I am sure he'll sell off every unentailed parcel to finance his gambling."

Then Marisol clamped a hand over her mouth. In her anger at this addlepated bumpkin, she'd forgotten he could be a murderer. If that acreage meant so much to Kimbrough that he'd kill Arvid over it, what was another tiny life? Especially after she'd practically promised that Boynton would be easier to deal with. She put her other hand on her stomach.

Carlinn didn't miss the protective gesture, nor the fear in her eyes, and he cursed again. He was furious that a pregnant woman was afraid of him, even more furious that she'd believe him a killer. "Dash it, ma'am," he shouted, "I do not murder innocent women and children. I did not even murder your husband! I cannot say I am sorry someone else did, but the fact is that I did not."

"How do I know that? You come in here in a rant and expect me to change public opinion. You follow no form of social conduct I've ever heard of. How do I know what you are capable of?"

"And how do I know you didn't kill the bounder yourself over some trinket or other?" he retorted.

"Trinket?" Marisol shrieked, pushed past her endurance. "You think I would kill my own husband over a pearl necklace or something? Was Lady Armbruster a trinket? Is my child's welfare a trinket?" she yelled, pushing mightily to get her ungainly body out of the cushions so she could be more on a level with this hulking clunch. Max ran to hide under the couch.

Seeing her struggle, Kimbrough naturally offered her his assistance. She put her right hand in his and said "Thank you" when she'd attained her footing. Then she hauled back with that same right hand and slapped him across the face so hard even the powerful earl reeled back. Or perhaps it was the surprise.

"My husband lies dead upstairs," the duchess was crying, "his mistress next door. I have been accused of murder by an odd little man in a red vest. My maid has given notice, and I am fat. But you . . . you are the worst of the lot!" She sank back to the sofa, her face in her hands, sobbing. "And now I have struck a man to whom I've never even been introduced!"

The earl held out his handkerchief and tried to speak past the dust of contrition in his throat. "Carlinn Kimbrough, ma'am, at your, ah, service."

Jeremiah Dimm wished he'd stayed in the dining room searching out more fallen pastries. He could have heard the whole conversation from there, so loud were these two, and without having to put his ear to any door. Then again, that red handprint on the stiff-rumped earl's cheek, even outlined by the tiny keyhole, sure warmed the cockles of the Runner's heart. Didn't help the case none, a' course, Dimm realized, but salute *that*, you sanctimonious prig!

Chapter Six

Arvid had been an indifferent traveler, restless, uncomfortable, impatient of delays. His child looked to follow in Arvid's unsettled path. No matter the finest sprung carriage, the slowest pace, the most careful avoidance of ruts in the road, the baby made Marisol's journey a misery, the same as Arvid would have done. At least the baby didn't get nasty and belligerent; neither did Arvid, for once, bouncing along in his ornately carved casket in the special funeral carriage up ahead. Boynton traveled next in his own coach with his valet and a mountain of valises, and the baggage wagon came after, with Mr. Dimm crammed between wardrobe trunks, delicacies from the London markets, household items from her own old home that the duchess did not wish to leave behind, and all the trappings she'd been gathering for the arrival of her child.

Dimm's daughter rode in the spacious crested carriage with Marisol and her aunt, thank goodness, for Sarah turned out to be a marvel with biscuits and peppermints and distracting chatter about her own large family and Ned Turner, the soldiering husband she wrote to every day.

Aunt Tess managed to sleep for most of the journey, her knitting fallen in her lap. Marisol was green with envy . . . or something. She was also jealous of her brother, who had chosen to ride alongside, or ahead, or on short cross-country excursions. That was the first thing she was going to do after the baby, Marisol vowed, ride with the wind down tree-shaded lanes, taking her jumps flying. The baby protested the flying part, too, so she sighed and pictured quiet strolls through the castle's rose gardens. Of course, that was in the spring, and who knew where any of them would be when the flowers bloomed? Except Arvid, of course.

Gardens, flowers, country rides, fresh air. It took Marisol a day and a night to recover from the journey before she could recall why she'd been so desperate to get to Berkshire in the first place. Then it took less than half an hour of raw, cold rain, winter-barren landscapes, and the drafty old barn of a relic, for reality to return with a thud. The thud of the dowager's cane, to be exact.

Arvid's mother had not moved to the Dower House on Marisol's marriage. There was no need, the older Duchess Denning had decided, since Arvid intended to spend as little time away from London as possible, and his mother was such an admirable manager of the estate and the household. She managed Arvid, didn't she?

The dowager obviously intended to keep on managing: assigning bedchambers, announcing dinner hours, selecting the hymns for Arvid's service and new curtains for the nursery. She punctuated each of her pronouncements with raps of her ebony cane on the marble floors that sent tremors through Marisol's aching head. The noise also set Max into a frenzy of yipping and lunging, so the dowager ordered the little dog banished to Aunt Tess's room, which offended that lady so much she chose to take her dinner upstairs on a tray. Marisol was too spent to argue.

At least there was no confrontation over the bedchambers. The dowager had moved to the recently renovated east wing when Arvid brought home his bride, so Marisol still occupied the duchess's suite, with its ill-fitted casement windows, antiquated furnishings, and resident pigeons outside in the battlements.

Dinner was another matter. The first night Marisol walked into the dining room on her brother's arm to see that Boynton sat at the head of the table and the dowager at the foot.

"Boynton is head of the family now, Marisol," the dowager declared, ignoring Marisol's own seniority, of however short duration. Marisol decided she was not as well recovered from the journey as she thought. She'd do better with dinner on a tray in her room also.

The next morning Marisol ordered a round table. She was willing to compromise, not buckle under to her mother-in-law's dictatorship. When the butler and housekeeper looked toward each other, and then allowed as how they'd best consult with Her Grace, Marisol reminded them that *she* was also Her Grace, for now, and possibly for years into the future. A round table it would be. Not for the state dining room, of course, but for the smaller room where the family ate. That night the dowager took dinner in *her* rooms. Unfortunately for Marisol's appetite, this left the younger widow alone with her brother and brother-in-law, who sniped at each other throughout. The funeral tomorrow would be a relief.

The man from Bow Street was finding his stay in Berkshire a real treat. He'd decided to put up at the inn in Pennington after being consigned to the stables by that nasty piece of work at the Castle, once Her Grace, Lady Marisol, that is, took to her bed. He hired himself a gig and called in at the pubs and farmsteads. Over hearty ales and fresh-baked breads, the locals were happy enough to talk about the gentry. Their "betters," they said with smiles and raised mugs.

No one had a good word to say about the late duke and less to say about the next, should it turn out to be that coxcomb Boynton. No one could think of anyone nearby with a reason to kill Duke Arvid, though, excepting that he was a miser, a lecher, and a snob. As far as absentee landlords went, that was the finest kind. He never came near Pennington much, so he never bothered them much.

Boynton scared the locals worse. Where Arvid had tried to make the most profit off his lands, Boynton could just wager the Pendenning holdings away, and with them the future of everyone in the little community of Pennington. The villagers were mostly agreed that if they had to have their lives in the hands of a gambler and they had their druthers, they'd pick a winner over a loser every time.

The young duchess and her babe were unknown factors to the country folk, and much would depend on who got named trustee for the little duke, if it be a boy, and if she got hanged.

Then there was Lord Kimbrough. No one hereabouts would hear a word against the earl. Could he commit cold-blooded murder? The vicar's wife would tie her garters on the main street first. Kimbrough was fair, generous, and not above having a pint or two with the lads after a hard day's work. Now *that* was a real gentleman.

Lord Kimbrough even made a point of finding Dimm at his inn and inviting the Runner to dinner one evening. A real dinner it was, too, not a batch of those pawky little bits of things swimming in sauces. The earl served an honest haunch of venison, mutton, and beef, with potatoes and turnips and peas, and no footman to scoop the platters away before a man had his fill. Kimbrough didn't get to that size and strength eating no lark's tongues, Dimm reflected contentedly. Besides, the Runner had already wangled a position in his lordship's stables for his younger boy, who had a real touch with horses. And he was in a fair way to landing a living for Cherry's brother, who was currently ministering to the lost souls of London's slums, at Dimm's expense. And that was all before dessert. Too bad that funeral was tomorrow.

Lord Kimbrough decided to attend the funeral after all. He wasn't going to at first, not to pay respects to a man he despised. But he was keenly aware of his responsibilities and knew that as magistrate, neighbor, fellow nobleman, and bordering landowner, by rights he should go. He wouldn't want to be thought lacking in courtesy to the duchess, either. Both duchesses, he amended. Besides, he didn't want anyone suggesting he stayed away because of a guilty conscience. He had absolutely nothing to feel guilty about, Carlinn told himself, at least nothing to do with Denning's murder. Making a recent widow cry, driving to tears a woman who was breeding, that was another matter. And then fleeing! Cow-handed and chickenhearted both!

His guilt must have shown, for even the amiable Dimm looked at him queerly, almost as if the Runner knew what a clumsy oaf Carlinn had been.

So he was going to Arvid Pendenning's last rites. There might even be some satisfaction seeing the bastard put in the ground he cared so little about. And, too, he had Dimm beside him, so he could help identify anyone else come to gloat. It was Dimm who pointed out the duchess's young brother, acting as one of the pallbearers. Laughton had the same fair coloring and the same patrician nose. With a little maturity and a bit of country cooking, the lad might be pleasant looking, as opposed to the sister. Carlinn recalled the duchess as looking aged beyond her twenty-one years and as if she'd been eating for two for all twenty-one of them. She wasn't present, of course, but would be waiting at the Castle with the other women to receive those wishing to express their condolences.

Kimbrough did not so wish. He'd done his duty to Arvid's memory, having sat through the Castle's private chaplain's droning attempt to find something nice to say about the blighter. Then he'd stood in the biting cold at the Pendenning burial grounds while the chaplain gave it a final go.

There were three distinct groups of mourners, Kimbrough noted as his mind wandered. One batch consisted of more relieved noblemen seen in one place than since Fou-Fou La Rue burned her journals. These were the men Dimm wanted identified, Arvid's gulls come to see if their notes were being called in. Then there were enough tallow-faced Captain Sharps to fleece every lamb in Berkshire. Boynton's friends, he supposed, come to support him in his grief—and to stake their claims to his future riches. The third group, a small gathering of tenants and local citizenry, stayed well away from the Londoners.

It was these last whose hands Kimbrough first shook when the cleric finally ran down. Then he moved among the knights, barons, and honorables, introducing Dimm when he could. Dimm in turn introduced him to young Laughton, who was pathetically glad of the opportunity, having little in common with any of the three disparate groups except his antipathy toward the deceased. On hearing the earl's name, Foster developed an instant case of hero worship for the retired army officer and begged Kimbrough to accompany the funeral party back to the Castle for refreshments.

Carlinn was torn. He'd satisfied the conventions; now he wanted to put this whole sorry mess behind him. But the boy was a pigeon among these wolves, especially with the fiery temper gossip said he had. Leaving the young marquis alone would be like sending a raw recruit out to the front line. Kimbrough couldn't do it, even if the bantling was one of the other murder suspects. He'd only have been defending his sibling. Kimbrough could understand that; he'd skewer anyone who offered harm to his own sister. So he accepted. And managed to get through half the curses he'd learned in the cavalry by the time a footman relieved him of his coat and gloves at Denning Castle.

Many of the grave-side mourners had refused Boynton's invitation to partake of the Castle's hospitality in favor of starting the trip back to London before the day was too advanced. Others chose to toast Arvid at a nearby tavern, where they might also get up a game of cards or two. The working people mostly went back to their farms and businesses. The company was thin, therefore, when Kimbrough and Dimm entered the large drawing room.

To one side gathered Boynton and his cronies, sampling Arvid's wine cellar. Kimbrough nodded. He'd just seen most of those fellows. Near the enormous fireplace the dowager held court, accepting sympathy from the local matrons, the squire's wife, and the mayor's sister, all her bosom bows among the neighboring gentry. The earl bowed and murmured something about being sorry. He was sorry he wasn't out riding his new chestnut stallion. But the dowager nodded and preened that the highest ranking gentleman in the shire—temporarily, naturally—had graced her son's obsequies. It was fitting, of course, but one never knew about Kimbrough. She ignored the Runner's presence entirely.

And finally, in a window embrasure across the vast room, sat Arvid's widow, her brother, and an older woman. They might have been lepers for all the attention paid them. A lesser woman might have retreated, taken to her rooms, but the duchess sat straight in her chair, chin raised. She was all in black, with a black lace veily thing on her head like those Spanish mantillas he'd seen on the Peninsula. Her hair was still down, loosely tied at the back of her neck. She had bottom, Carlinn had to give her that. And dignity.

"Coventry, that's what it is," Dimm whispered as they crossed the Aubusson expanse. "The dowager's got all the old biddies on her side, swearing the chit was responsible for Denning's death. If she didn't aim the pistol herself, according to the old besom, then it were the rackety brother. And it were the young duchess what forced Arvid to a life of sin in the first place."

"She couldn't conceive of Boynton being guilty?"

"No more'n you could picture your right hand up and cutting off your left. No, they got the gel drawn and quartered. She'll be an exile out here, iffen the dowager has her way. A' course, they'll all have to change their tunes when the baby's born, iffen it turns out to be the next duke. Or pay the piper. But that's months away."

"Do I detect a note of sympathy for Denning's doxy? I thought you chaps were supposed to be objective."

"I got daughters her age," Dimm said with a shrug, pausing to relieve a passing footman of a handful of toast squares spread with goose liver and fish eggs. "And her life couldn't of been easy, what I hear."

"She married him for his money and the title. That's what she got."

Dimm clucked his tongue. "Were things all that black and white, I'd be plumb out of a job."

There was no way she could get out of the room before he got to her. Heavens, there was no way she could get out of this chair in that amount of time. Unless the floor should open and swallow her up, she'd have to face the man she'd slapped. He'd deserved it, of course, barging into her drawing room like some ravening beast, but a lady should never lower herself to acting the fishwife, no matter the provocation. And then turning into a watering pot in front of a perfect stranger! At least he'd been gentleman enough to hand over his handkerchief and then leave before she disgraced herself further. Why did the barbarian have to show his second effort at proper conduct on this of all days?

He even looked more civilized. His clothes were well tailored if not absolutely bang up to the mark, without a single crease, spatter, or scent of the stables. His hair was combed, his eyes weren't shooting sparks, and his hands were wrapped around a wineglass instead of her throat. She should be safe.

"Marisol, have you met the Earl of Kimbrough?" Foster asked, eagerly drawing Carlinn closer to the little grouping.

"We've never been formally introduced," Kimbrough said before she could reply. "How do you do, Your Grace? May I take this opportunity to express my deepest regrets?"

Foster looked at him in astonishment and even Aunt Tess wondered aloud, "What's that? Did he say he was sorry Arvid was dead?"

He hadn't. He'd correctly apologized for their last meeting, Marisol understood. She nodded her head. "Thank you. This is a difficult time for all of us."

"Too kind," he murmured. There was more he wished to say, but not in front of her family and the Bow Street Runner. Dimm must have some skill in detection, for he winked at the earl and drew Laughton to the side with a question about one of Boynton's set.

"What's that?" Aunt Tess asked. "I hope they bring back some of those grilled oysters."

Speaking softly for once, and with a smile that quite transformed his face from passably attractive to positively stunning, he amazed Marisol further by apologizing more fully. Arvid had never apologized for anything, ever.

"I have no excuse for my actions," Kimbrough was saying, "except that I am used to being in control, Your Grace—of my circumstances, of my tongue, of my temper. Mostly of my privacy. But everything had gone beyond my control that day. I was thrust willy-nilly into a public spectacle of the type I most deplore. Still, I should never have taken my frustrations out on you. I sincerely apologize."

"And I am sure I would never have subjected you to such an ill-mannered, emotional display were I not suffering the same upset. So I believe we are even, my lord, unless, of course, you were the one who murdered my husband."

"Witch," he muttered even lower.

"What's that? They're playing whist? In a house of mourning? Why, I never!"

A proper twenty minutes later, the earl and the investigator took their leave.

While they waited for his curricle to be brought 'round Carlinn asked, "Did you discover anything new?"

Dimm pondered a moment. "Not much, less'n you count a partiality for lobster patties."

Chapter Seven

His nibs at Bow Street wasn't happy. No fresh scandal had rocked London, so the newspapers were still gnawing on the Denning case. With the principals out of town and no new facts coming to light, the editors were crying privileged treatment for the privileged class. Whitewash, they called it, with no one being brought to account. More like no vulgar headlines to sell more newspapers.

The reporters would lose interest soon enough, soon as there was some war news or a new sensation in the ton, some marchioness running off with her footman or something. Till then, his nibs wasn't happy. And when the boss wasn't happy, no one was happy, least of all Jeremiah Dimm, who was wearing out his shoe leather again, trying to dig up more evidence.

"But you can't just make facts. They is like rocks; you can find them, you can uncover them, but only time and nature can make one of the confounded things."

He went back over his notes. He retraced the paths on that fatal day of the brother, the neighbor, the wife's brother. He carefully checked the background of all Denning's associates, and he talked to the servants again at the duke's house. Her Grace's maid was staying with her mother, he learned, and the valet, Purvis, was helping to pack His Grace's belongings between visits to the employment agencies.

Dimm saw for himself all the reports that said no one had come to Lord Armbruster's love nest, not in a week of round-the-clock surveillance, so he went next door to Armbruster House, which was also draped in black, with its knocker off the door.

Lord Armbruster was still up north delivering his wife's body to her people in Cumberland, where he might convince some prelate she'd taken an accidental overdose of laudanum. There had been no reason to hold him in London any more than there'd been reason to detain the duchess or any of the others, despite the scandal sheets crying leniency for the aristocracy. Blast, you'd think this were France or something, Dimm considered, crossing that bit of roadway between the houses where Denning had met his Maker. Or unmaker. Deuce take it, the crime happened in the middle of the afternoon. Someone should have seen something! Or heard the shot.

"Oh no," Armbruster's butler contradicted him. "Our walls are very thick. His lordship would not want to hear the sounds of traffic or street vendors, don't you know. And then there was Lady Armbruster screaming. Of course that might have been after, but if before, we wouldn't have heard the shot, during. No, no one here knows anything."

But someone did. Lady Armbruster's maid was just finishing packing all of the dead woman's clothing into boxes when Dimm found her.

"You didn't happen to come by any suicide note, did you?" he asked for the eighth or ninth time, having searched for one himself before traveling to Berkshire. He had found enough writing in Lady

Armbruster's hand to know she hadn't sent the message to the duchess, unless she disguised her writing, of course, but a farewell note would have been Christmas and a promotion and lobster patties, all rolled into one. Especially if the lady had confessed to killing her lover before taking her own life.

"No, she were too sleepy to do any writing," the maid told him. "Right from the first. I didn't see her when she got up to take the rest of the bottle, but she couldn't of been thinking right, now could she? And just look at this mess." The maid waved her arms around the room. "And my lord intends to give it all to the poorhouse; he doesn't want to see any of it again."

"You mean he's not letting you have her clothes?"

Dimm interpreted her petulance aright, for the maid replied, "No, the bastard blames me for leaving the bottle with her. As if that's any of my job. And he's not even going to give me a good reference, he says. So what am I supposed to do now, I ask you?" She crammed a satin gown into a glove-sized space in the box. "I don't suppose you're on terms with Her Grace next door to put in a good word for me, are you? I heard Tyson didn't want to go to the country."

"The duchess already hired a new maid when I saw her in Berkshire." He didn't say it was his own daughter. "But maybe they won't suit. You never know."

"Well, here," she said, handing him a brightly colored shawl. "You take this, in case you hear of anything."

"I'm not sure . . ." he began.

"Oh, go on, his lordship owes me something, he does. I mean, I did try to stop Lady Armbruster from taking that first dose, I did. I told her right off that it wasn't good for the baby."

Dimm knew what to do with the pretty shawl; his widowed sister Cora who kept house for him and all their relations would look a treat in it. He wasn't so sure about this new bit of information. So he took his theories with him back to Berkshire, just about the time the will was going to be read.

"A baby? How sad." Marisol could not find it in her heart to feel sorry for the woman who had thrown her life away over a tawdry affair. But the poor, innocent baby was another matter. "But why?" she asked the Runner, as if Mr. Dimm would have the answers.

He was the one asking the questions, though. "I was hoping you could tell me, Your Grace. Did she say anything to you? Did your husband mention anything?"

"Goodness, Mr. Dimm, surely you know the spouse is always the last to find out about these things. Besides, Arvid hardly told me when he was leaving town for house parties and such. He'd never discuss more personal matters with a mere wife. But are you so sure the child was Arvid's? Did the maid say so?"

"No, twice. But why else would Lady Armbruster carry on about being ruined?"

"I wonder if Nessie were not simply mentally unbalanced. Why couldn't she just have passed the child off as Armbruster's? Ladies do it all the time. Ah, that is, I have heard such things happen." Embarrassed to have blurted such a scandalous statement—her aunt would have the vapors if she heard—Marisol offered the Runner more tea. "And do have another macaroon, Mr. Dimm. I am going to and I hate to eat alone. It makes me feel like a glutton, but I am always hungry."

Jeremiah was happy to humor a woman in such an interesting condition. As they nibbled away, though, he still pursued his line of inquiry. "Knowing Lady Armbruster was breeding, Your Grace, would you say she'd be more or less like to up and shoot the duke?"

"Killing Arvid wouldn't make Nessie any more or less *enceinte*. Of course, Arvid might have been threatening to tell her husband. I wouldn't put blackmail past him," she confided over another slice of poppyseed cake. "But they did not seem to be arguing when I saw them in the carriage."

"No, Your Grace, I didn't suppose they was." He took another gooseberry tart to help swallow the disappointment.

Lord Kimbrough was another disappointment. "I can't stand all those sweet things," he'd explained, but Dimm assured him the thick slices of bread and butter were more than adequate. The discouragement came when the earl said he did not believe either of the Armbrusters committed the crime.

"Nerissa Armbruster was your typically hysterical female. She would have fainted at the sight of all that blood. More so if she was in a delicate way." Carlinn burned his tongue, thinking of what the duchess had said about that euphemism, instead of sipping the hot tea carefully.

"Then what about his lordship? He finds out his wife is presenting him with a token of another man's affections, he's like to be a tad overset."

"But why should Armbruster kill Denning? He'd have done better to kill his whoring wife. Oh, I know you'll hear how these indiscretions are politely accepted in the ton, but that's after a man has his heir. Armbruster didn't, after—what? Five, six years of marriage. He does have cousins and such, I know, and I am sure he'd rather they step into his shoes than Denning's bastard. Besides, you said that maid had no way of knowing if Armbruster even knew his wife was breeding, much less who fathered the brat."

"It's a mess, all right," Dimm lamented. "I suppose all the Quality has to fret about who inherits, like this Denning argle-bargle. At least poor folks don't have that headache. By the way, my lord, who's your heir?"

Kimbrough put his cup down with a thump. "I have a cousin in Bath." A middle-aged, hypochondriac bachelor, but Dimm needn't know that. "And I am only seven-and-twenty, after all. Plenty of time to worry about the succession."

"Denning was only thirty-nine. Don't suppose he meant to cock up his toes yet either."

"By George, you're full of cheer today, Dimm. But buck up, maybe something will come out of the reading of the will this afternoon. Best have another cup of tea and some more to eat; the dowager's as cheeseparing as Arvid ever was."

"What's that man doing here?" the dowager demanded, banging her cane up and down on the Axminster carpet in the Castle's library. No one knew whether she meant the earl or the Runner.

Marisol thought Lord Kimbrough must be at the reading in his capacity as local magistrate, but Mr. Stenross, the second Mr. Stenross of Stenross, Stenross, and Dinkerly, the family's solicitors, announced that he had invited the earl on business pertaining to the will. The dowager's scowl deepened, as did Lord Kimbrough's. Mr. Dimm mumbled something about Crown investigation and took a position toward the rear wall, well out of the dowager's way.

"Shall I send for the servants now?" Marisol asked.

Mr. Stenross cleared his throat and shuffled his papers on the desk. "That, ah, will not be necessary."

By this everyone understood that Arvid had not provided for his long-term retainers, which boded ill for any lingering hopes that he might have had a generous moment while contemplating eternity. Aunt Tess reached for Marisol's hand. Foster put a hand on her shoulder, from where he stood behind his sister's chair.

Mr. Stenross seemed to feel elucidation was in order, as if anyone in the room needed a lesson in Arvid's mean, clutchfisted character.

"His Grace felt that the servants were being well compensated for their labors," Mr. Stenross explained uncomfortably. "Since none were due for retirement, he did not feel it necessary to provide pensions at this time."

"Yes, yes, man, we know he didn't intend to die just yet," Boynton said, forgetting to drawl. "Get on with it."

Mr. Stenross cleared his throat again and reshuffled his papers. "Getting on with it" was clearly beneath his dignity. Boynton moaned and Foster tightened his fingers on Marisol's shoulder.

"I must advise you that His Grace was very careful of his will, revising his codicils regularly. This document was meant to be an interim will, created for the purpose of expressing His Grace's wishes, should the sex of his progeny not be determined at the time of his demise."

"You mean he wrote a new will when Marisol got pregnant?" Foster asked, then flushed at his own outburst.

"Exactly." Mr. Stenross settled a pair of spectacles on his nose and began reading: " 'Being the last will and testament of Arvid Alexander Pendenning, Sixth Duke of Denning, Baron of Denton,' et cetera, et cetera. I shall skip over the technical paragraphs, but a copy of the document will be left here for your perusal, that there be no doubts of its authenticity or legality." He cleared his throat again. " 'To my mother who has been living at Denning Castle instead of the Dower House, conserving her own funds, I leave the annuity established under my father's will.' "

The dowager slumped in her chair and groaned.

Boynton tossed her a vinaigrette and leaned forward. "Go on, go on."

" 'Likewise, my brother already receives a sufficient allowance. Had he higher income, he would game deeper.' "

"Bastard!" Boynton shouted.

Mr. Stenross looked up.

"I didn't mean you. He can't do that, can he, if I'm his heir?"

The solicitor frowned. "These terms are conditional on the outcome of Her Grace's delivery, naturally." He turned back to the papers. " 'To my wife, Marisol Laughton Pendenning, I leave the sum of ten thousand pounds, should she fail to carry the infant to term or have a stillbirth, leaving me without issue.' "

Marisol gritted her teeth. Trust Arvid to consider every horrifying possibility. But they could live on ten thousand pounds, with the sale of her jewelry. She patted Aunt Tess's hand.

"Should my wife be delivered of a female child, I leave her ten thousand pounds a year until my daughter marries or reaches her majority, at which time the said daughter is to receive a dowry of fifty thousand pounds. The aforementioned annuity also terminates at my wife's remarriage.' "

Aunt Tess let go of Marisol's fingers in order to wipe her eyes. "I was so afraid he'd let us starve if you didn't provide the heir."

Mr. Stenross glared at her for the interruption. "Yes, the heir. Under both of the above conditions, His Grace's brother would inherit by law the title and all entailed property, including but not limited to Denning House in London, Denning Castle, Berkshire, the hunting box in Leicester, holdings in Jamaica, their incomes and earnings."

Boynton smiled, and even the dowager perked up, until Mr. Stenross went on. "I tried to advise His Grace concerning the disbursement of the unentailed property but the duke was adamant. The bank accounts, real estate investments, consols, et cetera, were his to do with as he wished."

"Yes, but we all know that's where the real wealth lies. Who gets it?" Boynton almost shredded the lace at his cuffs, in his excitement.

" 'If I die with no posthumous heir, neither my wife nor my brother is to have a farthing of the unentailed property,' " Mr. Stenross recited, disapproval evident in his voice, " 'which is to be used instead to establish a home for unwed mothers.' "

Boynton fainted dead away, falling off his chair at his mother's feet. Mr. Stenross's reading had to be suspended, which was a good thing since Marisol was tempted beyond reason to pick up the dowager's cane and beat Lord Kimbrough about the head to stop him from laughing so hard.

Chapter Eight

The reading continued, Boynton having been revived and fortified with several glasses of Arvid's finest claret. The earl and Mr. Dimm must have needed fortification also, for they partook just as liberally. Marisol wished that someone had offered her more than the tea she shared with her aunt and Mr. Stenross, to keep her hands from shaking so.

Mr. Stenross wiped his spectacles, cleared his throat a number of times, surveyed his audience to make sure he had their full attention, as if anyone might doze off during the disposition of Arvid's enormous fortune. He found his place and read: " 'If the child my legally wedded wife now carries is a male, my wife receives fifty thousand pounds in her own name, free and clear, to be used for her personal needs as well as those of her family. She is furthermore entitled to the income from the aforesaid unentailed property until our son comes of age to manage these holdings or until she remarries, whichever comes first.' " Mr. Stenross looked up as Foster let out a loud cheer. "The next clause establishes the firm of Stenross, Stenross, and Dinkerly as trustees for this property, since the holdings are extensive and also since Her Grace is an underage female."

Boynton, reclining on a sofa, managed to find a glimmer of hope there. "But that's all to do with the loose change. What about the entailed estate and all of its income? I mean, m'nevvy will need a guardian, won't he? Not even m'brother would be so havey-cavey as to leave it all in the hands of a slip of a girl and a pack of fusty old solicitors."

"Precisely. His Grace was very concerned about that very thing, that the will could be overturned on those grounds." Mr. Stenross was old enough to ignore Boynton's eruption, not fusty enough to let it slide. "Or that the estate might fall into unscrupulous hands. Therefore His Grace named a guardian"—Boynton adjusted his neckcloth; Foster stood to attention—"which is why I have asked Lord Kimbrough to attend today's reading. Due to Her Grace's young age and the infancy of the hypothetical posthumous heir, His Grace has named Carlinn Kimberly, Earl of Kimbrough, to stand as guardian to his minor son and administrator of the entailment."

"What?"

"That's outrageous!"

"I won't stand for it!"

"How could he?"

Marisol got Mr. Stenross's attention first. "Sir," she said, hating the quaver she heard in her own voice, "this must not be. I refuse to have this . . . stranger in charge of my son, having any say-so in his rearing."

"I am sorry, Your Grace, but you cannot refuse what was written into His Grace's will, nor would it be in your interests to contest this clause. By law, a female cannot own property or stand as guardian to an underage child. The law looks the other way at times, but not in the case of an estate of this size, when the infant has such standing among the nobility. The courts would appoint a guardian in any case, and you might find their selection even less to your taste."

Marisol found that hard to imagine. Her disagreement must have shown on her face, for Mr. Stenross continued: "With his reputation no court could find Lord Kimbrough an unfit guardian. I looked into it myself, at His Grace's request. He was insistent that certain parties not find grounds to overturn the will."

One of those parties was even now finishing off the bottle of claret.

Marisol twisted her handkerchief. There had to be a way out, besides having a girl child. "But his lordship knows nothing about children. He's not even married."

"And you know nothing about managing estates, Your Grace, begging your pardon."

"I cannot believe even Arvid could be so stupid as to pick a . . ."

Before she could think of anything terrible enough to describe her feelings for the brute, Kimbrough pushed himself away from the wall next to Mr. Dimm and strode up to the desk.

"The duchess might not be able to refuse myself as guardian, but I can and do. I refuse the offer. I never wanted anything to do with that reprobate Denning, and I want less to do with his ramshackle retinue. This hobble has naught to do with me, and I am leaving."

Mr. Stenross stopped him with a few quiet words before the earl could fling open the library door. "In return for your acceptance of the guardianship, His Grace signed over the deed to that parcel of land in dispute." Mr. Stenross held up a piece of parchment. "He conceded that the rechanneling of the water altered the boundaries, so the new land cannot be part of the entailment. Pending, of course, your overseeing the welfare of his son."

"Damn and blast!" Carlinn swore, hitting his fist

against the doorframe. "The makebait must have known I couldn't refuse, not with my people getting flooded out every rainstorm."

The solicitor was going on as if the earl's capitulation was never in question. "In answer to your question, Lord Boynton, concerning the interim period—"

"Interim be damned," Boynton shouted again. "I want to know what's to happen in the meantime! That whelp isn't due till when, Duchess?"

Marisol quietly replied, "After the first of the year."

Boynton's creditors were waiting on his doorstep at the Albany. "So what are we supposed to do in the meantime, besides sit around watching the egg hatch?"

"Everything is to continue as before, with expenses to be paid from the estate, overseen by myself." He anticipated Boynton's next question by saying, "There are also provisions for if the child does not survive to reach majority—"

"Stop it!" Marisol cried, putting her hands over her ears. "I do not want to hear those things! The child is not even born yet. How can you be discussing its death?"

"My apologies, Your Grace. Of course such details do not need to be mentioned at this time. I wished merely to illustrate that His Grace was very thorough."

"His Grace was a bounder of the first degree!" Boynton angrily declared. "Cutting out his own brother."

"No, it's all her fault," the dowager screamed, getting to her feet and waving her cane in Marisol's direction. "You two-faced slut! Arvid's mealy-mouthed, complacent little bride, all the while plotting behind his back. Yes, you and your lover here, plotting how to get rid of him and keep everything for yourselves." She stepped toward Marisol, still brandishing the cane. "You'll never get away with—"

"That will be enough, Your Grace." Kimbrough stood over the dowager and removed the cane from her hand, snapping it across his knee as if it were so much kindling. "There. My first job as guardian of the possible future duke. Your son was a cur and a scoundrel from childhood. I remember the hell he raised in the neighborhood when I was yet a schoolboy. Instead of blaming the duchess, rather blame yourself for raising him to believe he was above the law, above the dictates of polite society or moral conscience. If I have anything to do with the next duke—and, Duchess, I mean to have as little as possible, so you can stop shredding your handkerchief—the boy will learn his responsibilities as well as his rights. He'll find out what Arvid never understood: that he is not better than anyone else because he is Denning. He will be born hosed and shod, but he will have to earn respect."

The dowager took to her rooms; Boynton took to the bottle. Mr. Dimm was closeted with Mr. Stenross, going over those sections of the duke's will that Marisol had not wished to hear.

"Just what you could of figured," Dimm muttered. Obviously it was what Boynton figured, too, since his lordship hadn't bothered to stay to look at those passages. "The bastard cuts everyone off if the heir dies. The widow gets whatever's left of her fifty thousand, and Boynton gets the title and what goes with it, and not a groat more."

"And the home for unwed mothers gets the rest. Very commendable, I'm sure."

"That must be lawyer talk for spiteful, eh? That dirty dish didn't have a charitable bone in his body. Devil take it, though, none of this is getting me a better motive. And you say no one else was privy to the contents of the will anyways, right?"

"Are you questioning the integrity of my office?"

"Clerks has been known to take bribes." Although the ones at Stenross, Stenross, and Dinkerly hadn't, when Dimm sought to read the will aforetimes. Of course, 'twere always possible he hadn't offered enough of the ready.

Mr. Stenross was folding the papers back into their portfolio. He drew himself up and firmly stated: "The only way anyone could have known the contents of His Grace's will was if His Grace had so informed him. Or her."

"And judging by the shock we seen just now, no one had an inkling, or they were deuced fine actors." Which was all of a piece, since this whole hubble-bubble was enough of a farce to get billing at Drury Lane.

Since he had brought the Runner in his curricle, Lord Kimbrough was left to wait with the duchess and her aunt, awkwardly aware they'd be wishing him to Jericho. The aunt had moved closer to the fireplace with her knitting, booties this time. Blue ones. The duchess rang for tea.

"Thank you for coming to my assistance," Marisol said when he had been served, then rushed into her major concern: "Shall you truly leave me to raise my son?"

"Unless I see reason to interfere. I have a life of my own, you know. Managing my own estate is time-consuming enough, without having to worry over Denning's, much less the grooming of his heir." Carlinn vowed he wasn't going to get involved in the brat's upbringing. He wasn't going to let any Town belle dump her responsibilities off on his shoulders so she could resume her gay life in London, doing the social rounds.

"Thank you again," she said in relief, although he'd not offered any favors that he could see. "Isn't it odd that I'd be thought capable of rearing a daughter, but not a son?"

"Odd? Not at all. A boy needs a man's influence."

Marisol was silent, wondering what kind of influence her husband might have been. What if the child turned out to be like Arvid, even without his presence? She put down her plate, her appetite having flown, and pleated the fabric of her gown with nervous fingers.

And a woman needs a man, Carlinn thought when she went quiet. The jade was most likely thinking of the poor sod she'd snabble next to keep her in jewels and furs. Fifty thousand pounds and a proven breeder ought to put the duchess in contention, even if the high-nosed shrew had the tongue of a Billingsgate fishmonger. Of course, she'd have to get back her figure and her looks, or she'd frighten off the heartiest *parti*. Then again, he mused, perhaps she'd just take herself and her booty back to Town and set herself up as a dashing widow, going from dance partner to bed partner in the twinkle of a diamond bracelet. Yes, that was more likely, considering she'd already put off mourning for Denning, and him barely cold in the ground.

Marisol noticed when Kimbrough's brown eyes focused on her hands and the blue kerseymere material between them. She smoothed out her skirts and adjusted the black shawl at her elbows. "I only had three mourning gowns made up," she found herself explaining. Why she had to justify her wardrobe to this lumpkin in corduroy coat and unstarched cravat Marisol did not know, but she went on: "It seemed such a waste to order more for just the next month or two, when I'll hardly be seeing anyone anyway. Besides, it does annoy the dowager no end." She smiled then, and Carlinn suspected there might be dimples beneath the puffed chipmunk cheeks; something must have earned her the title of Incomparable.

He smiled back. Encouraged to try to make friends with the man who might have such impact in her son's life, she joked, "I decided to leave some black fabric for other widows, since my gowns take so much yardage."

Marisol was pleased to see a twinkle come to his eyes, and Carlinn was convinced that, yes, they were definitely dimples. "Now that you mention it, Duchess, are you sure you won't have twins? That would cause havoc with all the betting."

"Goodness, I'd better not. Arvid didn't make provision for that, did he? But the physician said no. I wish—" she began, but did not finish.

"For twins?"

"No, I wish no one cared whether my child is a boy or a girl, that I wasn't on exhibit like some empress giving birth to the royal heir. I wish no one else's future depended on my poor innocent babe."

She looked perilously close to tears again, Kimbrough thought in dismay. He quickly said, "Is the dowager causing you any difficulty? I heard her viperish tongue. Shall I go slay more dragons? Consider it part of my duty."

Marisol tried to smile. He really was being quite nice. "There is no need for such gallantry yet, my lord. Everything is awaiting the big event. If I have a boy, Her Grace will move to the Dower House, if I have to pay for the refurbishing myself. I'll pension off her servants and hire my own, who will owe me their loyalty. And if I have a girl, I shall simply leave. Another month or two of the dowager's unpleasantness won't matter. But there *is* something you can do, now that you were kind enough to offer."

Carlinn almost bit his own tongue off. Lud, what was coming next? Confound the woman and her blasted tears! He nodded, indicating that she should go on, but his lowered brow and clenched jaw were not encouraging.

"It's not a very large dragon, my lord, just that my brother and my brother-in-law are continually at daggers drawn. The situation will get worse as the bad weather keeps Foster in the house more, and his debts keep Boynton from returning to London. Their brangling cuts up my peace worse than the dowager ever does, for I don't dare leave the two of them alone together. Do you think you could spend some time with Foster, perhaps help him pick a regiment? Now that I know we can afford the colors Arvid promised him, Foster will have something to do, and will not feel so dependent."

"He needs schooling, the way he rushed out of here."

"He is feeling his youth. He could have been named guardian, were he older. And he should have been able to manage an estate, if ours hadn't been lost. Mostly I believe he holds himself responsible that we are all at Arvid's mercy, or lack thereof. He needs reassurance and advice, not Boynton's constant sniping. And he looks up to you."

"That's what comes of being so big."

"And humble, too. But you said yourself that a boy needs a man's influence."

His wayward tongue be double damned! Rolled up horse, foot, and gun. "I can see I'll have to weigh my every word around you, Duchess. But yes, if it will set your mind at ease, I will see what I can do. Might even put him to work exercising my old cavalry charger to shake the fidgets out of both of them. Old Beau is eating his head off, wondering what we're doing chasing foxes when we're supposed to be chasing Frenchies."

"Thank you. I know Foster will be thrilled, and I would appreciate it. And perhaps your sister might like to call while you are off drilling your new troops. I'd enjoy the company." She didn't say that the loneliness was almost unbearable, what with the dowager turning all the local women against her. She'd not had one visitor in the entire week since the funeral.

Carlinn picked a speck of lint off his sleeve. "I am afraid my sister is taking her new duties as chatelaine very seriously now that she is home from school. She is busy with menus and such, since she'll be having friends come to stay for the holidays."

"I see. Later, then, after the baby." Marisol saw, all right. She saw that this lummox didn't want his precious sister associating with the Coach Widow. The prig. So much for being her friend. "I doubt I'll feel like entertaining company anyway, so do not feel obliged to call, my lord. But thank you for coming. I am sure you will be notified if and when your services as guardian will be needed. Good day."

She had dismissed him! The Earl of Kimbrough found himself cooling his heels in the drafty hall of Denning Castle, his mouth hanging open. First she used dimples to soften him up, then tears to manipulate him into nursemaiding her scapegrace brother, then she showed him the door! That arrogant bitch!

Dimm was worried about the thunderclouds. Not the ones obscuring the sun, but the ones on Lord Kimbrough's face. The earl was driving the horses like all the hounds of hell were nipping at his heels, putting distance between him and Denning Castle. Or Denning's widow.

"If it's the dowager's words what has you so blue-deviled, pay them no never mind. I didn't take them to heart, so there's no reason for you to. The idea of you plotting with the duchess don't hold water."

"The idea of me throttling her does! She's the most infuriating female I've ever met, looking down her nose at anyone who doesn't take snuff with one hand. Hah!"

"Seems down to earth to me, for a gentry moll. Puts out a nice tea. Watch that there hay wagon, guv."

Kimbrough paid no attention to Dimm's words, either about Her Grace or the lumbering cart they passed with a scant inch to spare. "I don't know how I'm to maintain any degree of civility with her for minutes on end," the earl fumed, "and I'm looking at twenty-one years till the boy is grown. It's a life sentence!"

"But think of all the good you can do for the folks hereabouts if you get to manage that property. You said yourself Denning didn't take care of his people. Didn't even have a sawbones to look after them. Which reminds me, I have a nevvy at home what set out to medical school in Edinburgh. One year left of studies, he's got, but the money's run out. I'd wager he'd be willing to pledge his services for, say, five years, in exchange for his tuition. What do you think?"

"Done." The earl took the next corner on two wheels. "Hell and damnation, I'd almost rather the child be a girl. I'm sure I could buy that piece of land from the home for unwed mothers. Blast! If she lets a bunch of lightskirts come to Pennington, I'll murder her for sure."

"It's not as if Her Grace has any say in the matter, my lord. You might try praying though. By the bye, that brother-in-law of mine we talked of, the one in collars, is ready to move into that vicarage you mentioned. His wife and young 'uns is that excited to be getting out of the city." And out of Dimm's house.

His lordship grunted and flicked his whip over the horses' backs for more speed. Dimm held on with both hands. "What you need is a wife, milord."

"Why, do you just happen to have one of those stashed in your attics, too?"

"Not 'zactly, and you'd do better to keep your eyes on the road than sending me black looks like that."

"Oh, did you mean I need a woman's refining touch? Hah! That's just what I need on top of everything else, someone to nag about the polish on my boots or the smell of my cigar or the way I drive my cattle. I mean, a scandal and a murder charge and that aggravating female aren't enough? You'd saddle me with a prunes-and-prisms wife besides?"

"Devil a bit, guv. But you ain't thinking clearly, milord. Women die in childbirth all the time. Then there's always milk fever. What happens if Her Grace sticks her spoon in the wall any time these next five or ten years? You're stuck with a infant, your lordship, all on your own."

For the first time in twelve years, Carlinn put the curricle in the ditch.

Chapter Nine

Kimbrough kept his promise about Foster. He was a man of his word, Marisol conceded, whatever else she might think of his stiff-rumped earlship. And she thought of him more than was good for her or the baby, since his very name made her blood boil. Every enthusiastic encomium pouring from her brother's mouth grated against her nerves when she remembered how Kimbrough had denied her his sister's acquaintance. As if she'd contaminate the girl, for heaven's sake! He'd behaved like a doyenne pulling her skirts away from a mud puddle. And that sanctimonious snob was to be in charge of her son? No wonder she was in the doldrums.

The weather did not help, being raw and gray when it wasn't raw and rainy. Walks were more torture than pleasure. The wintery chill outside was nothing to the dowager's attitude inside, and the lack of congenial company was driving Marisol to distraction. She tried to keep busy renovating an apartment in the north tower, with Mr. Stenross's approval. The historic ducal suite was no place for a child and too drafty for its mother. But even that work was proceeding for the most part without the duchess, since the smell of paint made her queasy and the hammering of paneling gave her the headache. She only had to approve swatches of fabric from books and choose desks and chairs brought down from the attics for her inspection, there being no way she could navigate those steep steps and narrow aisles.

After that, there were only so many books she could read, letters she could write, little caps she could sew, comments about the weather she could shout to Aunt Tess to fill her days. She was reduced to playing with Max, for pity's sake!

For all that she was bored to flinders without his company, Marisol did not begrudge her brother his new interest. Kimbrough kept Foster busy and excited, sending him home physically exhausted, enough so that Boynton's acerbic comments at dinner fell on ears suddenly as deaf as Aunt Tess's, to Marisol's relief.

She was also relieved that the earl had taken her hint and not called, the high-handed, pompous prude. He was so worried about what people would say, it was laughable. Why, he fled the London social scene to avoid the gabble-grinders, she'd heard, burying himself in the country like a turnip putting down roots, the noddy. As if anyone's opinion mattered, not even his high-and-mighty lordship's. She did not care a bit that he didn't call for weeks after the reading of the will; it just showed what a rude, boorish clodpole he was. Of course, she heard about the carriage accident from her maid, but Foster assured her it was nothing.

Foster was too impressed by his hero to mention that Carlinn—they were on a first-name basis now—was suffering from abrasions and cracked ribs. Real men didn't whimper about their injuries. Besides, Foster would never let it be known that Carlinn was anything less than a top-of-the-trees whip. There had to have been ice on the road that evening. All Marisol knew was that the earl was letting Foster tool his curricle and pair—and bang-up bits of blood they were, too, according to her brother—and exercise his Thoroughbreds.

"And he's even writing his old commander about me. Cavalry, don't you know," Foster chattered happily. "Carlinn says that's the only way to go, especially for a chap hoping to win advancement in the field. Carlinn says I might hear shortly if there's an aide-de-camp position open."

Marisol was sick unto death of hearing what Carlinn said, but she smiled for Foster's sake. The rustic earl might be stiff and dull, without an ounce of cultured refinement in him, but at least he was steady. He wouldn't lead Foster into bad habits, like Boynton kept trying to do, daring the younger man into rash wagers. Since they were all pockets to let until the final disbursement of funds, nothing came of it, but Marisol could only be that much more appreciative of the earl's influence.

Boynton kept to his rooms for the most part . . . and to the bottle. When he wasn't in the stables trying to fleece the grooms of their wages, Arvid's brother and his shifty-eyed valet experimented with new ways of tying neckcloths. Occasionally he challenged Marisol to a hand of piquet for imaginary sums. They gave up on billiards when Marisol couldn't get close enough to the table.

The dowager, meanwhile, was suffering pangs of indecision. On the one hand, her daughter-in-law was a fallen woman, a pariah, and a murderess, deserving only of the cut direct. That's what she'd convinced her friends, so none of her cronies called. On the other hand, Marisol might be the mother of the next duke, controlling Denning Castle and all of its inhabitants. What to do? The dowager's decision was made easier by the lack of company she also felt. She couldn't accept invitations for dinner parties and cards, not after making a to-do about the trollop's lack of proper mourning, and the local matrons were hesitant about calling. They didn't want to get in the middle of the two duchesses either. So the dowager was forced to give Marisol grudging acceptance, to have a fourth at whist.

The Bow Street Runner was recovering from his concussion nicely. Just the occasional headache now, thank you, but a chap couldn't be too careful with head wounds, don't you know. He was staying on at the inn at the earl's expense, naturally, with two pretty chambermaids at his beck and call. This left the proprietor of the Three Feathers a shade shorthanded, so he agreed to give Dimm's niece a trial. Changing sheets at a country inn mightn't be precisely what Dimm would have chosen for the girl, but Suky was a pretty little thing with a head on her shoulders. If she didn't nab herself a handsome young farmer or such, his name wasn't Jeremiah Dimm. 'Sides, he told himself, it wasn't like she'd have any chance of getting into trouble, not with her strapping big cousin working in Lord Kimbrough's stables, another cousin fixed as the duchess's abigail, and her other uncle right now setting up as vicar one town over.

Dimm was doing just fine, keeping to his bed. A nice, slow recovery suited him to a cow's thumb. It didn't suit his nibs in London. Not by half. One week later Dimm's boss sent for the Runner and demanded results.

"I don't care who you arrest, just arrest someone. Charge the wife, by George—she had the most to gain just getting rid of that dastard. She'll never hang for it anyway, so there'll be no harm done."

" 'Cept the real killer will have got off easy. I can't do it, sir, sorry."

"Then somebody else! Surely you must have a prime suspect in mind. They are up in arms over this at Whitehall, that a nobleman can be gunned down in broad daylight and we cannot find the killer. Doesn't look good on our record, does it, Dimm?"

"No, sir."

"Good. Then what shall I tell the reporters?"

"Well, they all has alibis so thin you can poke a stick through them, but that Lord Armbruster won't name his. Man has something to hide, or I miss my guess."

"No, no, it couldn't have been Lord Armbruster. In fact, those men you had watching his flat in Half Moon Street have been reassigned. Waste of taxpayers' money, don't you know." His nibs shuffled some papers, without meeting Dimm's eyes.

"Begging your pardon, sir, but who gave that there order?"

"The prime minister himself, if you must know. So go find another suspect. Get on with it, man."

Jeremiah got on with it. He parked his son Gabriel in a carriage across the way from Armbruster's love nest. The boy had to learn surveillance work, didn't he?

"Facts is like rocks, my boy. The deeper they try to hide, the harder you got to dig."

The earl was licking his wounds. My word, he kept berating himself, how had he ever come to do such a corkbrained thing? Tipping over his carriage like the merest whipster. He deserved to suffer!

It was that woman's fault. Marisol Pendenning brought out the worst in him, that was all. He despised the way she put on airs, looking down on him as though he were lower than that foolish dog Max. She even talked to the mutt in warmer tones than she used to him. And no matter that she was the spoiled pet of a superficial society, she usually succeeded in making him feel like an unmannerly lout. Hell and tarnation, how was he going to face her now, with half his face rubbed raw from the accident? With his ribs strapped tight, he couldn't even make her a proper bow. Oh, how the witch would laugh at his comeuppance.

Unless he didn't come to call. Carlinn decided he'd rather she think him a craven than a clunch. Let her highness believe he stayed away because she'd disdained his company. That was better than the truth.

If he couldn't stop by to see how she did in that mausoleum of a castle, which he'd do for any neighbor in difficulty, at least he could keep his word about seeing to the brother. The boy was downright handy, in fact, cheerfully playing the role of carriage driver so the earl could get around the countryside on his estate business. Of course, young Laughton handled the ribbons like a novice, jolting Carlinn's aching ribs over every rut and ridge in the road.

Staying home was worse, for then he had to put up with Cousin Winifred's fussing over him. What the hell did Cousin Winifred—his father's cousin, actually—think lavender water was going to do for a busted rib? Or a posset? Or a mustard plaster, or any of the hundred other nostrums she tried to press on him?

His sister Bettina was worse, going into strong hysterics every time she saw his battered and bruised face. She was already nervous over her first house party, even if her guests were only three schoolmates and their mamas interrupting their journeys home for the holidays for a fortnight's visit. Those three matrons were crucial to her Season next year, Tina had confided, for without a mother of her own, and Cousin Winifred having lived in the country so long, she quite depended on the patronage of her friends' mamas to make the right connections.

In other words, an advantageous marriage. Gads, Carlinn asked himself, when had his sweet little sister turned into a conniving manipulator? When she approached womanhood, he answered his own question. Hair up, skirts down, gentlemen beware.

And her friends were worse, when they finally arrived. Giggling, simpering, batting their eyelashes and waving their fans around hard enough to make the candles flicker—and for him, a battered hulk of a gentleman farmer! He could see the calculating gleams in the mothers' eyes, too, assessing the furnishings at the Hall, the number of bedrooms, the quality of the food. They must have researched his income down to the last shilling; now they were calculating their chicks' chances. Carlinn was titled, wealthy, and unmarried, ergo he was fair game! Blast it, he felt like the fox with the hounds on his heels, and in his own house.

And Dimm thought he ought to get married! What, should he pick a bride from one of these chattering schoolgirls? He'd rather have four more broken ribs. The chits were as silly as peahens, his sister included, with more hair than wit. Blushes, yes, giggles aplenty. They possessed the usual insufficient talent to entertain but not enough sense to know it, and not a jot of intelligent conversation between the four of them. Gowns and beaux and next year's parties: that was the extent of their interests, and their mothers', their older sisters', and their ape-leader aunts' interests.

Jeremiah, when he went to bring the Runner some oranges from the hothouse, was sure they'd ripen with age. The chits, not the oranges. Carlinn was of the opinion that the town bronze they'd get next year would just add a superficial covering to superficial minds. Instead of being unspoiled schoolgirls, they'd have all the affectations of acknowledged beauties. He couldn't even think of picking a bride from the ranks of those . . . those incipient Coach Widows!

Mantraps in training, Foster's cow-handed driving, Aunt Winifred's coddling, Dimm's knowing chuckles, and a face that could scare birds out of trees—they were all too much to bear. Besides, he had another problem.

It was one thing to have young Laughton driving his curricle and running tame in his stable; it was quite another thing to invite him inside the house when there was a gaggle of susceptible young females in residence. Carlinn felt for the lad, really he did, and a wealthy wife could ease his way immeasurably. But these ninnyhammers were Kimbrough's guests. Their families trusted him to see they were not introduced to any scandal-ridden young scapegrace without a feather to fly with. Carlinn found himself making excuses to see less of the boy, steeling himself against Foster's wounded-pup expression.

Then Dimm announced he was being called back to London. Still feeling guilty over the older man's injury, Carlinn had the knacky idea of conveying the Runner into Town in style, in his own well-sprung traveling carriage. Of course, he and Foster would have to go along to make sure Mr. Dimm did not suffer any relapse. Carlinn could do some shopping—Christmas was just around the corner—and take the opportunity to introduce the young marquis to friends at the War Office.

A brilliant idea, the earl congratulated himself. He should have had it a sennight ago before the first of those plaguey females arrived. Of course, a week ago he couldn't have managed the stairs at the Pulteney, much less the carriage ride to Town. Still, it was a capital notion, if it was all right with Foster's sister.

Foster was so excited Marisol couldn't help but agree to the plan. He swore they'd be back in a week.

"Carlinn has to be back to see off his sister's houseguests. Bunch of hoydenish little schoolgirls, I gather. That's why he's running away. All the more lucky for me. I mean, Kimbrough putting in a good word for me will assure I get a quick posting and a crack regiment!"

So she kissed him goodbye, made sure he had her list of Christmas shopping commissions in his pocket, and wished him Godspeed. Then she went back inside and told herself how happy she was for Foster. Her beloved brother had a friend, he could get away from this oppressive atmosphere for a week, he was getting to go shopping, and he could go bounding down the steps so Lord Kimbrough didn't have to leave his cattle standing. If Foster weren't her brother, she would have hated him.

The little party arrived back at Denning Castle two days early. Foster did not bound up the stairs; he was half-carried into the hall between Lord Kimbrough and a young man in uniform. When Marisol got to the entry hall, the earl was helping Foster out of his greatcoat.

Both of Foster's eyes were swollen shut, his nose was covered in sticking plaster, and his lips were cracked and bloodied.

"My God," Marisol cried. "What have you done to him?" Then she started beating Lord Kimbrough about the head with the nearest thing to hand, which happened to be the slipper she was embroidering for Foster's Christmas present. "Wasn't killing my husband enough?"

Foster moaned. "Told you she wouldn't kick up a dust, didn't I?"

Chapter Ten

"Cut line, Mar," Foster gasped painfully through his split lips. "Not Carlinn. Lord Kimbrough wouldn't . . ." He took a sip from the flask the earl held to his mouth. Then Foster tipped his head back so he could look at Marisol through the slits of his eyes. " 'Sides, you work yourself into a swivet, you're going to drop the brat here in the hall."

Marisol was mortified at her brother's blunt speech, which drew Lord Kimbrough's startled glance to her enormously distended midsection, prodigiously more swollen than even the last time he'd seen her. Marisol felt all the more like a hot-air balloon with the crowd watching the inflating process. Blushing furiously, she tore her eyes off her brother and noticed Lord Kimbrough's face for the first time; his cheek and jaw were all discolored, too.

"I'm sorry." She lowered her hand that was still holding the slipper, embroidery threads trailing. "I never should have said what I did. I wasn't thinking, but—" She paused. "Never tell me you had another coach accident."

"No, blast it!" Carlinn shouted, still reeling from her attack. The woman actually continued to believe him capable of murder. Why, he hadn't suspected her in ages, not after getting to know her and her brother. She was imperious, and loyal, and something of a spitfire, but not a killer. Carlinn could picture her going at Arvid with a shoe, not a loaded pistol. How could she still suspect him?

Foster groaned. The earl gave him another sip from the flask. "He'll be more comfortable in his bed. I'll help him up the stairs, then we'll talk."

Marisol wanted to assist, but Foster's weight, those steep stairs—"Don't be a nodcock, Duchess. Your footman can show us the way." He put one of Foster's arms over his shoulder; the young man in army uniform took the other. "Oh, yes, I forgot. This is Joshua Dimm. He's another of Dimm's sons. Joshua was thinking of running off to join the army, to Mr. Dimm's regret and his family's sorrow. So we signed him on as Foster's batman, which should keep him from being cannon fodder. Joshua was invaluable on the trip home."

"Well then, thank you, Joshua, and welcome to Denning Castle. We are in your debt, it seems."

Joshua blushed and bobbed his head. He couldn't very well bow with Foster sagging in his arms. "Think nothing on it, Your Grace. I know my way around a sickroom. That's what comes of having a houseful of relatives and a cousin studying medicine. We'll have him right as a trivet afore the cat can lick her ear."

Marisol sent a message to the kitchens to prepare restorative broths, gruel, invalid foods—and a hearty tea. She was too anxious to wait for the earl's return downstairs, so she ate half the delicacies without him and had to send for more when he got to the parlor.

Carlinn sank exhausted into the chair she offered and gratefully accepted a cup of tea, but he declined further refreshment after he watched the duchess spread strawberry jam on a watercress sandwich.

"I apologize again," she said, oblivious of his fascinated gaze. "You have been kind to Foster, I know, and would not have hurt him. I can only plead a . . . a difficult time and beg your forgiveness."

Carlinn had always heard that women in the duchess's condition needed to be humored. He wouldn't point out, for instance, that most people did not put lemon, milk, sugar, and butter in their tea. The duchess, however, had no one to cater to her whims and relieve her fears. Carlinn did not count that doddery aunt or that dragon of a mother-in-law. And a fine lot of support she'd get from that man-milliner Boynton. He couldn't even support his gaming habit.

No, he shouldn't have taken Foster away, the earl realized now, as Her Grace sugared a cucumber sandwich. He swallowed and looked away. He definitely shouldn't have brought the boy home in this condition, giving her such a shock. And heaven only knew what would happen when he had to give her worse news, trying to explain what occurred in London. She was watching him now with those big blue eyes, waiting for him to begin. Oh hell, he should have told her he'd overturned another carriage.

"I took Foster to visit some friends of mine in the Home Guard," he began, "in case he wanted to change his mind about a cavalry unit. I thought you might rest easier with him staying on English soil."

Marisol nodded. Truly, the man could be thoughtful, when he thought about it.

"Foster met some acquaintances at the barracks and went off with them while I had dinner with an old comrade of mine. I thought he'd find more entertainment with the officers his own age, or I would have kept him with me."

"But he is a young man, not a child in leading strings. It was never your responsibility to look after him twenty-four hours a day."

"But I was supposed to be a good influence, remember? I should have guessed they would . . . At any rate, the sprigs did some heavy drinking."

"As young men are wont to do," she interrupted as the butler came in to ask if there was anything else Her Grace wished. "Yes, I'd absolutely adore some strawberries and clotted cream, please, Jeffers."

The butler bowed and withdrew, as if there was some way on this green earth he was going to produce fresh strawberries in December.

The duchess turned back to Kimbrough. "I'm sorry, my lord. You were feeling badly that the boys were in their cups. What happened then?"

Carlinn straightened his sleeve. "Then one of the others asked about the murder. I'm sorry, but it seems your name was mentioned in an insulting manner, and Foster felt he had to defend you."

"I see." She sat quietly thinking, and Carlinn did not disturb her for a time.

"He incapacitated half a platoon, if that's any consolation," he finally said, "and impressed a lot of the officers with his courage. He'll do well in the army."

"If he lives long enough to join up. He cannot go around brawling every time my name is mentioned." She pushed her cup away and reached for her handkerchief.

Kimbrough heard a sniffle, then another. He jumped to his feet. "Confound you, woman, don't you dare cry!"

Marisol looked up. He was towering over her, scowling fiercely. "Is that an order, sir?"

"Yes, blast it! I mean, no, of course not. Just don't. Please. It's, ah, not good for the baby." He grabbed up a dish of bonbons. "Here, try these."

She dabbed at her eyes. "Thank you, I am all right now. You say Foster is not badly injured?"

"The medico in London assured me nothing's broken, except his nose."

"Is it bad?"

"Nothing to worry about. In fact," the earl went on, relieved to have weathered the storm, "he'll most likely look better—not so snooty, if you know what I mean."

Marisol didn't. Foster had the Laughton Nose, the same one she had. She frowned.

Kimbrough hurried on: "He'll be uncomfortable for a time, and less than pretty to look at, but he'll make a full recovery. The surgeon says your brother's got a hard head."

"I could have told him that! Mayhap some good will come of this, though, if Foster learns not to jump into battle."

"At least not without a regiment to back him up."

The butler returned then with a dish of what appeared to be strawberry preserves atop a vanilla cake, the whole thing covered in dollops of thickened cream. "Cook sent this up, Your Grace, with her compliments. She apologizes, but it is the best she can do at this time."

The earl's mouth watered, seeing the extra dish and fork on the platter. Then the duchess sent it back! "I am sorry, Jeffers, I seem to have lost my appetite. You'd better eat it, lest Cook's nose get out of joint."

"Very well, Your Grace," Jeffers said. He bowed and left.

Marisol sat and twisted her hands in her lap. "Did Mr. Dimm have any news? That's the only way I can see this nightmare ending."

"No, more's the pity. You are right; none of us can relax until the crime is solved. Dimm was going on about facts being as slippery as eels the last time I saw him."

"Eels! I wonder if Cook has any pickled eels."

* * *

The earl called at Denning Castle twice that week before Christmas to see how Foster was faring. The marquis looked as if a carriage had rolled over him, but he was physically fit, and bored. Both times Kimbrough called, the duchess was resting in her chambers.

"The stairs, don't you know," Foster confided over the game of chess Kimbrough had offered by way of entertainment.

"Then I'll ask you to convey my greetings of the season to Her Grace now."

"Oh, we'll most likely see you at church Christmas Eve. The old girl is determined to get there. The dowager's chaplain is all well and good for saying grace and such, Marisol says, but it won't seem like Christmas if we don't go to services in the dark. I mean, you'd never know it was the holiday season around here at all. No greenery, no gewgaws, no kissing bough, no parties."

Foster was fondly recalling Christmases of his boyhood when the family was flush, even the elegant decorations that had prevailed at Denning's London town house in previous years.

Carlinn meanwhile was thinking that young Laughton might have been describing Kimbrough Hall, where every evergreen for miles around had been denuded of branches, every surface was covered with some berry or bow or porcelain cherub, and every neighbor, villager, and tenant was welcomed for carols and wassail. Every neighbor but the Denning ménage, who were in mourning, thank goodness. He moved a rook.

"Mourning, don't you know." Foster was unnecessarily explaining the lack of gaiety. "The dowager swears that even a single wreath would show disrespect for Arvid's memory." Foster made his move, then said, "That's just like Arvid, finding some way to ruin everyone's Christmas."

"If he can't enjoy the holiday, no one should, eh?"

"That's Arvid to the core. Not that Marisol isn't doing what she can, behind the dowager's back, of course."

"Of course."

Foster looked up at the other's dry tone. "She just made sure there was some mistletoe for the servants' hall, mincemeat pies, and a Christmas pudding, so all the tweenies and scullery maids can make their wishes. She made sure there were toys for all the tenants' children for Boxing Day. Nothing disrespectful or dishonest."

"Stubble it, bantling. I wasn't accusing the duchess of being anything more than strong-willed."

Foster's face reddened, not an attractive sight mixed with the purple and yellow. "Pardon. I shouldn't be so sensitive, I suppose."

"No, you shouldn't. The duchess is well able to defend herself when she needs." He studied the board.

Foster thought of Arvid again and dropped the piece he'd been about to move. "Sorry." Then he thought of Boynton and grinned, which hurt his split lips. "Ouch! But you should have seen Marisol light into that coxcomb Pendenning over the Yule log. She went on how the well-being of the whole house of Pendenning hinged on his going out to find a log that would burn till Twelfth Night. She said she didn't care who was duke, but her child wasn't going to suffer because Boynton was too lazy to help the servants find a suitable log. He was head of the household, no matter how temporarily, and he better start acting like it!"

Mulling over his move, Kimbrough allowed as how he'd dragged a huge tree limb home, too. "Silly superstition, but the house of Kimbrough should prosper, too."

"You should have seen Marisol carrying on. And you should have seen Boynton after, with his nose all red and his hands dirty. What a sight. But we do have a Yule log ready to be brought in when we get back from church Christmas Eve. The dowager disapproves, of course. She says we should worship here because we're in mourning and Marisol is too, ah . . ."

"Big with child?" Kimbrough supplied, declaring checkmate. "So naturally your sister is more determined than ever to get in the bumpy carriage and travel through the cold, dark night to a little unheated church. Why am I not surprised?"

The group from Denning Castle was not at midnight services after all. Lord Kimbrough drove his own party home, oversaw the lighting of the Yule log, and toasted everyone's health in wassail. Then he rode over in the direction of Denning Castle to see if anything was amiss.

That fancy London *accoucheur*'s timing, that's what was amiss. Half a mile away Kimbrough could see the castle on its hill, lights in half the windows, grooms riding off in every direction.

Foster nearly threw himself into the earl's arms in relief. "Thank heaven you've come. Marisol has been brought to bed two weeks early. The nearest physician is drunk with Christmas cheer, the next closest is down with influenza, and the local midwife is visiting her daughter in Oxford. I'm at my wit's end."

"You must be, if you're glad *I'm* here. Jupiter, what in the world do you propose I do? I mean, if it were a mare I'd have a go at the thing." He shrugged. "Surely one of the women . . ."

Foster poured the earl a drink with shaking hands. "My aunt's never had a baby. Neither has Marisol's abigail, the cook, or the housekeeper. The dowager had four, but forty years ago."

"I'm sure they still do things the same way." Carlinn tried to be reassuring, but found his own hand starting to tremble.

"That's what I said, but Marisol won't let the old bat near her, nor any of the local matrons like

Squire's wife. She says the dowager and her friends won't care if the baby dies, if it's a boy. She's out of her head, but maybe she has a point. I don't know. Lud, what am I going to do with her talking about dying and all?"

Foster looked as frightened as any green recruit facing the artillery for the first time. Kimbrough felt as if he'd already been shelled. Retreat wasn't possible, so he tried a delaying maneuver. "What have you done so far?"

"Well, Sarah, that's Marisol's abigail, sent for her aunt at the vicarage. That's Dimm's sister-in-law, and she's got three or four brats, I don't remember what Sarah said."

"Aha, that's the ticket. We only have to hold out till the reinforcements arrive! And Mrs. Vicar Hambley has four children. I saw them at church not two hours ago. She'll know what to do."

Foster was beyond rational thought. That was his sister upstairs, cursing her dead husband. "But what if Mrs. Hambley doesn't come in time?"

"Don't even think about it, lad. What else have you done?"

"Well, I sent for Dimm, too. Marisol might be dicked in the nob about someone trying to hurt the baby, but I had to humor her. He won't get here till tomorrow anyway."

"Rear guard never hurt. What else?"

"We put water on to boil. Everyone knows to do that much. And he"—Foster jerked his head toward the corner of the room where Boynton sat—"made another bowl of wassail."

"Excellent, excellent. Nothing like firing up the troops. So now all we do is wait. That's the hardest part of any campaign, the waiting. And there's one other thing a good soldier does before battle: He prays like the devil."

Upstairs a different kind of war was being waged. Marisol was trying to evict the dowager from her chambers, and the dowager was refusing to leave.

"If you can believe I'd harm my own grandson, I can believe you'd be so low as to switch babies to save your own skin. I am staying right here until I see that child with my own eyes."

Marisol was midway through swearing that she'd not let the baby come while her mother-in-law was in the room, when Mrs. Hambley calmly arrived and took over. First she rolled up her sleeves. "See? Nary a bairn stashed anywhere, Your Grace," she addressed the older woman. "And me a vicar's wife besides. I'd never have truck with such havey-cavey doings. What comes is God's will, and that's that, so you can go downstairs and keep the men-folks from drinking themselves stupid or you can sit in that corner out of the way quiet-like." Next she washed her hands and turned to Marisol. "While we get to work instead of this argle-bargle. And you save your energy for the baby, Your Grace, for from the size of him—or her—it's going to be a handful."

So Marisol stopped fretting about the dowager and concentrated instead on hoping that bastard Arvid burned in hell for doing this to her.

Downstairs the men paced. Then Foster dozed off in a chair and Boynton slipped in and out of a drunken stupor on the sofa. The Earl of Kimbrough found himself pacing alone, which made him so angry he paced harder and faster. What the bloody hell was he doing here anyway, and why was he the one staying up all night worrying over Arvid Pendenning's relicts? He'd just go on home. They could send a messenger.

Then a door slammed upstairs. Foster sat up with a jerk. More doors opened and closed. A woman screamed. Boynton got himself over to the nearly empty wassail bowl and started to pour out a cup. They all heard the next scream; they all bypassed the punch bowl and headed for the whiskey decanter.

There was one more scream and then, when at least two of the men were ready to tear their own hearts out if it would help, came the unmistakable sound of a new life welcoming the dawn of Christmas morning.

Boynton and Foster trailed Kimbrough into the vast, echoing marble hall. They stood there, staring up, for what seemed like hours more.

"For the love of God," Boynton shouted up the stairs, "what is it?"

There was one more shriek, a long, loud, high-pitched moan actually, the unmistakable sound of the dowager pulling her hair out.

Chapter Eleven

The earl paid a duty call two days later. The baby was his ward and all. He brought flowers from the Hall's conservatory for the duchess and a silver rattle he'd picked up in London for the occasion for the baby. It seemed the thing to do. He'd leave his offerings with the butler, play a game of chess with Foster, and be on his way, duty done.

Except the duchess wanted to see him. Upstairs, in her newly refurbished chambers. Carlinn found himself adjusting his neckcloth as he followed Jeffers up the stairs.

Marisol was propped up against the pillows of the large, sun-filled room. But the sun was not shining this day. Instead, the room was painted a soft lemony yellow and had flowered bed coverings and drapes so it reminded him of spring. The duchess wore a robe of amber velvet, buttoned to her chin, and a jonquil ribbon was threaded through the long blonde braid that lay over her shoulder. She looked weary and wan, but happier than he had ever seen her.

Nodding briefly at his arrival, the duchess turned her rapt gaze back to the bundle by her side.

"I wanted you to meet your ward, my lord," she said softly. "It's a boy."

"Yes, so I'd heard," Carlinn replied dryly. He could still hear Foster's whoops reverberating in his ears and the unpleasant sound of Boynton grinding his teeth into nubs. Then there had been the servants' cheers, the ringing of church bells, the messengers sent off to London, Boynton drumming his feet on the carpet. The day after Christmas brought Mr. Stenross with papers to sign, Foster with inquiries about his commission, foxed Boynton to be fished out of the village pond. You might say the earl had heard.

"And he's the most beautiful boy in the whole world," the duchess cooed. "Come look."

Lord Kimbrough took a cautious step closer to the bed. "Very nice, I'm sure. Congratulations."

"Silly, you can't see his face from there. Come closer."

She was right; the child looked like a pile of rags from this distance. He went up to the bed. It still looked like a pile of rags. Then the duchess peeled away a layer or two of wrappings. My word, he thought, he'd seen more appealing specimens crawl out from under a log! Worst of all, the red and wrinkled creature seemed already to possess the Laughton Nose. Great heaven, was that to be his job, too, to see that the child's nose got broken before he reached manhood? The duchess was looking up expectantly.

Carlinn coughed. "Er, handsome indeed. Fine big boy, I understand." That's what the aunt had said, that he was a strapping lad despite coming into the world two weeks early. To the earl the infant looked only slightly larger than a newborn foxhound pup, and not nearly as charming. He must have said the right thing, however, for the duchess was smiling blissfully.

"Have you, ah, selected a name for him?" the earl asked, rather than trying to come up with more Spanish coin. "I, ah, bought him a gift, but it needs to be monogrammed." He held out the tissue-wrapped parcel. Her maid took the flowers to put into a vase and drew a chair next to the bed for him. So much for a brief duty call.

Marisol uncovered the silver rattle. "How kind. Nolly will love it when he is a little older."

"Nolly? I know I said I wouldn't interfere, ma'am, but you really can't send your son through life with a name like Nolly. Why, he wouldn't survive public school."

"I know that, my lord. I'm not a total peagoose, you know. His name is Noel, for being born on Christmas day, but we can call him Nolly until he's bigger. The dowager is furious, of course."

"Of course. I suppose she thought the babe should be named after Arvid?"

"Yes, so that his memory would live on. As if I wanted any reminder of Arvid! I only pray Nolly has nothing of his father in him."

Nolly would have done better with Arvid's nose, Kimbrough decided, but he kept that thought to himself.

"The dowager then suggested, no, she *demanded* that I name him after the fifth duke, her husband Ajax. Everyone says Arvid's father was a worse scoundrel than Arvid ever managed to be. And Foster already bears our father's name. So it's Noel, for the holidays, that he should find joy and hope. Noel Alistaire Laughton Pendenning, seventh Duke of Denning. There's more, but all those titles and such can wait."

"I daresay. So is the dowager resigned, now that she has such a, er, fine grandson?"

"Oh no, we've already had words. I refuse to hire a wet nurse, you see, and she considers that unladylike and indecent." She looked up at him, challenging him to make a comment.

Kimbrough hadn't come through two years on the Peninsula without knowing when to keep his head down. He just nodded.

"And she thinks Nolly should be in the nursery."

Again she was daring him to exert his authority. "Ah, isn't that where infants usually go?"

"What, when he's so tiny and needs me so often? Why should he be alone, or with strangers, or worse, with that old woman who nursed Boynton?"

"Heaven forfend. For all we know, she's the one who first wrapped that coxcomb in puce swaddling clothes."

"You're teasing, but I am not. The woman is as deaf as Aunt Tess. What if Nolly were hungry or hurt?"

"Quite. But how will you manage?"

"Very well, thank you. Women have been caring for their own babies for centuries now, don't you know?"

"But they haven't been duchesses, I'd swear. Soon you'll have this great barn to manage, the dowager to dislodge. And you need your rest."

She nodded, tucking the baby back in his blankets. "My maid Sarah is a gem, for one thing. I cannot even imagine asking Tyson—she was my dresser in London—to help change Nolly's diapers. Tyson hated babies. And Sarah has a sister at home who is wonderful with children. Rebecca helped care for all of Vicar Hambley's brood and is now seeking a position, according to Mr. Dimm. We'll do fine until she arrives in a day or two."

"Oh, then you've seen Dimm?" He studied the tassel on his Hessians, wondering how much the Runner or Foster had said about the latest contretemps. He hoped the news hadn't upset the duchess; there was still childbed fever to be wary against. She didn't look ailing, just tired as she nuzzled the top of the infant's head.

She said, "Yes, Mr. Dimm called yesterday afternoon. Isn't it wonderful?"

"Wonderful? That Mr. Dimm called?"

"No, about the shooting. I don't mean that it's very wonderful for Lord Ashcroft, of course, or his family, but I didn't do it!"

It was too late; the fever had already affected her brain. "Pardon?"

"Don't be so buffleheaded. Your neighbor, Lord Ashcroft, was shot in his carriage on his way to Squire's house Christmas morning. And there is not a soul in England who can possibly accuse me of committing the crime. Isn't that fine?"

"Of all the addlepated ideas . . . It was a robbery gone bad, that's all. Ashcroft was only nicked. Nothing to do with you or Arvid or anything."

"Then why was Mr. Dimm asking Foster if he'd gone straight to bed after the baby was born? And asking Boynton if he'd gone directly to the village to get castaway?"

"Because as magistrate I asked him to assist our local constable, whose major investigation prior to this was finding whose cow ran through Widow Greenfield's front garden. Lud knows why I asked Dimm to help with the detective work, he's done so poorly with Arvid's murder, but I did. And he was asking us questions because he wanted to know if we saw anything that morning, that's all."

"Us? Weren't you home either?"

"No, I was keeping vigil here with your other suspects. Then I went home, across the fields, seeing no one. I let myself into my house, seeing no one, and slept alone in my bed until my sister woke me up to open Christmas presents. No alibi." He crossed his arms over his chest and glared.

"Oh. Well, as you say, it must have been a robbery. And Foster is too excited about his army career, and I told Boynton I'd pay his debts if the child was a boy, so there is no motive." She took her eyes off the baby long enough to notice his dark look. "And you are too well breeched, of course."

Kimbrough got to his feet. "Thank you, I think.

I'll just be going along then. There is a crime to investigate, don't you know, and I am magistrate."

She missed the sarcasm, staring again at the baby in her arms. "You know," she said, "I really could kill someone, I think. I mean, I used to believe I would never do such a thing. But now, with Nolly to protect, I do think I could." She looked up, and a cold, hard expression came over her face. "You might be Nolly's guardian, but I swear, if you ever harm a hair on his head, I'll—"

"Nolly doesn't have a hair on his head, you baconbrained Bedlamite! And I am not a murderer, a brute, or a child molester! What do you think, I'll have Nolly drawn and quartered if he soils his nappy?"

The infant started to cry. Marisol drew him closer. "Look at you, you're shouting! If you can shout at a tiny baby, you can do anything!"

"I am not shouting at the baby, madam; I am shouting at you!" Carlinn lowered his voice to a mere window-rattling whisper. "And yes, you aggravate my temper past bearing, but that's all, do you hear me? That's all! I can be angry without committing mayhem, Duchess. Lud knows you are pushing me to the limits, but I am not a violent man!" He stomped to the door. "Once and for all, I am not a murderer! And your child is not—" He was going to say "not beautiful," but the sight of her rocking the infant, whispering to him, made Carlinn regret even intending the slight. "Your child is not in any danger."

"Deuce take it, the woman is afraid of me!"

"Don't fatch yourself, my lord," Dimm consoled him, over a glass of the finest cognac it had ever been the Runner's pleasure to sip. "Females is unpredictable. They be especially changeable in Her Grace's condition, like with the tides. They got their humors, their moods."

"Yes, but that woman's moods are all bad! And

it's not just now, either. She's always been afraid of me."

"If you think on it, mayhap she has cause." Dimm held the stemmed goblet up to the fire's light, admiring the color of the spirits the way his lordship was doing, but not for too long before having another sip. "Figger this. For all she's a duchess, Her Grace is a weak little dab of a thing what couldn't protect herself from a flea. You're a big, imposing bloke what does shout some." He held up a hand before the earl could protest. "I know, my lord. You be used to yelling at the troops to make sure they heard you—to be obeyed. But she ain't no soldier."

"You make me sound like Attila the Hun. I'm a gentleman, confound it!"

"I can't say as that holds much weight with Her Grace neither. Look what examples of the breed she's known so far. That brother's just an unlicked cub with a quick fuse, but he'd use his fists afore his tongue every time. The father was a decent enough sort, from his rep, but he lost the family holdings so Her Grace had to take the highest bidder, Denning. Violent man, His Grace. No, don't surprise me none if she fears men."

"You're saying he— No, I don't want to know." Kimbrough swirled the cognac in its crystal. "That bastard."

"I'll drink to that." So he did, and the earl poured another glass for both of them. His lordship lit a cheroot, and Dimm had his pipe going, his feet propped on a hassock. Heaven couldn't match this, he figured, then begged his dead wife's pardon, God love her. As dusk fell, so did the level of the bottle. Dimm contemplated his host, sprawled in his leather chair, still glowering over his visit with Lady Marisol.

"A woman like that needs a man with a gentle touch, like a filly what's been broke to bridle too rough. Otherwise that filly won't let any man near her. Unrideable, don't you know."

"What, you think the duchess will never marry again?" In Kimbrough's experience, all women married again and again, given the chance.

"Hard to say. She won't have to, with her income, that's for sure. And it's just as sure that she'll have men buzzing around her like bees to a flower iffen she seems interested. Once she goes out and about, she could have her pick."

"Yes, of every loose screw in England."

"She be young, beautiful, and rich. What more could a decent chap want?"

"Your particular filly's got a dashed odd kick to her gallop. No discriminating gent's going to fall for those big blue eyes and forget the rest."

"No? It happens every day. Plenty."

"Not in the ton, it doesn't. And she won't marry any fortune hunter either, if I have my say."

"But you don't have any say-so, begging your pardon, milord. You be the boy's guardian, not Her Grace's."

"Exactly, and she's not taking my ward away to live with any basket scrambler."

Dimm whistled. "I see some rough sailing ahead, I do. Wouldn't want to be in the room when you tell Her Grace she can't marry where she wants this time around, if she wants."

"Nonsense. I wouldn't discuss it with her; I'd just warn the flat off. I'd be doing the skirter a favor anyway. Her Grace would make a hell of a wife." He got up to put another log on the fire.

Dimm shook his head. "I don't know why you two rub sparks off each other. Onct I got to know her, I found Her Grace a real lady. Loyal, quick-witted, pretty as a picture."

"A picture of a battleship in full sail, you mean. No, the woman I wed will be sleek. None of this running to fat, after. And she'll be biddable, by George, without all those moods and megrims."

"Been thinking of taking a wife then, have you?" Dimm wanted to know.

"I've been thinking of Arvid's going off so suddenly, that's what. And Lord Ashcroft getting shot. Something like that could happen to anyone."

"Uh-huh. If there be one thing certain, it's that life ain't."

"And then there's my sister and that blasted presentation. I can't like depending on acquaintances to chaperone her properly. A well-bred, socially acceptable wife could get Bettina fired off in style."

"No saying but what the right wife can ease a man's burdens. So you want one as won't ruffle your feathers, won't get snubbed by them hostesses at Almack's, and won't be real expensive to feed?"

Carlinn raised his glass in salute of the Runner's perspicacity. "That sounds ideal."

That sounded about like taking a broom to bed to Dimm, but he asked, "Where are you going to find this nonesuch, guv? Iffen you don't mind my asking."

Kimbrough waved the other man's demurral aside. They were old friends by now, he and the Runner, sharing cognac, sharing confidences. Less likely comradeships had formed, though at this precise moment he couldn't quite recall when. "My bride? She won't be in London, that's a sure bet. I don't want any polished Diamond who'll be as cold as a stone in bed and hard as a rock to m'sister and m'friends on the farms. And no spinster that didn't take, of course. None of those stammering debs will do or I'd have to bear-lead two chits through a Season. A country girl wouldn't have the enteer either, so no milkmaids for me."

"That do narrow the field some. Not too old, not too young, not from the country, not from the City. No wonder you ain't legshackled yet."

"Ah, ye of little faith. Such a paragon does indeed exist. My cousin Winifred's goddaughter is currently a leading light in Bath society, where she resides taking care of her ailing mother. Good sign, don't you know, when a chit knows her duty. She had a London Season three years ago and two offers since then as far as Cousin Winifred knows, so she's no ape-leader. Not an Incomparable, but not an antidote. That's the kind of woman I have in mind, one with a sense of responsibility who won't land me in the briars every step."

"And is she thin enough? Better yet, how plump is her ma? You can allus tell what kind of pup you're getting by looking at the kennel."

"Lady Sherville has kept her figure," was all the earl vouchsafed. Lady Sherville was as thin as a rail. Her daughter, unfortunately, was as flat-chested as a boy. Miss Edelia Sherville was well bred, well mannered, well connected, even well dowered. A man couldn't have everything.

"Well? When are you going to offer for the gel?"

Chapter Twelve

A man couldn't just rush into these things. Mortality might beckon and all but, dash it, a fellow had other responsibilities, too.

Now that the streambed land was his, Lord Kimbrough had to see about reclaiming those flooded fields. He had to consult with specialists, hire engineers, order equipment, and sign on work crews before he could think of leaving the project in the hands of his steward.

Then there was the steward for the Denning lands. The fellow seemed honest and capable, but the property and people were not in good heart. Arvid had been a harsh master, and a clutchfisted landlord. Both the steward and Kimbrough agreed improvements were long past due, but the earl didn't know the other man well enough to trust him with the decisions. Kimbrough was therefore obliged to meet with him nearly daily, to visit the fields to see conditions for himself, and to call on the tenants to hear their complaints, which were numerous and well founded.

Everywhere he looked, everyone he spoke to, gave

more evidence of Arvid's villainy and venery. The people, tenant farmers and villagers alike, were excited about the infant, but mostly they were pitifully eager to welcome a right 'un like the Earl of Kimbrough as liege. So Carlinn had to stop and toast the new duke with homemade wine or ale or cider at every farmstead and cottage, reassuring Arvid's people that *he* wasn't going to be an absentee manager. So he couldn't very well just hare off to Bath for the winter so soon after that.

Kimbrough also had to make sure that young Laughton was granted his commission, now that Foster was recovered enough from his injuries and the dibs were in tune. A few quick trips to London would see the deed accomplished, but Carlinn wasn't about to take his eyes off the feisty lad until he had him in uniform and under orders to abstain from brawling. Of course, then Foster and his batman Joshua needed to be outfitted and mounted. The earl couldn't send his ward's uncle and Dimm's boy off to war on Arvid's old break-downs, could he? Tattersall's was full of park-prads and highbred cattle that would bolt at the first sound of cannonfire. Luckily there were horse fairs in Berkshire.

There were also robberies in Berkshire. Lord Ashcroft's attacker struck another time, again only wounding his victim, another solitary gentleman driving alone in his carriage. The highwayman got away with a heavy purse, but left behind a good description of himself and his horse. The local constable, Mr. Dimm, and his lordship were all on the lookout. As magistrate, the earl felt it his duty to oversee the inquiry.

No, there was no hurry to get to Bath. Miss Edelia Sherville and her flat chest had gone all these years without being snatched up by some other lucky beau; she could wait a month or two. The earl told himself that Miss Sherville's lack of projection had nothing to do with his delay. He wanted a slender wife, didn't he? Besides, there was nothing wrong with Miss Sherville that an infant or two couldn't cure.

And the weather was bad.

Winter raged outside, and a storm blew through Denning Castle. Marisol was cleaning house. *Her* house. Foster went off to London. Boynton, his debts paid and his allowance increased, followed the Regent's set to Brighton. The dowager kept to her wing of the castle with joint pain, her nose in particular being out of joint. And Marisol lined up every last servant in the place, from butler to potboy.

"This castle and everything in it," she told the assembled staff, "now belongs to His Grace, the seventh Duke of Denning. The household, therefore, will function for His Grace's comfort and convenience, as I see fit. If there are any of you who take issue with this, please leave now so that we may avoid any future unpleasantness. For understand this," she pronounced, her chin lifted, her voice raised so the smallest scullery maid could hear in the back, "I will tolerate no insubordination. No disrespect toward my son, myself, my family, nor those I have hired to care for us. No disloyalty, no dereliction of duty to the duke, no disregard for his safety. Nothing. Is that understood?"

She waited to hear murmurs of assent. "Very well. I do not know my mother-in-law's plans at this moment, since she is ill with a sore throat."

"From eating too much crow," a voice in the rear of the ranks called out, and was hushed.

"If she chooses to take up residence in the Dower House, those of you who wish may apply to her for positions there. If she remains, she is also part of the duke's family and as such is entitled to the same respect. No more, and no less."

Not even the bootblack had to be told what that meant: Lady Marisol was in charge, plain and simple. Just for insurance, Marisol added, "Anyone who is less than loyal to the interests of His Grace shall have me to answer to. And the Earl of Kimbrough."

Marisol hated having to invoke the earl's name, but he was Nolly's guardian, after all. Let him be handy for something, even if it was striking terror into the hearts of recalcitrant retainers. She dismissed the staff.

Then every cupboard was turned out, every sheet inspected for mending. Unused rooms were shut off, and important chambers were restored and polished to a fare-thee-well. The castle's structure was inspected and made sound, eliminating drafts, smoking chimneys, and loose roofing tiles. Historic artifacts were catalogued and stored, or displayed out of reach as Marisol and the staff tried to think ahead.

The duchess was everywhere—the new duchess, that is. The old duchess stayed in her rooms suffering from back pain. She wanted to be back in command.

Lady Marisol, as she was called to avoid confusion, ran upstairs and down, from the attic to the cellars, with a hundred stops between. Sometimes she raced up and down the stairs to reach Nolly at his first whimper, but sometimes she just used those steep marble steps for the exercise. Besides the weather being too inclement for outdoor activities, Marisol needed to be within reach of her son at a moment's notice. Furthermore, she was determined to have her shape back before the spring, and the light muslins she so enjoyed. So she also ordered fewer courses served at dinner.

The dowager made her excuses from the table. A headache, this time, from banging it against the wall.

And Nolly thrived. How could he not, under his mother's adoration? He had his aunt Tess's knitted bonnets, booties, and blankets to keep him warm; Dimm's daughter Rebecca to see him clean and dry;

Her Grace's maid Sarah to listen for his cries; and Mrs. Vicar Hambley to lend advice and admiration. And of course Nolly had the smiles and pats and coos of a castleful of people dependent on him for their very livelihoods.

The only thing His Little Grace was missing—not that he suffered from the lack—was his grandmother's affection, for she was too ill. It was heart trouble. She didn't have one.

No peacock in his full plumage ever strutted as proudly as Foster in his brand-new scarlet regimentals.

"Oh dear," Marisol cried as she watched her beloved brother practice walking without tripping on his scabbard, "however am I going to let you go?" Foster wasn't just a little boy playing at soldier anymore; he was really going to go off to war this time, with real swords, real pistols.

"Don't be a gudgeon," he told her in that fond way brothers have. "You can't stop me now. 'Sides, it was you gave me the chance to go and make something of myself in the first place. Arvid never would have, by Jupiter. I'd still be like a dog begging for crumbs at his table. That's the way he wanted it, don't you know."

She knew that, but she also knew how much she was going to miss her brother, how much she was going to worry about him. Marisol wouldn't make Foster carry the burden of her anxieties, though, so she only told him how proud Nolly was going to be with a hero for an uncle.

"There," Foster teased. "I knew you couldn't keep the brat out of the conversation for two minutes! See, you won't miss me a whit, now that you've got Nolly to fuss over. Why, you've hardly noticed me this past month." He fondly chucked the sleeping baby under the chin.

"Not true!" Well, only partly true.

When Foster's orders had come, Marisol scheduled Nolly's christening for the week before her brother was to meet his troop ship, so he could stand as godfather. Aunt Tess would be godmother.

Marisol had sent out invitations to the ceremony at Reverend Hambley's little church and the reception at Denning Castle after, without much response. Still, she spent more time over her toilette than she had in ages. Sarah had transformed one of her old gowns for the occasion, trimming a lavender taffeta into half-mourning, with black ribbons and black rouleau at the hem. The maid had loosely coiled the duchess's thick blonde hair under a black ruched bonnet that trailed a long black veil, and both the bonnet and the gown's bodice were embellished with clusters of silk violets. Black gloves completed the outfit, which should have satisfied any but the highest sticklers. Since none of them had bothered responding to her invitation, Marisol was unconcerned. She felt almost attractive again.

They'd come to the church early, so she might feed Nolly in the little vestry in hopes that he'd sleep through the ceremony. Now she sat waiting, watching the church fill with a few of the tenants, a handful of servants, and the Reverend Hambley's brood. There were more of Jeremiah Dimm's relations here than there were of Nolly's, she calculated. So be it. These were the people who mattered, the ones who cared about her son.

Then Lord Kimbrough arrived. Marisol told herself she shouldn't have been surprised. Nolly was the earl's ward, after all, and Kimbrough was nothing if not punctilious about his duties. The earl had even dressed for the occasion, in Bath superfine and dove gray pantaloons. He was just too large a man for elegance, Marisol decided, but he did look bang up to the mark, as Foster would have said. Except for the frown, of course. Lord Kimbrough's scowls were nothing new to Marisol, but she did wonder if perhaps he was up in the boughs this time because she'd selected Foster to be godfather. The guardianship was enough for one man, she'd decided.

As Foster went out to shake the earl's hand, Marisol realized Kimbrough's forbidding countenance had nothing to do with her, for once. He was aggravated beyond bearing, she could tell from her place in the tiny chamber, at the necessity of introducing Foster to his family. Marisol's handsome scamp of a brother was making his formal bows over the hands of the earl's older cousin and his younger sister. His impressionable younger sister. The stunning little brunette was staring up at Foster, fading bruises and all, with open-mouthed admiration. The earl bustled her off into a pew, glaring.

Marisol grinned. Hoist with your own petard, my stiff-necked lord.

Her attention swung back to the door, through which a knot of gaily decorated gentlemen entered, laughing and comparing times for the journey. Boynton had come and brought some of his friends. "M'nevvy's christening, don't you know," she heard him tell Lord Kimbrough. "Couldn't miss it, so we made it into a race. I won a monkey on Cordell's grays. Use some of the flimsies to buy the boy a gift, don't you know. Can't imagine what he'd need now, of course, so I'll set the blunt aside for when he's ready for a pony, what?"

Ponies would grow wings if Boynton had that money when Nolly was old enough to ride, and everyone knew it. Even his friends all laughed. "No matter," Boynton said good-naturedly, "Prinny sent a gift. Youngest duke in the land, don't you know. Doubt it's paid for either, now I think on't. But it's the thought that matters, what?"

"What's he saying?" Aunt Tess asked, next to Marisol in the side room.

"Boynton's telling everyone that the Prince Regent sent a gift to Nolly."

"How lovely. Unless it's a portrait of himself. That's what he sent Lady Harrowsmith. She had to hang it in the infant's room, of course. The child had nightmares for years."

"It's the thought that counts," Marisol found herself repeating as another commotion at the doorway caught her attention.

Bugles should have been playing a fanfare. At the very least, a superior butler should have stood at the opposite end of a red carpet announcing the new arrival. No, the Regent hadn't decided to attend in person after all. The dowager had.

She swept in on her chaplain's arm, dressed head to toe in flowing black crepe. She accepted her son Boynton's kiss on the cheek and the other gentlemen's bows with a dismissing wave of her hand as she sailed toward the front pew. When Lord Kimbrough's sister swept her a deep curtsy as she passed, the dowager paused and patted the girl's hand. "Practice," was all she said. Even from her viewing place Marisol could see the girl's lower lip begin to tremble. Then Foster strolled by, retrieving one of the scarfs Her Grace had dropped, and winked at Bettina. The sun came out again on her face.

Oh dear, he isn't going to be happy, was all Marisol had time to think, before carriage after carriage deposited passengers at the steps of the little church. Where the dowager led, her fellow gorgons followed. And where those bejewelled, beturbanned, and befurred bastions of local society went, their husbands, sons, and daughters followed, willy-nilly.

Marisol quickly conferred with Sarah, who stepped outside with a message for their coachman, who sent a rider back to the Castle to warn Cook, who almost had apoplexy, that so many more guests were coming.

Then it was time. Marisol handed little Noel Alistaire Laughton Pendenning to his godparents and wept as Vicar Hambley said the prayers over him.

Nolly behaved, Foster stopped grinning at Lady Bettina, and the dowager nodded.

Later, everyone complimented Marisol on her beautiful baby, the refurbishing of the Castle, and the excellent refreshments. If some of the company privately found some of the offerings plain fare, Marisol was not surprised. Cook had excelled, but many of the dishes had been prepared for the servants' celebration later. The duchess promised them a better party tomorrow—and a bonus.

The excellent wines from Arvid's cellars compensated for the refreshments and kept the gathering in high spirits. None were higher than the dowager's as she held court in the Queen Anne drawing room, her grandson in her lap. Nolly's long white lace gown draped over the black crepe of her mourning. It was the gown Arvid and Boynton had worn, she told everyone, and their father and his before that. Of course, none of them had been such a fine boy as Noel.

And Marisol tried to hold back her tears some more, until Lord Kimbrough quietly handed her a handkerchief.

"Those better be tears of happiness," he commanded, but turning her so that his broad back shielded her from curious eyes.

"Yes, thank you. And thank you for coming. It was a wonderful day."

"I am happy for you," he told her, and meant it. This woman could send him into a rage with the curl of her lip, and her tears could turn his knees to blanc mange, but he truly was happy to see her on terms with her in-laws, accepted in the local society, and content. Yes, it was a good day, a happy occasion. Carlinn would have been more than satisfied, had it not been for the sight of his baby sister hanging on Foster Laughton's sleeve.

Blast! It was even more important that he get to

Bath. If Bettina fell for the first scarlet uniform she saw, it was time and past to see her Out. Why, he could even take her to Bath for a month or two, to get her feet wet in those smaller circles where enough of the Quality congregated for the winter. That's the ticket! He could go first to find accommodations and look things over, so to speak. That way it wouldn't be so obvious that he was looking over Miss Sherville. He needed a wife, he told himself. Bettina needed the example of a mature, responsible lady like Miss Edelia Sherville. He'd do it. As soon as the highwayman was caught.

Chapter Thirteen

The apprehension of the robber became even more crucial. One of Boynton's friends was set upon after leaving the christening party. The thief got away, and Sir Oswald returned to Denning Castle late that night, shaken and considerably lighter in the purse. Sir Oswald accepted Marisol's offer of a guest chamber for the night and her assurance that, since he was a guest of the Castle, the Castle would make good his loss. Sir Oswald did not protest as much as he ought, Foster felt, but there was no escaping the evidence of a bullet hole through the man's curly-brimmed beaver. While Rebecca, Nolly's nursemaid, offered to brew a special tisane for Sir Oswald, Marisol and Foster waited downstairs for the constable from the village, Dimm from the inn, and the magistrate from Kimbrough Hall.

Carlinn had just gone to bed, so he threw on his shirt and breeches and an old pair of boots and followed the messenger back to the Castle.

Sir Oswald's profile of the highwayman matched the previous description, but still did not match any of the known local miscreants: for the most part poachers, inebriates, and dealers in goods without excise stamps. This little section of Berkshire countryside was not known as a hotbed of crime, Lord Kimbrough tried to reassure the duchess.

"At least not until we Londoners arrived," Marisol replied, offering the earl sherry in the parlor after his interview with Sir Oswald and his later conference with Dimm and the constable. They had decided the night was too advanced to look for clues in the dark; they'd meet in the morning where Sir Oswald had been waylaid, but without much hope of success.

"I could see it on the faces of those ladies today," Marisol went on, "underneath their politeness. Thank goodness Foster will be on his way Tuesday. No one can accuse him of anything untoward."

Foster was pouring the drinks. He still wore his uniform, unbuttoned, and he ran a hand through his hair. "Dash it, I'm sorry to be going. I'd like to help in the hunt, find the dastard, and stop this infernal gabble-grinding."

"You'd do better to concentrate on stopping the Corsican, bantling," Kimbrough told the younger man, which brought a grin to Foster's lips.

Marisol could not be so easily diverted. She lay awake fretting after the earl left and the house had settled down, and that was how she came to hear the noise next door, in Nolly's room.

Marisol reached for a light, and knocked a book off the night table in her fumbling. She heard a muttered curse, then a cry from Rebecca, and a door closing. To hell with a candle, Marisol thought, flying to her son, calling his name loudly enough to wake everyone but Aunt Tess and the dowager in the far tower.

By the time the duchess reached the makeshift nursery, Rebecca was sitting up in bed, rubbing her eyes. Nolly was wailing, the nursery lamp was still glowing, and no one was in sight.

"I thought, that is, I couldn't be sure, Your Grace. I thought someone shook my shoulder, but I could have been dreaming, and then there was a noise."

Then there was a lot of noise, as Foster and servants came running. No one had seen anything.

They sent for Lord Kimbrough and Dimm.

The earl had been dreaming, and not pleasantly. Even in his sleep he knew he should be dreaming of Edelia Sherville. Life with her would be a sailboat ride on a tranquil day, everything smooth and peaceful, nothing to disturb the proper course. Instead his dreams found him tangled in the sails of a sinking ship in the middle of a raging gale, with a full-bodied siren with flowing gold locks beckoning him onto the rocky shoals. "Damn it," he cursed, waking in a sweat with his sheets strangling him, "that blasted woman has even invaded my dreams."

But it wasn't any blue-eyed siren calling him to his doom: it was his valet, with another urgent message from the Castle.

The shirt, the breeches, the boots, the same sleepy groom saddling a horse.

This time the duchess was in her own dishabille, a blue dressing gown buttoned over a lace-collared white lawn nightgown and a silly lace bonnet tied under her chin. And this time she was not merely fretful; she was frantic.

"The highwayman was in Nolly's room, I tell you! You have to do something!"

"Perhaps you had too much champagne this afternoon, Duchess, and that sherry on top of it led your dreams—" Since his own dreams had been far-fetched but all too vivid, he could well believe hers might be, too.

"I was not dreaming, I tell you. Someone was in

my son's room! And no, I do not believe in ghosts, before you ask me that absurdity."

"But the servants found no one, you said, and the maid wasn't certain. Your nerves have been overset and—"

"I am not a hysterical woman, so do not patronize me, my lord. There is a gunman loose, maybe two counting Arvid's murderer, and I want him found. Them. Whichever one was in Nolly's room. This is your province, Lord Kimbrough, so I demand you do something!"

Foster was upset, too. "Can't like to think about going off like this, leaving my sister all unprotected, with no man in the house unless you count that caper-merchant Boynton. I mean, what if the fellow is a madman?"

"Boynton? Are you accusing Boynton of being a Bedlamite?" He turned to Marisol. "Do you still consider your brother-in-law a suspect in Arvid's murder, trying to do away with his nephew now so he might succeed to the title?"

Marisol twitched at the belt of her robe. "I don't know what to think anymore. Boynton seemed thrilled with a raise in his allowance and a fresh start. I'd rather suspect your highwayman."

Kimbrough was pacing. He stopped and pounded on the mantel. "Begging your pardon, Duchess, and I swear I am not being patronizing, but what in bloody hell do you think a cove on the bridle lay was doing in the nipper's room?"

"Excuse me?"

"I apologize. Let me rephrase that. Why, if someone was in your son's room, do you think it was the highwayman?"

"Someone *was* in my son's room, and your highwayman has been going around robbing and shooting, that's why."

What kind of logic was that? He tried again. "But wouldn't the robber have gone after the silver plate or your jewels?"

Foster nodded. "He's got a point there, sis."

"There are white slavers and things. Gypsies steal children all the time."

"Not in Berkshire, they don't, Duchess. And if anyone wanted a child that badly, he could go to a hundred orphanages and poorhouses. No, I cannot believe this was the same man at all."

"He could have been trying to kidnap Nolly to hold him for ransom. I'd have paid anything to get him back. Everyone must have known that!" Marisol was starting to look damp-eyed, and her voice was quivering. Foster patted her hand.

"Please, Duchess, try not to get hys—ah, upset." Kimbrough might as well have asked the sun not to rise, which he could see it doing out the window just now.

"Don't get upset? What kind of unfeeling brute are you?"

"Now, sis, coming it too strong. His lordship's trying to be helpful."

"No, he's trying to shut me up so he can go back to sleep in his nice, warm, *safe* bed. How can I not be upset, I ask you, when someone might hurt my son? With Foster going off to war, he's the only thing I've got, the only child I'm likely ever to have."

"Don't make this a Cheltenham tragedy, ma'am," Carlinn said in exasperation. "Nothing is going to happen to your son, and you're bound to have a whole houseful of kiddies if you want."

She sniffed. "What, do you think any decent man would marry me now, after Arvid's scandal?"

Well, Carlinn wouldn't, but . . . "Of course, Duchess. You're young, well bred, wealthy."

"Of course, we mustn't forget the fortune," she snapped, having read his answer on Kimbrough's face, the puffed-up, prudish peer. "As if I would wed some down-at-heels fortune hunter. But none of this is pertinent to the matter, my lord. What are you going to do about the intruder in Nolly's room?"

First he suggested she have that yappy little dog Max sleep in the room to act as a warning device. Then he sent a message to Dimm, asking him if he knew an experienced bodyguard who would patrol the house and grounds. Those measures seemed to relieve Foster some, enabling him to resume packing while Kimbrough interviewed the servants again.

They all seemed genuinely distressed that anyone might think of harming the young master or upsetting the mistress, but they had no clues to offer. So he went to speak to Sir Oswald once more before the other's departure, in case the robbery victim recalled any helpful details. He did.

"About that little taradiddle last night . . . Didn't mean to frighten the girl, don't you know."

"The girl?"

"The nursemaid, the one who brought me the tisane. Thought she was extending an invite, don't you know. Didn't mean to set the house on its ear."

"You didn't mean to—? Why, you—!"

If Sir Oswald was shaken by the robbery, it was nothing to being shaken by the Earl of Kimbrough. The earl had the man off the ground and dangling by his shirt collar. Sir Oswald swore to leave the Castle, Berkshire, England, anything the earl wanted.

Kimbrough wanted all that plus an apology to the nursemaid and to Duchess Denning, and he wore a complacent grin while he watched the man grovel. Foster grinned, too, after he planted the man a facer and tossed him out the door. But the duchess didn't grin. She didn't even thank the earl. She merely took one look at his smirk of self-satisfaction and reminded him that the sun was up and there was still a murderous highwayman loose in his lordship's domain. Then she went back to bed.

Thunderation! Must he always appear no-account to the blasted female? And what should he care if the duchess thought him rude, arrogant, and incompetent? He cared. And so what if she nonsensically feared for her child's safety and even more foolishly feared him? So he'd do his damnedest to wipe that look of terror from her face, that's what. No woman should be afraid, Kimbrough told himself, not of her husband, not of strangers, certainly not of a bumbling blockhead like himself. Why, the code of chivalry honoring womankind ran so deep in his blood he might have been one of those wretched knights strewn around Denning Castle, clanking along in metal inexpressibles.

Obviously, what he had to do to restore a bit of luster to his armor was capture that thatchgallows on the high toby. There were no usable tracks to follow, no new directions to pursue, which only left setting a trap as a viable course. The makebait liked to prey on gentlemen traveling alone after dark, so the earl and Dimm decided that that's what he'd get.

They planned the trap for that very evening. Since the moon would be full, the highwayman was sure to be at his craft. Before going home for some much-needed rest in anticipation of a long night, Lord Kimbrough returned to Denning Castle. He only thought to relieve Her Grace's mind, he told himself. She would be happy to know that a plan was under way to capture the thief, and pleased that Dimm's son Gabriel, the one in training to be a Runner, was already on his way to safeguard the little duke. Dimm thought it would be good training for the lad, who was familiar with infants, and good for the baby to hear a deep voice now and again.

"Gor'blimey, little chap's being fawned on by five women at least. With that brother of Her Grace's gone, he'll need someone to teach him how to toss a ball and spin a hoop."

When the earl had last seen His Grace at the christening, Master Noel had needed nothing more than sour milk mopped off his chin. But if it eased the duchess's mind, one more Dimm on hand made no difference to Lord Kimbrough.

Marisol was indeed pleased that Nolly would have an armed guard by the end of the week. She was not quite as pleased with the earl's plan to act as bait for the robber. In fact, the approval, trust, and respect Carlinn thought to see in her eyes for once was missing altogether. In her eyes instead were enough fireworks to light up Vauxhall Gardens.

"No, not even you can be so chowderheaded, my lord," she said, fists clenched at her side. She didn't even offer him tea, she was so angry. "Then again, you must have been the gudgeon, for Mr. Dimm would never have devised such a reckless scheme. I am surprised he agreed to go along with it at all."

Dimm's agreement was hard-won, but Lord Kimbrough was not about to give the irate duchess more ammunition. "I thought you wanted me to apprehend the felon," he noted instead.

"Yes, to capture him, not offer him your head on a silver platter!" she shouted. "It's too dangerous, you jackanapes! Can't you see that, or are you so puffed up in your own conceit that you cannot comprehend an armed and desperate man winning out over the Earl of Kimbrough?"

"What, never say you are worried over me? And here I thought you'd be happy to see me gone."

"Don't be ridiculous," she said, puncturing what vanity the earl had left. "I am concerned for Nolly's sake only. What, pray, happens to him if the gentleman of the road does not behave in a gentlemanly fashion? What if he shoots you first, for instance, and then asks for your purse? What good is Dimm hiding in some bushes going to be then? And what good to my son are you going to be dead? The court will appoint another guardian, most likely Boynton. He is the Prince's friend, for heaven's sake. And you know what he is, what he'd do to

Nolly's estate." She crossed her arms over her now-heaving chest and pronounced, "You cannot do it."

Carlinn tore his eyes from that same generous bosom. "Dash it, Duchess, you cannot tell me what to do. You are not my wife, b'God."

"Heaven be praised for that mercy! And I pity the poor woman who takes on that thankless task. Of course, a wife might remind you of your responsibilities more."

Carlinn crossed his arms, too, more so he wouldn't be tempted to shake her than anything else. "You go too far, Duchess. I have made allowances for your sex, for your condition, even for the uncomfortable position you found yourself in with a virtual stranger thrust into your affairs. I have even tried to make excuses for your shrewish tongue. But I have *never* needed to be reminded of my duties, which is why I will not permit you to dictate my behavior, and why I will not permit a criminal to prey at will on my neighbors."

Marisol stormed over to the parlor door and threw it open hard enough to rock the panel on its hinges. "So you'll ride into danger with your pride for protection like any insolent, footloose bachelor. What about your responsibilities to Nolly, my lord? To your sister? You are even more of a jackass than I thought."

She left in a swirl of silk. The earl shook his head, wondering if that was the sound of the door slamming or the sound of his brains rattling loose in his skull. And here he'd thought she'd appreciate his efforts.

Lord Kimbrough and Jeremiah Dimm went ahead with the plan that night despite Her Grace's objections. The earl drove his curricle up and down the highways and country lanes, humming unconcernedly, while Dimm lay covered with a carriage blanket at his feet, pistol in hand.

It was a good plan, Carlinn told himself, not

reckless or devil-may-care. He cared very much to stay alive, thank you. He'd even sent reservations to the Ship Inn in Bath, so confident of the future was he. As Carlinn tooled his pair up a tree-lined lane, the perfect place for an ambush, he wondered how soon after his arrival in Bath he could call on Miss Sherville without being too obvious. He'd have a letter from Cousin Winifred, of course, her godmother, but it wouldn't do to raise expectations in her mama's hopeful breast until he was certain.

Fortunately the highwayman did not choose that particular spot to make his move for, unfortunately, that hopeful breast brought to mind not Miss Sherville's inadequate one, but the devilish duchess's milk-filled, rounded, mounded abundancy. The carriage hit a rut and Dimm cursed. Lud, the sooner he was wed the better.

The highwayman did not choose any other roadway Kimbrough drove that night either. It was a good idea, driving around with a lantern on his curricle like some perverse Diogenes seeking a dishonest man, but it didn't work. Nor did the earl's efforts to keep Duchess Denning out of his dreams when he finally sought his bed after midnight.

Chapter Fourteen

The urgent message came at three in the morning. There had been another incident at Denning Castle. With a scant two hours' sleep in two days, and that interrupted by extremely disturbing dreams, the earl could not generate the fever pitch of excitement he used to feel riding into battle. He didn't bother with a neckcloth or a waistcoat or a hairbrush. He just went. Lord Kimbrough was not in prime twig for more alarms.

Neither was Marisol. Her thoughts all night had been filled with images of the earl's bride, whoever she turned out to be, the poor dear. He'd bully her and shout at her and insist on having his pig-headed way about everything. The woman would be miserable, unless she admired broad shoulders and a firm jaw and a dedication to duty as immovable as a mountain, the widgeon.

Marisol pummeled her pillow. At least there was something she could force to her will. Of course, the pillow fought back, making lumps and hollows that kept her from a deep sleep. Tossing restlessly, she was easily roused by a slight noise next door. She waited to hear if it was Nolly stirring, or Rebecca checking on him, or even Max sounding an alarm. She heard nothing, and was about to drift back to sleep, chiding herself for a peagoose, wasting precious sleep time when Nolly would be up soon enough.

Then she did hear another noise: the sound of a door shutting.

"And don't tell me my imagination was working overtime, my lord," she told Kimbrough, "for someone was there. They knew enough to give Max a lamb chop to keep him quiet, and if I hadn't screamed, who knows what would have happened?"

Her scream had woken the baby, of course, and the weary servants who had to be up in a few hours, and Foster, who was to leave after breakfast. Even Boynton dashed to the rescue in his nightshirt, his hair in curl-papers. They found nothing but the lamb chop to signal an intruder.

The earl had the staff go outside with lanterns, looking for tracks under windows, signs of forced entry, anything. He made each one account for his or her time, then made them swear on the Bible they hadn't come next or nigh the infant. Then he ordered wine for the duchess; she must be more disturbed than he thought, for she didn't even rip up at him over his high-handed treatment of her servants. She merely amended his order to tea, with brandy for the gentlemen. Marisol was so pale, with purplish shadows under her eyes, her voice so subdued, that the earl almost forgave her for another night's missed rest.

What a damnable coil! Foster was in anguish over leaving in the midst of a family crisis. The young man's sense of honor couldn't permit him to abandon his sister in time of need, but he had his orders. Boynton, on the other hand, was packing to get out of this madhouse as soon as his valet could manage. Between the infant's caterwauling and his sister-in-law's fits and starts, a gent couldn't get his beauty sleep. Marisol meanwhile was asking the butler to find Arvid's hunting rifle. Lud, that was all they needed, Carlinn thought: a hysterical woman with a loaded weapon. She was wound so tight she'd likely shoot a crackling log in the hearth or a branch scraping along the window. Or him, for not protecting the infant.

Kimbrough could see the accusation in her eyes: He'd been out having a lovely drive around the countryside while some heinous malefactor was attempting to make off with her baby. He rubbed his eyes and tried to stifle a yawn. The sooner Dimm's son got here, the better.

Servants lit a fire in the parlor, the child was put back to sleep with a weary nursemaid, and Max was taken outside to be dosed with salts in case the lamb chop was poisoned. The footman who got that job was almost as aggravated with the earl as the duchess was. The servant couldn't show it, of course; Her Grace could. She practically ignored Kimbrough's presence while they waited for Mr. Dimm and the tea tray, as if she regretted sending for the nobleman and his useless suggestions.

Marisol was indeed avoiding looking at Lord Kimbrough who, with his unbuttoned shirt and ruffled hair, was looking barbaric and heroic and sleepy. His poor wife would have to look at that broad, hairy chest every night, if she was lucky. Marisol blushed at her own thoughts and dragged her mind back to Nolly. Maybe she should take him into her own bed? Nolly, she reminded herself, Nolly. At this rate her son was never going to reside in the nursery the dowager was so busily refurbishing for him. He'd never ride the rocking horse or play with the tin soldiers, for he'd have to be walled around with armed guards. But she would not weep. No, not a drop, at least until she was alone in her room, Nolly under one arm and a rifle under the other. Marisol made herself be strong for Foster, so he could go off and follow his own dream. And she had to show the earl she was no milk-and-water miss. She tucked a wayward curl back under her nightcap and poured out the tea as if she were entertaining Princess Lieven and Sally Jersey at an afternoon call.

The earl had to admire the chit's backbone. But how could she sit there so calmly when he was at his wit's end wondering what was to be done? Not that he thought the child was in any real danger; if someone truly wished the boy harm, there had been plenty of opportunities. He wondered if the duchess would feel safer at Kimbrough Hall. He could move her, infant, nursemaids, aunt, and all, but would he get any sleep whatsoever, knowing she was a few doors away? Botheration. Besides, he couldn't promise to keep her safe and then scamper off to Bath. What kind of watchdog would that be?

"A watchdog, that's what you need," he declared. "Not a barking lap-sitter like Max, but a real trained guard dog. The kind that stays out watching after sheep and cattle, defending them from wolves. Looking after one small baby can only be, well, child's play to a protective breed like that."

Marisol was dubious. A large, unkempt herd dog in Nolly's room? Besides, there hadn't been wolves in England in ages; she'd worry more the animal would swallow the baby. But Foster was nodding eagerly and the earl was going on, excited to have a plan of action. This plan seemed as harebrained as his notion of trapping the bandit, but Marisol didn't say anything. He meant well, and she didn't actually have to get the dog, so she nodded.

Then Kimbrough said, "Don't worry, I'll take care of finding just the perfect animal myself."

Before Marisol could voice her objections, Aunt Tess wandered in, a frilly mobcap askew on her gray hair. She frowned at her niece. "I saw all the lights, dears. Don't you think it is a trifle late for company?"

"This isn't a social call, Aunt Tess," Marisol explained, pouring a cup of tea for the older woman and speaking loudly. "I didn't want to wake you to another frightening event, but there has been another intruder in Nolly's room. Please don't be upset, Aunt Tess, but someone gave Max some food to keep him quiet. We don't think it was poisoned, but . . ."

"Poisoned?" Her aunt blinked. "Oh no, Cook would never leave poisoned food out on the table. Why, one of the servants might eat it. Much better to put the lamb chop on the floor behind the cupboard if you wish to kill rats. But I thought cheese . . ."

"Aunt Tess, you knew Max ate a lamb chop?"

"Of course, dear. Didn't I tell you Cook leaves a snack out for me? I don't sleep well at night. Old bones, don't you know. So I often take myself to the kitchen for some warm milk or whatever Cook leaves out. Tonight I thought Max was doing such a good job, he deserved a treat, too. And I did want to check on dear Nolly in case he needed another blanket. I thought he might like a lullaby or something, so you could sleep longer. You've been looking so tired, dear. But he was sleeping soundly, precious darling, so I tiptoed out."

"And you didn't hear me scream?"

Aunt Tess was stirring her tea. "What's that, dear?"

So Carlinn drove his curricle home as another dawn was breaking. He was exhausted, emotionally drained, confused by the feelings that warred in him. That's when the highwayman struck, of course.

The first shot startled the horses into rearing and kicking. Kimbrough had all he could do to keep the curricle upright. He certainly couldn't remove a hand from the ribbons to reach for his pistol in his greatcoat pocket. He fought the horses to a standstill, as per instructions.

"That's right, guv'nor, keep them steady. Hands on the reins where I can see them." The masked horseman rode over, a second pistol aimed straight at Carlinn's heart. "Now real slow, throw down your purse. And if you think to reach for a gun instead, you better be thinking fast, for I can't miss at this range."

It wasn't worth the gamble. He didn't have much money with him at any rate, and the thief already had his weapon cocked. Carlinn did as directed.

"Hell's fires!" the bandit cursed when he felt the lightness of Kimbrough's purse. "And not even a stickpin or a watch fob to pay for my time. Damn it!"

For a moment Carlinn feared being murdered for disappointing a deuced footpad. "Sorry," he said. "If I'd known your intentions, I would have been better prepared."

"I'm sure you would have, guv'nor. The local militia and a small cannon, eh?"

"No, just my pistol at the ready. I misdoubt you'd be so brazen were this a fair fight."

The highwayman laughed harshly. "Life ain't fair, m'lord, or haven't you heard?" With that he slapped the flank of the carriage horse nearest him, sending the curricle on another mad dash. He rode off into the woods while the earl struggled to halt the plunging team. If Kimbrough hadn't been a consummate fiddler, he'd never have brought the bays under control so quickly, nor managed to turn them in time to see which direction the rider had taken.

The dastard had gotten away with Carlinn's small purse and with a large portion of his pride, but he hadn't gotten clean away this time. The presunrise air was cold and frost lay on the ground, frost that kept a perfect set of hoofprints riding through the woods. When the earl had the horses calmed, he stepped down from the curricle, tied the bays to a bush to nibble, and followed those receding marks until he had a good idea where the bandit was heading.

This was his land they were on now, and Carlinn knew every inch and every abandoned gamekeeper's cottage. If he was mad before, he was outraged now; the maggot was using Kimbrough land for his hideout. Carlinn did not let his anger blind him to reason, however, so he went back to the curricle rather than going after the cutthroat on foot with only one round in his pistol. He drove home and changed his curricle for a fast horse, enlisted his stable staff, and sent riders off to fetch Dimm and Foster.

They all met at the marker that divided Kimbrough's property from Denning's, had a short conference, and followed the earl into the woods on foot. Some carried pistols, some pitchforks; all wore tired but determined expressions.

When they saw chimney smoke deep in the forest, the earl deployed his troops to encircle the small cottage he knew was there. "But remember," he whispered, "the man is dangerous. He is a hardened criminal who has nothing to lose now, for he can only hang once. No heroics," he especially warned Foster and his man Joshua, "and no one moves until I give the word."

They all nodded and took up positions surrounding the stone dwelling. The earl alone crept closer, dodging behind tree after tree until he was crouched almost beneath one of the narrow windows at the side of the house. He listened intently, then silently crept forward. He listened again. At last he straightened enough to peek through the window.

The glass was none too clean so he had a hard time making out the interior of the cottage. A bed, a stool, a sink, a cupboard. Then he saw a hand-hewn table, with two pistols lying on it alongside his purse. And finally, in the far corner, he spotted the dangerous, deadly, cold-blooded highwayman. Shaving. Pistol in hand, the earl wormed his way around to the front door, waving his cohorts nearer. When they were close behind him, he reared up, kicked the door in, and tumbled after it, landing next to the table holding the man's weapons, which he swept to the floor.

"Hands up, you son of a bitch."

The bandit, his back to them, slowly raised his hands, dropping the razor he'd been holding. Jeremiah Dimm kicked it away and gathered up the fallen pistols. "Evidence, don't you know," he said, then cleared his throat. "Pardon, milord, but this here's my line." He cleared his throat again and addressed the prisoner's back. "By the power vested in me by His Royal Highness King George, you is hereby arrested in the name of justice. Now turn around, you son of a bitch."

The man slowly turned, hands still in the air, to face at least five gun barrels. His own face, however, was still covered in soap lather.

"Shouldn't he wipe his face first, Da, before you take him in?" Joshua Dimm asked. "I want to see what he looks like."

So did Lord Kimbrough. He tossed the man a towel.

The highwayman scrubbed at his face, then made the earl a mocking bow. "Jack Windham, at your service."

"Windham? That label is on my list somewheres," the senior Dimm declared, reaching into his inner pocket for his notebook.

Foster was staring at the accused, a man not much older than his own twenty years. "Why, I know you. We played cards at Banning's place one night."

"I'm sure I lost. I always do. Do I owe you money,

then?" He jerked his head toward a box on the cupboard. "Help yourself."

Kimbrough's eyes were narrowed. "Windham, eh? Any relation to Lord—"

"My uncle," the man answered quickly, glancing at the crowd of stablehands in the doorway, mouths agape.

"What the bloody hell is any nephew of Lord—" Kimbrough began, to be interrupted by the Bow Street man.

"Aha! I got him now. This here is one of the blokes what lost so heavy to His Grace afore the murder. My man reported that Windham was with a doxy at the time."

"Patsy is a loyal thing, if a tad mercenary. And of course I was one of those whose vouchers Arvid Pendenning held. Why else do you think I would be doing this?"

Kimbrough shook his head. "You've taken to the high toby to pay a gaming debt?"

"Not just a gaming debt. Denning won everything I owned and then took my vowels. Honor was about all I had left, so I had to pay him off." Windham turned back to the tiny mirror and frowned. "I really do need a shave, old man. I don't suppose . . ."

The earl shouted to his back: "Turn and face me, sirrah, and tell me what honor there is in robbing and shooting innocent people!"

"I never meant to shoot Ashcroft, I swear. He threw his whip at me and my horse reared. The gun went off by accident. As for taking up the bridle lay—debtors' prison was a certainty, Tyburn tree was a gamble. I'm a gambler." Windham shrugged. "I thought the family name could stand my death better than my disgrace. And this was the only way I could pay Denning back, or his widow, as it turned out."

"Then I take it you never received Her Grace's note?"

Windham sneered. "Desperate criminals on the hideout seldom get regular mail delivery, my lord."

"Too bad, fool. She cancelled all of Arvid's debts. He cheated."

The highwayman threw the towel to the ground and stomped on it. "Blast! Then you mean I'm going to hang for nothing?"

"Why, no. You are going to hang for highway robbery, assaulting a peer of the realm, and possibly murdering Denning."

"You can't lay that on my dish, and I can prove it. I was on Hounslow Heath at the time, robbing two carriages. You want evidence?" He stepped toward the cupboard, with all the pistols following his move. He tipped the box onto the table and pawed through the contents. "Here's Lord Lithgow's snuffbox; this is Mr. Harriman-Browne's fob."

Dimm chewed on his pencil. "He's right. I remember thinking I was happy to get the Denning case 'stead of the robberies that same day. Still, we got us a confessed criminal."

"What we've got," Lord Kimbrough told the Runner, "is the nephew of one of the most highly placed men in government."

He whispered a name in Dimm's ear that had the older man sighing, "His nibs ain't going to be happy about this 'un a'tall."

Lord Kimbrough turned to Windham. "You say all of the booty is here? All the money you stole?"

"Of course, every shilling. A few more pigeons and I'd have enough to pay back my debt. I don't care that Denning cheated. I do not welsh on my debts to widows and orphans."

"Jackanapes," the earl muttered, feeling very old, very tired. He pulled Dimm out of the tiny house for a conference.

When they returned, Dimm collected the loot to be restored to its owners. Then he set off for London to collect the reward, if he could explain matters to his superior. Lord Kimbrough went home to pack. Then he traveled to Bristol that very morning with Foster and the younger Dimm, along with His Majesty's latest conscript for the Army.

Once he saw the official papers signed, the nodcock's uncle notified, and the ship's anchor raised, Carlinn took a room at an inn and slept for two days. He woke refreshed and reinstilled with a sense of mission. Bath was not far out of his way home. He'd stop and pay his respects to Miss Edelia Sherville. But somewhere between Bristol and Bath, the earl found just what he was looking for. And he couldn't very well call on Miss Sherville with a three-legged Border collie under his arm.

Chapter Fifteen

Max was in love. The little terrier followed the collie bitch around and did not let her out of his sight. One wave of Sal's tail sent the fluffball flying, so at least Max learned to mind his manners. For her part, Sal seemed to understand instantly what she was supposed to do. Carlinn did not even have to wrap the baby in lambskin, as the shepherd had advised, thank goodness, for he wasn't eager to sell that plan to the duchess.

The shepherd was sad to part with Sal, for he'd raised her from a pup, and her mother, too. But she'd been caught in a poacher's trap, and a three-legged dog was just no good out on the dales with the sheep. The herder hated to put a good dog down, but he was a working man who just couldn't keep a big, hungry animal as a pet. He already had a one-armed brother-in-law.

The deal pleased the sheepman, who went home that much richer, and Kimbrough, who'd convinced himself that making the duchess more comfortable in Berkshire was the right and proper thing for him to do. Somehow his guardianship of the infant overflowed its paper boundaries to include the mother's peace of mind. Carlinn refused to consider how that had come about.

Marisol wasn't sure she was comfortable with the collie at all. Sal was the best-mannered dog the duchess had ever seen, but that was not saying much, considering she was used to Arvid's barely civilized foxhounds or social lapdogs like Max. But Sal was devoted to Nolly. If he cried and no one came soon enough, the dog threw her head back and howled. If anyone entered the room, her hackles rose until Rebecca the nursemaid or Marisol told her "Friend." She knew who was allowed to bring things into the room, and who was allowed to carry the baby away. On her brief excursions away from the baby, to the kitchens or outside, she was restless and whiny, until she could lope with her peculiar gait back to Nolly's room, check the crib, and take up her position in front of the fire.

Marisol couldn't have asked for a better bodyguard for her son, especially with Dimm's son Gabriel to watch over the dog with a pistol at his side, just in case Sal forgot.

The highwayman was captured, Boynton had journeyed to a house party in Kent, and Sal recognized Aunt Tess as a friend. Marisol had nothing to worry about, except her brother, of course, and minor household matters. So unperturbed was the duchess, in fact, that the earl was able to convince her to go on a short outing, especially when he informed her in that blunt way of his that she looked like death on a dish, from lack of healthy outdoor color. They drove in his curricle to visit that flooded parcel of land, so Kimbrough might explain what the engineers had advised. She left Nolly for a whole hour. Even more astonishing, she spent that hour in the earl's company without once coming to cuffs with him.

So she thanked Lord Kimbrough and started getting out and about a little on her own. She didn't accept social invitations, both for Nolly's sake and as a sop to the dowager's mourning. But she did return a few of the local ladies' afternoon calls, she and Aunt Tess. Mostly the duchess enjoyed her brief visits to the child-filled vicarage, where she and Mrs. Hambley discussed the need for a larger school in the district, so girls as well as boys might learn their letters and possibly some skills to better their lives. With the work to be done for such a project, Marisol found that she needed a wet nurse after all. The dowager didn't gloat too much. And Marisol didn't wait too long before telling Sal the dowager was a friend.

Settling in to local life and motherhood, Marisol started thinking of gardens come spring. It was almost here now. The Kimberly ladies called once after the christening, and the London Season was all Bettina wanted to talk about. Marisol wouldn't miss it a bit.

Her letters to Foster were full of Nolly's latest accomplishments, of course, and the doings of the little village of Pennington, and her callers, especially Lady Bettina's wide-eyed fascination with everything to do with London. *"I wish you were here to chat with the girl,"* she wrote, *"since I cannot satisfy her curiosity with any pleasure on my part. London holds no fond memories. Certainly I was never as eager as Lady Bettina for my presentation. Her own brother says he dislikes everything about Town and doesn't want to think about it until he has to face her debut, next year."*

Marisol realized her letters would bore Foster; he hardly knew the Berkshire neighbors, and she didn't even have any London gossip to impart. By the time she got to the newspapers they were weeks out of date.

That's why she was so happy to greet Mr. Dimm when he called after a visit to the vicarage.

"Come to see how my boy Gabriel is doing with the dog and the babe, and if you've heard from that brother of yourn," he told her over a hearty tea, after admiring the baby's growth.

"Your house must seem empty now, with so many of the younger people finding employment here in Berkshire."

"Wouldn't say it was 'zactly lonely, not with my sister still keeping house and the occasional in-law dropping by. Then there's that boy we aren't sure who he goes to." He stacked a cucumber sandwich atop a watercress sandwich and put the whole in his mouth. "But it's getting so I can hear myself think nowadays, and that's no bad thing."

Curiosity made her ask if he had done any more thinking about Arvid's murder, and if people were still talking about her in London.

"I can't tell you 'bout the Quality, by Jupiter, but in my circles, they're talking a mite too much for my comfort. His nibs ain't happy that we've still got an open book on the case."

"Then there's nothing new?"

"Well, there is and there ain't. Jack Windham's alibi holds; so does Lord Armbruster's."

"Oh, you found Armbruster's ladybird?"

"Not 'zactly. I finally found who Lord Armbruster visits at that there love nest, but it ain't going to make a difference in the case."

"His, ah, bit of muslin vouched for him, then?"

"His bit o' muslin wears it for a cravat."

Marisol had to think about that for a minute. She quickly glanced in Aunt Tess's direction to make sure that her innocent aunt was still busy with her knitting. "Oh."

"Worse. Not only wasn't Armbruster not meeting a high-flyer, he was meeting the under secretary of the Exchequer. I figure that's why I was sent on vacation, like. Warned off. Hanging offense, don't you know."

Marisol didn't care about Lord Armbruster's hanging if it wasn't to be for Arvid's murder. "Perhaps that was why Lady Armbruster was so concerned when she found herself breeding."

"Right, Armbruster must of knowed he couldn't be the father. Might've been happy to have an heir, might've been furious. He swears he didn't know. My thinking is she hadn't told him yet, waiting on what Denning said that day. Still, Armbruster didn't kill her or the duke, so we're nowhere, 'cept I'm out of a job if I go near Armbruster again."

Marisol was disappointed, but not terribly so. She never thought quiet Lord Armbruster could have shot anyone. Then again, she never thought quiet Lord Armbruster could have . . .

"Oh, by the by," Dimm was saying, "do you have the address of the mother of that ladies' maid of yourn in London? The servants at Portman Square don't have it. I want to ask her a question or two again. Be surprised what people remembers when they have more time to think."

Marisol shook her head. "No, but the employment agency must. Or else they'll give you her new employer's address. She'll have a position by now, since I wrote her a good reference. Check there, or with Purvis, I suppose. Arvid's valet might know, though he must have a new direction by now, too."

"Not yet. The others say he's talking of emigrating to the colonies. Tired of waiting on swells, they say, but it might just be sour grapes that he ain't found a job."

"I wonder if Lord Kimbrough would consider taking Purvis on. Heaven knows the man looks like he dresses in the dark half the time."

"Been seeing much of his lordship?" Dimm asked casually as he made a selection from the pastry platter. "I called there, but he was out and about."

"No, we don't see much of him these days," Marisol said, angry to hear the petulance in her voice. "That is, I understand the earl is very busy. He is getting things ready so the county can survive his absence for a few weeks when he goes to Bath."

"Bath, eh? Taking the waters, is he?"

"Taking a wife, if gossip is correct. I am surprised you hadn't heard."

Dimm choked on his third macaroon.

Marisol never put much stock in the servants' grapevine, not even the almost infallible Dimm network, but she'd heard this rumor from the earl's own sister.

"He says he's going to see if there's a suitable house to let," Bettina grumbled. "As if I want to go to fusty old Bath. And Carlinn hates it there, too. He had to go once to recover from a wound, and I remember him complaining how there was no company except invalids and old ladies."

"Then why is your brother going, especially when he seems so busy having to oversee Nolly's property in addition to his own?" Marisol felt guilty at all the extra work pushed onto the earl's shoulders, broad though they might be. "He isn't feeling downpin enough to seek a cure or anything, is he? Those broken ribs from the curricle accident have healed, haven't they?"

Bettina laughed. "Carlinn? He's healthy as an ox. You must know he thrives on hard work. No, I'm afraid this latest start of his is my fault. Not exactly my fault, perhaps, but on my account. Carlinn told Cousin Winifred that he wished I had a female relation among the ton to take me in hand before I blotted my copybook."

"I'm sure that's not what he meant. He must have been wishing for someone who knew all the hostesses and all the rules, to take you around. That does make things easier."

"Yes, but then he said it was time he started thinking about setting up his nursery."

All of Marisol's recent warmer feelings for Kimbrough slipped away, leaving a knot of icy disdain behind. She forgot about the dog, and how the earl had helped Foster, and how conscientious he was about the Denning holdings. Kimbrough was going to seek a proper wife, was he? Someone who could produce both Bettina's successful Season and the necessary heirs. He'd most likely line up the eligible females and select the one with the best breeding, the widest hips, and the largest dowry. No, Kimbrough didn't need a wealthy wife, no more than Arvid had. The earl would want a more mature lady so she could chaperone Bettina, but otherwise it was the same. Another poor female would enter another cold, loveless relationship, where her lord and master made sure he got good return for his investment, then went his own way. Perhaps she'd shoot him.

"And then," Bettina was going on, "he asked Cousin Winifred about her goddaughter who lives in Bath. Edelia Sherville; do you know her?"

Marisol smiled. Edelia Sherville wouldn't have to shoot Kimbrough; she'd bore him to death. Yes, the duchess knew Miss Sherville; they had shared a Season. And yes, she was everything proper and correct. She was attractive, accomplished, well connected, and even well dowered, Marisol believed. She was also the most self-consequential person Marisol knew, after Kimbrough himself. What a perfect couple, two perfect jackasses! Truly it would be a match made in heaven; unfortunately they'd be living next door.

Marisol reproved herself for uncharitable thoughts. She didn't know why the thought of Lord Kimbrough's wedding should be distressing; surely the man was entitled to a happy marriage. And if Miss Sherville was his choice, well, Edelia was no green girl being sold on the Marriage Mart. She'd only accept Kimbrough if she wanted an oversized, fusty churl, or if she thought she could reform him. Marisol wished her good luck. She also wished, for Bettina's sake, that the earl had asked his cousin about her goddaughter merely out of curiosity or family feeling.

Carlinn had asked Cousin Winifred about Miss Sherville because he wanted to make sure she hadn't fallen into any bumblebroths or betrothals while he dithered in Berkshire.

"I'm sure I would have heard if she accepted any of her beaux, Carlinn, but what do you mean, has Edelia gotten into any hobbles? She's a lady, Cousin, not a hoyden. Edelia Sherville does *not* fall into scrapes."

Cousin Winifred's emphasis gave him pause, but not enough to change his plans. That was what he wanted: a wife above reproach. He packed, he left instructions with his staff, he held one last conference with the Denning bailiff, he paid his farewells to the duchess.

Marisol was in the morning room when he called, the baby kicking his legs in the air on the sofa next to her, the dog Sal at her feet. Carlinn paused in the doorway to admire the picture they made, the warmth shared between mother and child, the love that made Lady Marisol almost beautiful. Until the butler announced him. Then that mask of hauteur fell over her face. The chin rose, the nose went in the air, the duchess was back. He could almost see the strawberry leaves and ermine. Blister it, the woman changed moods as often as his sister changed her outfits. Today, he could tell, the duchess was as prickly as homespun drawers.

Marisol's greeting was cool, her wishes of Godspeed tepid, and her regards to his family perfunctory. Carlinn got up to leave after ten minutes, refusing tea because of the press of packing. The duchess wrapped the baby in his several blankets and picked him up to walk Kimbrough out. Before they reached the door, however, a huge commotion erupted in the hall beyond, with thuds, clunks, crashes, shrieks, and curses. The earl made to go see.

"No, my lord, please stay here. This is obviously a domestic crisis, and your presence will only embarrass the staff at such an awkward moment. I'll go. Here, you hold Nolly."

And she handed over the baby. Just like that.

"But, ma'am, I've never—"

"Then it's time you learned," she said from the doorway.

Carlinn looked down at the pile of blankets in his arms—the child weighed almost nothing—and said, "I cannot believe you'd trust me with him."

"I don't. I trust Sal. Stay, girl. And do not worry, my lord, you'll do fine. Just hold his head up." And she was gone.

Hold his head up? The last time someone said something like that they were talking about an artillery cannon. " 'Old 'er 'ead up, boys," some old, grizzled sergeant used to yell, warning the cannon was loaded. Lower the barrel and a live ball was liable to drop out among the troops. My God, he thought, holding the infant farther away from his body, what did the duchess have in mind?

Embarrassed servants be damned, Carlinn started to follow Marisol out the door. Sal had other ideas. Her orders were to stay. Stay she would. The big dog got between Kimbrough and the door. The fur on the back of her neck rose; the lips over the long white fangs lifted.

"Friend," Carlinn called in his cavalry-command voice.

"Grr." Sal marched to a different drummer.

The earl slowly backed up until he felt the sofa behind him. He sat, gingerly cradling the baby. The dog sat, tongue lolling, tail wagging. "Good dog. Good baby."

But the baby wasn't being good. He was starting to screw up his face and turn red. Oh God. Carlinn jumped to his feet and started pacing, three-legged

Sal following with her eyes. The movement calmed the baby some, but his arms and legs were thrashing in the blankets. "Want the coverings off, do you, old chap? Can't blame you. She's got you done up like a straitjacket."

But when he started to place the baby down, Nolly started to cry and Sal started to whimper. Carlinn snatched him up again. Like trying to juggle eggs, the earl tried to unwind the constricting blankets. And keep Nolly's head up. And keep walking, but not toward the door. "And don't drop it, whatever you do," his lordship muttered to himself, wishing he had another hand to wipe the sweat off his forehead. Why did they have to wrap the creature in so many layers? It was deuced warm in here.

Finally the baby was more or less free, except for the death-grip Kimbrough had on him. Nolly turned his face into Carlinn's chest, got a mouthful of blue superfine, and started sucking. "Dear Lord, not that!" He shifted the light weight around, so Nolly was more or less upright, and close enough to get a fold of the earl's neckcloth in his mouth. "No!" Carlinn almost shouted, but caught himself in time when he saw furrows appear on the little brow, making Nolly look like a thoughtful old man. He stuck his thumb in the baby's mouth. "It's the best I can do, old chap. Don't blame me; blame her for leaving you."

Nolly wrapped his hand around the earl's thumb and looked up at him. The gray-blue eyes stared into Lord Kimbrough's brown ones almost assessingly, as if wondering just what kind of guardian he was going to be if he couldn't provide a snack. The earl was mesmerized by that clear stare, the tiny fingers, the downy hair, and petal-smooth skin. The infant smelled of talcum and weighed next to nothing, and frowned his disapproval like the most superior of aristocrats. Like his mother. And he was so soft, like his mother.

Then Nolly spit out the earl's thumb, with a quantity of drool, and smiled up at him.

"As changeable as your mother, too, Your Grace," Carlinn said, grinning back and thinking that he was right to get to Bath. The sooner he offered for Miss Sherville, the sooner he could have one of these all his own. One without that Laughton Nose. And hopefully one that didn't leave a damp streak down his fawn breeches.

Chapter Sixteen

Bath was as awful as he recalled, only worse. This time Kimbrough wasn't recuperating, so he didn't spend his time bathing or resting. Without those activities, there was hardly anything to do, as the clerk at the White Hart informed him. The Pump Room, the Tea Room, the Upper Rooms, the Lower Rooms, the Gardens: That was Bath. Slow walks and promenades, twice-weekly assemblies, once-weekly musicales, card parties. If the pools weren't so crowded with gout-ridden oldsters, he'd go swimming anyway. And Bath was everything he hated about London, only smaller and not so smelly, except at low tide. Here was all that constant bowing and hat-tipping, changing one's clothes by the hour, being surveyed and audited, all without the escape of the gentlemen's clubs.

There were coffee houses, to be sure, but some doddery old windbag was liable to interrupt Kimbrough's newspaper reading to ask his opinion on the latest war news. He didn't know the latest war news; London papers took longer to get here than they did to Berkshire.

On a walk through Sydney Gardens, he was just as likely to be accosted by retired officers as retiring spinsters, women of a certain age, women of uncertain incomes. Were there no youngish gentlemen in the town?

Carlinn's original plan was to happen upon Miss Sherville by luck—and a bribe to the hotel clerk to find which giddy entertainment she'd be enjoying—but he changed his mind. Another day dawdling around would have him complaining of his rheumatics. Besides, who could make tittle-tattle out of a duty call to his cousin's goddaughter?

The six simpering matrons in the Sherville drawing room, that was who. Six pairs of eyes watched him cross the room to the Sherville ladies, to express his cousin Winifred's greetings and regard for Lady Sherville's health.

"Why, 'tis as tiresome as ever, as I'm sure Winifred must know. I just wrote her last week. But I do find the Bath climate salubrious."

Salubrious? Carlinn found the climate about as healthful as the air around that bog he was draining. Right now, in the overheated drawing room, he was finding the atmosphere positively oppressive. Or was that because of the six pairs of watchful eyes? Lud, how he wished he could loosen that blasted neckcloth!

"So what brings you to Bath, Kimbrough? Can't be your health; you're looking disgustingly robust."

He wasn't sure whether to apologize to Lady Sherville or say thank you, so he just explained the mission he'd created.

"Oh no," Miss Sherville exclaimed, "you mustn't bring Miss Kimberly to Bath now. It is the summer which is positively gay for the younger set. The Regent's crowd flocks to Brighton, but families and such come to Bath. Sydney Gardens are at their finest then."

So were his mother's perennial borders. What, should he give up the fishing and riding and the most productive time on the agricultural estates? And why did Edelia's words make him feel old? From what he'd seen, though, Edelia was correct. Tina would be miserable in Bath, where a horseback ride required a day's outing.

From what he'd seen of Miss Sherville, however, he was correct in making Bath his destination. She was lovely in her morning gown of oyster-shell luster, fashionable without being flashy. Every auburn hair was in place on top of her head; there wasn't a single curl to tempt a man to tuck it back. She had a small, slightly rounded nose, thank goodness, and pleasant hazel eyes. Those wide-set eyes bespoke neither a dewy-eyed virgin nor a fiery temptress, but a chaste, clear-gazed maiden who wouldn't play her husband false. She even modestly lowered her eyes under his scrutiny.

His own gaze dropped, then rose. Better not dwell on that distressingly untempting neckline.

The proper twenty minutes for a social call passed quickly, with no interruptions for babies or dogs or importunate relations. His seat was immediately taken by a clerical gentleman who posed a question about last week's sermon, and an ex–India colonel took Miss Sherville's other side with a mention of the war news. Politics and religion; now those were fitting topics for the drawing room, not all that twaddle about fashions and balls his sister was always prattling on about, nor the latest crim. con. stories that surrounded Denning Castle.

Before leaving, he asked if Miss Sherville would walk out with him to give advice on renting a property, in case he decided to take a place for the summer. Which he would do if Berkshire or Hell froze in July, whichever came first. But the six pairs of eyes were nodding and passing their scrutiny over to the two newcomers, so his request must seem plausible.

Miss Sherville highly recommended those residences in the Royal Crescent as the most fashionable. They were also the most closely connected, cheek-by-jowl dwellings he'd seen outside a London slum. They were elegant, of course, and pleasing to the eye, but there was no land! Just the cursed endless hills they were climbing up and down at a snail's pace, to suit the speed of the female in black who trailed behind. Carlinn didn't know if she was a maid or a paid companion, for he'd never been introduced, but Sal could have taken lessons in watchdogging from the old crow.

That night he had a dance with Miss Sherville at the Assembly Rooms. Just one, for she was promised for the rest to a clutch of middle-aged Romeos with pomaded locks, creaking corsets, and snuff-stained fingers. Two were even in wheeled Bath chairs. Kimbrough assessed the competition while doing the pretty by every wallflower and widow in the room; he wasn't worried. He also wasn't tired when the Assembly ended at the stroke of eleven. So he was happy to walk back to his hotel rather than take one of those dratted sedan chairs where the polemen grunted at his weight with every step, hoping for a bigger tip.

The following morning he made one loop of the Pump Room with Miss Sherville on his arm to fetch her mother a glass of the foul waters, before his arm and company were politely but carefully dismissed. In the afternoon, he took one cup of tea before his allotted time was expired. He played one hand of cards with her that night before partners were switched. No, there would not be idle gossip about Edelia Sherville. There would also be no getting closer to the female without a formal declaration.

Damn and blast, he couldn't just propose. He wasn't ready. Besides, a woman expected to be courted. Circumspection was all well and good, but the devil take it if he was going to act the mooncalf under the eyes of every Bath tabby.

But how could he get to know her, to see if they

would suit, if they were never alone? And how many days was the deuced thing going to take before he could go home?

He suggested a ride out of the city. She thought her mother would be delighted for the drive. A shopping expedition? The lending library? Miss Sherville organized a party of her friends, with luncheon at one of the coffee houses. Such conduct would have been considered fast in a girl his sister's age, Edelia confessed, straight-faced, but she considered herself above the most confining social strictures.

Then why the hell wouldn't she step an inch off the path at Sydney Gardens? For heaven's sake, Duchess Denning was willing to sleep with a rifle at her side and thumbed her nose at society by not wearing full mourning. And the duchess drove out with him with no chaperone and entertained him in her nightrail without blushing. Granted, Lady Marisol was a married woman, a mother, a widow, but she couldn't be much older than Edelia Sherville. In fact, she seemed much younger, except in experience. Kimbrough reminded himself that he didn't want an experienced bride, a woman of the world. He wanted just what Miss Edelia Sherville offered: a dignified gentlewoman who understood the proprieties.

Then he reminded himself again. And again the next day.

Never before had Lord Kimbrough appreciated the mayhem that entered his life with the introduction to Duchess Denning. Never before had he received one of her urgent summonses with such delight. Actually the duchess hadn't requested his presence back in Berkshire at all, nor had she suggested the groom ride neck or nothing to deliver the message. She'd just written to inform him of the occurrence, but no one in Bath had to know that.

"I am saddened to have to shorten my visit with nothing settled," he hinted to Miss Sherville, her mother, the six members of the Greek chorus, and the ever-present black-clad dragon. "The rental property, of course. But there is an emergency in Berkshire; a neighbor needs my help. The messenger almost rode his horse into the ground to get to me, so I must leave at once. Thank you for making my stay in Bath so pleasant. Farewell." Miss Sherville permitted him to take her hand and kiss the fingers, which was the closest he'd come to intimacy with the woman in a sennight.

Carlinn left Bath faster than Marisol's messenger had entered it. And happier.

The emergency in Berkshire was that Foster Laughton was home, and a hero. He was wounded, Marisol wrote, but the doctors were optimistic. She hadn't wanted Lord Kimbrough to hear the news elsewhere and be concerned. So he wasn't, and took his time on the return, not pushing his horses, not taking chances with bad weather or muddy roads. Freedom was a heady brew and Carlinn was going to enjoy every last drop.

He supposed the duchess expected him to entertain the lad, or speak to the War Office about a promotion now that Foster had distinguished himself. Perhaps he would.

Or perhaps he'd have the young marquis drawn and quartered.

"Bloody hell," Kimbrough shouted when he saw how matters stood. "Why didn't you tell me to hurry back?"

The duchess slammed the door in his face and went back to the room where Foster lay on a sofa. The baby gurgled over some toys on a blanket on the floor, and Aunt Tess knitted in the corner. Sal kept watch from the hearth, and Max chased a ball of yarn. And there, leaning over the sofa, hanging on the invalid's every word, bringing him lemonade or a cool cloth for his head or a book to be read aloud or a guessing game, was not the nursemaid, not milady's abigail, but Kimbrough's own little sister! Entertain young Laughton be damned! Carlinn would see him entertained in the afterlife, if he didn't stop ogling Bettina's chest when she leaned over that way. And where the deuce was Cousin Winifred? Was ever a man so besieged by rattle-pated females?

Foster, it seemed—and Kimbrough read the newspapers to verify the details—was indeed a hero. His troop ship, in convoy, had caught fire just two days before landing in Lisbon. The fire was not due to any enemy cannonade, but to a carelessly smoking seaman in the munitions cargo hold. Suddenly there was pandemonium aboard the ship, with explosions and burning sails, flying sparks, falling masts.

The captain's dying words were "Abandon ship" so the first mate and half the navy crew did, leaving the army recruits and their few inexperienced officers to fend for themselves. Men were trampled in the stampede for the longboats; others just jumped overboard. Then Foster proved his mettle. He ordered his batman Joshua and the highwayman Jack Windham to stand by the lifeboat lifts, pistols in hand, to make sure the men made an orderly retreat.

Foster, meanwhile, went below, dragging injured naval officers and enlisted men up on deck to be carried to the boats and safety. When everyone he could find in the smoke and flames was away, he had Joshua and Windham launch the remaining boats, manned or not, so the men in the water could be rescued. The three of them rowed and rowed, for hours, it seemed, prying panicked soldiers away from burning debris. Over Joshua's protests, Foster even dove into the water to haul out exhausted swimmers until another of the convoy ships got close enough to send out boats.

All the survivors were taken aboard the second

ship, which proceeded on to Lisbon and the army surgeons. The uninjured and those whose wounds were minor were sent to join their units; the more seriously hurt were left on board and returned straightaway to England. Jack Windham would get his preferment in Portugal; Foster Laughton was a war hero, without his feet ever touching foreign soil.

Now he was home being feted by the neighborhood, as helpless as Nolly, his burned arms and chest swathed in gauze and ointments. Joshua Dimm had been promoted, but sent home to care for his officer, who needed to be fed, dressed, and diverted from his pain and discomfort. Foster's favorite diversion, it seemed, was Bettina Kimberly.

"Damn and blast!" her brother cursed again. "You should have seen the look on the little snirp's face," he told his cousin, who was home with a head cold. That was why she wasn't chaperoning Bettina, although Winifred had thought the duchess, her aunt, and the dowager ample protection from one bedridden soldier. She guessed not, with Cousin Carlinn wearing a hole in the Aubusson carpet with his angry pacing.

"She looked like one of those martyrs in the stained glass windows who's just been told he's going to heaven. Why, I couldn't loosen her from the boy's side with a pry bar. I was right. She needs a firmer hand at the reins." He kept pacing. Cousin Winifred blew her nose, hoping she'd be well enough on the morrow to go visit dear Foster and precious Noel. Carlinn's next words intruded on her thoughts of calves' foot jelly and mustard plasters.

"Your goddaughter Edelia was so helpful to me in Bath, showing me around, introducing me to her friends, that I thought I should repay the favor."

"I'm sure a note would not come amiss. Edelia would never expect anything more. She is a very polite sort of girl."

"Yes, and that's even more reason I thought you

might want to invite her for a visit. She'd be a good influence on Bettina. Show her how to go on, that kind of thing."

Somehow he'd gone from a thank-you note to an invitation while Winifred sneezed. She blinked. "You want me to invite her here?"

"Of course. Nothing out of the ordinary in that; you're her godmama. If I were to extend the invite, naturally tongues would wag, perhaps expectations might even be raised in certain quarters. But it cannot be pleasant for her in that musty old town with those octogenarians for company. And her mother is amply cared for, so Miss Sherville can enjoy a vacation away from the dismal place. Lud knows she deserves one."

"Here? You expect me to invite Edelia Sherville here? In the middle of winter?"

"It's not wintery at all," Carlinn said, ignoring the cold wind that had his ears stinging during the ride home. "Why, it's almost April. Before you know it, there will be flowers, and fishing."

"Fishing? You really think Edelia will enjoy fishing? You did say you had a chance to meet her, didn't you?"

"Puttering around the garden, then, or going for long rides to pick wildflowers. You know, spring in the countryside. What could be more lovely?"

"To Edelia? The assemblies and teas and card parties and musicales her letters are full of."

"Yes, but she must like the country somewhat, mustn't she?" It was time he found out, for he did not intend to spend another day of his time in Bath. London was entirely out of the question. "She does ride, I hope?"

Winifred wiped her nose and tried to recall if Edelia had ever mentioned a horse in her letters. There was that horse-faced Miss Kilborn who visited Bath last month and came away engaged to a dyspeptic viscount. "Bath is very hilly, you know. But yes, Edelia did take her turns in Rotten Row during her Season, I'm sure. You mustn't expect a delicate female like my goddaughter to spend all day in the saddle the way you do though, out and about on the property from morning till night. I expect she wouldn't even approve of Bettina's neck-or-nothing style. Edelia wasn't raised in the country, Cousin, so she is liable to have different interests. I don't think she'll come."

Carlinn thought of the jackstraws who made up Miss Sherville's court, that pasty-faced baronet with the rasping cough, the prosy cleric, or the jug-eared widower with four children. It did not take any great degree of vanity for him to say, "She'll come."

Chapter Seventeen

She came. Edelia Sherville was no country-woman, but she was no fool, either. She was prepared to admire the bucolic beauties, from a distance, of course, and endure. This was her ticket back to London. Oh, how she missed the theater, the opera, the balls, and the shops. Oh, how she cursed her mother's ill health that made their residence in Bath so necessary. Oh, how she regretted not accepting any of those offers that she'd turned down in her first Season, hoping to make a better match in her second.

"Oh, how lovely," she enthused as Lord Kimbrough pointed out the view of the formal gardens from the glass doors in the library. Would she like to stroll there? How silly, but her slippers would be ruined. A ride about the estate later? She had in mind doing a watercolor of the ornamental lake, as seen through her bedroom window. A walk through the home woods searching for the first daffodils? She had promised her mother to practice the pianoforte faithfully.

Edelia was happy to accept Kimbrough's offer of

a drive into the village to visit the shops—until she saw the shops. All three of them, if you didn't count the butcher. But she did enjoy sitting up beside the handsome earl, so expertly tooling his elegant rig down the roads. She'd have enjoyed it more, had there been anyone of distinction to notice their passing instead of the cows and their equally bovine keepers. And the inn, where she'd felt the need for a restorative cup of tea before the return trip, did not even boast a private parlor. Miss Sherville sipped her beverage quickly and downed her sweet roll in haste, before the blacksmith or some such took a seat next to her. Mama would be horrified.

The earl was pleased. "There, you should come out more. The fresh air does wonders for the appetite and puts roses in your cheeks."

Miss Sherville spent the rest of the day in her room applying Denmark Lotion to her skin.

Cousin Winifred also spent a great deal of time in her chambers. Miss Austen's new work having arrived on her difficult goddaughter's heels, Winifred decided to have a relapse, leaving Edelia's entertainment—and chaperonage—to the earl and his sister.

"La, I don't know what Mama would say. Of course I realize manners are less strict in the country, but a girl can never be too careful."

"Miss Sherville, I assure you, you are in no danger of being compromised." Bludgeoned, maybe, not compromised. Perhaps the visit was not a good idea, Carlinn decided, coming at a time when he was too busy to devote himself to Miss Sherville's amusement. Work on the streambed was continuing, as well as the improvements on the Denning properties. And the occasional chess game did seem to get Foster's mind off the pain he was undoubtedly suffering.

The earl's busy schedule and Cousin Winifred's retreat left Edelia more and more in the company of Bettina, whom she considered a hoydenish schoolgirl in the throes of calf-love. Miss Sherville was having nothing of such Turkish treatment, especially when she could turn it to her own advantage.

"Your sister is left to her own devices too much, my lord," she did not hesitate to inform her host, cornering him in his estate office. "A young girl like that needs to be more strictly supervised. Why, she should be preparing her wardrobe for her Season in London, not coming home with her skirts all muddied. I would be happy to lend my advice, if you agree Lady Bettina should pay a visit to Reading to have some new gowns made up."

"Tina knows she has but to send for Madame Molyneaux if she needs anything, and besides, she's not to make her come-out until next fall." He shuffled some papers. She didn't take the hint.

"The fall? Next year?" There went Miss Sherville's hopes for an early wedding. "But never tell me you'll present her at the Little Season? Why, she's old enough to be presented right now."

"I see no reason to rush young girls into these things. Besides, I'm sure some dashing young man will come sweep her off her feet the minute she shows her face at Almack's, and I'm not ready to part with her yet."

No one had swept *her* off her feet, Miss Sherville thought bitterly. Out of sheer spite she told him, "If you are not careful, she will form an entirely unsuitable connection here in the country and she will never make her curtsies at Almack's at all."

"Laughton? No, I am convinced she'll outgrow her infatuation for the boy. Especially if I don't come down the heavy and make him seem like forbidden fruit." That was the duchess's wisdom talking; Carlinn would have tossed his sister into the nearest carriage headed for the Antipodes else. "It's only hero-worship, after all."

"Lieutenant Laughton? The marquis is well

enough, I suppose, now that he's made a mark for himself. Not a feather to fly with, of course. But it's the sister I was referring to. The Coach Widow. Absolutely ineligible."

A pencil snapped in Kimbrough's hands. "She is innocent," was all he said.

"Of the murder, perhaps. But what of the rest? Why, I hear she's not even in full mourning for her dead husband."

"The situation was out of the ordinary." Kimbrough uncomfortably found himself making excuses for the duchess. "And there is the baby to consider. He likes bright colors. Why, you should see him with Mr. Dimm's waistcoat, and these gold buttons of mine were a big hit this . . ."

Miss Sherville's painted-on eyebrows were raised almost to her hairline.

Edelia resumed her attack over luncheon, when Bettina announced she was going to visit at Denning Castle that afternoon. She had promised to read to Lieutenant Foster, she declared, challenging anyone to gainsay her.

"But perhaps Miss Sherville would rather meet some of the other neighbors, Tina." Carlinn tried for diplomacy.

"Then perhaps you should take her, brother dear," his sister shot back, still angry with him over his early words about Foster, even more furious that he and Cousin Winifred were foisting this porcelain princess off on her.

"Maybe we could all go call on Denning Castle tomorrow. You really must see it, Miss Sherville, for it truly is a singular bit of architectural history, with its restored battlements and—"

"No, thank you. I am sorry I must refuse to meet your neighbors, but it is not at all the thing, as I have mentioned. And you, Lady Bettina, would do well to heed my example. A girl cannot be too careful of her reputation if she wishes to have a successful Season. You should guard your name better, for a female is also known by her associates."

Cousin Winifred, who had joined them for luncheon, stepped in before Tina could retort. "I am sure the duchess is unexceptional. My stars, you should see the wonderful work she's doing with the local schools and helping the vicar see to the needy."

"Schools? The needy? The woman is a pariah, a social outcast. Of course she has to bury herself here in the country, busy with good works."

"Marisol is a true lady!" Bettina cried, throwing down her napkin.

Her brother quelled the incipient tantrum with a frown, then he turned his lowering look to Miss Sherville. In a quiet voice, he said, "Denning Castle has suffered enough from gossip and ill will. The Duchess has proved to be an asset to this community, and as such deserves our respect. Foster Laughton is lying wounded in his country's service. But even if she were less of a lady, and her brother a cad, Noel Pendenning is still my ward, requiring my attention to his welfare. Therefore my family"—his eyes moved first to Bettina, then to Cousin Winifred, before coming to rest on Edelia, who was patting her mouth with a serviette—"shall all visit Denning Castle tomorrow, with the duchess's permission, of course. You, Miss Sherville, are welcome to accompany us."

Edelia stalled, folding the napkin into tidy corners. Kimbrough was furious, she could tell, and that little minx Bettina was smirking. Even her own godmother had turned against her. If she didn't pay that call on Denning Castle, she may as well pack her bags and return to Bath. Instead she smiled, showing all her perfect teeth. "La, I do keep forgetting that country standards are not so exacting. I can see you are all won over to poor Marisol's side. Oh, didn't I tell you we were acquainted from our first Season together? Lovely girl. I really must pay my respects now that I am in the vicinity, mustn't I?"

"What's a dog doing here?" Edelia hissed into the ear of the lady next to her on the sofa. All those suits of armor, battle-axes, and maces were off-putting enough, but a big hairy creature that was crippled besides? Edelia's idea of a house dog was more that shaggy little thing dancing around in search of crumbs, not Cerberus guarding the gates of Hades. She sat rigid on her side of the couch, afraid of moving lest she draw the beast's attention to herself.

"What's that?" Miss Laughton asked loudly enough that she—and everyone else—could hear. "What about the dog?"

Lord Kimbrough leaned over. "That's just Sal. She minds the baby. She won't bother you unless you threaten Nolly."

That brought to mind another source of Miss Sherville's discomfort. Babies were to be brought forth, admired, then dismissed. What was this one doing here, at tea? She whispered to the earl, "Why is it not in the nursery?"

"Nolly? Oh, he's our local entertainment, aren't you, my lad?"

The earl plucked the infant out of its mother's arms while Bettina wailed, "Unfair! It was my turn!"

Edelia couldn't believe her eyes; they were nearly fighting over possession of that damp, squirmy article. If that weren't bad enough, on top of the dog, Kimbrough was dangling the child in front of her rose-colored muslin gown, which must already be covered in dog hair.

"Would you like to hold him?" the earl was offering, as if he held the Crown Jewels instead of a grubby brat.

"No. No, thank you." Cute? Edelia had never seen anything less appealing, unless it was the sight of that Lieutenant Laughton, recumbent on the opposite sofa. Edelia couldn't bear to look at him, with his bare patches of raw, red flesh. The least they could do for company was cover him up in more than the bandages and dressing gown he now wore. Miss Sherville turned her eyes away.

Unfortunately they landed on an unprepossessing little man in a red waistcoat and tight-fitting unmentionables. When Kimbrough caught her direction, he explained that Mr. Dimm was with Bow Street, but he was here today to see his son, who had come home from the army with the lieutenant. His son-in-law, married to Lady Marisol's maid, had also been on the hospital ship carrying the wounded home from the Peninsula. Ned Turner was abovestairs now. Another of Dimm's sons, Kimbrough went on with a straight face and a twinkle in his eyes Edelia was too offended to see, was the fellow in the corner with the pistol in his pocket.

Edelia needed all of her upbringing to stifle the scream in her throat. How could Marisol have permitted herself to sink so low, she wondered, turning her parlor into a nursery, a sickroom, a kennel, a thieves' den? Murder was one thing, but such a lapse of proper conduct was quite beyond the pale. And she was sadly off her looks, Edelia was gratified to see, positively blowzy. To think she, Edelia Sherville, had been jealous of the twit for capturing Arvid Pendenning in her first Season.

At least the dowager duchess was there representing good ton, Edelia was relieved to see, and in full mourning, too. Her Grace was acquainted with Miss Sherville's mama and many of the other Bath biddies, so there was news to relate and messages to convey. Edelia could politely ignore the rest of the room's occupants, instead of continuing her previous impolite disdain.

Soon the gathering had divided into other smaller groups. Aunt Tess and Cousin Winifred were vying with the tea tray for Mr. Dimm's attention; Foster and Bettina were engrossed in a book whose title neither of them knew or cared. Rebecca the nursemaid came for the now-sleepy baby, and left accompanied by the big dog and the bodyguard.

Lord Kimbrough asked Marisol to walk apart with him, to discuss a new tenant for one of the vacant cottages, he told the others. When they were at the other end of the room, ostensibly admiring an ancient tapestry on the wall, he apologized for inflicting Miss Sherville on her and her family.

"Think nothing of it, my lord. I assure you, I am more than familiar with Edelia's kind. Be happy the Hambleys did not drop in, children and all. Miss Sherville might never have recovered." She thought he muttered "Too bad," but must have misunderstood. "I suspect she is simply out of her element here. My, ah, casual style is not what she is used to, in Bath or in London."

"About London, Duchess. I'm sorry to have to inform you that you'll have to change your plans about London."

"My plans? I have none that I know of."

He ignored her protests, concentrating on the difficult news he had to impart. "According to Miss Sherville, and I have no reason to doubt she is *au courant* with the current tittle-tattle, word about your lack of mourning is common knowledge, along with tales of Arvid's indiscretions." He stepped closer to the tapestry, examining a section depicting blackamoors leading tigers on leashes. "None of the mess has been forgotten. You will not be received. I was informed by Lady Sherville herself that I was tolerated only because I was a man and could be forgiven my part in the imbroglio. The rumor mill will not deal as kindly with you."

Marisol shook her head, dislodging a curl from its ribbon. "You were tolerated, my lord, because you are a wealthy bachelor peer. I am a wealthy widowed duchess. I would be accepted eventually by all but the highest sticklers, unless they had a son or brother to settle, but thank you for your concern. And I must remember to thank Miss Sherville for hers," she added dryly. "However, I have no intention of putting my luck to the test. I do not plan to go to London anytime soon."

"Of course you do. It's your way of life," he insisted.

"What, leave Nolly and my responsibilities here for the pleasures of Town?"

"That's what every other woman would do." It was certainly what Edelia Sherville would do, and they both knew it.

"Thank you, my lord, for the thought. And I am sure Edelia will be relieved that you consider a true lady most at home in London. But I can only repeat, *this* is my home. I am not Edelia Sherville."

Together their eyes moved across the room to where Edelia was still in conversation with the dowager, still turning her back on the rest of the company as if they were beneath her.

Carlinn couldn't help contrasting the auburn beauty with the blonde at his side. Edelia was perfectly groomed, *point device* in thin, low-cut muslin, and shivering, while Marisol wore a soft dark blue merino with long sleeves and a high collar. She looked warm, comfortable, inviting. He wiped that last thought from his mind and turned back to the tapestry. One tiger was leaping, in the midst of capturing a rabbit for all eternity. Somehow he knew how the rabbit must feel.

"I apologize again. I should have known better."

"What, the Earl of Kimbrough apologizing twice in one day? Unheard of!" She smiled to lighten his mood. "Besides, I might want to go up to Town next year or so, do the shops, the opera, and such. It would be infinitely more comfortable to have Arvid's murder solved and forgotten. It's too bad Dimm cannot find any more clues."

Together they looked toward the trio around the

tea table. "Though I do not know how he expects to uncover any evidence in London when he spends most of his time here in Berkshire flirting with Aunt Tess."

"What, are you matchmaking there, too, Duchess?" Carlinn demanded.

Her smile disappeared. Her chin rose. "That is none of your concern, my lord. You can try to keep your sister from a misalliance, but my aunt and Mr. Dimm are none of your affair."

"My, how easily you fly into the boughs, Duchess." He tapped her nose with one finger. "I was teasing. I meant to save Mr. Dimm for Cousin Winifred."

They shared a laugh, but Carlinn noticed how quickly her smile faded. He thought she must still be troubled over the talk about her reputation. And she was looking tired, he realized, rebuking himself for battening his entire family and difficult guest on her at one time. How could she not be exhausted, looking after Foster, the baby, and the new school? And her maid was no help, with the abigail's husband also needing nursing. "Have you been getting out at all, Duchess, other than your parish work?" he wanted to know.

"What, going to parties and such? Now that would set the county on its ear. I do keep to some kind of mourning, you know."

"Yes, but you are entitled to some pleasure, too. How would you feel about a small dinner party among neighbors at Kimbrough Hall? The adult Hambleys, Squire and his sons, perhaps a few others. No one could find fault with that."

No one but Miss Sherville, who had turned to watch them, obviously impatient with her neglectful escort. Carlinn sincerely believed the duchess needed time away from the infant and the invalid; he also believed it was time he established mastery of his own household. If Miss Sherville did not like his friends . . .

Marisol also looked to Edelia, and felt the other woman's barely concealed loathing. A night out sounded marvelous, but what pleasure could there be in seeing that jealous cat sitting at Kimbrough's right hand?

"Come, your brother can't have all the valor in the family."

But she didn't have to decide. The dinner party was cancelled when the note arrived at Denning Castle. *If you care about Denning's brat,* the message began.

Chapter Eighteen

If you care about Denning's brat, the note read, *leave 200 pounds in Hyde Park at 5 P.M. Tuesday next*. Below was a rough sketch of the park with an arrow to one path, an *x* marking the third bench past an ink blot. No, that must be a landmark of some kind, a big tree or a monument. Marisol could not quite recall that particular footpath; she was more familiar with the carriage ways along Rotten Row. No matter, she'd search out that third bench as if her life depended on it—or Nolly's.

"You'll what?" the earl yelled, not believing his ears. "You'll go pay this cockamamie ransom demand when they don't even have the boy? Are your attics to let, woman?"

"Don't you dare shout at me! And yes, I'll go give them anything they want so they leave us alone."

"Leave you alone? This is only the beginning. If you pay them now, you might as well put them on your payroll! I've never heard a more paperskulled idea. I forbid it!"

"You cannot forbid me anything, my lord. I have my own accounts to draw from."

The earl tore his neckcloth off and threw it to the ground, so he could shout louder, it seemed. "You nimwit, this is not a kidnapping, this is just extortion! You don't pay someone for making threats!"

Marisol jumped to her feet and stood glaring at Lord Kimbrough. "What would you have me do, wait until they harm Nolly, then pay them? Now that is being penny-wise and pound-foolish in the extreme, my lord."

"This has nothing to do with money, for heaven's sake!"

"It has everything to do with money! I have it, and they want it! Two hundred pounds is a small price to pay for my son's safety."

"And that's another thing. What kind of maggoty blackmailer asks for two hundred pounds when they have to know you're worth thousands? You cannot do it."

"I can and must!" She stomped her foot for emphasis. "I'll get that money to Hyde Park with or without your approval."

"That's fine," he said with a sneer. "The duchess is back in command. You'll ignore my advice just to prove your superiority. What will you do, flounce off to London and leave Nolly here unprotected? Then again, you've hardly left him out of your sight for his—what? four months?"

"Nearly five. Some kind of guardian you are," she muttered, "not knowing your ward's age."

"Just so. Nearly five months. So what do you intend, to take him with you to Town? You might as well hand him over to these cockleheaded criminals now, along with his fortune, for there is no way to protect him in London."

"I hadn't thought of that," she said quietly, sitting down again.

Carlinn sat beside her and took her hands in his. "I know, Duchess. You're only thinking with your heart, not your head. But you can't, for Nolly's sake. A threat like this is meant to arouse fear, that's all. If you give in, they've won without doing more than writing a letter. We can keep Nolly safe here; you know we can."

An army of relatives, trusted servants, and dogs surrounded the baby. He was never left unattended by less than two people and one dog. He was never brought into a room without it being checked for lurkers first and never taken outside except in a phalanx of adults. The grounds were patrolled regularly, the village was on the alert for strangers, and Marisol kept her embroidery scissors on a ribbon around her neck. Even Lord Kimbrough had taken to carrying his pistol with him, and Dimm's son Gabriel was never out of shouting distance, with his ready weapon.

"Nolly is safe, until someone shoots Mr. Dimm's son to get to mine! We cannot live like this, Carlinn!" Neither of them noticed her use of his first name, nor that he still held her hands. She felt better for his strength; he felt better for giving what reassurance he could. "Don't ask me to live in fear for the rest of my life, my lord. I cannot do it."

"Of course not. Dimm and I have a plan to capture the extortionists."

Marisol groaned. "Oh no, not another trap. I won't let you use Nolly as bait; I swear I won't."

"You really do get mushbrained under pressure, don't you? You'd never find a place on Old Hooky's staff, that's for sure. If he's hoping for aide-de-camp, Foster had better hope he didn't inherit your skitterwits along with your nose."

"What's wrong with my nose?" she asked, diverted as he intended. "And my wits, of course?"

Carlinn patted her hands, got up, and was already pacing. "Your wits have gone begging, my girl, if you think I'd endanger Nolly in the least. No, we'll leave the ransom under the bench, all right, but it will not be real money."

"Yes, it will," she insisted. "Otherwise they

might be angry enough to follow through with the threats!"

He frowned at her. "Blasted pigheaded female." But he kept pacing. "Then we—Dimm and I—stand back and watch who comes to fetch the loot. Then we follow the fake money—"

"No!"

"The real money then, in case the pick-up person is merely a messenger. We see where he delivers the package and, *voilà*, we have the blackmailers."

"What does Mr. Dimm think?" Marisol asked, doubt coloring the question.

"He thinks we might even find Arvid's murderer at the end of the trail. He's off checking now, but he is almost positive that the handwriting on this note matches the message that sent you out to Denning's carriage that day. There's got to be a connection. He also thinks that the demand of two hundred pounds is peculiar."

"It's so low?"

"Right. It eliminates suspects like Boynton. He gambles away more than that before lunch."

"Are you still suspicious of Boynton? I thought he was content now."

"He's still the one with the most to gain if . . ." He let that thought trail away. "But not for two hundred pounds. He'd hit you up in person if that was all he needed. I thought it might be a good idea to send for him anyway, where we could watch him, just to make sure."

"I'll write asking him to come stand watch over Nolly. He never leaves without hinting about some tailor's bill or a new pair of boots, so he'll come."

The earl nodded. "Dimm says the low demand sounds more like some poor sod needs the money to get out of town or something, like Arvid's valet going to the colonies. Dimm doesn't suspect the man—he had nothing to gain except unemployment—but Dimm is looking into ship departures for next week and recent bookings. Maybe he'll turn up something there and we never have to bother with the ransom."

"You keep saying 'we.' You and Dimm have already decided on this plan, then? You weren't even going to consult me?"

"Now don't go getting on your high horse, Duchess. Of course we were. I am. Right now."

"It's too dangerous. And they'll be expecting me."

"No, the note just said leave the money, not that you had to be there. I doubt they'd be wanting to see anyone who might recognize them."

"But that's all the more reason I should go!"

"Definitely not! And don't argue, or I'll have you bound and gagged. Foster gave me permission. He's already aggravated he cannot go help since he cannot hold a pistol or make the carriage ride, so sitting on you is his job. Besides, I need you to stay here to help entertain Miss Sherville."

"I'd rather face the blackmailers."

Kimbrough grinned. "So would I."

Edelia thought Lord Kimbrough's taking himself off to London a capital idea. In fact, she, his sister, and his cousin could all accompany him. She knew he wouldn't wish to leave the women under his protection alone in a neighborhood of such desperate goings-on.

"What, you think you will be safer in London? With all the raff and scaff of the metropolis?"

"But you will be there to protect us, my lord," she flattered, batting her lashes.

"I'm sorry, but I shall be too involved in this effort to trap the hoodlums to be a proper escort."

Edelia wasn't giving up. "Then we'll have time to do the shops and see the sights. You wouldn't wish your sister to appear the gapeseed when she does go up to Town, staring at everything like a cabbagehead. This would be the perfect opportunity for her to gain a bit of Town bronze before the ton returns."

"Miss Sherville, thank you for being concerned for my sister's welfare, but this is not a social call I am paying. It is a very serious matter, possibly even perilous, and will take my full attention. I could not think of having you or Bettina in London at the time."

"And just what am I supposed to do for the remainder of my visit then, with my host nowhere in view?" she demanded.

What she was *supposed* to do was be a gracious guest to her godmother, who had, in fact, issued the invitation. She was supposed, Kimbrough thought, to go for walks and rides and visits to the neighbors, none of which she'd been content with so far. One more week and she'd be back in Bath, thank heaven. Thank heaven twice that he hadn't made any commitment.

To Miss Sherville, the invitation had been as good as an offer. There was no way she was going to wring that proposal out of the slowtop if he wasn't even in the county, though. And for certain she was not going to stay by herself in this benighted place where the nearest neighbors were up to their eyebrows in havey-cavey doings. Not if there was no chance of bringing the Elusive Earl up to scratch. "Perhaps it would be better if I shortened my visit."

"You must please yourself, of course, but I was hoping you would be a companion to the duchess in this trying time. You said you were old friends. I'm sure she'd find comfort in that."

Marisol Laughton? Edelia should sit holding that frumpy blonde's hand? Marisol was the one who married a rich duke and now seemed to have a rich earl sitting in her pocket. "Don't you think you are taking your guardianship of the boy a little too seriously?" she asked spitefully. "I mean, extending your care to the child's mother? That really should be the prerogative of her brother . . . or her husband."

The earl loosened his suddenly tight shirt collar. "Her husband is dead, Miss Sherville, and her brother is incapacitated. I am only doing what any gentleman would do in my place."

"How lucky for Her Grace," Edelia sniped, sure now she had lost the battle. "I think I should prefer to go home. Rather than being a comfort, the duchess must find guests an unwanted burden at this difficult time." To say nothing of dangerous. Edelia had no intention of stepping foot in Denning Castle again, not with armed guards and vicious dogs and puking infants who were subject to kidnapping. "Good manners dictate that I cut short my visit under the circumstances."

"But I cannot accompany you home at this time, Miss Sherville. I can put a carriage at your disposal, and outriders, if that is your wish, but I have no male escort to offer. My sister and my cousin feel needed here, helping to look after Foster, so you would only have your maid for chaperone. It is not what I can like, but if you insist . . ."

Edelia was thinking on it. Traveling back to Bath without an engagement ring wasn't what she could like, escorted or no. If she stayed, she might have another go at getting him up to the mark when he returned from London. On the other hand, Kimbrough might be highly titled, as handsome as he could stare, and as rich as Croesus, but there was no denying he was as firmly planted in the Berkshire soil as an old oak tree. With a few squirrels in his upper branches. Oh, he might drag himself to London for his sister's presentation, if the chit didn't run off with that Laughton boy to follow the drum. But after that? He'd stay right here in the country with his outré neighbors, forever and ever. Earl or no earl, Bath was preferable to that.

Miss Sherville was still trying to decide where her best interests lay the day before Kimbrough was to leave for London. Then Lord Boynton came to call. She'd stay. What elegance of fashion, what address, what fulsome compliments he paid!

"What? You've got the Sherville heiress next door, Marisol? 'Pon rep, I knew my luck had changed with old Arvid's passing. She's Golden Ball Sherville's only child, don't you know. And that Grosvenor Square house they own is just sitting there empty. With the father dead and the mother in Bath there wouldn't even be in-law problems. Could even set up my own private gaming hell. Dash it, I always said you were the best of sisters-in-law! Thankee for sending for me, m'dear."

Marisol sipped at her ratafia. "But, Boynton, I didn't send for you about Miss Sherville. It's Nolly's future I'm concerned over, not yours. You've waited this long to marry an heiress. It never occurred to me that you'd be interested."

"Time comes for all men to bite the bullet, m'dear. You've been more than generous, but I can't live off m'sister-in-law forever, don't you know. That's what they make wives for." Boynton patted her shoulder. "And don't worry your pretty head about the little chap, m'dear. Makes frown lines. Tell you what, I'll fork over the two hundred pounds myself. I'm flush this week, what? Better yet, I'll give you a draft on my bank. That way you can set someone to watching the bank when your culprit tries to cash the check. Of course, we'd have cancelled payment by then anyway. I do it all the time." Boynton was grimacing at his waistcoat. "Coral will never do for calling on an auburn-haired beauty. What do you think, m'dear, should I change into the white marcella or the puce brocade?"

Marisol bit her lip. "I'm not sure Miss Sherville shares your enthusiasm for fashion," she hinted. "Edelia is a very proper sort of female."

Boynton adjusted the black arm band he wore. "Right, the gray satin stripe."

Chapter Nineteen

"Traps is like women," according to another of Jeremiah Dimm's teachings. "They's some what puts out lures, and they's some what plays hard to get. The ones what turn their backs are the ones what get a man every time. Now, you take lions. You want to trap a lion, you can set out some bait and hope he shows up for you to get a net on. Else you can try to chase him into a corner somewheres, hoping he doesn't turn on you. Or you can do what the natives do, and use your noodle. You find a path your big tabby takes. You dig a deep hole, then you cover it over with leaves and branches, so it looks natural, undisturbed. You put out your bait. Then you go away. You turn your back, he shows up, you got him, and he ain't got you."

Kimbrough wondered how many lions the Bow Street Runner had ever seen, much less captured. Then again, he also wondered how many crooks Mr. Dimm had captured.

The money was the bait. The absence of armed guards and sentinels was the big pit. Natural and undisturbed, that was the key. The plan was foolproof.

So Carlinn set out for Hyde Park at the fashionable hour. Of all of London's absurd conventions, he considered, this one was right there with Venetian breakfasts that took place in the afternoon. A man couldn't really ride in the park, the lanes were so congested, and driving a carriage was worse, with all the stopping to raise your hat or bow. Bowing in a curricle was a boneheaded idea in the first place; keeping highbred carriage horses standing around was worse. Most ludicrous of all was walking, for on foot you were then obliged to make chitchat with every passing toady or climber, or pretend to ignore them by striking up conversations with mere acquaintances. Either way, you never made progress, so why bother going for a walk in the first place? To be seen, of course, which was the whole point of the Promenade. Which was why Lord Kimbrough never went on the strut, even when he was in Town.

But here he was, bowing and tipping his hat, smiling at dowagers airing their pugs in landaus, and sidestepping young gamecocks atop more horse than they could handle. And it wasn't even the height of the Season. He could see whispering behind fans as he passed by, speculation in gamblers' eyes. They all wanted to know what he was doing in Town; luckily his reputation kept them from asking. The earl kept walking, swinging his cane as if he hadn't a care in the world, as if he weren't cursing every last popinjay among them. Natural and unperturbed, hah!

He moved through the knots of carriages, horsemen, and strollers, and set out for less congested areas of the park. Following the map, he took a path that paralleled the Serpentine, where nursemaids and their charges were feeding the ducks and a small boy was sailing a toy ship. Carlinn thought of his ward. This folderol was worth it for Nolly's sake, and Marisol's.

He passed an area less cultivated, where laughter from the bushes told him young couples were enjoying the seclusion. Here he could even notice that the trees were coming into bud and the grass was definitely greener. The whole of winter had gone by without removing his name, or hers, from society's list of suspects in Denning's murder. He quickened his step.

One more turnoff and he was back to a path made too narrow for horses by the benches on either side. Fewer pedestrians walked here, and those who passed were not of the same class as those near the park gates or on the carriage ring. Here was a young woman pushing a pram, a student eating an apple as he pored over a book, and a uniformed park employee scything the grass.

There was the monument, a verdigris knight on a charger so thick with pigeon droppings Carlinn couldn't read the plaque. He walked on, whistling. On the first bench past the monument, a gentleman in an old-fashioned bagwig sat feeding squirrels out of a sack. On the second bench a grandmotherly woman was reading a story to a schoolboy in short pants. The fourth bench held the prone form of a tattered old man whose snores almost toppled the bottle of Blue Ruin by his side. The third bench was blessedly empty. Relieved, Carlinn sat there for a bit, polishing the brim of his beaver hat with a handkerchief until a distant clock struck the hour. Five o'clock. He checked his watch on its fob. Goodness, time to go change for dinner. He replaced the timepiece, replaced the handkerchief, and almost by accident dislodged a small, sealed parcel from his inner pocket. The packet managed to slip under the bench while Carlinn gathered his cane and his hat. He set the hat on his head just so, as if he didn't have to doff it a hundred times before quitting the park. Then, swinging his cane and whistling, he ambled back toward the park gates where everyone and his uncle could see the Elusive Earl heading home. Natural and undisturbed, that was the ticket.

He got into his closed coach and had the driver pull away. Two blocks later he pulled the check-string and ordered the man to turn around, to go back and pull up opposite the gate and wait.

Carlinn had recourse to the flask in the door pocket while he sat there, wishing that he could have been the one to hide in the park waiting for the quarry to tumble into their ditch.

The first one to knock on the coach door and come inside was the young park attendant, scythe and all. "Quitting time," said Jeremiah's youngest son, who was currently employed in his lordship's stables. "Da said it would look peculiar-like was I to stay on. No one's picked up the package yet, though."

The grandmotherly woman, Dimm's sister Cora, stepped up to the coach next, assisted by that young boy some cousin had dropped off in Hill Street, Kensington, and forgotten to fetch. The lad was happy to scramble up beside the coachman, meat pasty in hand, after seeing his aunt seated across from the earl.

"No one would keep a boy out on a park bench past his dinner hour," Dimm's sister declared, "so Jeremiah signalled us to leave. Thank goodness, for I swear we read that story till the sprout knows it by heart. Oh, and the parcel is still there."

They waited some more, until the student, Dimm's nephew studying his anatomy text, reported in. "It's getting too dark to read by, my lord. Uncle waved me off. No one has approached that third bench since you left."

Carlinn put them all in a hackney and sent them home. He drummed his fingers on the door handle. Deuce take it, their pit-trap was growing shallower by the minute. That lion could climb right out again, after taking the bait.

The gentleman feeding the squirrels rapped on

the carriage. "Sorry, can't stay any longer," he said when Carlinn opened the door. "Important meeting at Whitehall. I've been out of nuts for hours anyway, my lord."

"Thank you, your nibs, ah, your honor. I really appreciate your making this effort."

"Like to see this case closed, my lord. Like to see every case closed. Won't happen tonight, by George."

"No, sir, it doesn't appear that way."

The chief magistrate shook his hand and shut the door again.

It was full dark when Dimm climbed into the coach, brushing off his coat and offering the earl a swallow of Blue Ruin. Kimbrough grimaced a refusal. "Did they come?"

"I allus said, no trap is foolproof. They must of recognized one of us, though I don't see how. But they ain't coming today or they'd of been here."

"Hell and confound it. No, they won't come in the dark when we could have constables behind every bush. I suppose I'll just take the money back to the duchess and wait to hear from the extortionists again."

Dimm wiped his mouth on his shirt sleeve. "Well, it's like this, guv. I promised Her Grace I'd leave the brass no matter what, so you'll have a hard time giving it back."

"You mean to say you left two hundred pounds out there for some beggar to find, if the squirrels don't get it first? We'll never know if the blackmailers got the blunt or not, dash it!"

"I promised Her Grace," Dimm repeated.

So Kimbrough took one of the carriage lanterns and picked his path back through the park, avoiding the calling cards left by the carriage horses, staying well away from the banks of the Serpentine, and brandishing his pistol instead of his cane to discourage those who hunted in the park at night. He turned down three propositions from prostitutes, two pleas from paupers, and one approach from a nearsighted pickpocket before reaching the turnoff to the smaller path.

He doused the lantern and stealthily picked his way to the statue, taking up a position near the horse's tail, peering down the path. The packet gleamed white in the darkness, undisturbed by anything but a passing mongrel who sniffed at it, then moved on before Kimbrough had to shout him away. A doxy went by, a sailor on either arm, then a drunk, weaving his way down the path, grabbing onto each bench in passing.

Carlinn held his breath. The blackmailer? No, just a drunk finding his way into the bushes to cast up his accounts. If the fellow didn't land in the Serpentine, 'twould be amazing. If none of the cutpurses and footpads got to him, 'twould be a miracle.

The moon rose, and Carlinn's ire. His fingers on the metal horse's rump were turning blue and, blast, no one was coming to fetch the blood money. He picked it up and went home.

"You did what? Of course they wouldn't come while you were standing there. They must have seen you!"

"Your Grace, no one saw me but some pigeons. I had to throw out a perfectly good hat. They were not coming, period."

"You don't know that! Oh, how could you have taken the money? I mean, so what if you didn't catch them? That wasn't the point!" Marisol jabbed the needle through the gown she was embroidering for Nolly, then back up through the thin fabric. She set those tiny stitches at so furious a pace she never noticed that she was sewing her own gown to the baby's dress.

Carlinn was pacing, as usual. "Oh, sit down, you impossible man. It's enough that you have jeopardized my child's life; you don't have to give me *mal de mer* besides."

"Let me tell you, Duchess, that I did not stand behind the tail end of a metal mount out in the cold for two hours just to put a blight on your life." He sat, but restlessly, drumming his fingers on the chair arm. "It was no pleasure, by Jupiter. And no one was going to come along but some beggar looking for a bench under which to sleep. Your blunt would have made him happy, but that's all. The blackmailers would still be as greedy. Meanwhile, Nolly is safe. Your tormentors will come back, never fear."

"What if they don't? I'll never be able to sleep nights, worrying."

She didn't look well either, he noticed now that he was facing her. Pale and drawn, the duchess seemed to have lost more weight just since he'd been gone. Her dress hung loosely and her hair was more mussed than usual, too. Lord Kimbrough was the last person to quibble over clothes and appearances; he was sitting in Her Grace's parlor in his riding clothes, after all, but he'd been anxious to relate the news. Still, proprieties aside, the duchess's loose and untamed hairstyle, with a ribbon holding back only some of the blonde curls, was disconcerting to him. Not that he would have found fault with the style in a mistress, mind. Instead of reaching out and touching the silky length, he drummed his fingers harder. Dash it, he would not allow her to get to him.

"By the way," he told her, reminded, "Dimm's staying on in London, but he said to tell you he hasn't managed to locate your old maid yet."

Marisol noticed his intense gaze and grimace, and tucked her hair back into its ribbon. She raised her chin. By the stars, Marisol was not going to apologize to him for her appearance, even though she found herself wishing she were in looks for his visit. Besides, if Kimbrough could sit in all his dirt on the dowager's crocodile-legged sofa, then she could leave her hair down when her head ached with fretting. Furthermore, if his clothes could be so unstylish as to give his arms ample room to move, then she needn't be exercised over the fit of hers until she'd regained her figure. It seemed foolish to have her maid alter every gown every week, especially with Sarah so busy. Marisol thought that perhaps next month she'd be ready for a new wardrobe, when Arvid would be dead for six months. Six months was not proper mourning, not by half, but it was all she was willing to give, here in the country. By next month she should have a new maid, too.

"Yes, my Sarah's husband is mending. He wants to go back to Yorkshire where his family has a small textile mill. He'll have a job waiting, unlike so many injured veterans. I am glad for him, of course, but I am sorry to lose Sarah. They won't be ready to travel for a while, but I thought that if Tyson hadn't found a new position, she'd consider returning to my employ, even if I am just a country matron now, quite beneath her dignity."

Marisol Pendenning could never be less than lovely even in her undress, Kimbrough was thinking, putting his first impressions entirely out of his mind. If only he could rid his imagination as easily of thoughts of her undressed altogether. . . . He got up and looked out the window. He was *not* pacing. He was checking the weather. The sky was not quite as blue as her— Thunderation, he was no moonling! He went back to the sofa.

"Dimm says the agency you mentioned hasn't seen the woman, but they gave him her mother's address. He called, but got no information there either. They haven't seen her since Christmas. That valet of Denning's who was supposed to be sweet on her is packing for America, quite openly, nothing furtive. He says he asked Eleanor Tyson to marry him after the murder, but she refused. He hasn't seen her since, he swears, but Dimm isn't sure he's telling the truth on that, for fear of getting her in trouble."

"With Dimm? What kind of trouble could that be? All he wants is to pass on my offer of a job. Certes, it's no big thing. Mr. Dimm says he knows a likely candidate for the position."

"Oh, I'm sure he knows two or three, all relatives of his."

"Blast!" Marisol had just realized she'd sewn the baby's gown to the front of her dress. "Now look what you've made me do, I'm so upset. And using swear words! I never swear, dash it." She started to cut all the stitches she'd just sewn, mortified to look like such a cake in front of him. And the wretch was grinning! "I do wish you'd left the money!"

"Somehow I knew we'd get back to that," he said with resignation. "I did what I thought was best."

"But it wasn't, and you gave your word, to leave real money and all. How could you do such a thing? You listen to me, nod, then go your own way," she complained, as women had for years. "What kind of behavior is that?"

Indefensible, of course, so he didn't try. "I've a bone to pick with you, too. You said this thing between my sister and your brother was only puppy love, childish infatuation."

"Of course it is. Foster is ill and bored and Bettina is sweet and attentive. Helping to care for him gives Bettina a sense of being needed, like a mature woman. Having her admiration restores the pride Foster lost to Arvid and even to you, who stands as his nephew's guardian. Still, he is only twenty and army-mad. He's not ready to take a wife. And Bettina is only seventeen and has seen nothing of the world. Don't worry."

"Strange, you don't listen to me when I tell you not to worry about Nolly. Besides, if there is nothing to worry about, why is Tina suddenly claiming that a London Season is not so important anymore?"

"Perhaps because Edelia is still here, and Boynton now, too. You did tell me to send for my brother-in-law, you know. I'm sorry to have to tell you, and I hope you aren't put out, but those two are as close as inkle-weavers. Edelia even comes to visit Foster now, in the guise of chaperoning your sister in the afternoons when Boynton is between his late breakfast and his early dressing for dinner. London is all the two of them talk about, the latest *on dits*, the newest fashions. Bettina is sensible enough to grasp the shallowness of the tonnish life in Town. It's enough to give anyone a disgust of the place."

"I should take her to Hyde Park at night then to see the pigeons. It would finish the job and I'd never have to go back."

Except to deliver the second ransom demand, of course.

Chapter Twenty

This time the note demanded four hundred pounds brought to the same place, same time, that Friday, without the Runners. It was her last chance to save the little bastard, the message said, sending chills through Marisol's heart. Anyone who could speak so vilely of Nolly could be capable of anything.

She hugged him the harder, and patted the golden curls on his head while he played with the ribbon in her hair. That there were creatures so base they could threaten such a precious little innocent made the world an uglier place. "Don't worry, my angel, the earl won't let anything happen to you." Somehow, to Marisol's surprise, she'd come to believe it was true. Pigheaded and overbearing he might be, but Lord Kimbrough could be trusted. She'd thought never to accept another man's word for anything, never to let another male have authority over her, but the earl was different. He really wasn't like Arvid at all.

This time he swore to leave the money and walk away, after a furious discussion over who should put up the additional pounds. Carlinn felt the blunt should come from him, since his mishandling of the first attempt had raised the ante. Marisol was adamant the duke's estate should defend the duke, that the earl should have no more burden placed on him beyond that of messenger. Resenting the designation of errand boy, Kimbrough had protested. He stormed and he shouted, he paced and he scowled, but he took her money. Arvid would have gone his own way regardless of her objections, and would have flown into an ungovernable rage at her first sign of disagreement. He would never have conceded, or smiled at her afterward. And Arvid's smile never reached his eyes and never warmed her heart, the way Kimbrough's did. "Ah, Nolly," she whispered, tickling the baby's ear, "too bad his lordship is such a stickler for the niceties."

Such a stickler was the earl that he offered to escort Miss Sherville home the very afternoon the note arrived. Her departure date had come and gone, her mother must be missing her, and she should not be subject to more shabby treatment of a missing host. If they hurried, and he rode through the night on the return, he could be in London on time.

Such sacrifice was not needed. Lord Boynton had offered to see Miss Sherville and her maid removed to Bath, at her chosen pace, which involved frequent stops, reservations in advance at the finest inns, and elegant repasts along the way. At the earl's expense, of course.

"Think nothing of it, Boynton," Carlinn told the older man. "You'll be doing me a favor, saving me the trip to Bath. The least I can do is spring for the tab."

Boynton took out an enameled snuffbox and offered it to the earl, who shook his head. When Boynton had succeeded in opening the box with one hand, taking out a judicious pinch, then sneezing into a lace handkerchief—none of which impressed the earl—he said, "Deuced good of you. And can't say I blame you about not wanting to go to Bath. Devilish dull kind of place. Wouldn't be caught dead there, m'self. Actually, suppose I would. Be caught dead, that is. They say it's where old reprobates like m'self go to die. Don't want to end m'days playing silver loo with the biddies, though. Got a better notion, if it don't throw a rub in your plans."

"My plans? What have my plans got to do with anything?"

"Your plans for Miss Sherville. Between gentlemen, don't you know. Wouldn't want to be cutting you out or anything."

Carlinn was able to assure the other man that not only did he have the earl's approval, he had his blessing. "Then Miss Sherville won't feel her trip to Berkshire was a waste. That is, she does reciprocate your regard, doesn't she?"

Boynton puffed out his chest, buckram wadding notwithstanding. "I do believe so, Kimbrough, I do believe. Haven't wanted to put it to the touch yet, of course, not without your leave. You had first choice, what?"

"Sporting of you, I'm sure." Carlinn coughed to cover a laugh.

Boynton didn't seem to notice. "Now that you're giving me a clear field, I'll take the plunge. I mean, Arvid's cocking up his toes like that and all, and my not getting any younger, give a chap pause, by Jupiter. Miss Sherville's a handsome female, what? And knows how to dress. Looks good on m'arm, don't you know. Will look better in that empty house of theirs in Grosvenor Square."

"Ah, part of the dowry, is it? I understood there was enough to purchase any number of London houses."

"Quite, but there's no reason to be wasting all that brass. Need it to keep up appearances, don't you know. Style is everything. Miss Sherville agrees. Well-bred female, thinks just as she ought. Well favored, well dowered; what more could a chap ask?"

Well endowed, Carlinn thought to himself, thinking of another female's soft, womanly shape. Aloud, he just said, "I wish you well."

"And you too, boy-o, happy hunting."

"Hunting? Oh, you mean the ransom note."

Boynton placed his finger alongside his nose. "If that's how you want to put it. Between gentlemen, don't you know. But it happens to the best of us, Kimbrough. Plain as the nose on your face your turn has come, even if you ain't ready to admit it."

Carlinn did have to admit that he knew exactly what Boynton was referring to, but that was as far as he was going. Lud, if this old court card was making book on his fate, Kimbrough's carefully controlled facade must be slipping. It wouldn't do. No, it wouldn't do at all. And it was all that woman's fault. As soon as this ransom mess was taken care of, he'd put her from his mind once and for all. Of course, he'd do his damnedest to see those bastard blackmailers brought to book, and Arvid's murderer, too, so her peace of mind was restored and her name was cleared, so that no one, ever, would think of her as less than a lady. The most infuriatingly exciting, enticing, affectionate, courageous, and beautiful lady of his experience . . . but it wouldn't do.

Dimm was to stay outside the park. He wore his red waistcoat and kept in plain sight, hobbling back and forth near the park entrance. The extra poundage he'd gained recently, from all those fancy teas and lavish dinners, only exacerbated the problem.

"I allus said policing was nine-tenths footwork, but this beats the Dutch. And what am I doing? Nobbut showing the bastards where I ain't." So he limped across the street to the earl's carriage and climbed up next to the driver. He even opened his coat so the redbreast was more visible. "I should be in the park making an arrest," he muttered. To which the driver commented that he'd like to see the day Dimm did anything to earn his keep. Dimm chewed on the stem of his pipe.

Lord Kimbrough was once more making his obeisance at Society's feet. This time the park was even more crowded, the warmer weather drawing the Quality back to London like ants to a picnic. He smiled, he bowed, he refused invitations to innumerable parties and innumerable beds. Behind him he could almost hear the wheels of speculation turning. What in the world was the Elusive Earl doing in London twice in a month? He was only seen in the park, so it couldn't be business; therefore it must be pleasure. A woman, they concluded, quizzing every female to whom he nodded.

Hope even flared that it wasn't a particular woman who drew the earl to Town, but the search for one. A plump matron trailing simpering misses behind her like a row of ducklings even dared suggest he attend her Sylvia's come-out, for they were sure to have much in common. He doubted that. One hard look from the earl had Sylvia—the one in cerise—quaking like a pudding. He moved on, delighted to leave the main thoroughfares behind.

He strode across the grass instead of on the verge by the bridle paths, to avoid the horseback set, nodcocks who called themselves Corinthians because they could sit a fractious beast that didn't belong in the park in the first place, or the peahens trying to show off their seats, their trailing riding habits, and their eligibility all at once.

Bah! Thank goodness not every gentlewoman cared to put herself on display. If he wanted to see fancy equestrian acts, he'd go to Astley's, and if he wanted a bed-warmer, he'd go to Mother Lil's or the opera house greenroom. And if he wanted a wife, well, he wouldn't go back to Bath, that was for sure.

Carlinn checked his watch. Right now what he wanted was to get the parcel to the designated bench. He hurried past the riverbanks where children fed the ducks and the shallows where boys sailed paper boats. At last he was in those deeper reaches of the park that stayed less congested. As he took the final turning, he was pleased to note that the statue was actually being washed down by a park attendant with mop and bucket and damp uniform, not that it would stay clean for long. He was also relieved to see most of the benches were empty. A maid and her young man were enjoying their afternoon off on one of the seats, and a dignified older gentleman read his newspaper on another. A youngish woman in a poke bonnet that hid most of her face sat on the bench opposite the third, rocking a perambulator. She wasn't having much success getting the baby to sleep, Carlinn noted, for he could hear the infant's wails from beyond the monument. He thought for a moment how lucky they were in Nolly. The little duke never carried on that way. Of course, he had any number of adults to cater to his every whimper, but Noel truly was a well-behaved child. Not that Carlinn considered himself any kind of expert, naturally.

He sat on the third bench and checked his watch again and waited for the church bells to mark the hour. The woman across from him was busy with the fussing baby, her head bent over the carriage. Good. At the first stroke of the chime, he removed the packet from his inner pocket. Heavier and bulkier this time, the parcel contained the additional money, plus a plea from Marisol to take the money with her blessings but leave her son alone. Kimbrough slipped the package beneath his seat at the third chime. By the fourth he was on his feet, ready to leave.

Just as the church bells struck the fifth gong,

however, a different noise sounded. "Runaway!" someone shouted back along the bridle paths, and " 'Ware, loose horse." Women were screaming, men were yelling, and hooves were pounding nearer.

The young swain had hustled his sweetheart behind the bench, Carlinn quickly ascertained, and the old gent was on his feet, ready to bolt. The park attendant dropped his mop and came out from behind the statue, peering back toward the intersection. The woman with the baby was shrieking, setting the infant to howling again, on top of the other cries. Carlinn hurriedly grabbed the woman's arm in one hand and the pram's handle in the other and dragged them both over to his side of the path, behind the bench where he could protect them.

"He's coming this way!" the park employee hollered just as a mighty gray stallion, sides flecked with foam and blood, thundered down the path. The uniformed man dove for his bucket of soapy water to toss in the runaway's face, which didn't stop the horse for a second. Then he grabbed for the reins and almost got trampled, without success. The old man waved his newspaper at the brute, and still the animal kept coming without the slightest pause. The bookish-looking beau started out from behind his bench while his companion screamed, but Carlinn ordered, "Get back, you fool!"

Making sure the mother and infant were safely behind him and the concrete bench, the earl stepped onto the tanbark, right in the stallion's way. "No!" He shouted, "Whoa, sir," in tones so loud, so firm, so used to being obeyed, that they finally penetrated the frenzied beast's terrified mind. At least the animal slowed enough to think about running down the large man in his path. The gray's hesitation was long enough for Carlinn to lunge for the trailing reins and wrap them around his fist, digging his heels in the ground as the stallion plunged and tossed his head. By this time the maintenance man was able to grab the cheek strap on the stallion's bridle and add his weight to the earl's to bring the panicked horse to a stop.

"Good boy, good lad," Carlinn crooned, running his hand along the heaving side, where blood flowed from what looked like a bullet crease. "You'll be fine now," he told the animal. "I am sure your rider will be coming along any minute now to take you home."

"I'll walk him a bit, shall I, milord, to cool him off?" offered the park attendant.

"Yes, he's too spent to get up to more trouble. Good job, Isaac."

"And you, milord," said the grinning boy, actually Dimm's son from Kimbrough's own stables.

Carlinn turned around as more people hurried down the path now that the danger was past. The young couple, Dimm's niece Suky from the inn and her brother who was clerking for Stenross, Stenross, and Dinkerly, were helping the older gentleman, Mr. Stenross himself, pick up his newspapers. And the mother and baby carriage were—gone. So was the extortion money.

Diddled, by damn!

"Well, I hope you're satisfied, Your Grace," the earl grumbled. "They've got the money and all we've got for the effort is one scarred stallion." No one had claimed the horse, naturally, especially when he was deposited at the police stable. So Kimbrough took the gray home. He had too hard a time finding a mount up to his weight to leave this one languishing in gaol.

"No," Marisol told him, pouring out the tea. "We've got a little peace of mind and that's worth every bit of the four hundred pounds. Maybe if they read my note, they'll see how much Nolly means to me and leave us alone. If that woman with the baby really was the culprit, she'll understand. I feel much better about the situation now."

She was looking better, too, since he'd sent a note ahead informing her that the money was delivered. Marisol was wearing a blue silk gown that almost matched the color of her eyes, and it clung to her figure enough that he could see she hadn't lost too much weight, only enough to reveal a narrow waist, well-formed legs, and a still-ample bosom.

"In truth, now I can sleep at night without waking up every hour to listen for Nolly's breathing or Sal's growls. I thank you for that, my lord."

He waved aside her gratitude. "You might try calling me Kimbrough then, or Carlinn. I do think we know each other well enough by now, Duchess. You even know how to fix my tea the way I like, without asking."

Marisol found herself blushing like a schoolgirl. She sipped her tea to hide the embarrassment. "And I am sick to death of being *your grace*ed. Please call me Marisol, my—Carlinn." With a faint tinge of color still in her cheeks, Marisol changed the subject away from the personal: "Do you think this will be the last of the threats, then?"

"Only time will tell, but you are an easy mark. The female could not have been acting alone—remember the stallion—hence you cannot bank on her maternal feelings winning the day. I would not want us to relax our vigilance entirely, but yes, I believe you can rest easier."

Kimbrough went home to get his own much-needed rest, but sleep did not come. He kept thinking of lovely Marisol— No, "Duchess" seemed to suit better, especially when she was acting the gracious lady, thanking him for his efforts. He lay in his bed, thinking of her waking up every hour, in his arms, thanking him for his efforts. Every hour ought to do it, for a start. And oh, the efforts he'd go to for her had him breaking out in a sweat. Strange, he'd never once thought of taking Edelia

Chapter Twenty-one

"A bastard? You mean I went through all that and almost got trampled for Arvid Pendenning's bastard?"

"Yes, and I paid four hundred pounds for him. Isn't he precious?"

Well, no, he wasn't. He was dark and scrawny, with Arvid's narrow eyes and pouty expression. His name was Arlen, the note said, and he was three weeks old. He was also a fussy baby who wouldn't eat well, according to the wet nurse, and hardly slept, according to everyone else in the house. Arlen was quickly settled into the nursery, out of earshot. Poor Sal was in despair, trying to keep her new little herd together and under her watchful eye. Rather than make the crippled dog go up and down the stairs all day, Marisol had brought both children into the morning room, where her maid Sarah was rocking Arlen in a cradle and she was singing to Nolly, to give the exhausted nursemaid Rebecca time for a nap.

When Lord Kimbrough was announced, Marisol dismissed the maid, telling her to go spend time with her recuperating husband. The earl approached the cradle and peered down at the new infant. It was Denning's, unmistakably. One could tell from the petulant curl to the infant's lip. "Fertile bastard, Denning. Sowing his seed in three women at once. His wife, his married mistress, this other woman. Who knows how many other little butter stamps might turn up."

"I wonder who she was, poor thing, that she had to give up her baby." Marisol carried Nolly over to the earl's side and looked down at her husband's illegitimate child. Nolly crammed a fistful of her Norwich silk shawl into his mouth while she was staring into the cradle, wondering if the woman missed Arvid, if he had been kind to her.

"She must be from the lower orders," Carlinn speculated, "that she needed money. A wealthy woman would have gone off somewhere to have the child in secret, then put him out to an orphanage or foster home. If she couldn't, ah, get rid of the problem beforehand."

"I suppose we'll never know. Do you think you could recognize her again?"

Carlinn looked up and started to extricate the shawl's fringe from his ward's mouth. "Silly lad. A gentleman might devour a beautiful lady with his eyes; he doesn't try to swallow her apparel." He turned back to Marisol, who was smiling at his flummery. "No, I cannot say I'd know the woman again. Her bonnet hid most of her face, and then she kept her head down. Not that I would have recognized Denning's lightskirt anyway."

"Mr. Dimm might have. I suppose that's why she wrote that no Runners should come to the park. What does he think? He never mentioned that Arvid had another woman in keeping. I wonder if he knew."

"He didn't say, just that he was going to Bristol on a hunch. Something about wrapping a string around a stone or such."

When the new baby started mewing, Marisol handed Nolly to the earl, as casually as she'd hand him her cape or gloves. She bent to pick up Arlen before he could work himself into a red-faced squall. "Hush, poppet, hush. Everything is going to be all right now. I know you miss your mama, but we are trying our best."

"The doxy didn't seem to have any better luck with the brat than you. Maybe that's why she gave him away." The earl was bouncing Nolly in his arms, getting chuckles and gurgles. "Now, this is what a baby should be!"

"Of course. Too bad they can't all be dukes." Marisol laughed, sitting again and rocking the infant in her arms. Sal dropped down at her feet, tail thumping against the carpet. "I wonder what the mother would have done if we hadn't paid her?"

"Sold him to gypsies, or left him on some parish doorstep, I suppose."

"And we'd never have known. We'd have kept thinking someone meant to hurt Nolly, when the unfortunate girl only wanted Arvid's son to be taken in."

"If that was meant to remind me that I counseled against paying their demands, I stand rebuked." He was dangling his watch in front of Nolly, and told the boy, "Your mother's a hard woman, Your Grace. She never forgets a fellow's lapses, and never misses a chance to gloat. You'd better eat all your porridge or you'll hear about it the rest of your life, how you could have been as big as Uncle Carlinn if you'd only listened to your mama."

He smiled over at Marisol, who really wished he'd stop teasing; it did peculiar things to her insides, like turning them to jelly. "But you were right that Nolly was in no danger," she admitted.

"Ah, a gracious concession. Did you hear that, Duke? In the past six months I have been right one whole time! Amazing, isn't it?"

"Gudgeon, you've been everything wise and kind and brave, and well you know it. I'd tell you how I have come to appreciate you, but shan't, for fear of swelling your head even further."

"A compliment, almost. Nolly, my lad, I think she likes me!" And he tossed the laughing child up into the air.

Blushing furiously, Marisol ordered him not to play so roughly unless he wanted his shirtfront decorated in a fashion Brummell could never approve. Carlinn hastily replaced the child on his lap, where Nolly was content to play with the gold buttons on his waistcoat.

Marisol had rocked Arlen back to sleep in her arms, and now hummed softly to him. Lord Kimbrough watched and listened, until a fierce jealousy swept through him. Denning had two children now, and he was dead! As the earl stared at the duchess, the infant's dark hair a contrast to her golden curls, he got even angrier that it was Denning's child she was cuddling, Denning's bastard besides.

"You cannot keep him, you know."

That brought Marisol's head up with a jerk. The infant thrashed a bit, but stayed quiet. "Excuse me?"

"You cannot keep him, I said. It's too much of a burden. Nolly already takes much of your time and attention. Think of him."

"Are you suggesting I would neglect my son?" she asked, her voice dangerously low.

"No, of course not. I'm only saying that you have enough on your plate without Denning's bastard, too. Why, it will be hard enough to reestablish yourself in Society as is. The ton will forget everything in time if you let them, even Arvid and his lovers, but dragging around the duke's baseborn brat will remind them all over again. You know they won't think kindly of you for making them admit such things happen."

"Why do you persist in this humgudgeon about my vying for Society's approval? I am content here, where I have family and friends and worthwhile endeavors. Let them sneer at me in London. I do not care."

"Very well, I believe you, but think about the boy then. He'll never be accepted. You cannot pass him off as your own; he'll never be anything more than Arvid's bastard, second-rate goods. And his whole life he'll look to Noel, the duke, the heir, the favored son. No boy could help being envious, jealous, no matter what you do for him. That's a hell of a legacy for Arvid to leave the boy, a terrible thing to do to a child. You couldn't be so selfish. You must not keep him."

"Are you quite finished now, my lord?" Her tones could have turned Bath's hot springs to ice. "Are you done with telling me what I may and may not do, even though you have absolutely no authority over me?"

Carlinn kept his eyes on Nolly. "Good intentions. Only thinking of you and the boy," he muttered.

"Are you through? Are you ready to listen to what *I* have decided about Arlen?"

He nodded. But he did whisper in Nolly's ear, "Hard as nails. Remember, I warned you."

Marisol cleared her throat. "Rather than being selfish, my lord, I have been drowning in guilt that I cannot warm to this child the way I ought. I look at him and I see Arvid, his perfidy, his nastiness. I see a mother no better than she ought to be, maybe even a murderess. Little Arlen is not to blame, of course, but he is not an easy child either. Perhaps if he were soft and sweet . . . but he is not. Fortunately my maid Sarah is good with him, better than Rebecca, Nolly's nanny. And Sarah has asked if she and her husband can take Arlen with them when they go to Yorkshire. Her husband's injury—Well, the doctors are not certain there will be children for them. Sarah and Ned want to change his name to Leonard and make him their own son, no one's cast-off by-blow. I would be his godmother, and pay for his schooling and such."

"And I'll stand for his first pony! Brilliant, my dear, brilliant! I should have known you'd do what was best for everyone."

"Yes, you should have," she said dryly, then added, "We have sent for Mr. Stenross, to check into the technical aspects of the thing so there is never a question about Arl—Leonard's legal parents, and we'll wait to speak to Mr. Dimm. What if he finds the mother and she wants the infant back?"

"She sold him, for heaven's sake. She won't want him returned. At most she might demand more money, but baby-selling is still a crime, if nothing else. We can threaten her with gaol if she won't sign Stenross's papers. The problem is if he doesn't find her and the woman sells information to the papers, just to hurt you."

"Me? None of this was my misdeed! I didn't bear an illegitimate child, I didn't kill my lover, and I didn't trade my son for a sack of gold!"

"Yes, but people will talk. You can't like being the latest *on dit* forever."

No, *he* couldn't stand being the brunt of tittle-tattle, Marisol knew. Kimbrough was the one who was so concerned with the proprieties that he'd be mortified to find his name in the gossip columns again. He was just like the dowager, who couldn't get Arlen out of the house fast enough, lest she be reminded of her own son's debauchery. And Kimbrough's sister's come-out would be ruined by the hint of scandal, old or new. Carlinn would never do anything to reflect poorly on Bettina's chances of making a brilliant match. He'd never do anything to tarnish his family name or cut up his peaceful existence.

That night it was Marisol's own crying that kept her awake.

Carlinn rode out early the next morning, as was his habit. He took the new gray to evaluate the stallion's recovery, and was pleased to see that the horse was skittish, not mean. A firm hand was enough to keep him under control, even when a rabbit ran across his path. He'd be a safe enough mount as long as the rider didn't lose concentration. The blackmailers could have got him cheap, though, for the otherwise magnificent animal must have been a hazard in the city. With a gun being fired purposely near him, or at him, the wonder was that no one was killed. It was also curious that no one had seen or heard the shooting. Dimm's relatives and associates were still looking into it.

Carlinn rode toward the Castle, expecting to be invited in for a second breakfast. He left the stallion at the Denning stables, after giving instructions for its tending, and carefully brushed off his boots on the way to the front door. Her Grace was sleeping late this morning, however, according to the butler, and asked not to be disturbed. Nolly, Carlinn's second choice, was having a bath, then a nap. So the earl asked after Foster, and was shown up. Foster's smile of welcome only dimmed a bit when he realized the earl was by himself.

"Deuced good to see you, my lord. Dashed flat sitting around, I can tell you. Can't even read the newspapers without someone turning the pages; I tried doing it with my teeth. Only got newsprint on my nose."

"Would you like me to read to you then? I have a bit of time." The longer he stayed, the more likely that Marisol would be up and about. "You must be wanting to hear the latest war news."

Foster rubbed his bandaged hand along the counterpane of his bed. "Well, ah, thing is, your sister kindly offered to stop by this afternoon and do the reading." His face cleared. "But how about a game of chess? I almost had you beat last time. I'm afraid you'll still have to make the moves for me; can't bend the fingers yet with all these wrappings the sawbones insists on. The doctor says soon though. He thinks I can rejoin the regiment before summer. Isn't that capital?"

"Summer in the Peninsula is hot and buggy, full of diseases and mud. Are you sure you want to go? I mean, you've done your bit for king and country already. White or black?"

"But there's bound to be action this summer and I mean to be in the thick of things this time, not on some blasted ship. I had white last time; you can open."

"Your sister will worry." He moved his first man.

Foster was studying the board. "That didn't stop you from going, did it? I mean, all the chaps have mothers and sisters and wives and sweethearts."

"Sometimes all of them. Where do you want to move?"

A few turns later, Carlinn's mind started to wander as he waited for Foster to call his play. Was she stirring yet? Would she come check on her brother before going downstairs? He straightened his cravat. Foster cleared his throat.

"Your turn, Carlinn."

"What? Oh, sorry." He studied the board.

While he pondered his next move, Foster cleared his throat again, which did not aid his lordship's concentration. He looked up.

Foster was rubbing at the bandages again. "I've been meaning to ask permission to write to your sister when I go," he said. "Good a time as any."

"Pardon, you want my permission to write to Bettina?"

"Well, I wouldn't want to do anything harum-scarum and give you a disgust of me. It's not the thing, don't you know, for a young miss to be getting correspondence from a man who is not related."

Carlinn allowed as how he might have heard of such a convention. His sarcasm was wasted on Foster, who was intent on making his case.

"Thing is, my intentions are honorable. Not soon, of course. Tina should have her Season. Dance holes in her slippers, don't you know. I've never been a dab hand at cutting a caper, and she's looking forward to it. I'd lay odds she'll be a regular Toast, too."

Carlinn wouldn't take the bet. Bettina was pretty and gay and rich. She'd be a success. Such a success that he had to ask: "Aren't you afraid all those Town beaux might turn her head?"

"It's a chance I'll have to take. That way we'll both know she's sure. Then I'll be asking your permission to pay my addresses. When the war is over, of course."

"And I'd be proud to give it, after you've both seen a bit more of the world, and if you both are of like minds then."

Foster nodded his head and turned back to the board. Then he looked sideways at the earl and queried, "Anything you'd like to ask me before I go?"

Carlinn reached for his knight, then reconsidered. "Like what, chub?"

"Like permission to address *my* sister?"

The knight fell out of his hand onto the floor. "You're beginning to let this courtship nonsense go to your head, bantling. Either that or the hero business."

"Then perhaps I should be asking your intentions, my lord." Foster was only partway teasing. "An eligible bachelor running tame in the household, making morning calls before breakfast—that type of thing can't be good for my sister's reputation."

"You're putting your ugly Laughton nose where it don't belong, Lieutenant," Carlinn barked.

Foster hadn't been in the army long enough to jump when so addressed. Nor had he ever served under Major Lord Kimbrough, for which he thanked his lucky stars. Therefore, he valiantly—or foolhardily—proceeded. "What's the matter with my nose except that new bump in it? I mean, it ain't like Wellesley's honker. Marisol's got the same beak and everyone says she's a beauty. Looks like Noel will have it, too, and I've heard you say he's a handsome lad. Anyway, I thought it was my job to ask about your intentions. Head of the family and all that, don't you know." He grinned. "Luckily I'm not shipping out just yet. You have another month to get your courage to the sticking point."

Kimbrough knocked over the chessboard in his hurry to leave.

Grace for the world, you were always so good to me. But he—"

"Why don't we wait for his lordship to get here?" Dimm suggested. "Magistrate and such. That way we can all hear all of it at once and figger what's to be done."

When Kimbrough arrived, Foster came down, but the dowager took to her bed, preferring not to know any more than she had to. Sarah and her Ned stood quietly in a corner while Aunt Tess was furiously knitting close to the fireplace, where she couldn't hear much, not that her location mattered for that. Marisol would explain things to her later, she said, but little Leonard would need lots of sweaters in Yorkshire now. She refused to consider any other option. The babies were not present. Marisol couldn't bear the thought of Nolly in the room with someone who had sold her own child. Tyson hadn't even asked about Arlen's welfare.

When everyone was assembled, Dimm had his son Gabriel bring in another man, in handcuffs.

"Purvis? Is it really you?" Marisol found that her hands were shaking. She'd written such glowing references for these two, while all the time they'd been plotting her ruin. How could she have been so mistaken, thinking Tyson merely disloyal when the woman was a desperate criminal? To have an affair with her employer, right under his wife's nose, and then perhaps kill him—or have her other lover, the valet, do it—were not the usual functions of milady's abigail. Marisol tried to steady her hands by clasping them together in her lap.

Lord Kimbrough brought her a glass of sherry and stood behind her seat, his strong hand on her shoulder. "Let's hear the whole thing then, Mr. Dimm, before we jump to conclusions."

"Well," the Runner began, "my part of the story starts in Bristol. Purvis here had his name on a ship's waybill, going to the colonies by Robin's barn. The embargo, don't you know. So I weren't half surprised to see him. Then the abigail shows up, the one what's been missing for four, five months. And she's got passage money, too. Wasn't hard to figger."

"But why?" Marisol asked. "I don't understand."

Tyson started to cry. "I swear I never meant to harm anyone." She put her hands over her eyes.

Purvis awkwardly set his manacled wrists at her waist. "Hush, Nell, I'll tell it. It's like this, Your Grace, my lord. I asked Nell, that's short for Eleanor, to be my wife, and she said yes. But His Grace, he said no. He didn't believe servants should marry, he said."

"That's just like the dastard," Foster muttered from the opposite sofa. Lord Kimbrough poured him a sherry, too, which Foster managed to clutch in his bandaged hands.

Purvis went on: "So I waited a bit and then asked him again, seeing as how he was in a rare good humor, what with the baby coming and all. Your baby, Your Grace. The heir, that made him happy to be cutting out Lord Boynton finally. And the duke, he said maybe we could marry, maybe we couldn't. He'd think about it." Purvis stared at his feet. "But he was thinking that if I wanted Nell so bad, he'd maybe better take a second look."

"Oh no."

Purvis nodded. "Yes. I'm sorry, but Your Grace was getting big with the child, and sickly, so his eye was wandering even more than usual. And he did look at Nell. A right pretty lass, my Nell is, too," he said, patting her back with his shackled hands. "And His Grace told Nell she didn't have any choice."

"You should have come to me, Tyson. Eleanor."

The maid looked at the duchess through tear-swollen eyes. "But I saw how he was with you. Everyone knew how he took his temper out on you, poor lady. If you'd crossed him over me, it would only make things worse. I was that worried about you and your baby," she said bitterly.

Now Marisol looked away, embarrassed to have so much dirty linen washed in front of Lord Kimbrough. Understanding, he tightened his grip on her shoulder.

"So I didn't fight him, Your Grace," Eleanor went on. "He said that he'd let us marry when he was done. If I resisted, he said, or cried foul or anything, he swore we'd both be dismissed. So it wasn't rape."

"Of course it was. You had no choice. It was against your will."

"But Purvis didn't see it that way," she said sadly.

"I told you I was sorry, Nell. It was just that at first I couldn't . . ."

"You were not to blame, Eleanor," Marisol insisted with a dirty look to Purvis. "Go on."

"Well, then I found I was increasing, too. When I told His Grace, he laughed and said now I could marry Purvis, and get out. He wouldn't keep either of us on. But Purvis, he didn't want me anymore."

The swine. To Marisol's thinking, there was not much to choose from between Purvis and Arvid. Her glare at the valet spoke volumes.

"But how could I support a wife and child without a position, Your Grace? It wasn't even my child! At least he should have paid. . . ."

"So you made sure he did, eh?" Foster held his glass between two hands and saluted the valet.

It was Marisol who asked, "Which one of you . . . ?"

The maid replied: "First I wrote that note to you, just to get even. Purvis told me where the duke would be and who with. His Grace was bragging something fierce. I wanted you to see what kind of animal he was."

"Oh, I knew, I already knew," Marisol whispered.

"But most I wanted to shame him in front of a real lady, his own wife."

Purvis took up the tale: "When Nell told me

what she'd done, I feared he'd get in a rage, Your Grace. The duke didn't like anyone getting in the way of his pleasures, if you know what I mean. I knew he had taken to carrying that pistol, so I went out to stop you."

"You wanted to protect me?" Marisol asked.

"Yes, and Nell, too, if he figured out she'd written the note. But I was too late. You'd come and gone and so had Lady Armbruster. His Grace was in a rare snit all right. I'd never seen him in such a taking. He was screaming like a banshee, saying I must have been the one to send you after him like that, Your Grace, and I'd pay for it, and you'd pay for it, too. I knew he meant it."

Marisol's shoulder was aching where Carlinn's fingers were digging into the flesh. She patted his hand and he relaxed a bit, but she knew that if Arvid Pendenning were alive and in the room right then, he'd be wishing he were dead again. Hell had to be less painful than what the earl would have done to him.

Purvis shook his head. "I couldn't take his threats no more, Your Grace, my lord. That muckworm, ruining everyone's life that way, and making me turn my back on the finest woman I ever knew. So I told him I was going to marry Nell even if she carried his seed, and if he didn't give us our fair pay, and something to see us by until I could find a place, I'd go to the newspapers and the magistrates and to Lord Armbruster next door. And he laughed. He didn't care, don't you see? He knew he couldn't be arrested for taking liberties with a common maid or withholding pay from unsatisfactory servants. And fornication was as ordinary among the gentry as fleas on a dog. There was nothing I could do."

"So you shot him?"

"No. I didn't have any weapon. I spit on him instead, to show him what I thought of his idea of *noblesse oblige*. I worked for other gentlemen before.

I knew what was right and honorable, and he was none of it. So I spit on him, right in his face."

"Good for you, man," Foster cheered.

Purvis ignored the interruption, still directing his narrative toward Marisol. "You know how he liked everything about him to be perfect?" She nodded. "I thought he'd go off in an apoplexy right there, but instead he took out the pistol and started waving that gun around like a madman. I was afraid it would go off, so I put my hand on his wrist, to keep it pointed away from me. His Grace, he twisted away, screaming at me to take my hands off him like he was god and I was manure. I held on, though, and the gun went off. He was dead, I could see, so there was no point in calling for help. I went back inside but everyone was still at supper, except Nell. No one saw me coming or going, so I kept mum."

"But you could have come forward during the investigation. It was self-defense."

He shook his head at her naiveté. "Who believes a valet? 'Sides, they'd want to know why I didn't speak up first time 'round. I couldn't take the chance, not with Nell depending on me. So I kept my mouth shut. I'm right sorry blame fell on any of you, Your Grace, Lord Kimbrough, Lord Laughton, but what was I to do?"

No one had an answer, so the valet went on: "I had enough put by to emigrate, and a cousin in the colonies who would help us get settled. I thought we could get away if I just kept quiet long enough."

Nell interrupted. "But I couldn't go on a sea journey, not in the middle of winter, not in my condition. Besides, every time he looked at me, I could see Purvis thinking of how I'd lain with His Grace. He didn't mean to, but it made me feel dirty all over again. So I went off on my own with what I had. Said my husband was with the army, and I had no family to care for me. Took rooms in Richmond where no one knew me, and had the baby."

"Who looked like Arvid."

"And who fussed and cried no matter what I did. And I wanted to go off with Purvis, to start a new life without any reminders, and without throwing myself on his charity in case he changed his mind again."

"So you decided to sell us the baby." Marisol couldn't keep the disapproval from her voice.

" 'Twas that or dump him on some church steps and hope for the best. An ocean voyage wouldn't have been healthy for him, and we were going to set up a little haberdashery out west, not near the big cities. Purvis's cousin had written that there was money to be made there, but it was rough and dangerous, with red Indians and all. I couldn't take a baby into that, not after his warning."

"And you needed more money to set up the little business," Kimbrough suggested.

"I figured the duke owed us. Purvis agreed."

"We never meant for you to think we'd harm the little duke," the valet put in. "We neither of us ever meant you ill, Your Grace."

"Yes, I can see. My husband was more evil than even I suspected. All of this can be laid at his door. But what's to be done now, Mr. Dimm? These people were as much victims as criminals."

" 'Spect that's up to a jury, Your Grace."

Lord Kimbrough was thinking ahead to that trial. The press would be lapping up the details like a cat at a milk saucer. Marisol would have to testify, all about finding Denning with Lady Armbruster. She'd have to listen as the sordid details of her miserable marriage were made public. "Must we really have a court case, all the additional notoriety?" he asked. "It was self-defense, we all know it was, and Arvid had it coming. I'd have killed him myself if I knew what he'd done to— Why can't these people just keep going? They're not a danger to anyone else, and they've paid in all the anguish they've suffered at that dastard's hands."

Marisol looked hopeful, but Dimm scratched his head. "I don't know 'bout taking the law into our own hands that way."

"But if I stand by the decision as magistrate? Purvis and Tyson could sign confessions so if they ever came back they could be tried, and legal adoption papers so they'd never have a claim on the boy. It's like deportation to Botany Bay, only in the other direction and with better chance of survival at the end. We can just say Arvid was accidentally killed by a self-inflicted gunshot wound while in a towering rage at his valet. Even the press will accept such a story."

"His nibs might buy it at that, 'specially if it doesn't stir up another hornet's nest at the rumor mill. Just might work."

The manservant pleaded: "There's another boat leaving next week. We can be on it and you'll never hear from either of us again. I swear it, Your Grace."

"And I," Tyson promised.

Everyone's eyes turned to the duchess, as if to leave the decision to her, for revenge or retribution. "Let them go," she said, "after they sign all the papers."

She accepted their undoubtedly heartfelt gratitude, but could do no more than extend her wishes for a safe journey before leaving the room. They'd suffered, but so had she, and at their hands. Besides, neither had inquired about the baby's future. Tyson hadn't even asked to see her son.

Marisol went upstairs to him and to her own child. She dismissed Rebecca and the maid assigned to help in the nursery, leaving her alone with the sleeping babies and the dogs.

It was over, blessedly over. Tyson and Purvis would be on their way by nightfall. Sarah would leave with her Ned and Leonard in a few days, while Dimm's niece Suky from the inn would take Sarah's place as lady's maid. Foster was nearly well enough to rejoin his unit, and Bettina would go off to her Season . . . and his lordship would resume his search for a perfect wife.

Marisol and Nolly would finally be alone to start their real life together, just the two of them and Aunt Tess and the dowager.

"And you, Sal." The collie thumped her tail on the floor. The terrier whined. "And you, Max."

Lord, maybe she should emigrate, too, rather than stay in Berkshire waiting for him to bring home an impeccable bride like Edelia Sherville. Marisol sighed, knowing there was no place on earth far enough away to escape her own breaking heart.

Chapter Twenty-three

"I have decided to keep Nolly at Kimbrough Hall," the earl declared one afternoon a few days later.

"You what?" Marisol fairly shrieked.

Carlinn studied his fingernails. "My right as guardian, don't you know. I think it will be better for the boy. He needs a man's influence."

The duchess was livid. "He's barely six months old. What are you going to do, take him to a cock fight?"

"And this place," the earl continued, waving one hand around, "is totally unsuitable for a young boy. Dangerous with all those turrets and towers and arrow niches, to say nothing of the broadswords, maces, and battle-axes all over the place. He's sure to get nightmares," he lied through his teeth, thinking the Castle every boy's fantasy playhouse come true. Why, that central bannister was enough to tempt him, even at his age and dignity. He went on: "And then there are all the artifacts that could be damaged."

"Everything dangerous or fragile has already

been put in storage or above the reach of a small child," she said through gritted teeth, wishing she had one of those battle-axes to hand right then.

"No, the little duke is better off with me, at the Hall."

"Better? Why you—you self-righteous toad! You can't even play with Nolly without making him cast up his accounts! And you think you know what is better for my son? You despicable cad, you monster! And you even gave your word not to interfere with his upbringing! I'll fight you in the courts, you bounder! I'll never give him up!"

"I know."

Marisol replaced the china shepherdess she'd been clutching, preparatory to letting it fly. "You know? You did this just to upset me?"

"And you do rise to the bait so charmingly, my pet. I particularly liked that 'self-righteous toad.' But I was not just trying to set the sparks flying. I do know that you'd never part with Nolly, and I would never ask you to."

"What are you saying, Carlinn?"

"What I am saying, no, asking, in my usual bumbling way, is if you would make me the happiest of men, and Nolly's father."

"You are asking me to marry you, just to get Nolly?"

"Now, that is a particularly goosish thing to say, Duchess. Granted the lad is the most adorable, perfect creature ever placed on earth, but even I draw the limits somewhere."

"But—but why, then?" she stuttered, completely baffled.

"Because I think I have loved you forever, and don't want to be apart from you for another day. Because I think of you all the time and wish to spend the rest of my life trying to make you happy."

"But you thought I was shallow and scandalous, a bad influence on your sister. You even thought I was a suspect in Arvid's murder."

"So I was a fool. That cannot come as a surprise; lud knows you've told me often enough. And Tyson forgave Purvis for far greater sins," he added hopefully, staring at her lowered head.

"And far be it from me to be less gracious than my maid?"

"Exactly. Besides, I did buy you this in London, even before we had Purvis's confession." He held out a small box and opened the lid to reveal a gold ring set with small diamonds around a sapphire. "There's the official Kimbrough heirloom engagement ring, but I wanted you to have something all your own. This one matches your eyes." He knelt on the carpet before her so he could see her face. "Blast it, I hate when you cry!" He jumped up and tossed her his handkerchief.

"I know," she blubbered into the square of fabric. "I'm sorry."

"Deuce take it, I'm the one who should be apologizing." He was pacing in his agitation. "I dared to hope . . . that is, I regret if my—my importunities have caused you discomfort. Forget I ever said anything."

"Oh, no, that's not it at all. It's just that you've made me the happiest of women."

"I have? You are? Then I can take it that it's a yes to my question?"

"Oh, yes. I have loved you for ever so long, but never thought—"

Whatever the duchess thought was lost in his embrace. There was no thinking, only feeling, the warmth and magic of his touch, the promised passion, the tender affection and gentle strength and the faintest scent of lemon. If Marisol had to describe heaven, this was it.

"Lud, I've been wanting to do this for ages," he admitted when they paused to catch their breaths. Somehow Marisol was sitting on his lap, on the sofa, their arms entangled. She tucked her head under his chin and gave a sigh of contentment.

"Dash it," he complained, stroking her back, "I'll never understand how you can go from screeching wildcat to purring kitten in the blink of an eye. Do you suppose I might figure it out if I have the next forty or fifty years?"

"You can try, my lord."

"Don't you think you can call me Carlinn, Duchess? But you won't be a duchess much longer, will you? Shall you mind being called Countess instead, my love?"

" 'My love' sounds best of all!" Which required another long interval of less verbal communication.

"What would you have done if I'd said no?" Marisol asked later.

"Oh, I'd camp on your doorstep, frighten away all your other suitors, teach Nolly to say Papa Carl."

She laughed, then turned serious. "And you truly don't care about all the gossip?"

"The gossips can say whatever they want, as long as you say you love me."

"I'll say it over and over, from every rooftop, every day, even if you get more odiously swell-headed."

"And I swear to try not to be too proud that the most wonderful woman in England returns my affection. I'll do anything for you, my love."

"Even move to London?"

Marisol almost found herself dumped on the floor, Carlinn sat up so suddenly. "Good grief, Marisol, you can't want that, do you?"

"Of course not, I just wanted to see you fly into a pelter, my love."

"Touché. But there is Tina's presentation to be considered. We'll have to attend to that."

"Perhaps Nolly and I can stay in the country?"

"What, and make me face the dragons on my own? Not on your life, my girl. Besides, I have no intention of leaving you alone for more than an hour or two, here and there. Anyway, I doubt we'll have much trouble, not with my sister's prattling on about Foster this and Foster that."

"Shall you mind? He hasn't much to offer but his title and his character and what I can provide. Once the war is over, he'll be just another bankrupt aristocrat."

"But Tina comes into a handsome property from our mother when she marries. Foster will have plenty to do handling that. It will give me more time to see to ours."

"Now, that has a nice ring to it. Ours," she repeated dreamily, her head on his shoulder.

He kissed the top of her very disordered curls. "My dear, shall you mind that I'm just a country gentleman, without all those fancy manners? One who looks after his lands instead of his wardrobe? Shall you mind that I didn't woo you with flowers and candy and poems?"

Marisol pretended to think. He didn't give her much time to come to a conclusion. "Too bad. I'll bring you puppies and kittens and new strains of oat and all my love instead."

"Now that you mention it, I do believe that Sal is the only gift you've bestowed on me before today. But what woman could ask for more than what you've offered now? Your name, your ring, your love. I suppose I shall just have to be content, my foolish darling."

After another interval, during which Marisol's hair became thoroughly disheveled, and Carlinn's too, she said wonderingly, "I thought you wanted a proper lady like Edelia Sherville."

"No, I thought I should have a cold, decorous wife like Edelia Sherville. There is a big difference between what I wanted and what I was prepared to accept. I always wanted a lively, loving lady. With a big chest."

Marisol was surprised she could still blush, with said chest being half exposed. "I'm not proper like

Edelia. I'll never make you a perfect wife, you know."

"You're not perfect? Ssh, don't tell anyone. I've been calling it from the church steeple that you are. Except for your nose, of course."

"My nose? What's wrong with my nose?"

"Nothing, my love. It's perfect for kissing." So he did, then asked, "Are you sure you'll be able to put up with me? I know I can be high-handed and dictatorial."

"I'll try, my lord," she answered between kisses of reassurance. "And if not, well, I'll shoot you, of course."

"Sometimes facts is like a boulder," Jeremiah Dimm commented to himself. "They sits right out there, obvious like, and wait for you to stub your toe on 'em."

The Bow Street Runner was in his soft chair, feet up, pipe going, a mug of ale by his side. The little house in Kensington was as quiet and snug as a bear's winter cave. Life was good.

His nibs was happy, for once. He liked the way the Denning murder was tied up so neatly without ruffling any feathers among the peacocks of Mayfair. He was so happy, in fact, that Dimm was promoted to Senior Inspector, and given a healthy bonus. That bonus money was enough to get that last youngster, that cousin's boy, off to school. An architect, he said he wanted to be. Dimm puffed on his pipe and nodded. The boy'd be plying his trade just about the time Lord Kimbrough'd be needing an extension at that manor house of his, what with the way the earl and Her Grace were carrying on.

Now there was a tricky piece of work, Dimm reflected. Arresting Jack Windham, solving the Denning murder—those were child's play compared to getting those two prickly swells together. They were made for each other, any fool could have seen that. But getting them to see eye-to-eye, now that took a real detective. Be damned if that wasn't the high-water mark of his career.

And now his first grandson was the son of a duke, by George. A'course, that was only for private knowing. It was enough that the rest of the world knew little Leonard was having a duchess for a godmother. Countess weren't half bad neither. And the rest of Dimm's brood was fixed for life better than he ever hoped. All those nieces and nephews, sons and daughters, getting established in Berkshire. Even Gabriel was staying on at Lord Kimbrough's invite, as assistant constable with his own little apartment above the one-cell gaolhouse.

That left only Dimm's sister Cora here in Kensington, and Jeremiah had it in mind that Mr. Stenross was a lonely widower. Dimm took another puff on his pipe and raised his mug to his own beloved Cherry, God keep her soul.

He went back to considering the new Lady Kimbrough's offer of the position of caretaker for Denning Castle. He'd have his own cottage by the gatehouse, and a whole staff to look after. And, the countess had added by way of incentive, Mr. Dimm would be right there in Berkshire amid all his sons and daughters, nieces, nephews, and Hambley in-laws.

Dimm blew a smoke ring up to the ceiling and smiled, there in the peace and contentment of his empty house. He'd think some more about her ladyship's offer. Next week.

An Angel for the Earl

To Ruth Cavin, Harvey Klinger, Barbara Dicks,
and Melinda Helfer. Thank you.

Chapter One

Miss Lucinda Faire was eloping with the man of her dreams. Captain Leon Anders was abducting one of Derby's leading heiresses. Obviously, this was not a marriage of true minds.

Lucinda's first inkling that her dreams were about to be shattered came when the handsome officer ignored her company in the hired coach in favor of the silver flask he pulled from his scarlet coat. Not only was Leon drinking in front of a lady, but he had not thought to provide his beloved with anything to ward off the morning chill in the damp, drafty carriage. Having crept from her house before first light, Lucinda naturally hadn't broken her fast. She would not complain, though, lest dear Leon think her the peagoose she undoubtedly was for not even saving a roll from her dinner to carry along the way. Of course a kind word from dear Leon would have warmed her to the core, the way his sweet whispers always did in their stolen moments together. He must be too concerned with their flight to Gretna, she excused him, or perhaps all gentlemen were that cranky in the morning. Heaven knew her father was.

Lucinda settled back in her corner of the coach, a smile on her lips, prepared to enjoy every moment of the grandest adventure of her seventeen years. No, she amended, this was the *only* adventure in her seventeen constricted, confined, and uncompromisingly correct years. Her parents had seen to that, the same way they were seeing to her marriage to Lord Halbersham, an ancient, curmudgeonly neighbor who spouted piety while his servants went cold and hungry.

Which reminded Lucinda of her present discomfort. "Leon, do you think we might stop soon to refresh ourselves? Perhaps at the next change?"

"What, are your attics to let?" her beloved growled. "Do you want your father to find us before nightfall?"

Well, no, but she couldn't help thinking that ten minutes spent sipping a cup of hot tea and ordering warm bricks for their feet would not make that much difference. Her father wouldn't even think to look for Lucinda until she did not arrive promptly for the noon meal, so sure was he that she'd be at her chores or practicing the harp. She drew her serviceable gray wool cloak more snugly about herself and studied her adored Captain Anders.

For once the sight of her soon-to-be-spouse did not send chills down Lucinda's spine. Perhaps that was because there were already so many chills down her spine and elsewhere, one more couldn't be noticed. Or perhaps the dark stubble on his jaw and the bloodshot cast to his eyes lent him an unfamiliar, harsh look. Lucinda was only used to the fair-haired, blue-eyed Adonis who had stolen her heart that day at the haberdasher's when he smiled just for her, plain little Lucinda Faire.

Leon was not smiling now, nor when they finally stopped to change the horses close to midday, and

Lucinda made to follow him from the coach into the posting house.

"Get back in there, you nodcock," he snapped, looking over his shoulder at the busy inn yard. "Do you want to chance being recognized this close to your home? One more red-coated soldier won't draw anyone's attention, but think of your father coming to ask after a blondish chit in a gray cloak, for pity's sake." Lucinda's hazel eyes had grown wide in her face at his abrupt speech, so Captain Anders drew his gloved hand down the side of her cheek. "Hush now, sweetings. I'll bring back a nuncheon fit for a princess. My own princess." That won him back a weak smile, so he shut the door behind him, adding, "I am only thinking of your reputation."

Then why hadn't he pulled the window shades? Lucinda could not help wondering. And worrying about her reputation in the middle of a scandalous elopement seemed just a tad hypocritical. She tried her best to bury such disloyal thoughts. Dear Leon was simply as nervous and anxious as she was. This eloping business was not nearly as romantical as she'd imagined.

Captain Anders must have refilled his flask at the inn, for he kept sipping at it during the long afternoon, slouched in his corner across from her. As the bricks at her feet cooled off, Lucinda stared at the bleak, wintry countryside rather than at the reddening, scowling face of her beloved. Finally she fell asleep, huddled in her cape.

"Wake up, Lucinda." Leon was shaking her shoulder none too gently. "We're at the inn where we'll spend the night."

Lucinda shook her head to clear her mind, dislodging a pale curl or two. "But . . . but it's still light out. We can travel for another hour at least and gain that many miles on my father's pursuit."

"These horses are tired and the driver says there is not another suitable inn for hours more. We'd be forced to put up at a hedgerow tavern or some such."

"But that means we'll be two nights on the road, not one, without even a maid to chaperone. You were so concerned about my reputation at luncheon, what—"

"I said this is where we'll stay, dash it. Don't argue, you plaguey chit. Now, get down, and fix your hair. You look like a schoolgirl."

Stunned and still sleep-fuddled, Lucinda could only stumble after him. He took her arm as they passed the innkeeper, smiled as the man bowed, and hustled her up the stairs.

"There was only the one room, so I said we were man and wife. Less explaining that way, anywise."

"But I cannot share the room with you!"

He ignored her squawked protest. "Less expense, too. I ain't made of brass, you know. How much blunt did you bring along anyway?"

Lucinda reached into her reticule. "Just what's left from my pocket money. You know Father does not give me an allowance or anything." She held out a handful of coins. "Will it be enough for another room?"

He took the coins. "We're on our way to Gretna, blast it, so stop being so deuced missish. I can't abide a prosy female."

"Leon, I . . . I think you may have had too much to drink."

"And what would you know about it, Miss Prunes-and-Prisms? Oh, go take your cloak off and sit down. The innkeep promised dinner soon. Try to act like a starry-eyed bride and not some frightened fawn, or he'll throw us out." The captain shrugged out of his uniform coat without a by-your-leave and tossed it onto the bed before sprawling into the room's only comfortable-looking chair.

Lucinda picked up the scarlet jacket and hung it in the clothespress with her cloak. At least the room appeared clean, boasting a linen-laid table, and chairs, and even a vase of flowers on the stone mantelpiece. Best of all, there was a sofa near the fireplace. A sofa that looked too short for Leon's tall frame, she noted with a twinge of satisfaction, thinking of the uncomfortable night he'd have in store.

Once again Lucinda's and the captain's thoughts were not marching in step.

"You're going to sleep where?" she gasped after dinner when he'd made his plans evident. "Not on your life!"

"Come on now, sweetings. What can a night or two matter?" He was holding her in his arms, stroking her back, whispering in her ear.

Perhaps a night or two in anticipation of their vows was not such a big thing after all, Lucinda was starting to think, when the captain kissed her. His mouth was wet and cold, and smelled of wine and brandy. It mattered. A lot. He was holding her so tightly she felt suffocated. She pushed him away. "No," she declared, shoving him away again when he dragged her back into his embrace and started drooling wet kisses on her neck. For a girl's first experience at lovemaking, this left something to be desired. Not only did her hero seem to have feet of clay, but those feet were set in quicksand.

"Come on, sweetings." Leon was panting. "We have to make sure you're well and truly compromised before your father finds us, else he's liable to drag you back home and hope to scotch any rumors."

"Stop that, Captain!" Lucinda slapped away a hand that was straying where no man's hand had ever strayed. "And I do not wish to be compromised. In fact, I am thinking that perhaps we were too hasty about this elopement after all. We should have gone to my father, explained your prospects—"

"What prospects were those, sweetings?" he asked with a sneer. "Everyone knows the only prospects I have are hopes of getting your skint of a father to part with some of his blunt."

The sinking feeling in Lucinda's stomach had nothing to do with the inferior dinner she'd just eaten. "My father's money? You . . . you don't love me at all, do you?"

"Don't come the innocent with me, girl. You would have come away with anyone who saved you from old Halbersham."

"No, I lo—" Miss Faire's pride kept her from uttering the fatal words. She raised her chin. "I have reconsidered. I no longer wish to marry you, compromised or not."

He laughed. "Who's talking of marriage? You think I intend to marry a drab little dumpling of a chit like you? You're even greener than I thought."

Lucinda still hadn't grasped the depths of his infamy. "You planned this whole fake elopement just to ruin me?"

"That's only incidental, and no great treat either, I can tell you," he said, adding insult to injury, waving his hand vaguely at her limp blond hair, the plain gray traveling dress that did nothing to improve a short, squat figure. The captain's lip curled in derision. "And they say there's no such thing as a homely heiress."

She slapped him. "You, sirrah, are no gentleman. I am going home."

Rubbing his cheek with one hand, the captain shoved her into a chair with the other. "You're not going anywhere until your father gets here with my blunt. That's right, I left him a note explaining right where you'll be and how much he'll have to pay to get you back, and to keep my lips sealed."

"My father will make you marry me," Lucinda cried, horrified at his admission, dismayed at the thought of spending the rest of her life with such a villain.

"Not when I show him my marriage lines. My Fiona's waiting for me in Liverpool."

"Then he'll kill you."

"That old man? He can challenge, but I'm a crack shot."

If she had a pistol, Lucinda thought she might use it herself. "He'll have you arrested for abducting a minor. He'll . . . he'll ruin your career." Lucinda was running out of dire threats.

Anders just snickered and raised a bottle to his lips. Some of the wine dribbled out the side of his mouth. "Think again, little dab, he'll never make more of a scandalbroth by calling for the constables. And my army career has been over for years. The uniform just made my new, ah, profession more successful."

Cardsharping, usury, highway robbery? Lucinda didn't even ask. "My father will see that you never get away with this. And you won't get a farthing out of him."

"Oh, he'll pay. They all do."

All? Lucinda choked back tears of rage and heartbreak. She'd been seven kinds of fool, but she wasn't going to make it eight by staying here one second longer.

Once more Miss Faire and her erstwhile fiancé had a major difference of opinion. As usual, the opinion of the stronger personality, or the stronger person, held sway. Anders dragged Lucinda back from the door by a fistful of the unfashionable gray gown, which ripped down the front as she wrenched out of his clasp. She was crying in earnest now, fear suddenly mingling with the welter of emotions. "Let me go!" she screamed when he grabbed for her again, trying to hit him, claw him, kick him, bite him, anything to get away.

"Shut up, bitch." He slapped her, jerking her head back. Lucinda screamed, and thought she heard hollers in the hallway so she screamed again. Leon shook her, hard, then pressed his slimy lips to hers.

Lucinda pushed him away with all her strength,

which was nothing compared to the captain's, except that he was the worse for drink and unsteady on his feet. He staggered back, cursing loudly. Then his foot struck the bottle he'd dropped. He toppled backward with a yell that was abruptly replaced by a sickening thud as his head hit the corner of the stone mantelpiece. Captain Anders collapsed the rest of the way to the floor while Lucinda shouted his name.

"Leon? Captain? My God, Leon, you can't be dead!"

The dirty dish won that argument, too.

The room was filled with people almost before Captain Anders hit the floor. The innkeeper was shouting for boys to ride to the doctor, the magistrate, the undertaker. His wife was squealing about never having such goings-on under her roof, and death being bad for business, and she should have known such a handsome rogue had no decent business with any milk-and-water miss. One of the maids fainted, two of the lady guests called for their carriages and reckonings, and a young buck who'd been in the taproom swore he'd heard the whole thing and was just about to rescue the young lady. The merchant in the room next door concurred the dastard had got what he deserved, but never mentioned a thought about coming to the damsel's aid.

And there was blood everywhere. On the floor, on the hearth, on Lucinda's hands, on her gown, on her mouth where he'd struck her. And mostly there was blood spattered all over Leon, so someone covered him up with a blanket from the bed. No matter; Lucinda still saw him. Someone put another blanket around her shoulders to cover up her torn dress. Someone else, one of the messengers, she thought, or perhaps the doctor, put a glass into her hand. She drank.

Then the magistrate came and asked a great

many questions, which everyone else seemed to want to answer.

"I killed him," she interrupted in a voice as dead as the captain. "My name is Lucinda Faire, of Fairview Manor, Derby. I did not mean to, but I killed him."

"No, you didn't, my dear," the magistrate replied. "The fireplace killed him. You were only trying to get away, self-defense and all that." The magistrate was only a local squire. He was not about to set himself up against Sir Malcolm Faire, the richest man in Derby, not over some loose screw who should have hung for his crimes. After all, the magistrate had daughters of his own. "Death by misadventure, we'll call it. There'll have to be an inquest, but don't worry, your papa will come and handle all the details. I already sent for him. Why don't you wait downstairs in the private parlor? You'll be more comfortable there than up here with the, uh, mess."

Her father was coming. The magistrate had sent for him; Leon had sent for him. Leon did not love her; her father did not love her either, but he was her father. He'd take her home, where she could burn this gown and have a bath to rid herself of the stench of Leon and this place and the blood. Nanny would put something on her cut lip. But there was no reason for Sir Malcolm to see Leon or this second-rate inn or the blood. Sir Malcolm hated anything tawdry or unkempt, anything that did not fit into his orderly universe.

So Lucinda decided to go home. She was bound to meet up with her father on the road, and anything was better than staying here, with Leon upstairs. The blanket still around her shoulders in lieu of her cape, Miss Lucinda Faire walked out the unattended front door of the inn, gathered the reins of a horse left tied there in the excitement, mounted with the aid of a handy barrel, and rode into the pitch-black night.

* * *

The doctor was not hopeful. "She is badly concussed from the blow to her head when she fell off the horse, and then there is the congestion of her lungs from lying out in the cold all night and half the day. The most worrisome, however, is that your daughter has not regained consciousness for two days. I fear that the shock from the other, ah, unfortunate events have sapped her will to live. Coupled with the physical injuries, I cannot be optimistic in my prognosis." The physician did order her hair cut, lest the heavy tresses drain what energy the poor girl maintained, and he did bleed her, to relieve the swelling. "That's all I can do, Sir Malcolm. If she does not wake up on her own . . ." He shrugged. "Now we can only pray."

"Pray for the devil to claim his spawn," Sir Malcolm muttered as he sent the doctor on his way.

Sir Malcolm never did ride toward the inn. When the captain's note was delivered, he sent his wife to search the girl's room. She'd packed a valise; no one came and forced her to run off with a blackguard extortionist. He tore up the note. When the messenger came from the magistrate, babbling about how Captain Anders was dead, his daughter Lucinda responsible, Sir Malcolm replied, "I have no daughter." And when they brought her battered, frozen body home, he almost had them deliver her to the poorhouse or the church or the livery stable, he cared not which. Only his wife's whispered "What will the neighbors think?" kept him from slamming the door on the poor fool of a magistrate who'd spent hours searching the countryside for the jade.

Lady Edwina looked at her husband across her daughter's still form in the big bed. "No one will have her now, not even Halbersham."

"No matter, you heard the doctor. If she hasn't woken by now, she likely won't. If the fever does not carry her off, she'll waste away unless someone spoons sustenance into her. Likely a futile effort anyway," he said. Sir Malcolm glared over at Lucinda's old nanny. "So we need not try too hard. Is that clear?"

Lady Edwina wrung her thin hands. "Oh, the shame of it all. There's no dressing this up in clean linen, not with half the county hearing about it already. What will I tell our friends?"

"Nothing. We simply won't receive anyone for the week or two this should take. Then we can go away."

They left the darkened room, discussing the merits of Jamaica versus Greece. Only Lucinda's old nanny stayed behind, weeping.

Chapter Two

Kieren Somerfield, sixth and possibly last earl of Stanford, was a tidy person. He conscientiously wiped his Hessians on a faded Turkey runner in the marbled hall of Stanford House, Grosvenor Square, and carefully draped his caped greatcoat over the back of a Queen Anne chair that was missing an arm. Sweeping the lamp left burning there for him in an arc, he made sure everything in the grand entry was in order: no valuable pictures on the wall, no ornate candle sconces, no Chinese urns filled with hothouse flowers. Kerry shrugged his broad shoulders. Poverty as usual. He made his way to the study at the rear of the house, one of the few rooms in the mansion currently in use.

'Twas easier to keep clean this way, more considerate of Demby, his man-of-all-jobs, few-of-them-by-choice. The earl owed his only servant so many months' back wages, Demby must be staying on for room and board. That and the scarcity of positions for a groom whose hands shook so badly he took half a day to tack up a horse, or a valet so palsied 'twould be a death sentence to ask him to shave you. The neckcloths Demby tied more likely ended under the earl's ear, and his cooking more often landed on the kitchen floor than on the table. The man had sworn off drink, though, and did manage to get Stanford's clothes pressed, his mail delivered, his bed made up, the stable mucked out, and his watch redeemed from the jeweler when the dibs were in tune.

The earl hadn't known the hour for some weeks now. It was obviously time to get his life in order.

In his study Kerry rekindled the fire, then gathered scraps of paper from his desk, his drawers, his pockets. Fastidious as ever, he made neat stacks of the letters and notes.

The first pile was for tradesmen's bills, complete with dunning notices for payments in arrears: the grocer, the vintner, his clubs, a coal dealer. A great percentage of these bills were from the finest tailors, bootmakers, and hatters in London. The earl was very particular in his dress, particularly for a man with pockets to let.

The next bundle was for debts of honor. He smoothed out the crumpled notes from his pocket and penciled in some figures on others. These were gaming debts, vowels, chits—fortunes owed to other members of the sporting class. Since inheriting his father's honors, along with the fifth earl's debts and mortgages, Kerry had made his living by his wits. They'd gone begging, too. His horses were like to trip at the gate, aces seemed to have a magnetic attraction to his opponents, and the dice could be round, for all the mains he hit. Hell, these days if he wagered the sun would rise on the morrow, likely the world would end today. But somebody would be around to collect, he was sure.

He got up to pour himself a brandy from the decanter left on the mantel. When he got back, the stack of vouchers on his desk looked even taller. Taller than his own six feet, taller than a mountain. Kerry swallowed down his glass and tried, unsuccessfully, to recall if there was any gudgeon on earth who owed him money.

The next batch of papers were all official-looking documents. The earl did not need to read the letters from his bank enumerating his mortgages or the interest payments due. The bank wrote to him often enough that he had the figures memorized. As for his account balance, well, the bank did not waste postage when there was nothing to report. Downy birds, those banking fellows, his lordship thought, pouring another glassful. They watched every last groat.

The final pile consisted of letters, which took another brandy to open and read. His steward at his seat in Wiltshire reported two more of the few remaining tenants—and their rents—moved off to better-yielding lands, half the fall harvest lost to flooding, and the roof of Stanford Abbey itself about to collapse.

The dowager Lady Stanford, Kerry's loving mother, wrote a brief, affectionate letter in which she fondly recalled that Kerry's properties were in disrepair, the earldom was in danger of extinction, and his way of life was not conducive to a doting mama's mental well-being, but she was, as always, contributing what assistance she could. Of course, those were not the exact words she used. Hers were more like *gudgeon*, *popinjay*, and *wastrel*, with demands he marry an heiress posthaste, before she was forced to pawn her last piece of jewelry just to keep a roof over her aching head. And, by the way, she'd concluded, all of the housemaids had left because Aunt Clara was talking to Uncle Nigel again.

Uncle Nigel, his father's younger brother, had gone overboard on a fishing expedition when Kerry was barely seven, some twenty years ago. Aunt Clara was positive Nigel's spirit haunted Stanford Abbey, waiting for her to join him in the Great Beyond. As expected, Aunt Clara's letter was full of Uncle Nigel's advice and pronouncements: Nigel thinks the roof tiles can be repaired, Nigel thinks the south quarter fields can be drained into a ditch across the home woods. If Uncle Nigel knew so much, Kerry wondered, how come he never learned to swim? And why the deuce did he have to leave his widow without a feather to fly with? In Kerry's poor, dilapidated nest, no less.

Aunt Clara's final remark, that his mother was keeping company with a smuggler, he ignored. The Countess of Stanford and a personage called Goldy Flint? Even Kerry's befuddled mind rebelled at that notion. The woman was as queer as Dick's hatband, that was all. The two widows cordially loathed each other, giving Kerry another excuse to avoid visits to the ancestral pile, if overwhelming debts and impossible demands were not enough.

The papers were all neatly arranged, corner to corner across the desk. On the top of the piles of bills and notices the earl placed his assets: the last bottle of brandy, a handful of coins from his pocket, and some lint. He opened the bottom drawer of the desk. He had no way of repaying his debts, no stake to make another wager, nothing to send to keep the abbey from crumbling into dust. No heir, no hope. He did have his father's prized dueling pistols. Kerry tenderly placed one of the silver-sided Mantons in the exact center of the desk.

"Drat. He said this task was hard, not impossible."

"Demby? Is that you, man?" The Earl of Stanford squinted into the shadows at the other end of the room.

"And I should have known better than to believe that devil. There isn't a male anywhere a girl can trust, living or dead."

"Demby, if you've brought one of your dollymops into my study, I'll—" Kerry's words were cut off by a cough as his nose and throat were assailed by an awful stench. "Gads, something must have died in the chimney. I wonder if the sweeps will come on credit," he muttered as he went to open a window. The smell of rotten eggs and boiling tar abated somewhat, mingling with London's usual rank odors. He took a deep breath of the cold night air to clear his eyes and his lungs—and his head.

"That's right, enjoy the cold now; it's the last you'll know for a long, long while if I can't do my job."

Kerry spun around. There *was* a woman in the room, and what a woman. This wasn't one of Demby's barmaids either, not if he was any judge of the demimondaine. This luscious creature had to be one of the highest-flying birds of paradise on three continents. She was small, but shaped like a goddess, with flame-colored hair trailing down her back. The shimmering red-gold gown she wore was so sheer, he could see the nipples painted to match her lips and her nails and her toes. Gads, the brazen baggage was barefoot. Kerry licked his suddenly dry lips. "I am sorry, *chérie*—you'll never know how sorry—but I just cannot afford your services tonight. I do admire your, ah, initiative, though."

"Afford my . . . ?" She gasped, which served to lower the neckline of her gown into near nonexistence. "You think I'm a . . . Oh, my, I'll *never* succeed."

"*Au contraire*, my dear, I think you'll be a bigger success than Little Harry. You could have every buck in London at your feet in a sennight, if that's your goal."

"Well, it isn't. My assignment is to lead you to the path of righteousness!"

Kerry laughed till tears came to his eyes. "Congratulations, my dear. That's the cleverest remark I've ever heard come out of a whore's mouth."

"I am not a . . . what you said, and this is not a laughing matter, my lord. Your whole life, for all eternity, could be decided tonight, and mine along with it. I just *have* to get you to renounce your life of sin."

"You? Ma'am, I beg to tell you, you make a very unlikely evangelical. Why, you could lead the Archbishop of Canterbury straight to hell with one blink of those incredible green eyes."

"Me? Drab little Lucinda Faire?"

"Fishing for compliments, are you? Drab? Have you looked at yourself recently?"

"Well, no. You see, I have this problem with mirrors. I can tell, however, that this dress is like nothing I've ever owned." She ran her hands along the silky material over her thighs. His lordship didn't breathe again until she murmured, "It feels rather nice."

Rather nice? Kerry swallowed, hard.

Lucinda was twirling one of those fiery curls in her hand. "And I am sure my hair was never so red, just a streaky kind of blond. And it never took a curl like this. It must be the heat."

His lordship was fairly overheated himself, watching her. Before he grew too uncomfortable, he tried to get her to leave again. "This has been pleasant, miss, a truly novel approach, but I really have other business tonight, as I am sure you must also. If you would just come this way . . ."

Instead of following him toward the door, the female seemed to drift toward his desk. Her hand reached out for his pistol. "I killed a man, you know."

By Zeus, she was a Bedlamite! What a shame, for such a beauty. She must be someone's mad relative escaped from confinement. Zounds, he didn't want to send her into hysterics by shouting for Demby. He didn't want to end up shot either. "Miss, please, come away from there. That's a very delicate mechanism."

"Will you listen?"

"Yes, yes, anything."

Lucinda stepped away from the desk, but floated

gracefully out of his reach. "I did kill a man, truly," she began, and started to tell Lord Stanford about how her parents were very strict, and how they had arranged her marriage to a crotchety old man.

"I'm sure they meant well," he said, trying to hurry the tale along and not believing a word of it, or this whole bizarre occurrence. "The road to hell, you know. Paved with good intentions."

"No, it's not. It's paved with rakes and libertines, reaching and grabbing and slobbering over you." Then she told him about Captain Anders and the elopement with a sadness in her voice he couldn't help wishing gone. When she got to the part of how Anders confessed it was all a pack of lies to get her father's money, and how he wanted to ruin her to complete the plot, Kerry found himself wishing the bounder were still alive, so he could shoot him.

An actress, that's what she was, he decided, gathering his thoughts again, an incredible actress who almost had him believing that farrago of nonsense. She'd gone from seductress to lunatic to innocent child in a matter of moments. One of his friends must have hired her for his entertainment. Kerry smiled at the thought of what kind of entertainment was in store, if she was as talented in bed as she was in the drawing room. Then her words drew him back.

"So I hit my head. Now, for all intents and purposes, my father's especially, I am dead."

"Dead? You mean you're a ghost?" Actress, he'd believe, prostitute definitely, but this was too much. She was back to being dicked in the nob.

"No, not exactly a ghost, since I'm not precisely dead yet. You see, things have been fairly slow at the Gates these days, what with the peace talks and the new smallpox inoculation, so they decided to hear my case before the fact, as it were."

"They?" Kerry had heard one should always humor a madman. "What happened to St. Peter?"

"Oh, he took the pleasant job of welcoming new

arrivals. He leaves the messy details of deciding who goes where for the women to handle. Typical male, don't you know."

Kerry's mouth was hanging open by now. He could only repeat: "The women?"

"Oh, yes, they run everything. Anyway, St. Joan was there, and St. Ermintrude, and that Queen Medea for the opposition. But they couldn't decide. I *did* disobey my parents, and I *did* cause Captain Anders's death, directly or not." She paused and looked down at the hands clasped in her lap. In a near whisper she confessed, "And I did know lust. I wanted him to kiss me, at first."

"A kiss? You call that lust? Why, every red-blooded female—"

"So I was destined for hell," Lucinda interrupted. "But I had led an exemplary life before then, and I was truly sorry Captain Anders was dead. I could not regret pushing him, of course, only the result of it. So the angels struck a bargain with the demonesses." She looked up and smiled, showing perfect dimples. "I can go to heaven if I save you from hell."

Chapter Three

"Hell and damnation!"

"Exactly, my lord." She was smiling now, pleased with his understanding.

"You mean you expect me to believe that a parcel of females, all martyrs and murderesses, got together and decided my fate?"

"And mine, my lord."

He ignored that. "You're saying that females run the show there? What about God? What's He doing while all this is going on?"

"He? I'm afraid you're not ready for all of this yet, my lord."

"But I am more than ready to be shut of this fustian nonsense. I really must ask you to leave, miss. I don't know how you got in—it's not like Demby to be so careless—and if someone paid you, tell him it was an excellent joke while it lasted. But let me give you some advice, ma'am, if you wish to continue your career, whichever career you choose. Do drop the missionary gobbledygook. You're liable to be labeled a reformer, and no one is comfortable around a moralizing zealot, especially any gentleman you'd like to encourage. No one takes that religion stuff seriously these days."

"Sad, isn't it?" Her tone was wistful, but she did move toward the door in a graceful, gliding sort of motion.

Relieved the female was finally taking his hint, which was more an outright request, the earl vowed he'd have Demby's head in the morning if he found the man had let her in.

Lucinda paused at the sofa where she'd been sitting. She bent over to pick up her slippers, then kept bending until her softly rounded derriere was in the air, wiggling as she searched for something else underneath the furniture. Kerry loosened his cravat before he strangled. Damn, she was good. Too bad she was queer in the attic, and too bad he was punting on the River Tick. If the chimney sweeps didn't take credit, bits of muslin never did!

"Oh, my," Lucinda exclaimed, blowing a dustball back under the couch. "Haven't you ever heard that cleanliness is next to godliness?" Still bending, she wiped her hand along the length of one shapely hip.

Kerry clenched his teeth, murmuring something about the devil preaching gospel, and almost reached out to thrust her forcibly from the room before he was tempted past endurance. Then he caught the gleam of something under the sofa. Along with another fluff of dust was a shiny yellowboy, two crumpled pound notes, and the diamond stickpin he had thought lost in some boudoir or other ages ago.

"By George, that's marvelous!" he exclaimed, retrieving the bounty as she stood. He rose and held out one of the pound notes. "Here, you keep this, for bringing such luck."

She shook her head. "Luck had nothing to do with it, my lord. I told you, I'm here to—"

Kieren, Lord Stanford, that nonpareil among the Corinthian set and paragon of fashion, was already back on all fours, searching beneath the rest of the furniture. "Blast, only a silver button."

The woman was gone when he straightened up. Kerry shrugged. She had been a diverting interlude, no denying, but now he had business to attend to. Two pounds, a golden guinea, and a stickpin weren't much of a fortune, but they more than tripled his current holdings. He couldn't begin to pay off even the smallest of his obligations, but now he had a stake. Not much of one, for certain, but enough, with Lady Luck on his side. Or whoever that peculiar ladybird was.

His lordship went to bed for a short sleep, blessing Demby's careless housekeeping. His dreams may have been filled with scarlet women, but he still woke refreshed and eager. A bath, a change of clothes, some of Demby's wretched coffee with the grounds still floating in it, and he was ready. He left the two pound notes with his servant for safekeeping. "And do see about the chimneys, Demby, that odor was appalling."

Manton's shooting gallery was thin of custom so early in the morning, but there were enough sportsmen practicing their aim to offer a bit of competition.

"Shall we make a little wager on the results, gentlemen?" The earl was priming his father's silver-sided pistols.

"With what, Stanford? I'm still waiting on that monkey you owe me from last week at Crockford's." Lord Thurston curled his lip.

"The end of the month, dear fellow, the end of the month. No, I meant a friendly little bet, just to keep the practice session interesting. I say, that's a pretty little trinket you have in your neckcloth. Not an heirloom or anything, is it? No? Then care to chance it against my diamond?"

The earl couldn't lose, not today, not with his father's perfectly balanced pistols, a clear eye, and that lucky gold piece in his pocket. Soon he had a collection of stickpins, snuffboxes, and silver shoe buckles, a magpie's horde indeed. Kerry whistled all the way to Reyerson's, one of the lesser Bond Street jewelers.

Lucinda, meanwhile, was at the lending library doing research. Two matrons vowed to take their trade elsewhere, and one purple-turbaned dowager had to have feathers burnt under her nose, so bad was the smell. A rat must have died in the wainscoting, one of the harried clerks suggested as he reshelved books no one admitted to taking down. *Paradise Lost* and Dante's *Inferno* were not the usual fare for the ladies who came to Hookham's for the latest Minerva Press offerings.

Reyerson's was not as distinguished as Rundell and Bridges, but it was more discreet, catering to the bucks and bloods of the ton, rather than the beaus. The losers at Manton's would know where to go if they wished to ransom their trifles; that was the accepted thing, and Reyerson was accommodating. A fellow didn't run so much a chance of meeting his mother's correspondents while he redeemed his watch there, either.

Kerry had his watch, his diamond stickpin, and a purse that jingled cheerfully when he turned to leave the premises.

"By Jupiter, it's Stanford! Just the chap I was hoping to see!"

"You were? That is, delighted to see you, too, Fortnam. Been out of town, have you?" The earl's mind worked frantically, trying to recall his old friend's name on any of the betting slips he owed. "The end of the month—"

"Just in town for a day or two, don't you know, never believed I'd run into you like this. Congratulate me, man, I'm married."

Fortnam could have demanded the deed to

Stanford Abbey and Kerry would have been less surprised. "Leg-shackled, you? I never thought I'd see the day!"

"Yes, I know, more's the pity. I can't believe I waited so long. Kerry, it's the best thing that's ever happened to me."

They shook hands again. "Thrilled for you, Fortnam. Who's the lucky lady? Do I know her?"

"No, and you never shall if I have my way, not with your reputation with married women. She's from the provinces, never even had a come-out, never wants one, she says."

"A gem beyond price." The earl stared pointedly at the gaudy bracelet in his friend's hand. Fortnam's ruddy cheeks got redder.

"Not at all the thing for Frederica, of course. It's a parting gift for Mimi."

"What, never say you are giving up the delightful Mimi, and for a mere wife?"

Fortnam laughed. "Just you wait, my boy. It'll happen to you someday. But that reminds me why I was so glad to see you. Here." And he took out his checkbook and wrote a draft on his bank for a hundred pounds. "Remember that old wager we had over who would turn benedict first? I'm more than happy to pay up. No, don't argue. I know you're going to say to keep the money for a wedding gift, but I really want to settle up the best bet I ever lost."

Kerry was just staring at the note in his hand. A hundred pounds? "I don't know what to say. I—"

"That's all right, Stanford, I know you can't believe it's me touting parson's mousetrap, but you really ought to try it. Of course, my Frederica is divine. You ought to find an angel for yourself, man."

A hundred pounds? "I believe I may have met one just last night."

The stickpin money went to purchasing a pretty tea service for the newlyweds; half the hundred pounds went to Demby, for safekeeping.

"And I don't care what the blasted chimney sweep said, something's wrong with this fireplace that's stinking up the room. Call in another if you have to."

When he shut the window—demned waste, letting his coal heat all of London—that woman was there again. Her gown didn't seem quite as sheer, or quite so skimpy. Perhaps it was a trick of the daylight, for she certainly hadn't lost any of her allure. "My, you are persistent," he said, thinking of the fifty pounds in his pocket. He really needed it for the card game later, but . . . "What is the price, anyway?"

"To keep your soul from eternal damnation? They wouldn't give me specifics, so I've been trying to find out."

Kerry ran his fingers through his carefully arranged brown curls. "Persistence be damned. Not that moralizing tripe again, I pray you. Just name a figure."

"It's too bad you are not a Papist," Lucinda went on as if he had not spoken. "You could simply confess your sins, sincerely repenting them, of course, and be spared the hellfires."

The earl lit a cigarillo, a sure sign of his frustration, that he might smoke in front of a lady—no, a female, even—without asking permission. "Ma'am, you are sin personified, and I confess I am already burning for you. The only thing I might repent beyond the cost is having to listen to any more of this claptrap. Sincerely."

Lucinda stamped her foot. "Oh, how am I going to make you pay attention?"

Kerry inhaled deeply on the cigarillo. "I assure you, *chérie*, you have my complete and total attention." Then he watched as the lightskirt bit her lip in concentration, muttering words he thought sounded like *rattle-pated rake* and *bone-headed bounder*. This dasher was certainly adding new dimensions to the oldest profession.

He exhaled in a perfect ring. Lucinda's scowl turned into a smile as she waved her arm through the smoke without disturbing the circle. Kerry blinked. "Excellent, ma'am, although I did have more in mind than parlor tricks."

"Oh, you must have buckram wadding where your brain is supposed to be! I know, touch me."

"At last."

Now, a gentleman would have reached out in a gentle caress along her cheek, or a soft stroke on her bare upper arm. Stanford was well past the stage for gallantry. He reached to wrap his hand around one of those enticingly round, milk-white globes that were barely concealed by the bodice of her gown. And touched nothing. His fingers tingled, but there was nothing in them. Nothing.

Lucinda gasped and swung her arm back. Kerry didn't duck; he knew he deserved the slap. Her hand came around and he felt the air whoosh by, and that same tingle, but no contact. Nothing. Silently Kerry reached out again, this time gingerly, respectfully. He tried to touch her arm, tried to feel one of those silky red curls, even the fabric of her gown. Lucinda let him, standing still, and even reached toward him, as if to smooth away the frown lines between Kerry's eyes. The hair on the back of his neck rose, the way it did when he was out in a lightning storm, then he felt light-headed, as if he were about to faint. He sat down in a hurry.

"My God, I didn't know my imagination was that good!" was all he could say when he could speak again.

Lucinda nearly ground her teeth in aggravation. "It's not, you clunch. I am not a product of your muddled mind, not even a night dream. I found the diamond stickpin for you, remember?"

"Then you're a . . . ghost?"

"I told you, I'm not dead yet. I'm just between positions right now, somewhat like an unemployed governess."

"Not an angel?"

"And never like to be if you don't show a little more cooperation, my lord."

Kerry got up and poured himself a brandy. His hands were shaking worse than Demby's. Still, he managed to get most of the liquid down his throat before sinking back into his chair at the desk. Lucinda was sitting atop the cherrywood surface, swinging her bare feet.

"So you're a minion of the devil," he asked, "here to save my soul? I thought it was the other way round."

"Heaven knows the devil doesn't need any more souls. And I am not quite consigned to hell yet either, so they gave me the opportunity to save both of us."

"Uh, are you so sure I'm destined for Hades?"

"My lord, do lust, gluttony, vanity, and sloth mean anything to you?"

"I think you have just described the Prince Regent."

"Gambling? Gossiping?"

He was glad he'd thought to bring the bottle with him so he didn't have to get up again. He didn't bother pouring into a glass either. "And every other gentleman of fashion in London. It's not so bad."

"It's not so good. Can't you see, the tonnish life is leading you to perdition."

"Dash it, if I'm so wicked, then why did they even bother sending you? Assuming, of course, that any of this is real."

"They sent me because they thought there might be hope for you. Someone spoke on your behalf."

"Must be Uncle Nigel. He speaks to everyone. Well, I hope you can help with this mess." His hand indicated the bills and such still in neat piles on the desk in front of him.

"That's nothing compared to the mess your immortal soul is in."

The drink was taking effect. The earl flashed

Lucinda a sweet smile. "Then one more sin won't matter. What did you say your name was?"

She sat up straighter and stopped swinging her legs. "Miss Lucinda Faire, my lord."

"I'll never accept you as a prim and proper Miss Lucinda Faire. Why, if St. Peter ever got a glimpse of those ankles, he'd never let you out of the Pearly Gates."

Lucinda thought she blushed, but without a mirror, of course, she couldn't be sure. "I have already been taken in by two silver-tongued devils: the one who got me into this fix in the first place, and the one who set me the impossible task of reforming a confirmed hellraker. So don't waste the effort of turning me up sweet, my lord. You may call me Lucinda, Lord Stanford, since we are to be such close companions."

"And I am Kerry to my friends and fellow fiends, Lucinda. No, Lucy, that's better. Ah, Lucy Faire, how clever. Let's have another drink to toast the partnership."

"Demby, do you believe in ghosts? Angels, devils, any of those spirit things?"

The earl's loyal servant removed the decanter from Lord Stanford's limp fingers without spilling more than a drop, so low was the level of brandy remaining. "No, my lord," Demby grumbled on his way to fetch a pot of coffee, "but I do believe in the demon in the bottle."

Chapter Four

"I'll never touch another drop of liquor," Kerry swore, clutching his throbbing temples. Demby's hands, all four of them, were shaking worse than usual as he held out a tray with some noxious brew guaranteed to cure the earl, if it didn't kill him first. The motion of the tray was making Kerry seasick, and the rattling of the cup was hammering stakes through his eyeballs. "God, I need a drink," he groaned.

"No, my lord, you need a clear head for tonight. Remember?"

His lordship couldn't remember his name right then, only a recurring nightmare about the most beautiful woman who never existed. He shook his head, a definite mistake. When the walls stopped revolving, he grabbed for the cup before Demby sloshed the entire contents onto the carpet. "Tonight. Right, the game. I still have fifty pounds, don't I? And my lucky gold piece? Don't worry, Demby, we'll come around."

"We'd better, my lord."

* * *

A few recuperative hours later, Lord Stanford was on his way to hell. Gillespie's gaming hell, to be exact. He eschewed Whites and his other clubs, where too many members held his vouchers, and the exclusive gambling dens where the stakes were too high for his present circumstances. Gillespie's was perfect: respectable enough that he'd find enough gentlemen mixed in with the cardsharps and ivory-tuners, not so refined that every player was already a creditor.

The rooms were dingy, dark, and overheated. The smell of stale wine and stale bodies hung over the tables, mingling with clouds of smoke. Fevered eyes and feral smiles greeted the earl as he passed by the roulette wheels, the dicing tables. He wouldn't want to spend eternity here, Kerry thought with a grin, but for tonight Gillespie's was ideal.

He played at vingt-et-un for half an hour or so, winning some, losing less. He did better at the hazard table, steadily increasing his rolls of house markers, wagering conservatively, and moving on as soon as his luck shifted. The roulette tables never interested him before, but this evening he placed a rouleau on red. And won, doubling his bet. He left both wager and winnings on red, and won again. And a third time.

The other gamesters were quiet, waiting to see what he did. The croupier was watching with raised eyebrows. Kerry started to move his stacks of markers over to the black box, when he chanced to look up. "Lucy?"

"Milord?" the dealer was ready to spin. Lucy was shaking her head. He left the chips where they were.

"Lucky, I meant to say. Red has been lucky for me."

"Number twenty-seven, odd, red."

Dazed, Lord Stanford gathered his considerable take onto a tray a waiter provided and followed Lucy into the shadows. She was in that same carmine gown that could have been painted on her. For some reason he found himself standing in front of her, shielding the view from the sight of the hardened libertines at the tables.

"What the bloody hell are you doing here?" he demanded in a harsh whisper.

"You could at least mind your tongue in front of a lady," she replied, not even looking at him but gazing over his shoulder around the room in wide-eyed innocence.

"This is no place for a lady!"

"Nor a gentleman with hopes of salvation," she reminded him.

"My only hope is to win a fortune, which I cannot do with you here to distract me."

"Are they really enjoying themselves?" She waved one hand at the scowling gamblers hunched over the hazard table. Kerry refused to see that her hand passed through his shoulder, leaving a slight vibration.

"Yes, and I would be, too, if you'd just go spread the gospel to some other poor soul." He turned his back and purposefully strode into Gillespie's second parlor, where smaller groups of men were gathered at card tables. Kerry sat at the faro table, determined to ignore what he didn't like. His concentration was off though, and he lost. Faro was too much a game of chance anyway. He stood and looked around and, right on time, spotted Lord Malverne, his quarry.

Malverne was well-to-pass, a heavy gambler, and none too needle-witted, by all accounts, although he won with enough frequency to keep him coming back. Sitting with him were two younger men, green but eager to lose the tidy bundles in front of them. No need to worry about taking vowels at this table. Kerry asked if he could sit in, and the youngest of the players, Wilson-Todd's cub, Kerry thought, nodded eagerly.

The other youngster dropped out shortly, the

stakes quickly growing too high for his resources, and his seat was taken by a cit with mended cuffs. He did not last long, nor the sideburned lieutenant who went down heavily for three hands, nor the grinning sot who wagered his whole roll on one hand, and lost. Young Wilson-Todd, Chas he called himself, was holding his own, while Kerry and Malverne were steady winners. Bystanders started to gather in a circle around the table, making side bets, some of which Kerry covered, extending his own winnings.

At a pause for a new player to take his seat and a fresh deck to be opened, Kerry took a sip of the excellent sherry at his elbow. He choked on it. Across from him, right behind Malverne, stood the flame-haired Lucy.

"Go away!" he shouted.

The tulip about to take up his hand rose in his seat. "I say, if you feel that way—"

"I told you, women do not belong here!"

The foppish gentleman in his yellow cossack trousers started to sputter. "I say, are you insultin' my manhood, sir?"

Kerry noticed him for the first time. "Who in tarnation is talking to you? Sit down and mind your own business!"

The dandy gulped, Adam's apple bobbing, but he stayed in his seat as directed. Malverne looked to Wilson-Todd, shrugged, and commenced the deal.

No one was staring at Lucy. Kerry couldn't believe it. He watched all the faces, those checking their cards, those making bets behind the chairs. Not a single slobbering smile was fixed on her half-naked chest, not one ogling eyeball was admiring her silk-draped legs.

"Your bet, Stanford."

They didn't see her, ergo she didn't exist. Kerry dragged his eyes away from the creamy white skin of her shoulders and concentrated on his cards. *He* didn't see her, therefore she didn't exist. Then why was the tobacco smoke taking on a burning pitch odor?

He lost that hand badly, and the next, trying not to consider the odds of red coming up four times in a row on a roulette wheel. Tarnation, he had to get himself in hand. He couldn't afford to lose from lack of concentration. By all that was holy, he couldn't afford to lose, period.

The next rounds went better as the deal progressed around the table, other players taking hands in the game, the bets getting larger, the pots in the center growing. Chatter died down as the ante rose. Wilson-Todd mopped the sweat beading on his forehead, another chap turned his jacket inside out for better luck, and a third player believed that serious gaming demanded serious drinking. He was seeking inspiration in a bottle of Blue Ruin. Malverne kept fussing with the lace at his collar, nervously picking at the picot at his shirtsleeves. 'Twas his deal and his call. "Match."

"Raise."

"Fold."

"See your raise."

Kerry fingered the yellow-boy in his pocket and raised the bet again. So it went, in near silence, until only Malverne and Stanford were still playing for an enormous pot. Kerry's turn came again. His hand was good, not great. Pulling out of the game now would end his hopes for a big coup this night; staying in could cost him much of his holdings. Was Malverne bluffing? Kerry stared across the table, trying to look into the older man's eyes. What he saw was Lucy, leaning over the old roué's shoulders, her breasts practically spilling out of her gown into the dastard's lap.

"Hell and tarnation!"

"That's what I keep telling you, my lord."

Kerry looked around. They were all staring at *him*, not at her. Malverne was smiling. "Your call, Stanford."

The earl started to say "I—" but Lucy interrupted. "Did you know he has three aces?"

Kerry threw his cards down and jumped to his feet, his chair crashing to the floor behind him, drawing the attention of everyone in the room. He didn't care. "Blast it, that's cheating! You may think I am steeped in depravity, but I consider myself a gentleman and I will not play in a rigged game!"

At which Lord Malverne jumped up, threw down *his* hand—the three aces and two others which fell out of his sleeve—and ran out of the room before anyone knew what was happening or could stop him. Besides congratulations on his canny insight and gratitude for keeping them all from being gulled, Lord Stanford was also unanimously awarded the pot, and a considerable share of the cash Lord Malverne had left behind in his haste. That loose screw wouldn't dare show his face at Gillespie's to collect his booty, nor anywhere else in London, for that matter.

Kerry couldn't wait to get back to Stanford House to count his winnings. He even took a hansom cab, lest he be set upon by footpads. Once home, he made sure Demby was asleep, the rooms were all empty, the doors and windows all locked. Then he spread the gold, silver, and paper currency on his desk, ready to make his usual neat piles.

"They say 'tis easier to thread a camel through the eye of a needle than for a rich man to get into heaven."

Kerry groaned, then coughed at the fetid air. "Oh, no, not you again. You do not exist."

"Don't be any more foolish than you have to be, my lord. Am I not sitting right here in your leather chair?"

She was, right where there had been no one an instant before. He was sure the door was still locked; he was sure she was still the most exquisite creature a tired, overwrought mind could conjure up. If he could give her such kissable lips, he wondered, why, by all the saints, couldn't he get her to keep them closed?

"Of course I exist," Lucinda was repeating in some exasperation herself. "Well, for the next fortnight or so anyway. Which is not a great deal of time, after you have frittered away the last twenty-seven years. We absolutely have to come to some kind of accommodation here. Now, I've been taking notes." She pulled a sheet of paper out of the wall. Kerry sat down and poured a drink. Then he pushed it away and lit a cigarillo instead.

Lucinda wrinkled her nose. "Filthy habit, that. Anyway, the way I have reasoned it, we need some guidelines. I mean, you don't seem to see anything wrong with your way of life, and *they* don't see much right with it."

Lucy consulted her paper while the earl sat bemused. "I thought we'd start here, my lord. Do stop me if you recognize any of this. . . . 'I am the Lord thy God, thou shalt have no other God before me. Thou shalt have no graven images or bowing to other gods.' " She stared at the mounds of gold in front of Kerry, the coins he'd been idly trickling through his fingers. "So much for idolatry."

"God damn!" he protested.

" 'Do not take my name in vain.' Humph. 'Remember the sabbath day and keep it holy.' "

"I do. I went to church just a Sunday or two ago."

"That was a month ago, and you went only to collect the money Mortimer Greenstreet owed you. Then the two of you went to a prizefight. The next Sunday you stayed abed all day, still castaway from the evening before. The one after that you stayed abed with—"

"Enough! So I don't pay lip service to the mumbo jumbo they serve up in church."

"Hmm. 'Honor thy father and mother.' "

"Got you there," he said with a grin. "I wasn't the one who ran away from home."

"No, but you never *go* home."

"I am a good son," he blustered, although he couldn't keep from glancing to his mother's last letter right there on the top of the nuisance pile.

Lucinda had no need to read his correspondence. "The way you honor your father by caring for his ancestral property, begetting an heir to carry on his line? The way you listen to a lonely old woman's cries for your attention?"

"Ma'am, m'father was a basket scrambler of epic proportions. He ran the property into the ground and saddled me with more debts than I can repay in a lifetime. And m'mother's a fishwife."

"That's honor?" She went on before he could answer: 'Thou shalt not kill.' "

"Ah-ha! I never—"

"What about that duel with Sir Swindon? He died of your gunshot wound."

"He died of an infection, and he was a bounder anyway! He stole that opera dancer right out from under me, literally. And it was a fair fight. He had the choice of weapons."

Lucinda consulted her list again. "Strange, it doesn't mention opera dancers anywhere. Oh, here. 'Thou shalt not commit adultery.' "

There was silence at the other side of the desk.

" 'Thou shalt not steal.' "

"There. I've never taken anything that didn't belong to me in my life, unless you're going back to some apples in the vicar's orchard when I was seven. You wouldn't hang a boy for that, would you, much less send him to hell?"

Lucinda gestured to the pile of tradesmen's bills, some of them years overdue. "What do you call that other than theft of services? How do you think the tailor and the baker feed *their* children? By letting them steal apples?"

His lordship had no answer. Lucy went on: " 'Nor bear false witness.' All that gossiping at White's can't be the truth. Even tucked away in Derby we heard how many a young deb's reputation was ruined by some careless bragging at the clubs. Are you going to tell me you never took part?"

"What, and bear false witness?" he asked impatiently. "What's next?"

" 'Thou shalt not covet thy neighbor's—' "

"Uh-oh."

" 'Wife, nor his house nor his fields.' "

"Well, there, I never coveted anyone's house or fields. Don't even see much good in my own acres, with farming such a dirty, unproductive business. And I can't help it if those old sticks keep marrying lasses twenty years younger than themselves." Kerry leaned back in his chair with his head cushioned on his crossed arms. "There, I didn't do so badly, did I?"

Lucinda did a quick tally. "Not only have you broken every one of the ten commandments, you've managed to justify your actions to yourself. You have no remorse." She sighed. "This is going to be a busy two weeks."

Chapter Five

"Demby, did you ever hallucinate? You know, see visions when you were in your cups?"

"Aye, my lord, all the time." Demby was holding out a fresh neckcloth. Kerry took it before the thing lost its starch from being fluttered about. "Great slimy monsters they were, too, slithery, snaky things, crawling all over."

"No gorgeous females?"

"Criminy, an' I saw gorgeous females, I'd still be drinking, begging your pardon, my lord."

Buckskin breeches molding his muscular legs, a coat of blue superfine stretched across his wide shoulders, and the neckcloth tied in a new knot, the windfall, the Earl of Stanford was ready to meet the day.

And a fine day it was, too. No clouds for once, no wind, and no interfering female, imaginary or otherwise. Kerry stepped jauntily out of the door of Stanford House. As usual, he did leave half of last night's winnings with Demby for safekeeping, but this time with instructions to put at least something on account on all of the tradesmen's bills, and to pay off the smallest and longest overdue.

Whistling, Lord Stanford was off to the races. A minor meeting was to be held at the oval near Warringdon, just outside Richmond. Lovely, brisk weather, superior horseflesh, convivial company—not even Lucy Faire could find fault with the day's entertainment.

Of course some of the races were fixed. Everyone knew the jockeys were frequently paid to lose apurpose, and often enough horses were nobbled, drugged or injured so they couldn't run the course. Still, it was the sport of kings, and a downy cove could win a king's ransom with judicious betting, inside tips, and a bit of luck. Kerry considered himself an excellent judge of horseflesh, he'd made friends with a paddock watchman, and his luck was definitely in.

The track was crowded, rough wagons alongside racing curricles, countrymen and clerks rubbing shoulders with turf rats and toffs.

Kerry found a boy to hold his horses, then made his way through the spectators, keeping a wary eye out for pickpockets and anyone who might wish to lighten his purse by demanding repayment of debts.

Lemuel, the guard, was holding fast to the gate, making sure no unauthorized persons had access to the horses. A few coins loosened his tongue.

"The rider of Aldebaran in the first was out here havin' a confab with Six Fingers O'Sullivan, then he went in passin' somethin' out among the other jockeys. An' in the second race, that Frenchy what trains Lord Finsterer's nags went 'round checkin' all the stalls, lookin' for some missin' tack." Lemuel placed his finger alongside his nose, and his other hand out.

Kerry filled the open palm and went off to place his wagers. He was careful not to put too much of the ready with any one bet taker, lest he change the odds on Aldebaran in the first or Lord Finsterer's Nightdancer in the second.

Aldebaran came in second. That threw off Kerry's parlaying calculations, but not by much. The day was still early. Then Nightdancer's jockey fell off partway through the last turn. His saddle slipped. Rumor around the track had it that Finsterer was too much a nipcheese to buy new leathers.

Kerry went back to Lemuel.

Lemuel scratched his head. "Well, in the third, that big gray do be the favorite on account of his trainin' times, but they ain't got him off to a good start yet. He don't like other horses next to or nigh him, so he'll balk at the gate."

The gray hated other horses near him so much that he finished ten lengths ahead of his nearest competitor. Kerry's long shot must have disliked the other runners, too; he stayed a long, long way behind them.

Lemuel whispered that Ruffles in the fourth had been given something to make him run faster; he was a sure thing. The only sure thing was that Ruffles dropped dead around the first bend, along with Kerry's hopes of amassing a fortune. He was losing too much on each bet and on Lemuel's misinformation, and there were only three races left.

"Blast, I'll pick my own losers."

He studied the horses, he studied the odds. He listened to track talk and carriage chatter, about this beast's sire, that gelding's last outing, a third one's rumored blind eye. Two minutes to start, and he hadn't placed a bet. "The devil take it," he swore.

And Lucy winked back at him across the track with a saucy smile. He rubbed his eyes. This was broad daylight and he hadn't had a drink all day. She could not be here. True, there were a few women scattered about, bachelor fare with escorts or looking for escorts. One or two ladies sat in their carriages, watching the races through opera glasses, well protected from the elements and the masses. No female ever strolled by herself through a race meet—hell, through the race track itself—daintily picking her way through the dirt and the droppings, twirling a red parasol over her shoulder. Lucy did, the sun shining gold in her red curls, and a matching ostrich plume curling along her right cheek. She winked at him again.

Lud, he was losing his mind.

"Last bets, gentlemen. Last bets."

He read the chalk board one more time. There at number five was a horse he hadn't noticed before, Devil's Handmaiden. He looked to the field, quickly scanning the numbers on the jockeys' backs. Number five was a smallish roan mare with the sun making golden glints on her red back. He put fifty pounds on her to win.

"But, gov, she's goin' off at thirty to one. That little filly don't stand a chance."

So he bet seventy-five pounds and put that oddsmaker out of business for the day. Kerry's winnings were enough to pay off a few more of his debts if he quit then, which, of course, he had no intention of doing.

He strolled down to the paddock to inspect the horses for the sixth race. Lemuel had a tip about the number seven horse, Riddles, how his name was really Faradiddle, a winner at last month's meet. "A few white-wash socks, a new name, and much better odds."

"What about that black gelding over there, number three?" Kerry wanted to know.

"Look at 'im, covered in sweat already. Nervous as a new bride. Why, that horse'll wear hisself out before the start. Now, Faradiddle outran 'em all a few weeks back."

Something about the black appealed to Kerry though, the small, intelligent head, the flowing muscles, the jockey's scarlet silks. He went back and consulted the betting boards. Number three's odds were ten to one. He placed a substantial sum on Riddles, or whatever the horse's name was today, to come in second. The bulk of his earlier winnings he placed with various bookmakers on number three, Impy, to win. Then he held his breath until the homestretch, where, unbelievably, Riddles and Impy were racing neck and neck. Impy took the lead, then Riddles. Lord Stanford screamed himself hoarse, almost willing the black to get his nose across the finish line first. Somebody must have been listening, for the black stretched his neck out just so, at just the last second.

The seventh and last race. Kerry was *that* close to having the wherewithal to pay off most of his debts; he could almost taste the freedom. But no horse looked promising and Lemuel had no tips. No names struck a chord. There was Bething's Folly, Minor Indiscretion, and Loyal Companion, but none seemed to speak to Kerry. Perhaps that was a sign he should take his winnings and go back to the baize tables. At least the cards required something beyond intuition or luck.

The earl was turning to make his way back to his curricle when he heard an angry shout from the crowd behind him. The favorite's name was being erased from the chalk boards and a new name was being entered in its stead, Salvation. Furious, the mob kept up their howl. No one had ever heard of the horse or even knew what it looked like. The jockey, Luke someone, was equally unknown, and the bookmakers couldn't begin to figure odds long enough.

No matter. Kerry smiled and put every last shilling on Salvation. And practically cried when the horse was led out of the paddock area and onto the track. Salvation was gray except for a white muzzle, sunken-chested, and stumbling. Why, it would be a miracle if Salvation managed to save himself from the glue pot for another day. He managed to amble to the starting line, facing in the wrong direction, while the other jockeys made jokes. Salvation's jockey appeared to be foxed, weaving around in the saddle and having trouble staying aboard. The crowd laughed, of course. None of them had any money on a superstitious, hallucinatory whim. Of course.

The jockey finally managed to get the ancient horse turned around and everyone settled down for the start of the race. No one else but Kerry seemed to notice that the scarlet-clad jockey had an ostrich feather in his cap. His? Kerry wasn't even surprised when Lucy smiled going around the nearest turn, dropping the reins and her whip—no, her parasol—to wave at him. His only surprise was that the officials didn't stop the race when she leaned forward to whisper in the horse's ear and the old nag started to fly toward the finish line. Literally. Oh, God. Kerry prayed for Salvation like no sinner ever had.

Half the money went to Demby for safekeeping as usual, after he paid off the rest of the household bills. With a celebratory bottle of champagne and a new stock of cigarillos, Lord Stanford joyfully prepared to pay his gambling debts.

"Fifty pounds to Cholly Spofford. . . . A monkey to Lord Cheyne. Devil a bit, I still think the match should have gone to the Dutchman. . . . Seventy-five for the curricle race I could have won but for that herd of cows . . ."

"Isn't it nice to know that now you can give up gaming?"

"Give up—Lucy?" The earl scanned the shadows of his study. There she was on the sofa, her feet tucked up beneath her. He thought for a moment what a charming domestic scene they made, he settling accounts and she at her embroidery. Except, of course, that he was paying gaming debts and she was dressed in a gown that could make a whore blush, and the room smelled of brimstone. And he was a rational, clear-thinking Englishman, and she didn't really exist.

"I'd kiss you for today's work, angel," he told her, "if you were real."

Lucinda knotted a thread and bit it off with her teeth. "Why are you so afraid to admit I exist?"

"Because if you exist, if you are who and what you say you are, I am crazy." Carrying his glass and the bottle, Kerry took a seat across from her near the fire, where he could drink in her incredible beauty.

"You'd rather consider yourself insane than headed for hell?"

He was watching her graceful fingers dart in and out of the fabric, rather than listening to her words. "What's that you're working on?"

"An altar cloth. The devil makes work for idle hands."

He laughed. "You? A painted harlot sewing on an altar cloth?"

"Why not?" she asked with a scowl. "*You* aren't aiding my cause any. And I do wish you'd get it out of your mind that I am a fallen woman. I mean, fallen from grace is one thing, but fallen off the primrose path is quite another. I strayed only that once, you know. Before that I was strictly trained in all the genteel arts like music and sewing and watercolors. I'll have you know that before meeting you I'd never been to a horse race or a card party."

Staring at shoulders that were almost bare except for two ribbons and a lock of hair, he sneered. "Somehow I cannot feel responsible for corrupting an innocent."

"I do realize from your, ah, admiration that I do not appear the proper young lady right now. No man has ever looked at me that way before, not even Captain Anders. While such, ah, attention cannot help but gratify my vanity, this"—she indicated her body, her clothes—"is merely the devil's handiwork. I do not intend to spend eternity looking like a doxy."

With that businesslike pronouncement, the needlework vanished and a piece of paper appeared in her hand. "How do you feel about 'God, King, and Country'?"

"Pardon me?"

" 'God, King, and Country.' You know, what the crusaders shouted before battles. I still believe we need some kind of credo, a workable system to get you into heaven. It worked for all those feudal types."

"It did? I mean, they were bloody-minded bastards. I'll thank you not to put me in any clanking armor for all eternity. I'm no blasted fanatic, b'God. And as for the king, the man is a hopeless lunatic. Everyone knows that. Would dancing with him on the parapets in my nightshirt show my moral fiber?"

"And country?"

"They wouldn't let me join up, blister it. The heir and all that, last in the line. I would have gone," he said, raising his chin.

"But you could have served your country by taking your seat in Parliament, and you never did."

"What, argue endless politics with those old bagwigs?" He had another sip of the champagne, then put the glass down. "I'm sorry, I never thought. Would you care for some champagne? I could fetch another glass if you'd prefer."

"I've never tasted champagne," she answered with a hint of regret. "But even if it were possible, the last thing I need is another vice."

"What, a tiny sip of wine? That cannot be so great a sin. And while we're talking about that, I don't see why I cannot go on as I have been, sowing my wild oats like every other buck in town. Soon enough I'll have to settle down, set up my nursery, take my seat, be an upright citizen. That's the natural way of things. Even m'father got religion before he died."

"Haven't you been listening? You might have another forty or fifty years to balance out your current dissolution, but I need you reformed now, in the two weeks or so before I die."

"You're wrong, you know. I have listened to you. I just haven't believed all the fustian. The doctor thought you could wake up anytime if you really wanted to. So why give yourself two weeks? You could have the same thirty or forty years to embroider altar cloths. That's a better bet than putting your money on me. Besides, there's champagne and waltzing. I wager you've never waltzed either. Why die if you don't have to?"

"There is no reason for me to live. I'd have no family, no friends, no resources, not even any references to get a position. Those pleasures you speak of are for the privileged, not destitute females with no reputations. Once my father casts me out, I'd have to become what you think I am, or starve. I'd rather die. Especially if I have hopes for a better life after, with your help, thank you."

"I still don't understand. If you are here to win me over to the side of the angels, why in hell are you in the guise of the devil's daughter?"

"It's because of the odds against my succeeding. Now, there's something in your ken."

"They gamble in heaven? Hallelujah."

"Of course not, silly. But purgatory has a special place for gamblers where they win all the time, so there's no pleasure in it."

"So the odds against my reforming are not good?"

"You've heard of a snowball in hell? So won't you please try?"

"Certainly, as soon as I see my tailor."

"Tailor!" she cried, clenching her fists. Of all the uncooperative, disaccomodating fribbles. "With all those bills and closets full of frippery waistcoats and such? I'm going to hell in two weeks and you're going to the tailor?"

"Certes, my dear, I need to be fitted for a strait-jacket."

Chapter Six

After spending the evening tracking down one creditor after another through all the clubs and gambling parlors of London, Lord Stanford sank into a contented sleep. A few hours later, unhappily, he awoke to an embarrassing dampness in his sheets for the first time in years.

A woman. He needed a woman, was all. Once the stress and strain of all those debts was lifted from his mind, his body had reasserted its own needs. He hadn't kept a regular mistress since Claudine, last year, and hadn't even partaken of the offerings of widows or wandering wives in months. Even those free spirits expected a show of gratitude his finances did not permit. Hell, in the past weeks a hasty doorway coupling with a Haymarket whore was above his touch, if not beneath his dignity. *That's* why he was seeing visions of half-naked women all the time, awake and asleep. Relieved to have a satisfactory explanation, Kerry got up and pulled on his clothes.

Fortnam's Mimi might still be available and in need of consolation, he thought. But demireps like

Mimi expected to be treated like ladies. One didn't call without an appointment, especially at three in the morning. He could always go down to Covent Garden and pick up a streetwalker. They were out all night. But who knew what else he might pick up there?

So Lil's place it would be. The girls were clean, the sheets were fresh, and Lil's cellar was superb—not that he meant to overindulge. Never again, once he started hallucinating.

Lil gave him an effusive welcome. Of course she did, word having spread through town that the dashing young earl was flush in the pocket again. In fact, tonight's surge of business could be credited to his account, what with at least three or four of his former note-holders spreading his rhino at Lil's.

"And lucky money I heard, too. The best kind, my lord. May Lady Luck stay looking over your shoulder, dearie, as long as one of my girls is sitting on your lap!" And she cackled so loudly, the bruiser by the front door came charging into the parlor. Lil dismissed the bully with one beringed hand. "So what's your pleasure tonight, my lord? Being so late and all, a lot of the girls is already in bed. Asleep, that is." She laughed again. "They'd be more'n happy to have you wake 'em, I'm sure, if you don't see what you want down here."

Kerry was already looking over the sleepy-eyed girls in the gilt-and-fringe-decorated parlor. They looked tired and pale despite the painted smiles trying to win his attention. He chided himself for being disappointed. What did he expect at Lil's, some pink-cheeked charmer with dewy eyes?

"I was, uh, hoping for a redhead," he heard himself saying. "Young, but, ah . . ."

"Bosomy?" Lil didn't go into this business yesterday. "I have just the girl for you. She's new and eager to please. You go on up with our Sally here. I'll send Lucille along in just a minute or two."

Lucille? Kerry gave the maid Sally a coin, but

she couldn't tell him anything about the girl, she was that new. He hung his jacket over the back of the small room's only chair, then started pacing. Not even noticing the faded wallpaper or the patched quilt on the bed, he paced until the door opened, then shut behind his lady of the evening.

Lucille. She was eager, all right, eager to tear him apart with her long, blood-red fingernails. Kerry'd heard of someone being so mad they smoked; he used to think it was a figure of speech.

Putrid fumes and fiery sparks billowed out of Lucy's mouth, nose, and ears. Red flame glittered in her green eyes.

"Uh, jealous, my pet?" Kerry bluffed. "If I thought for a second you'd have—"

"How dare you?" she roared, sending roils of smoke toward the ceiling.

Kerry backed up across the little bedchamber until his knees hit the narrow bed. He sat down and edged as far as possible away from this raging fury. If he'd still had doubts about her story, he was a believer now.

"That's right, cower. Cringe, you puny lordling. Where is the arrogant cynicism now? If I don't exist, why are your knees shaking? If you conjured me up from the depths of your depraved mind, why can't you conjure me into your bed? Why?" she ranted. "I'll tell you why, you boil on the butt of humanity. Because *I*, Miss Lucinda Faire, late of Fairview Manor, Derby, currently teetering on the brink of the River Styx, am in charge here."

Lucy clamped a hand over her mouth, suddenly aghast at what she'd said. Whatever happened to meek and dutiful little Miss Lucinda? She didn't recognize herself in this body, this virago, this . . . this bordello. This last restored some of her indignation, especially since she could see her outburst had finally penetrated his lordship's social veneer.

"I have been very patient," she went on in a milder tone, "waiting for you to see the error of your ways. Realizing that you are only a product of your times, and a male besides, I forgave your pride and pigheadedness. I have tolerated your insobriety, even your blasphemy. And I actually abetted you in your gambling, thinking that was the quickest way to set your mind on higher matters. But whoring? Whoring I shall not tolerate!"

By now Lord Stanford deduced that he wasn't about to be smoked like a kipper. Lucy needed him alive and kicking bad habits. He mopped his brow. "I, ah, did thank you for your assistance at the racetrack, you know."

Lucy was not appeased. "You'd better cherish your appreciation, my lord, for that was the last time. From now on, you bet, you lose." She crossed her arms over her chest.

Even in these circumstances Kerry noticed her chest was particularly generous. He smiled. "Cut line, Lucy, I didn't always lose, even without your help."

"You will now."

Somehow he believed her, not that he wouldn't test her assertion at the first opportunity. "But if I am not to support myself by wagering, how do you propose I live? Does highway robbery suit your notions of morality any better than gambling?"

"Don't be goosish." Lucy was studying the room. Her nose wrinkled at the damp gray towel, the chipped basin and unmatched pitcher.

The earl stood up, trying not to be embarrassed in front of her at the dirt in the corners, the darned coverlet, and cracked mirror. This wasn't his house, after all, just because he visited. "Now who is being goosish? You must know *my* father wasn't any nabob, Miss Lucinda Faire of Fairview Manor. All he left me were debts and obligations."

"And your heritage. It's past time you took up the reins of your responsibilities, my lord."

"What, become a country squire?"

"There are worse things."

“Not for me there aren’t. Oh, I enjoy the horses and the open spaces, but waking at cock’s crow and riding all day pall after a while. Furthermore, in case there is something you didn’t know about my personal life, Stanford Abbey needs a major investment of funds just to make the mortgages, much less a living. Needless to say, without gambling I have no chance to find that kind of gold.”

“I do know you haven’t yet tried hard work.”

He gave her a smile. “You think gaming is easy? Besides, the abbey doesn’t require another strong back, it requires a degree of expertise I haven’t got.”

“Then learn,” she said in exasperation. “If you can understand the rules and percentages for all those silly card games, surely you can manage to figure out crop rotation and irrigation.”

“My father never did.”

“Is that what you want *your* son to say? Oh, bother.” She seemed to be looking for something, searching for nonexistent pockets or a dangling reticule. Finally she pulled a piece of paper from the air above her head. “Ah-ha. The code of chivalry.”

“Now you’re the one with attics to let. What in blazes does the code of chivalry have to do with mangel-wurzels and milch cows?”

“See, you do know something about agriculture.” Lucinda was studying her notes, biting her lower lip in a way that made Kerry wish she really were Lucille, his belle de nuit.

“Don’t you even think it, sirrah,” she said, reading either his mind or the bulge in his breeches. “And the code of chivalry is another doctrine of conduct, one it might behoove you to consider as a modus vivendi.”

“What, more medieval dogma? Are you going to bring back chastity belts, too?”

“One or the other might have kept you out of such a place as this.”

There was an unmistakable note of disdain in

Lucy's voice that robbed him of the last amorous thoughts, but not regrets for what might have been. "And what's so wrong with a house of accommodation? It's just a service like any other, buyers and sellers. No one is injured."

" 'Chivalry,' " she read, " 'a canon dedicated to the protection of the weak, defense of the innocent, reverence for the purity of women.' "

"Here? Weak, innocent, pure? Were you born under a cabbage leaf? Prostitution is a trade the girls pick, like becoming a seamstress, only with more chance of advancement."

Lucy shook her head sadly. "Wickedness must weaken your mind, too. Come with me." And she took his hand. That is, she made his hand tingle, so he followed her.

Lucy led him down the deserted hall, around a corner, and up a flight of uncarpeted stairs. Motioning for silence, she pushed open one of the doors there. By the light of the hall candle, Kerry could see a room no bigger than a closet really, with a pitched roof that made it impossible to stand in, filled wall to wall with a ragged mattress. Three girls slept under one thin blanket, tumbled together like kittens.

"The one on the end is Lucille," Lucy whispered, nudging him forward.

Feeling like some kind of voyeur, Kerry ducked his head and took two steps into the room. Yes, there was the red hair, only it seemed to be the dead color of henna dye rather than auburn or carroty or Lucy's vibrant gold-streaked red. They'd forgotten to dye the chit's eyebrows, which were still pale brown. But she was young; Lil hadn't misled him about that. Sixteen perhaps, unless it wasn't just the innocence of slumber making her seem a veritable babe.

"Fifteen," Lucy whispered, "and fresh from the country. The family's farm fell under the enclosures, her brothers went to the mines. Lucille knew a girl who had a position as a housemaid in London, so her mother sold her wedding ring for the girl's coach fare. Lil met the coach."

Kerry could still see the tear tracks down the girl's cheeks. "My God, I didn't know—" But of course he did. He'd heard the stories, even joked how the girls got younger every year. "What can I do?" he asked helplessly.

"For Lucille? Nothing." He put a gold coin under her pillow anyway, before backing out of the room. There was a small chance she'd find it before one of the other girls did, or Lil.

"But you can do much for all the rest of the Lucilles," Lucy was going on as she preceded him down the steps, then down the carpeted public stairway and out to the cold night air. "You can speak out in Parliament against child prostitution. You can see that legitimate employment agencies meet the coaches. You can convince your friends that prostitution is degrading and that celibacy is a virtue. You can—"

Kerry was stopped in his tracks. "Hold fast, Lucy. I thought I just had to be a better man, not perform miracles!"

Lucy laughed and took his hand, which was an eerie feeling, but nice once one got used to it. "I have great hopes for you, my lord."

His watch at Lil's being over, the burly doorman took himself off to the Three Feathers for a heavy wet.

"Bash any heads tonight, 'Arry? Toss any sots in the alley?"

"Nah, more's the pity. Quiet night."

"Any fancy toffs come by, then?"

"Yeah, the Earl Stanford what they was sayin' had such a run o' luck this week. Must be true. 'E didn't even bat an eye when Lil doubled the goin' rate. Even tossed me a coin just for offerin' to call a hackney for 'im. Said 'e'd rather walk though."

The Three Feathers was shortly an empty nest as every cutpurse and footpad in the neighborhood lit out after the easy mark.

Kerry was deep in thought when the first assailant struck. He never heard the villain creep up behind him with a club in his hand, and he never turned around when the scoundrel slipped on a patch of ice—the only patch of ice in London that night—and knocked himself to flinders.

The next attackers worked in a pair. Except that one of them pulled his knife too soon and nicked his mate, who gave him an elbow in the breadbasket, which started a melee that distracted the next set of thugs into betting on the outcome.

Kerry kept walking, thinking of injustice, poverty, and the fate of unprotected innocents. Chivalry, almost, except that he wanted a woman more than ever. He didn't notice how a streetlamp somehow got between him and a tossed rock, or how a slavering pit bull decided to claim the block behind him as its own territory.

He didn't see the rat as big as a house cat run over Dirty Sal's foot, causing her to drop her pistol. He did hear her screaming, however. With thoughts of damsels in distress that would have cheered Dirty Sal no end, he turned in time to see two men coming at him with cudgels.

Lucinda decided to let the earl handle this attack on his own. She'd heard somewhere that men liked to feel important. Still ashamed of her own emotional outburst and shocking display of raw power—a lady never indulged in such disgraceful exhibits—Lucy felt she owed the earl a sop to his pride. Besides, he did need an outlet for some of that masuline energy, for she was going to make him toe the line, come hell or high water. She only hoped the ruffians didn't damage the earl's handsome face.

Kerry fended off the assault without raising a sweat. He did skin the knuckles of his right hand on one lowlife's chin, and ripped the sleeve of his greatcoat tossing the other into the side of a building, blast it. He'd finally got the curst topcoat paid for. Demby was no good at repairs, and the earl had to thread the needle for him anyway. Maybe he should just take up tailoring, now that he was renouncing gambling. Or perhaps he could become a prizefighter. Heaven knew he'd need some thrills in his life if he was to give up wine, wenching, and wagering. What other excitement was there?

So he went home and burned the house down.

Chapter Seven

He didn't mean to start the fire, of course. Kerry just lit his cigarillo and sprawled back in his comfortable chair to contemplate his dreary future. Thinking of ways to circumvent those strictures—he hadn't precisely given his word to abandon the life of a London gentleman; there had been no chance yet to see if he could win a wager—he remembered the smoke and sparks coming from Lucy. Gads, she was magnificent when she was angry. Of course, he'd do his best never to provoke her again, but wondered if such a passionate nature carried over to other situations. Those heaving breasts, the flushed cheeks . . .

Of course she did have that freakish layer of prudery. The earl contemplated trying his hand at a little reform himself. After all, even a saint should experience a few of life's finer things before giving them up. Thinking of some of those finer things, he fell asleep.

When his head hit the armrest, Lord Stanford awakened enough to take himself upstairs to bed, where the dream continued. Oh, my, yes. There was

Lucy calling his name, desperately urging him to hurry. There was that tingle, a frisson, a warm quiver to his face, his bare chest where she was grabbing at him in her frenzy. And there was that wretched smoke. How the devil did anyone make love with their eyes streaming and their throats gasping for fresh air? He coughed and sat up, awake.

"Thank goodness! There's not a minute to spare! Now, hurry!"

The room was filled with smoke and a distraught Lucy, trying to tug at him. He didn't see any flames, but the heat was uncomfortable and the smoke was unbreatheable. Staggering to the window, he threw it open and took deep cleansing breaths.

"Hurry! The fire!"

Kerry didn't wait for another warning. He grabbed up his coat, his purse, some papers, and his boots before hurtling down the stairs. That's when he saw the flames coming from his study and traveling along the faded Aubusson down the hall. The dry-as-dust wainscoting was smoldering, the ancient paper was curling off the walls. He ran through the great hall toward the front doors, away from the flames and thick smoke, glad for once that the place was no longer filled with priceless treasures.

Outside he shouted "Fire! Fire!" to draw the attention of the watch, who ran off to alert the fire brigade. He drew on his boots and his greatcoat, stuffing the papers and such in his pockets, and thought of going back for his father's Mantons.

Lucy was fluttering around the earl, anxiously patting him to make sure he was intact. "No, no, you mustn't. The whole place could burst into flames at any minute!"

Kerry supposed she was right. Besides, now he could buy a new pair if he had to. "Oh, my God, Demby!"

Racing around the side of the house, Kerry tried the service door. It was locked, of course. He tore off for the kitchen entrance at the rear of the house, and didn't even bother trying the handle. He just stepped back, then kicked the door in with his booted foot. Lucy was already inside, on her way to the apartment Demby kept near the kitchen, what would have been the housekeeper's rooms. "Hurry!"

The smoke was as bad here as on the upper story, the fire having traveled down the bare wooden servants' stairs. Kerry took two deep inhalations before plunging into the fire cloud.

Demby was in his bed, not stirring at Kerry's shout. Not breathing at all, in fact. The earl lifted the smaller man from the bed, blankets and all, and over to the window. Blessing the ground floor, he shoved his valet-cum-housekeeper out the window onto the shrubbery, and leapt out after him, dragging Demby to a safer distance away from the house.

"Breathe, man, breathe," he urged the gray-skinned man, shaking Demby's thin shoulders in a futile effort to jolt air into the man's lungs.

"The kiss of life," Lucy directed. "Give him the kiss of life!"

Kerry stared at her blankly. "The what?"

"Breathe into his mouth, you dolt! Hurry!"

The earl looked at his servant's unshaven face, straggly beard, stained mustache, and yellow teeth. "Like hell."

"Confound you for a gutless jackaninny, just do it."

So he did, and shook Demby again for good measure. Demby started to cough and wheeze and gasp for air, but he was breathing.

Lucy was radiant. "You did it," she cried, clapping her hands. "You saved his life! You endangered your own to save a fellow man, and then gave him your very breath! Oh, they have to appreciate this up there. Such a noble act has to cancel some of the wickedness, it just has to. So generous, so selfless, so—"

"So where's my stash?" Kerry thundered, shaking poor Demby again.

"Under the bed," Demby rasped. "With my collection."

Kerry dashed back into the house while Lucy shrieked like a banshee about his jeopardizing her chance for heaven with his recklessness and greed.

There were two boxes under the bed, so Kerry dropped both out the window before hurtling after, just as something in the kitchen exploded with a roar and a burst of new flames.

The fire brigade had arrived by then, in time to get a good view of the flames while their captain dickered with Demby over his lordship's lapsed fire protection policy.

Kerry opened his purse into the captain's hand. A new policy was instantly in effect.

"Exceptin' your lordship might also be interested in a benefit lottery we be holdin'. For the widows and young'uns of us brave firefighters, don't you know, what has fallen in the line of duty. Drawin's soon, and we only be sellin' a fixed number of tickets, so chances are pretty good."

"Better than the chances of any of your brave boys putting out my fire if I don't take a ticket, I suppose," the earl muttered, emptying his purse into the waiting palm. The captain whistled his men to work.

Demby was sitting up against the garden gate, blankets still draped over his shoulders. He was staring into one of the boxes, his stricken face looking more ghastly than it did when he wasn't breathing.

"Not the money, man, tell me the money is safe!" Kerry begged, falling to his knees next to the servant.

"No, my lord, your property is secure." He indicated the other box, where a household account ledger rested atop a leather pouch. "It's my, ah, collection."

"Deuce take it, I'm sorry if anything got damaged when I threw the box from the window. Didn't seem much choice at the time, you know."

"Of course not, my lord. And I believe the damage was done by the heat, not the fall." He held the box out with hands that shook less than usual.

Kerry looked in, then stirred the contents with one finger. "Uh, you were collecting candle stubs? I mean, I know it's been bellows to mend for a bit, but candle stubs?"

"Not candle stubs, my lord, wax carvings. Figurines I was going to have cast in bronze when we were in the chips again. Pewter, anyway. Here." And he unwrapped a piece of flannel to reveal a brass dragon small enough to fit in the earl's hand.

"Why, this is exquisite. Too bad it's not jade or ivory. Wherever did you come by such a fine piece of workmanship?"

"I had it cast the last time the dibs were in tune, you recall, when we did so well at Newmarket last year."

"You mean this is from one of the candle stubs? Uh, wax carvings? You're saying you did this? With a knife?"

"A chisel, actually."

"With your palsy?"

Demby took the statuette back with hands that didn't tremble at all. He coughed, as if there were still a residue of smoke in his chest. "The tremors passed when I stopped drinking, which is what cost me my apprentice mason job in the first place. I didn't like being a valet, my lord. Or a groom, or a cook, butler, footman, whatever. While you believed me incapable of performing all those duties, I had more time for my carving."

"Blast it, I hired you as a man-of-all-work," Stanford complained.

"But you never paid me, my lord."

What could the earl say? For one of the first times in his life he said he was sorry. "And for your collection melting. Lord only knows how, but I'll make it up some way."

"You already did, my lord, you saved my life. Besides, while I was lying there more dead than alive, an angel came and told me we'll come about."

"She wasn't wearing a red dress, by any chance, was she?"

"You know, I wondered about that very same thing."

Kerry sent Demby off to a hotel while he in his shirt-sleeves went to help the firefighters, carrying buckets and hoses. He even went with them to have a mulled ale after, to warm up. Just one. The captain said it was too soon and too dark to assess the destruction, but guessed it likely that the worst damage was from the smoke and water. The fire hadn't really spread yet, so the structure should be sound. Of course, it would take most of Kerry's remaining funds just to get the place clean and livable again, to say nothing of his clothes, household necessities, and buying the firemen a few more rounds.

He decided to bed down in the stables for the night rather than follow Demby to the hotel, thinking to guard against any looters bacon-brained enough to believe there was anything of value left in Stanford House.

He was counting the money Demby had been keeping, adding in the remnants from his purse and his pockets. He added the fireman's benevolent lottery ticket to the pile.

"You won't win, you know." Lucinda was sitting on an overturned bucket in the corner of the empty stall his lordship had selected as the evening's bedchamber.

She looked younger somehow, or perhaps the lantern glow made her hair seem more gold, less red. The sight of her still took his breath away, and not just because she'd appeared out of nowhere. "How can you be sure?" he asked.

"I just saved your life. Can't you trust me?"

"I never got a chance to thank you for that either. The firemen said it was a miracle the smoke didn't kill me."

"There's no need to look so humble." Lucy thought Lord Stanford was looking even more handsome than ever, in fact, brown curls all tousled and a smudge on one cheek. No wonder the man found it so easy being a rake. "I cannot very well save your soul without saving your life. Speaking of souls, no one has yet gone to heaven on a wager, so you may as well give poor Demby that raffle ticket to get his mind off his loss. We have nobler considerations."

"We do?" Still, he put the printed ticket away in the box, then shuddered as Lucy produced a thick sheaf of papers. "By Jupiter, ma'am, you don't intend to start reading me sermons, do you?"

"Would they do any good? I have it on high authority that you never paid proper attention to one before, so I misdoubt you'd start at this late date. I had thought to find defense of sorts for your behavior here." She tapped the papers. "The British legal code. Such things usually hold little sway with my, ah, superiors, but I thought if we proved you a model citizen . . ."

"That's the ticket. You can tell the lady judges I'm a regular upright law-abider. Never boxed a charley, never cried 'Fire!' in a public place, except tonight of course."

"Hmm. Do you know they have laws here in London about herding cattle through the streets, laws about crossing sweeps and sidewalk vendors and where Gypsies may camp? I'm afraid there is also a law about making duels illegal."

"The magistrate wrote it up as a hunting accident."

"And they did pass the Seditions Act."

"What, should I go to jail for saying the king is insane?"

"You did tell Lord Sidmouth that we were losing the war due to inefficiency, and you have mentioned that England would be better off with a few more bordellos than with any of Prinny's pavilion schemes."

"A man's entitled to his opinion."

"Not according to this law, he's not. But no matter." She sighed and tossed the papers into the hereafter. "The laws are very clear about arson."

"Arson? I never—"

"Your cigarillo did when you fell asleep and dropped it under the chair. Willful negligence. Leading to loss of property and endangering lives."

"I see what you're about. You're trying to get me to swear off tobacco."

"It's a filthy habit. See where it's led? And just think what would happen if Demby had died. The entire hallelujah choir couldn't keep you from hell."

The earl did not have any of his cigarillos with him, so it was an easy promise to make, but then he recalled that fiercesome display Lucy had put on at Lil's. Not above a little bargaining himself, he offered, "I'll stop smoking if you will."

Lucinda blushed. "I am truly sorry for enacting such a scene. I'm . . . just not myself these days. Yes, I'll agree to that. Shall we shake hands on it?"

The feeling of warmth traveled right up Kerry's arm to bring a smile to his face. "You know, you look different. Your hair, your dress. Something."

"Yes, isn't it wonderful?" Lucinda grinned back. "I even have a petticoat!" She clapped her hands to her mouth at the indiscretion. "Oh, dear, I shouldn't have said that. But I couldn't help feeling my attire wasn't at all the thing. But now . . . It's the odds, you know."

“The odds?”

“Yes, your chances of getting to heaven! You saved Demby's life and I got an undergarment!”

And a softer face, an inch higher décolletage, and satin slippers instead of decadent Roman sandals. Kerry sighed. Now he couldn't see the outline of her legs through the sheer gown. This business of reforming wasn't all a bed of roses.

Chapter Eight

Stanford House was salvageable, just. The stairs were unsafe, the parquet floors were buckled from the fire brigade's enthusiastic application of water, the wood paneling was soot-blackened, and the plaster ceilings were cracked from the heat and in danger of collapsing. On the other hand, the engineer reported cheerily, this was a fine opportunity to repair the dry rot on the upper story, the ill-fitting casements, and the antiquated kitchen.

Twitching in Lord Stanford's hands, not so cheerily, was an urge to strangle the fellow. The mandatory renovations alone would swallow his last shilling, leaving him with an unfurnished mansion, a fire-sale wardrobe, Demby, dry rot, and empty pockets. His watch and diamond stickpin might bring enough for new draperies, so the neighbors couldn't look in and see the Earl of Stanford sitting naked on the floor.

There was less than no chance of his borrowing another fortune either, with no unmortgaged collateral to put up, no future income to pledge away.

Deuce take it, he'd gone only one whole day without being in debt, besides.

Then again, he could just board up Stanford House and move to a hotel until his money ran out. Afterward he could batten on his friends, going from house party to hunting box as many of the ton did. Kieren Somerfield, hanger-on, left a sour taste in his mouth.

Blast, he was in as bad a case as ever, only colder. Sitting in the remains of his study with the windows open, Kerry huddled in his greatcoat, wishing for a drink. The last of his wine had been rescued by the fire brigade—liberated, more like it—and the kitchen was in no condition to produce even hot coffee. 'Twould take a squad of hardworking lackeys weeks to restore the kitchen to its former disreputable condition. Months, if they were under Demby's direction.

Kerry took out his gold coin, his lucky coin—hah!—and tossed it in the air. Heads he went ahead with the repairs, tails he abandoned the old pile. The coin slipped out of his hands on the downward arc, however, and rolled into a pile of debris, his former cherrywood desk.

Botheration, he thought, getting down on his hands and knees in the wet muck. He couldn't afford to let a ha'penny get away, much less a guinea. He'd wager it was the last he'd see for some time. Wager? What was it the chit had said about him betting?

Kerry found the coin and tossed it to his other hand. "Heads," he called. The coin showed tails. "Heads" again. Tails again. He called "heads" seven times, and got the reverse seven times. So he called "tails," and heads came up.

"Now do you believe me," Lucinda asked crossly, "or are you going to sit on the filthy floor all day, playing, when there's so much else to be done?"

Kerry scrambled to his feet and brushed off his breeches as best he could. Lucinda was perched on the window ledge, her dainty feet dangling into the room. She wore no pelisse, not even a shawl over that silky red gown, but Kerry's temperature rose a few degrees just looking at her. "Did you expect me to start mopping the floors, ma'am?"

"I didn't expect you to sit around feeling sorry for yourself."

"God damn, I'm not—"

"And I thought we agreed that you would give up blasphemy?"

"*We* didn't agree to anything, if I recall. You made demands and threats; I listened, that's all."

"Of all the thick-skulled, stubborn mules . . . I suppose some of us cannot rise in the face of adversity."

"And I suppose some of us expect too much from others. Riding to heaven on my shirttails, indeed! Well, ma'am, let me tell you, you'd better find another driver. I cannot go around saving people from burning buildings and I cannot be giving alms to the poor, because I am one of them. So good deeds just aren't going to pull your chestnuts out of the fire. As for the rest, you'd better stop right now trying to make me what I'm not, for it won't fadge. I am a gentleman and I live by a gentleman's code. That's always been enough for me, and it shall have to do for you, too. The lady patronesses of Almack's are satisfied; I expect those inquisitors of yours can't be higher sticklers."

Lucy smiled in delight. "Then there is such a thing after all! I searched everywhere and couldn't find any gentleman's code written out."

"What kind of peahen looks for honor in a book?"

"Perhaps one who hasn't found it in the gentlemen of her acquaintance. Could you explain it to me?"

Kerry leaned against a bookcase long since emptied of anything but racing journals and old newspapers. He thought a moment. "Well, a gentleman keeps his word. That's the most important thing, so you can trust a chap if he makes you a promise. Like an I.O.U. That's play and pay, debts of honor when you put your name to them. And you can't cheat, of course."

"Is the whole thing concerned with gambling, then? They won't be happy about that."

He crossed his arms over his chest. "Of course not. There are lots of finer points to it, like always being dressed appropriately to the occasion."

Lucinda's lip curled. "I'm sure they'll be impressed with that."

"And the things fathers teach their sons at an early age: never pick on anyone smaller than you; don't foul your nest."

"Don't . . . ?"

Kerry picked a bit of dirt off the sleeve of his coat. "Don't bring loose women home to your mother. In later years, don't introduce your wife and your mistress."

"My, those are finer points."

"Never strike a woman," he went on with gritted teeth, "no matter the provocation."

"That's it?" Lucinda asked in amazement. "You cannot cheat at cards, but it's all right if you cheat on your wife as long as you're dressed correctly and she's not looking? Oh, and if she complains, you mustn't hit her. No wonder there are so few of your type in heaven!"

"That's not all of it," he practically shouted. "Ladies must be shown respect at all times, even if they are shrewish, nagging fiends from hell."

"Ladies, as opposed to serving girls or opera dancers?"

"All females deserve a gentleman's courtesy, some just more than others."

"And virgins?" she asked curiously.

"Virgins are to be avoided like the plague. Their virtue's such a fragile thing, a gentleman can find himself honor-bound to make an offer if he sneezes in their direction. Like being here alone with you.

If you were a real girl, which you're not, thank goodness, your reputation would be so tarnished after being with a libertine like me, I'd have to marry you. That would be the only honorable thing to do."

"Is that why you never married? You never compromised a lady?"

"I stay out of parson's mousetrap out of choice, not because I haven't been forced into it. Blast, you are sounding like my mother. I thought we were talking of honor, not marriage."

"Oh, I thought you mentioned something about fathers and sons. I don't suppose honor has anything to do with carrying on the family lines and all that."

Kerry looked away. "A gentleman is expected to perpetuate his name, yes. But not until he's damned ready!"

A pencil appeared in Lucy's hand. She licked the point before setting it to paper. "Now, let me see. You did give your word not to smoke."

"We shook hands on it, yes."

"And wagering?"

"I'm not gudgeon enough to bet when I can't win. It's only for two weeks or so anyway, isn't it?"

"I don't think that's the spirit of the thing. I'll mark that one with a question. Drinking?"

"To excess? I can't afford to. Besides, I got deathly ill last time."

"And you will next time, too." She left a blank and went on. "Cursing?"

"Damn—dash it, I'll try if it will end your nattering on about it."

"So I have your word on that?"

"To try, yes. I can't swear to minding my tongue every blo—blessed minute, but I'll try."

"And women." She made a big check next to that entry.

"Now, hold line, Lucy. You're the one who laid down the law there. I never promised any such thing. I mean, a female devil breathing smoke down a fellow's back can put paid to his desire. And if you're going to pop up anytime I feel randy and find myself a willing partner, well, that can limit my raking, all right. But I ain't turning monkish for you, by Go—by George. Not you nor the apostles altogether could keep me from lusting after a pretty girl." He turned away. "It might help if you stopped swinging your legs like that, though."

"Oh, dear." Lucinda stood up and smoothed out her skirts. "It's hard to remember sometimes. The freedom can be quite intoxicating, it seems. Of course no lady . . . but then, our particular situation . . . the familiarity and all. You must admit the circumstance is unique."

"To say the least," he concurred, grinning now at her efforts to look the proper female, when she wore no gloves, had no hairpins to bring order to her tumbled curls, and possessed no fichu to stuff in the low neckline of her gown.

Lucinda made her hands stop fluttering and simply stood erect, recalling days with a backboard. "So what have you decided to do about the fire damage, my lord?"

"Actually I was hoping you could wave your magic wand and restore Stanford House to its former glory, from crystal chandeliers to priceless carpets."

"I think you are confusing me with a fairy godmother or a genie in a bottle. They don't exist, you know," she told him as if imparting a great truth.

"But angels and devils and miscellaneous in-between sorts do?"

"Of course. I thought we'd covered all that before. Oh, you were just teasing, weren't you? No one has ever . . . Anyway, my assignment is to help make you a better person, not improve your living conditions. So where will you start?"

The earl ran a hand through his hair. "Hang it, I haven't the foggiest. I'm tempted to shut the place up and take lodgings. Be cheaper in the long run, rather than sinking everything I own into this barracks. Foolish for just one man. My mother hates London; she'll never come."

"Why don't you sell it if you care so little?"

He laughed without humor. "Don't you think my father would have sold it ages ago if it weren't part of the entail? Besides, who said I don't care about the old wreck? I simply cannot afford it. Were I to start restorations, just paying for the materials would strain my finances so that I couldn't afford a place to sleep in the meantime. I'd be back in the stables. I don't care what you have to say about mangers and such, I am not spending another night with my horses."

"But if Stanford House were in good repair, you could rent it out for the season at some exorbitant fee that would cover the cost of refurbishing the mansion. Grosvenor Square is the prime location to launch debutantes, you know. A few years of that and everything would be paid for."

"Fine, and what am I supposed to do during those few years, hire myself as majordomo in my own house?"

"You could go home."

"I am home, or what's left of it."

"The Abbey. Wiltshire. You could leave while repairs are being made here, go see about your estates, make something of them. I know you can if you only try."

Kerry looked at her through narrowed eyes. "That's what you wanted from the first, isn't it, to get me away from the temptations of the city? You think I'll turn into a dutiful son if I'm out of the fleshpot, that I'll take tea with the vicar and his wife, marry some bran-faced squire's daughter, and raise a parcel of God-fearing, law-abiding, frugal farmers. I begin to think this whole fire business suits you to a cow's thumb."

"*I* wasn't the one who fell asleep with a lit cigar in my hand," she retorted.

He still looked suspicious, but said, "It makes no never mind. I cannot bring this place up to any kind of standard, and I cannot hope to do anything at all for the Abbey. If you knew anything about mortgages and such, you'd know that every shilling the place earns has to go to the bank just to pay the interest on the loans. I was hoping to put it off for my mother's lifetime, but sooner or later I am going to have to petition to break the entailment so I can sell the blasted place, just to meet the obligations."

"You'd sell your son's birthright?"

"The devil take it, I don't have any son!"

"And aren't likely to at this rate," she muttered, then: "Hmm. What's this, do you think?" She was staring at a water-stained picture that had peeled back in its frame.

"Just one of my father's hunting prints, nothing even remotely valuable. He cut them out of magazines, just to fill the wall space once the paintings were gone."

"No, not the print. The painting under it."

Kerry came over. "What painting? Let me see." He scraped off the rest of the hunting print. "By George, there really is a painting under there. I can see why the governor covered the thing up. Deuced offputting, all that blood and gore."

"He seems familiar," Lucinda said, standing so close to Kerry she could have touched him, if she could have touched him.

"Who, the poor martyr chap on the cross? Did you ever get to meet . . . ?"

"No, the artist's name. Cannoli, is it?"

Kerry grabbed the picture down off the wall, frame and all, and rushed over to the window. "My God, it is! Lucy, this is the missing masterpiece from the Italian school. Cannoli taught Leonardo! Why, if this is genuine, it's worth a fortune! My father must have covered it up to hide it from his creditors, then forgot to tell anyone."

"Is it part of the entailment?" Lucinda called to him as he raced around the room, ripping scenes of horses and hounds out of frames. He brought two more oil paintings over to the window, though neither was as distinguished as the Cannoli.

"None of the furnishings were ever mentioned in the legal papers; that's how my father managed to dispose of so many antiques. I wonder why he kept these."

"For you, I suppose."

"Lucy, do you know what this means? I'll have to have them appraised, of course, but, my word, the missing masterpiece! Lucy, I could kiss you!"

And he forgot that there really wasn't any body there, and did. And felt something. It wasn't flesh and blood, but it was warm and it sent shivers through him. Lucy must have felt something, too, for she blushed like any pure maiden. Then she disappeared, like any phantasm.

Chapter Nine

The solicitor was nearly as excited as the earl.

"My lord, I cannot tell you how pleased I am. Why, the firm of Stenross and Stenross has been serving the Somerfields since our inception. I cannot express my sorrow over the recent situation. You *have* received my communications, haven't you?"

Kerry studied his fingernails.

"About the bank and the Abbey home woods? How they are demanding the trees be cut down and sold to pay something toward the debts? The wood being the last unentailed asset, they are growing quite insistent."

The deer and the quail, the yule logs and the tree houses—the debts. "That will no longer be necessary."

"Indeed, indeed." The elderly man polished his spectacles. "The paintings will have to be authenticated, of course, but I believe we might expect in excess of five thousand pounds. I think I have a buyer for the Cannoli among my own clients, a very well-respected collector, don't you know, so we might avoid public auction and all the notoriety that entails."

"I'm sure you'll think of everything, Mr. Stenross. I have always found your company to be most efficient and discreet."

The solicitor preened. "Too kind, my lord. The profit from the sale of the Cannoli *is* to satisfy some of the outstanding interest on the Abbey mortgage, then?" If Mr. Stenross sounded hesitant, he was all too aware of the Stanford flaw, a fatal tendency to gamble away any income.

"Yes, and this other piece"—another massacred saint, this one sprouting arrows like a hedgehog—"should bring in enough to complete the repairs to the Grosvenor Square house. I'll leave it with you, if you don't mind, along with what funds I can spare now, and ask you to look over the bills as they come due."

Mr. Stenross rubbed his hands. "Of course, of course, my lord. I can have my son oversee the whole project if you wish. He gets restless in these stuffy offices, don't you know."

"That will be excellent. Thank you again."

"We are always happy to serve." Especially when the serving involved saving one of the noble houses, both the structure and the succession. Mr. Stenross was one of those who still believed that the aristocracy was one of England's treasures, to be preserved for future generations like any other decrepit landmark. "And the third painting, my lord? I do not recognize the name, but the style is very popular right now. It should bring in enough to make some of those needful repairs at the Abbey." He was hopeful; things had been going so well, the earl being so reasonable, so responsible, so unlike himself.

His lordship shook his head.

"Then may I suggest the Consols?" Stenross put forward. "A bit of steady income here and there never comes amiss." That was optimism indeed.

The earl was still studying the third picture. A saint—he had a gold halo—was on the ground amid some shrubbery and flowers. He was asleep this time, Kerry thought, for there was no blood, and the figure wore a contented smile. A cherub with rosy cheeks and flaxen curls floated overhead, like a guardian angel watching out for bandits or wolves or Romans. Something about the cherub reminded the earl of Lucy; perhaps it was the innocence around the eyes. "No," he heard himself saying, "I do not want to put this one on the block unless I have to. Lock it away somewhere, will you, until Stanford House is ready for it. If it's possible, I'd like to save this one . . . for my son." There, that should at least earn Lucy a hairpin. He felt good, until the other man started beaming.

"Oh, my lord, that's the finest news I could have heard. I never believed—that is, let me extend my heartiest congratulations and wish you every—"

"Not yet, Stenross," the earl interrupted the other's effusions. "I meant someday. And if I find myself up the River Tick before then, well, the painting will have to go. Is that clear?"

"Of course, of course, but let us pray for the best, shall we? Now, my lord, where might I send information regarding the sale of the other two, and questions that might arise about the work at Stanford House? Have you found lodgings yet, or shall you be staying with friends?"

The earl cleared his throat. "You may, ah, send all communications to me at Stanford Abbey, Wiltshire. I'll stop there awhile and look into the mess. Only for the duration of the hammering and painting in Grosvenor Square, you understand."

Not only did Lucy appear with her hair tamed from its wanton look—to the earl's mixed feelings—but now she had a bonnet. A tiny, saucy hat with a cherry bow at her cheek, it was just the thing for a curricle ride out of town.

"And you won't be cold? I could have bricks . . ."

She just laughed.

The earl had spent a busy morning after conferring with Mr. Stenross's son about the repairs. He hired the contracting firm young Mr. Stenross had recommended, and called at one or two furniture warehouses. He visited his tailor, who welcomed him with delight, having received payment in full just the day before. Stanford was promised at least three sets of clothes, for evening, riding, and daytime, within the week. He also purchased ready-made shirts for the first time in his life, and a supply of cravats, handkerchiefs, and smallclothes. Locke luckily had a beaver hat that suited him, and the glovers had two pairs that fit almost perfectly. Demby would just have to do his best with the earl's sooty shoes and boots; there wasn't time to be fitted for new ones.

Demby would follow later in a hired carriage with the new clothes and whatever was reclaimable of the earl's smoke-permeated wardrobe; Kerry was eager to be off, now that he had made the decision.

He planned to make the trip in easy stages, not caring to leave his champion matched bays in indifferent hands, not wanting to arrive with job horses.

Lucy joined him outside of London, after the bays had run the fidgets out. Thank goodness, for the earl's hands jerked at the reins when she suddenly appeared by his side on the curricle's narrow seat. After bringing the high-bred cattle back under control, Kerry was able to appreciate his companion's glowing smile. This wasn't such a bad idea after all, stopping in at the Abbey, if it ended all that nagging and brought the chit so much pleasure. He supposed he'd wake up from this bizarre dream someday, but for now he could just enjoy her excitement.

"You see, I've never driven in a curricle before. How I used to envy those lucky girls out for rides with their dashing beaus, to be sitting so high and going so fast. And the fortunate men, to have control of such exquisite horses. None were as fine as yours, of course."

For a moment Kerry was tempted to offer her the reins, which was astounding since he had never let a female touch the ribbons of his carriage yet. What was even more astounding was that he forgot she wasn't really there. She was in Derby, waiting for Gabriel to blow his horn. He shook his head.

"You didn't have any beaus to take you driving? I cannot believe all the men of Derby are wantwits."

She giggled. "Oh, I do not believe I was very attractive to the gentlemen, being plump and pale and dowdy. But that wouldn't have mattered. Papa did not believe in fast horses, you see, or in dashing young men. He thought they were all fortune hunters. He also believed that fancy dresses and jewels encouraged a miss to put on airs, and that dancing encouraged young people in licentiousness. So I was never permitted to attend the local assemblies and such, where I could have met those whips."

"Deuce take it, no wonder you ran off with a loose screw like Anders."

"I do hope I would have made a wiser choice had I more experience, but I think I would have run away with anyone, rather than marry Lord Halbersham. He was old and mean, with hair in his nose, and had buried three wives before."

"Good grief, why would your father accept his offer? You were—you are—young enough to wait for others. And with a decent dowry, even plain girls find better partis than that."

"His title was higher than ours."

"Begging your pardon, but your father sounds a curst rum touch."

"Oh, no, he is a good man. Everyone says so. He supports the local foundling hospital and gives money to the church for new pews. His tenants are treated fairly and the servants always have enough to eat. Father is a great believer in noblesse oblige, the responsibilities of the privileged class to look after those who depend on them."

"I *have* heard the term, ma'am," Kerry said with a distinct chill in his voice.

"Oh? Then of course you have schools for your tenants' children. My father did not believe in education for the lower orders; no matter how I tried to convince him otherwise, he held that it gave them ideas above their station."

The horses suddenly pulled at their bits. Kerry forced himself to relax. "Demmed cow-handed driving," he muttered. "That's what comes of having a woman aboard." When the horses were in stride again, he continued: "My tenants are in the care of my bailiff, Wilmott. I am sure he sees to their needs."

"Then *I* am sure there is a school. And a doctor, of course."

"Wilmott manages as he sees fit. Competent fellow, been with me for years."

"If he is so competent, how come your rents have been declining for those same years and tenants keep moving on?"

"Damn—dash it, the whole nation's been in a decline, haven't you heard? It's not *my* fault farm prices are down. And I don't have the funds to do anything about the other stuff, roofs and floods and outdated equipment. You've seen the way I live. Hell, my tenants are most likely living better than I do."

"Then I take it there is no school," Lucinda commented softly, which was the last conversation for a while.

Late in the afternoon, when Kerry was thinking of seeking accommodations for the night, Lucinda told him to take a farm track off to the right.

"What, is there an inn there? I prefer one on the main road that's more used to dealing with fine horseflesh."

"Just turn here, do."

"Oh, you need to use the necessary. Why didn't you say so? I could have pulled over anytime these last miles. Strange, I wouldn't have thought a ghost or whatever would have to—"

"Just drive!" she ordered, blushing furiously.

He turned, but kept teasing. "After all, you don't eat or drink, do you?"

She wasn't listening. That is, she was listening, but not to him. Then he could hear the noise, too, screams coming from a short distance away.

"What . . . ?"

Lucy told him to keep going; the shouting sounded closer. He pulled the horses to a walk, and felt for the pistol in his pocket. When they rounded a bend in the narrow road he could see a group of boys gathered around a smallish pond. The place looked to be the perfect swimming hole—if it were summer and if the boys knew how to swim. Apparently they didn't, for they were shouting on the bank while one of their number bobbed up and down in the water.

"Hell and damnation!" Kerry swore while Lucy urged him to hurry. He jumped out of the curricle, leaving the bays to stand alone—thank goodness they were tired—and ran toward the scene. The boys on land fled into the surrounding woods, likely afraid of being caught playing too near the water, Kerry supposed. The figure in the pond was barely struggling. "Hang on," the earl shouted, looking for a long branch or something to hold out to the boy.

"You'll have to go in after him," Lucy yelled.

"Dammit, you're the supernatural one of us," Kerry yelled back, throwing his greatcoat to the ground, "why can't you part the waters or something?"

He jumped in, boots and all, and swam the short distance to the center of the pond. He couldn't see the child anywhere.

"He's gone down, just ahead of you," Lucy called from shore.

The earl dove, came up for air, and dove again. This time his hands touched something, so he hung on and kicked upward. He got to the surface, raised the dead weight in his arms, and started to turn the air blue with his curses.

"You promised!" Lucy screamed, holding her hands over her ears.

"It's a bloody dog!" Kerry roared back. "I ruined my only set of clothes and my Hessians for a dog!" And he prepared to throw the animal back into the depths.

Lucy shrieked, "Don't! It's one of God's creatures, you heartless libertine!"

Kerry was already wet, and he already had the animal in his arms, so he swam closer to the bank and then waded ashore, dropping the small hound-mix at Lucy's feet. "Here." He even untied the rock from around the pup's neck before returning to the curricle to check on his bays and dry himself off with the lap robe. He was pulling on one of the new ready-made shirts from his valise, when Lucy called to him.

"Kerry, he's not breathing!" Her eyes were huge, imploring.

"That's your department, angel. I did what I could."

"Kerry, please." A tear was starting to trickle down one cheek, leaving a path through the rouge.

"What do you expect me to— Oh, no, not the kiss-of-life bit again. Demby was bad enough, Lucy, but a dog? Never!"

The dog was whiskery and wet and smelled of swamp. Worse, when Kerry was done, the mutt crawled over and licked Lucy's hand.

"Of all the ungrateful— How come he can see you and no one else can?"

"He can see me only now, while he's so close to

death. He'll forget in a minute and won't notice me at all."

Sure enough, the dog, no more than a puppy really, soon whimpered to Kerry, wagging his tail.

"Oh, no, you don't," the earl commanded. "You go find a softer touch. Go on home now, sir."

"He hasn't got a home. He's been living in the woods, close to starvation. If he goes near that farm again, those boys will only try to drown him again, or the farmer will shoot him for bothering the chickens."

"Damn and blast, woman, what do you expect me to do about it?"

So the dog sat between them on the curricle's seat while the earl carefully backed the horses and returned them to the main road.

"He's cold."

Kerry looked down, and the dog was indeed shivering. "With all the heat at your command, can't you . . . ? No, I suppose not. That would be too easy." Soon the puppy was nestled next to the earl's second-to-last clean shirt, buttoned under his greatcoat. No respectable hostelry would take him in like this, the earl considered, so he'd be bedding down in a stable somewhere with his horses after all. But the rouge was gone entirely from Lucy's creamy cheeks, and her lips were now a natural pink color, spread in a happy grin. Kerry felt warm, despite the weather, his wet boots, and the damp dog.

"And it's only a few days until Demby gets here with the rest of my things anyway," the earl conceded.

"Demby's not coming, my lord. He'll send your clothes and belongings when he gets a chance, I suppose."

"Not coming? What gammon is this? Of course Demby is coming."

Lucy bit her lip. "Uh, remember that lottery ticket you gave him?"

Chapter Ten

"Just look at you! Is this any way to enter a lady's drawing room? And without telling us you were coming!"

"Hello, Mother. I am delighted to see you, too," Kerry said, lightly kissing the powdered cheek Lady Margaret Stanford reluctantly offered.

Her nose wrinkled. "What's that odor? And what is that creature with you?"

"It's my new valet. Shall we set a style, do you think? His name is Lucky."

"Oh, you're still a tease." Aunt Clara chuckled, opening her arms for a hug, then thinking better of it. She shrugged and permitted the embrace, so she could whisper in his ear: "Nigel says you'll need your sense of humor around this place."

"I see that everything is the same here." The same overheated drawing room, the same caustic tongue, and the same superfluity of servants, with one coming to take the dog to the kitchen, one to fetch tea, one to notify the housekeeper to see to the master's bedroom. Even the same Aunt Clara, still all draped in mourning crepe for Uncle Nigel after twenty years.

"Nothing is the same, which you would know if you read my letters," the dowager Lady Stanford announced. "We have had to close the east wing due to dampness, cancel the annual open house because the grounds are in such deplorable condition, and I am ashamed to show my face in church after the vicar was nearly killed by a falling roof tile. I have been suffering from an agitation of the nerves for weeks now."

Kerry was suffering from days in an open carriage, nights in various barns, and an incipient head cold. He spoke a little more sharply than he intended: "It's a wonder you don't choose to reside in the dower house, then, if this one distresses you so."

"What, that pawky place? I could hardly entertain. Besides, think of the expense of operating two houses."

Kerry thought of his mother supporting herself on her own widow's pension and leaving this pile with a mere caretaking staff. Talk of pipe dreams! The only abode suitable for the Countess of Stanford, according to the Countess of Stanford, was Stanford Abbey, every moldy corner of it. Then again, if the dowager chose to use her annuity to keep the Abbey in appearances, how could he argue? Of course, he hadn't seen much evidence of her contributions. The drive was so pitted he had to get down and lead his pair through the ruts, for fear of damaging the curricle's wheels. His first view of the Abbey itself, with its hodgepodge of styles and additions, also showed boarded windows, ropes across areas presumably in danger from flying tiles, and shrubbery gone wild. Doors were hanging loose on the stable, and the large indoor staff was in shabby livery.

"Everything will be fine now that you are home, Kieren. We shall open the ballroom and the conservatory, of course. Rehire the gardeners, order new draperies for the public rooms, and—"

"Hold, Mother. If you wish to apply your widow's pension to the improvements, I'll be forever in your debt, for I haven't resources for any of those things."

Lady Stanford did not offer a penny more of her substantial income. "Of course you do. We heard all about your winning at the races."

Kerry wondered how they could have heard so quickly. He glanced at Aunt Clara's nodding gray head. Did she really hear from Uncle Nigel? He'd have to ask Lucy about that.

"I'm sorry to disappoint you, Mother, but I had some necessary expenses of my own. And you cannot have heard of the fire at Stanford House." Or the paintings, he hoped. "My finances are already strained."

"Then why did you come home?" his loving mother asked ungraciously. "I'm already at the edge of ruin, trying to hold house for you while you live the high life in London."

Where Kerry wished he'd stayed. "I know, Mother, and I truly appreciate your generosity. I fully intend to repay you, though I cannot see how at this moment. I came as you requested, to see if there is anything to be done to make the properties more profitable."

"I am sure Wilmott is wringing every shilling out of the place already," Lady Stanford told him angrily.

"Nigel says he's cheating you, Kerry," Aunt Clara put in, earning her a scowl from the dowager.

"That's neither here nor there, Kieren. You'll not make a go of farming. Your father never managed to. You'll just have to marry a rich female. Even your father managed *that*." She spoke with more than her usual degree of bitterness, then cracked her lined face into a smile. "At least you're better favored than the old windbag was. The local girls will be tripping over themselves for an introduction. Naturally I'll make sure you meet only the ones with generous portions. With your looks and the title and my careful attention to those details of dowries, we'll have Stanford Abbey in prime twig in no time."

"Mother, I have no inten—" Kerry began to object.

"Don't think I mean to hang on your coattails either. When I know you are secure, and my accounts have been settled, I'll take a little place in Bath. After a year or two, of course. Your new countess will need me here to show her how to go on before that."

"Mother—"

"Now, let me see, there's Westcott's girl. They were hoping to bring that duke up to scratch, but nothing came of it. And Lady Prudlow's granddaughters will be visiting her for the holidays. We'll have to hold a ball, I think. Yes, that should do it, rather than waiting for invitations." Suddenly the dowager's lined face crumpled in mid-strategy. "My jewels! How can I entertain all those well-dowered females without my jewels? I'll look no-account to Lady Prudlow and that shrewish Isabella Westcott. Oh, how can I ever show my face in the neighborhood without a tiara?" she sobbed.

Clara shook her head but went for the vinaigrette. Kerry took his mother's hand—ringless, he noted with remorse—and swore to make things right. He very carefully did not swear to marry an heiress, but he did vow to do his utmost to recover the jewels his mother had so selflessly sacrificed on his behalf. "Right after dinner I'll start going over Wilmott's books and see—"

"Dinner!" the dowager shrieked. "We're having company for dinner. Look at the time, and I'm not dressed. You must be tired from your journey, Kieren, so I'll have the housekeeper send a tray to your room."

Aunt Clara loudly whispered, "Goldy Flint is coming, the smuggler. I told you so."

"Mr. Gideon Flint is a retired wine merchant, I'll have you know. But if you do not wish to sit to table with us tonight, I shall make your excuses. No place has been laid for you anyway," she sniped, "since you did not see fit to notify us of your visit."

"I am sure a place can be laid for the head of the household, Mother. I'll leave you to dress, then, and see what I can do about repairing my wardrobe. I wouldn't want to embarrass your company by appearing in all my dirt."

Kerry needn't have worried; his odd ensemble fit right in. Aunt Clara was in her unrelieved black, looking like a plump little crow. Lady Stanford wore feathers and flounces, ribbons and ruffles, any number of gewgaws designed to camouflage her lack of jewels. Mr. Flint, whose sobriquet actually came from a gold tooth, not the amazing amount of fobs and pendants he had dangling from his expansive chest, was likewise overdressed in white satin knee breeches. The breeches looked like sausage casings, with the prosperous Mr. Flint stuffed and ready for the pan. His waistcoat was cerise with, naturally, gold embroidery, and his coat was pale blue satin. He resembled nothing so much as a masquerade-goer dressed as a hot-air balloon.

Kerry would have traded. His own outfit, hastily assembled by one of the ubiquitous footmen pressed into valet duty, was culled from the attic trunks. The brocaded lemon and scarlet frock coat was his father's, so it pulled across his shoulders and gaped across his waist. He would have left it unbuttoned except the only waistcoat the doltish footman could find in a hurry was the butler's Sunday best, complete with gravy stains. The peach satin smallclothes were Uncle Nigel's, twenty years in mothballs, and smelling like thirty. Kerry's shoes were a pair he'd outgrown in his university days, so pinched unmercifully. At least the shirt and stockings were new.

The earl was tempted to wonder if Mr. Flint's wardrobe had been lost in a fire, too, except his style of speech seemed to match his style of dress. Without so much as a by-your-leave, the nabob—he could be a pirate, for all Kerry knew—joined the dowager in a discussion of the local debutantes.

"I was wondering your opinion of this wine," Kerry interrupted, to put paid to this conversation, especially in front of the waiting footmen. He also wanted to see if the old rasher of wind knew anything about vintages at all.

"Don't worry about the wine, my boy. I made sure your mother has only the best. You put your mind to finding a wealthy gel, eh?" Goldy crammed another forkful of stuffed prawns into his mouth before turning back to the dowager. "I think your best bet is Westcott's chit, Margie. Five thousand a year, and more if that aunt names her beneficiary."

Margie? No one had ever called Margaret, Countess Stanford, anything but My Lady in Kerry's lifetime. Not even his father. Now some fat old free trader was calling her by diminutives? Aunt Clara was right, by George. His mother was so lonely, so desperate for company, she was taking up with a wine merchant. And a deuced good one, to judge by the Madeira. Meantime, the mushroom was discussing his, the Earl of Stanford's, marriage prospects!

"Wedding a female for her money is a caddish thing to do," he stated in a pause of their conversation. "Degrading for both parties. I do not believe in marriages of convenience." How could he, after knowing Lucy's story?

Aunt Clara was silently applauding, but his mother was astounded. "Don't be a jackanapes. It's the way of the world. And how else can you hope to bring this place about? It's not as though you've gone and thrown your heart over the windmill like some ninnyhammer either." She pointedly ignored her sister-in-law. "So you might as well marry a rich girl."

"Your mother's in the right of it, lad," Mr. Flint put in. "Fellow's got to think with his head, not just his ba—heart. No one said all heiresses have to be antidotes. Leave it to your mother to find you a pretty one. 'Sides, there's not a girl on this earth so platter-faced she wouldn't look bonny in a countess's tiara."

The dowager's fork clattered onto her plate and her lip started to tremble.

"Aunt Clara," Kerry said loudly, "I know you believe in ghosts, but do you believe there is a heaven and hell?" That was the first topic that came to mind, being on his own mind often these days.

"I do not know about hell," Aunt Clara answered after a moment's reflection. "I have never known anyone that bad. But of course there is heaven, dear. Uncle Nigel is only waiting to go until I join him there."

The dowager was over her lapse and glaring. Not only had Kerry exposed Mr. Flint to Clara's dottiness, but religion was *not* a proper subject for the dinner table. Kerry raised his wineglass to her. "And you, Mother, what think you of the afterlife?"

"I cannot imagine anything drearier than spending the rest of eternity in heaven with one's poor relations"—a frown toward Aunt Clara—"unless it's spending it in hell with your father. I refuse to contemplate either."

"And no reason you should, at your tender years." Mr. Flint reached out a fat hand and patted the dowager's arm. Kerry almost choked and Aunt Clara smirked.

"And you, Mr. Flint? Have you thought about the hereafter?"

Gideon took a long swallow of wine. "Well, m'lord, I've thought about it, all right. I like to be prepared, don't you know. It's always paid in my business. I *think* those stories about reward and punishment are tales to scare the kiddies. Just in case there are fleecy clouds, though, with dancing girls and flowing wines, I've been paying my dues at the church."

"You hope to buy your way into heaven?"

"No, they say you can't take it with you. This way it'll be waiting there for me."

After dinner Mr. Flint excused himself. "Hope you don't mind my leaving you to take your port alone, m'lord. Lady Stanford expects me in the parlor, don't you know. We get up a hand or two of piquet. Helps to pass the time."

Kerry had been thinking of a way to warn the man off. The chap was as vulgar as a Punch-and-Judy skit, and as likable, but Lady Stanford and a midnight-merchant? Preposterous. "Fine, fine," he said. "You go on and join the ladies. I wanted to start looking over the books this evening anyway. We'll be too busy for such quiet evenings for some time now, I expect, with the countess planning that ball to entertain every eligible female in the county. Enjoy the card game while you may. You will likely be the last company we invite for a while." There, he congratulated himself, that wasn't too broad a hint.

It was so narrow, Mr. Flint missed it entirely. "Oh, I ain't company, m'lord. Margie treats me like one of the family. You can call me Goldy, lad."

Lucy was ecstatic. "What a wonderful place! It's perfect!"

"Perfect? It's shabby and run-down, overstaffed and undersupervised. These ledgers resemble the Rosetta stone, and the bailiff has been robbing me blind. My aunt has bats in her bell tower, my mother is on the verge of the misalliance of the century with a free-booter who has the run of the place, and you think it's perfect?"

"Oh, yes! Think of all the opportunities to do good deeds!"

Chapter Eleven

The ledger books were not improved by the earl's staying up all night to pore over them. Neither was his cold. The fireplace in his bedchamber wasn't working, according to a footman who reported that chimneys in the unused chambers were not cleaned in the interests of economy, milord. Milord snapped back that economies could dashed well begin in the servants' hall, not his bedchamber. Which conversation, dutifully reported below stairs, had the staff spending a restless night, too, fearful of losing positions or what few comforts the Abbey offered.

Unable to sleep, the glum footmen heard their master talking to himself downstairs in the estate office half the night. Two handed in their resignations before breakfast. Why wait to be dismissed when the employer was not only a nipfarthing, but touched in the upper works besides? Cook huddled in her cot all night with the cooking sherry, praying to be delivered from the Abbey ghosts, so breakfast didn't promise to be any great shakes anyway.

Without coffee Kerry had even less success deciphering the books. For the life of him, he couldn't see where Wilmott was putting the dowager's money to use. His pride nagged at him, that his mother was using her own pension to pay for his household expenses. Every manly sensibility was offended, as if he'd been hiding behind a woman's skirts, living as a gigolo, marrying for money. Furthermore, if her income were intact, she might take herself off to Bath, to meet gout-ridden generals and dyspeptic dukes. Anything but wealthy merchants of questionable backgrounds.

Lady Stanford never went to London, she said, because she could not tolerate the endless embarrassing gossip about her only son and his raffish ways, which she managed to keep very well informed about here in the country. Kerry suspected the dowager's rustication was also caused by an embarrassment of funds. She could not make a splash in the metropolis, and she liked being a big fish in the small pond of Derby society. Kerry made a note to write to Mr. Stenross, inquiring into the exact specifications of his mother's pension. Meanwhile, the idea of sending Lady Stanford to Bath appealed to Lord Stanford, and not just to get her away from Goldy Flint.

So where was the dowager's money going? Was she paying servants' wages off the books, or merchants' bills in cash that was never recorded in the household accounts? Absurd, considering the amounts charged to the estate. There appeared to be enough servants to keep the Tower of London clean and enough foodstuffs to satisfy the Carlton House set. For two elderly ladies? No, Wilmott had to be inflating the expenses and pocketing the dowager's cash, then draining the estate income to pay the bills. No wonder the mortgages were never met. No wonder Kerry never saw a shilling of profit.

Wilmott had to go. At worst he was a crook; at best he was an inefficient manager and a terrible bookkeeper.

Wilmott came to give his notice before Kerry even sent for him.

"Now that you're here, my lord, I can leave with a free conscience. I did my best for you, with no thanks. The land's gone to ruin while you and yourn live high on the hog, and it ain't right, I tell you. Disheartening to a fellow it is, to see his work gone for naught but gaming debts and fancy togs. Did you answer when I wrote as how the income had to go back into the property for improvements? Nary a word. And when I said expenses were too high? Nary a word. Well, now you're back to see for yourself, and good riddance to you, I say. I've had an offer from a gentleman t'other side of the county. Wants to raise sheep. Be a relief to work for someone who wants to raise anything but Cain. And don't worry about paying my salary, you haven't for the last two quarters anyway."

When the echo of the slamming door died, Lord Stanford hunched forward and put his head in his hands. Either the fellow was a fine actor, or Kerry's last chance of making sense out of the estate business had just deserted him. He blew his nose and made a note to pay the man his back wages if he did, indeed, deserve them. Lud, he needed a drink.

"You need some hot soup and a warm bed," Lucy told him, appearing at the end of his desk, looking concerned.

He blew his nose again. "No. Too much to do. I don't suppose you know any magic tricks to fix this mess?" He waved a hand at the ledgers. "I know, you're a demon, not a wizard. Maybe I'd do better to go upstairs and ask Uncle Nigel's advice."

"About Uncle Nigel . . ."

"Not now, Lucy, I've got to do some thinking."

Kerry's immediate concerns were finding an honest, intelligent bailiff, redeeming his mother's jewels, which debt weighed heavily on his mind, and visiting the local haberdashery. The haberdasher came first.

The drive through his property to the village of Standing Falls made him realize like nothing before the extent of his difficulties. A new waistcoat he could afford, and trousers and a superfine coat that needed only minor tailoring. But the fallen roofs, the deserted cottages, the shoeless children, the unfriendly faces on people he'd known all his life—how could he ever hope to fix all that?

Lucy wanted to talk about the Golden Rule. "You know, do unto others . . ."

"I know that, blast it. Don't you think I'd like to make everything right? Or have you painted me so black that I don't care about the plight of these people? It's a wonder you haven't given up on me, then," he added morosely, falling deeper into the doldrums with every new reminder of the poverty around them.

"You could afford to smile, at least. I'm sure *you'd* feel better if people were pleasant to you."

So he waved and tried to smile, with his red, drippy nose and heavy head. The villagers just shook their heads. Drink must have addled the rake's brain box, on top of everything else. Grinning like a fool and talking to hisself. No hope there.

Kerry felt better after the visit to the haberdasher's, especially when his cash payment brought the first sign of friendliness he'd seen. Vanity might be a sin, but a fellow's amour propre suffered grievously in castoffs. Now he was ready to face the shopkeeper in Farley whose chits he held, in place of his mother's jewels. Redeeming the diamonds might take the last of his latest windfall, but a grown man should not stand indebted to his own mother.

Gilmore's on Center Street was almost as discreet as the jeweler Kerry patronized in London when temporarily in dun territory. There was a silver tea service in the window—Kerry was relieved not to recognize the inscribed crest—and some gilt-framed portraits hanging on the walls over shelves of vases, epergnes, and candelabra. Glass cases with velvet-lined shelves held rows of timepieces, snuffboxes, and any kind of jewelry a lovesick swain might purchase to win a lady's heart, any kind of trinket a down-at-the-heels lady might pop to earn a few pounds.

The shop wasn't terribly busy. A young country-dressed couple was looking at rings; a foppish gentleman of middling years in yellow cossack trousers was surveying a tray of quizzing glasses.

Mr. Gilmore left the coxcomb experimenting with each of the lenses to greet his newest—and most prestigious-looking—customer. Kerry's stature and bearing proclaimed his nobility, even if his Hessians would never be the same and his many-caped greatcoat still showed dog footprints. The bespectacled shopkeeper was even more delighted when Kerry presented his card.

"The Earl of Stanford," he read loudly, when Kerry's intention in handing over the card was to maintain his anonymity. Gilmore even bowed at the waist, in case any of his other clientele missed the aristocratic presence in the little shop. The dandy inspected Kerry through one of the looking glasses, like some new specimen of insect, until the earl glared back at him.

"Just so, milord, honored indeed," Gilmore was prattling. "You must be here for her ladyship's diamonds."

"Yes," Kerry replied, trying for a bit of subtlety. "I understand she brought them in to be cleaned."

"Cleaned, is it?" Gilmore chuckled as he wiped his spectacles. "That's the first time I've heard it called that. I'll just fetch them from out back. I never do put her ladyship's goods up for sale, you know, for she always manages to buy them back before any big party. I suppose you'll be having a ball up at the Abbey, now you're to home."

Kerry did not respond, wasting a haughty set-down stare at the gabble-grinder's back. Mr. Gilmore was too excited at having a real earl in his store to notice the icy silence. "Too bad about the gambling," he shouted from behind the partitioning curtain. "They say it's like a disease."

"You, sir, are impertinent," the Earl of Stanford snapped back when Gilmore placed the necklace, bracelet, ring, and tiara on the counter. Gads, first Wilmott, now this bumpkin of a shopkeeper. Did every rustic feel free to comment on Kerry's gaming habits? He turned to scowl at the young couple, who were looking at him as if he were an ax murderer. He almost shouted that his debts were all paid and he'd given up the practice, by Jupiter. And if the man-milliner didn't stop viewing Kerry through that eyepiece, he'd soon find his one enlarged orb closed by Kerry's fist. As for the counter-jumper, no, that was beneath the earl's dignity. He took out his wallet, eager to get this transaction over and done with.

When Kerry turned back to lay his blunt on the glass case, his motions were arrested by the sight of Lucy sitting on the counter, hammering at his mother's diamond necklace with her shoe.

"What the deuce are you doing now? Put that down, I say!"

At which the tulip dropped the three quizzing glasses he'd been stuffing in his pocket while Gilmore's attention was on the earl. He fled, Gilmore in pursuit calling for the watch. The young couple shook their heads and left.

Unaware, Lucy was battering away at the diamonds, to absolutely no avail, of course, since her shoe kept passing right through them. Kerry snatched the necklace out of her reach anyway, and held it up to the window to make sure there was no damage. Then he reached for one of the quizzing glasses the would-be thief had dropped and studied the diamonds even more closely.

"By all that's holy, they're paste!"

"Of course they are, my lord," Gilmore said, returning and mopping his bald head while he caught his breath. "Do you think I would lend the countess this mere pittance if they were real?" The pittance he indicated was almost Kerry's entire bankroll. "Her ladyship would never pawn her real jewels, just the ones she wears every day without fear of losing them." He put the necklace, ring, and bracelet into a velvet pouch, the tiara in a wooden box. "I'm sure the originals are safe at home in your vault."

Kerry was certain they were not; why would the dowager have the vapors over her copies when she had the originals to wear for that blasted ball she was planning?

Mr. Gilmore was going on: "But forgive me, my lord, I have not expressed my gratitude for your alert intervention. The thief got away, but you saved me a tidy sum in trinkets. I am in your debt."

Kerry noticed that the man did not feel indebted enough to hand back the outrageous sum he'd just pocketed for paste diamonds. Paste, for pity's sake!

"And to show my appreciation," the storekeeper was saying, "I'll give you back the rubies at no interest."

"The rubies, you say! They're entailed! Mother could never put them on tick."

"Austrian crystals, this set."

Kerry forked over the last of his ready for glass rubies, and cursed the entire ride home while Lucy's cheeks got redder. Embarrassment or returning rouge, he didn't know which, and he didn't care right then.

The real jewels were not in the vault, of course. What were there instead were receipts for gaming slips—Kerry recognized them well—in payment of which his mother had pledged her rings, bracelets, necklaces, and the diamond tiara. And *his* ruby parure and the Stanford engagement ring.

"I'll strangle her. I'll put my hands around her scrawny neck and I'll—"

"The Chinese philosopher Confucius phrased the Golden Rule in the negative: do not do to others what you wouldn't like done to you."

The dowager hadn't been pawning her valuables to make ends meet, she'd been meeting gambling debts. Worst of all, the name on the receipts, the person now in possession of his mother's jewelry, and the Stanford rubies, was none other than Gideon Flint.

"Why, that . . . that dastard. That's how he got so rich, not by smuggling at all, but by diddling wealthy widows out of their gems. And that's why she lets a loose screw like that run tame at the Abbey. She's so much in his debt, she daren't say no."

"I thought she was just lonely," Lucy put in, still bending over the safe.

Kerry was *almost* too distraught to notice her rounded rear end, but he wasn't dead yet, so he paused in his ranting to admire the view. Backsliding had its advantages; Lucy wore no shift or petticoat. He sighed.

"It doesn't matter what methods that bounder used to win her trust. He holds those vouchers and I'm back in debt. I cannot let my mother be beholden to such a blackguard. Who knows what liberties a pirate like that might take? How in blue blazes I'm supposed to redeem those jewels, I'll never know. And here I was, finally caught up on the mortgages. I even thought I'd have some brass to invest in the Abbey like everyone's always nattering at me to do, so the estate could start paying again."

"Did you know Uncle Nigel had shares in a copper mine in Haiti?" Lucy straightened up, but her hair was all undone. Kerry's hands itched to run through the silky tresses, watching the red turn to gold. He sighed again—he was doing that a lot lately—and bent to look into the safe. He pulled out a partnership deed.

"Good try, Lucy, but the paper is useless. I remember my father raging on about Nigel's West Indies bubble. My uncle put most of his capital in the venture and never saw a ha'penny back. The thing went bust in slave uprisings. And even if it hadn't, his shares reverted to his partners when he drowned."

"About Uncle Nigel . . ."

"No, some worthless copper mine shares can't help me now. It's looking more and more like the home woods have to go after all. Or my horses."

Chapter Twelve

Both. Kerry was going to have to sell off the timber stand after all, and the string of hunters he kept stabled at the Abbey. A quick ride around the home farm to burn off some of his fury before confronting his mother showed him how much needed to done. Even his inexperienced eye put the cost at well over what he could realize from the price of his horses. He hadn't been able to afford the hunt last year anyway; this year looked to be no different. Why should he have the nags eating their heads off in the stables, requiring grooms and exercise boys, when he had better use for the money?

Kerry surprised himself by realizing that he wouldn't mind half so much selling off his stable in order to make an investment in the future. A new plow, say, or having a work crew come in to dig that drainage ditch. But to pay his mother's gambling debts to a rogue of a neighbor who most likely fuzzed the cards besides? Now, *that* was a waste of fine horseflesh, like the prime goer under him right now. To say nothing of that woodland where his tree house still leaned precariously among the branches. Hell and tarnation!

Stanford kept riding at a furious pace, past his property line, past the small farms, past the little village, until he could see a large house on a hill. Lord Humboldt's derelict old place used to be the neighborhood's haunted house, attracting small boys who would dare each other to knock on the door or snatch a fallen chestnut from the big tree beside the windows. Now the mansion was all in lights as dusk fell, with every pane of glass shining, every shrub manicured into precision. Goldy Flint had put his money to good use.

Not quite sure of his own intentions, the earl rode up the graveled carriage path. He couldn't call the cit out; affairs of honor were for gentlemen. If there was one thing Flint wasn't, that was it. Kerry could land the man a facer, though, he thought with eager anticipation, after demanding to know the price to redeem the Stanford rubies. At this moment Lord Stanford was so angry at both his mother and her cardsharp friend that he was willing to let the dastard keep the diamonds, let the countess wear paste.

"The lands come first." Kerry almost fell off his horse when he heard himself say that aloud. He was too used to Lucy's presence. But where had such sentiment come from? Not two days ago he'd happily have consigned the estate to perdition. Must be that plaguey chit's influence there, too, making him act like a mooncalf.

Two grooms rushed forward to take his horse, and two footmen pulled open the double doors at the entrance to Flint's abode. A very proper butler in powdered wig bowed the earl into the marble hall. How many widows had the rogue swindled, Kerry wondered, to afford such a display? He snapped his riding crop against his leg.

Fortunately for Mr. Gideon Flint, the man was not at home at present. The butler informed Lord

Stanford that his employer was away on business for a few days but was certain to call on Lady Stanford at his return, unless his lordship wished to leave a message?

His lordship wished to leave a few broken noses, but he merely nodded politely and returned to his horse, which had been rubbed down and walked.

Blast! But he should have known, Kerry told himself. 'Twas a full moon; likely the old scoundrel was out on a smuggling run. Either that or he'd already heard from the servants' grapevine or that toady Gilmore that the earl was onto his lay.

The countess had certainly been apprised of the earl's foray to Gilmore's and his subsequent fury. She had taken to her room with a severe megrim, her maid reported, caused by overexhaustion with plans for the ball. Short of breath and faint-headed, she was much too ill to grant her son an interview.

"Too faint-hearted, more like," he muttered. He did direct the maid to extend his sympathy. "And tell your mistress I would not for the world have Lady Stanford jeopardize her health, so I insist there shall be no ball. I have already canceled her order for invitations." There, that should take care of that bit of nonsense, too. Undoubtedly the countess would be too weak—and too furious—to descend for dinner either, so Kerry made his excuses to Aunt Clara and rode into town to the local tavern.

The village of Standing Falls used to boast an inn and two pubs. But that was when the mill was operating, when produce wagons and delivery carts and fancy carriages made frequent trips through the village, when every house on the main street was occupied. In other words, when Stanford Abbey was prosperous and supporting the local economy. Now Standing Falls was more fallen than standing. Half the cottages were deserted, the Stanford Arms posting inn was long boarded up, and only one unprepossessing alehouse remained. The church deacons might have been gladdened at the demise of the watering places, except that the house of worship had not escaped the overall decline: the broken church steps were replaced with a series of planks and barrels.

Kerry stepped around the makeshift stairs after leaving his horse at the livery, and made his way to the building under the sign of a torrent of liquid pouring into a mug. The Falls had been at the corner before his birth, serving generations of farmers. Now it served the needs of fieldworkers, servants, tradesmen, and gentry alike.

Some of all were represented this raw November evening. A party of well-to-pass but undistinguished travelers sat at the large table at the center of the room, quietly conferring among themselves over dinner. Kerry had noted their well-appointed carriage at the livery. A red-coated soldier was slumped over his drink at the inglenook, while a clerk of some sort made notes in a pad on the opposite side of the hearth amid numerous satchels and parcels. The local blacksmith and another man Kerry did not recognize were at one end of the long plank bar, and a group of thick-soled farmers were at the other end, warming their hands over mugs of steaming ale.

No one stirred at Kerry's entry beyond a few disinterested glances, so he took a table in the corner, his back to the wall. After a longer-than-polite interval the barkeep, who was also the tavern owner, called from behind the stained wood counter, "What can I do for you, your lordship?"

The blacksmith grunted. A few of the other heads turned, then went back to their drinks.

"Good evening, Ned. And you, Charlie," with a nod to the brawny smith. "I'll have a pint and a menu."

"It's pigeon pie, steak and kidneys, or stew, same as it's been every night for dogs' years. 'Course I don't expect you to recall that, your lordship, seeing as it's been—what? Two, three years since you been here in the neighborhood?"

One of the farmers snickered, his back to the earl. Kerry ordered the steak and kidneys and then started to eat in silence after Ned slammed a dish on the table in front of him. Tacit hostility was better than any more comments about gaming debts, he supposed. And the food was good, hot, and filling, even if it was the plainest fare he'd had in ages.

One or two of the farmers left for their own suppers, and a herder came in with his dog, proceeding to share a bowl of stew with the animal. Kerry was beginning to wish he'd brought the drowned mutt Lucky along; at least he'd have someone to talk to over the meal. Of course he could go back to the Abbey and chat with Aunt Clara. Or Uncle Nigel.

The toffs at the center table were preparing to leave, wrapping mufflers, drawing on gloves, settling their bill, when Kerry next chanced to look up as an odd odor reached his nostrils. The sheepdog? The blacksmith's pipe? The ages-old pigeon pie? No, there was Lucy, looking as wanton and as luscious as ever, patting the shoulder of the redcoat near the fire.

"Stop that!" Kerry shouted in what he was horrified to discover was a loud, jealous-sounding voice that drew the attention of everyone in the room. The earl ignored the startled looks, staring beyond them at Lucy trying to brush back the soldier's hair. He did manage to lower his voice as he asked, "What the hell are you doing here? You don't belong where men are drinking!"

" 'Ere now, who are you to be insultin' one of our brave boys?" Charlie the blacksmith demanded, and one of the farmers, one of Kerry's own tenants, he thought, muttered, " 'At's right, Charlie. Ask him where *he* was during the war."

The gentlemen who were getting ready to depart

looked at one another and shrugged, then hurried about their leavetaking before the scene got ugly.

Kerry gathered his wits back from where they'd gone begging at Lucy's half-bare chest, and apologized to the room at large. "No, no, never meant to insult anyone, especially a soldier. I was just, ah, woolgathering about something else entirely. Here, Ned, pour the fellow a drink on me. In fact, buy one for everyone."

Charlie sat back on his stool, and even the sheepdog's hair lay flat again. Lucy still scowled at the earl when Ned roused the soldier enough to put a fresh glass into his left hand. Now Kerry noticed that the other sleeve was pinned up where his right arm was missing altogether. Oh, God.

"Can't you see he doesn't need another drink?" Lucy chided, trying ineffectually to stop the soldier from spilling the ale in his lap.

"Maybe he'd do better with coffee, Ned, or some hot food." Kerry reached for another coin, but all that was left was his lucky gold piece. He put it on the table.

"Keep your blunt," the barkeep said. "The lieutenant's meals are free. He lost his arm saving my nevvy's life in that heathen place."

The lieutenant may have lost his arm, but Lucy had found it for him. To the earl's horror, she was walking around the soldier with a limp, bare arm, trying somehow to affix it to his shoulder.

"Do you mean that all those missing limbs are waiting for their owners in heaven?" Kerry choked out.

One of the farmers crossed himself and Charlie shook his head. "They was right at the Abbey. Few cards short of a full deck."

But the veteran looked up and smiled sweetly at Kerry. "What a charming thought. That's something to look forward to, at any rate." He lifted his coffee cup in salute. "Thank you, Stanford."

"Johnny? John Norris? Is that really you? Of

course it is. Man, it's been ages." It had been almost ten years, in fact, since Kieren Somerfield had played cricket with the squire's sons on the village green. Kerry'd gone on to the university and then his life in London; Ralph had taken over his father's place right there in Wiltshire, but John had gone off to join the army.

"I'm deuced sorry about your arm, Johnny, and my, uh, tactlessness. I've been in a brown study here, coming home and all." To say nothing of Lucy, who seemed to be checking the clerk's baggage on the other side of the fireplace.

Johnny waved away his apologies. "Welcome back, then, my lord, and take a seat." He indicated the bench next to him.

"It's always been Kerry, John," the earl replied as he carried his drink over and sat down. "So what are you doing now?"

"Drinking. What else is there to do for a one-armed man with no prospects?"

Kerry lifted his own glass. "At least you've got a good excuse."

"Yes, I've heard of your difficulties."

The earl took another swallow. "Everyone has. I'm thinking of selling off my stables. Do you think Ralph would be interested? He used to be horse-mad."

"Still is, and still can't tell a Thoroughbred from a tinker's mule. If your cattle are as bang up to the mark as ever, I bet he'll snap them up in a flash. Be happy to talk to him about it if you wish, get back to you tomorrow."

"Thank you, I'd appreciate that." Ralph Norris would treat the nags well, at least, and he could afford to pay top dollar. Not that it made parting with the horses any easier. Not that it would solve enough of Kerry's problems.

"Not enough, eh?" Johnny asked.

Kerry figured he wasn't a mind reader, just up on the local gossip. "Not by half."

"What you need is an heiress," Lieutenant Norris firmly stated.

"Not you, too, Johnny. That's all I'm hearing, find some fubsy-faced chit whose father's got deep pockets. Old Lady Prudlow's trotting out two well-heeled antidotes again this year."

"Felicia Westcott's not fubsy-faced, and the marquis is warm enough for your needs," Johnny insisted.

"If she's such a paragon, why don't you try for her?"

"What, a second son with no title and no prospects but m'brother's charity? Old man Westcott's too downy a cove for that."

"You're right, my outlook is brighter," Kerry said bitterly. "I at least have the option of selling my title when all else fails. What will you do? Go into government work?"

"A desk job? Never. And the army is done with me, so that ends that career. I intended to be a gentleman farmer, help m'brother run the place, that kind of thing. But I depress his wife. Breeding, don't you know. Sensitive type. And big brother doesn't think I'm capable now that I have only one arm. Doesn't want me out and about lest I hurt myself worse, he says." He threw the mug of coffee into the fire, where it hissed, and called for another ale. "Do you know the best part? All those months of recuperation, lying there, do you know what I did? I read farm journals. Everything I could get my hands on, all about Coke and his new ideas, seed presses and crop rotation. Funny, huh?"

Kerry didn't laugh. "I wish someone would teach me half that stuff."

"Pigs."

Kerry looked around to see who Johnny was calling names. If his foxed young friend was starting a fight, Kerry hoped he didn't pick on the blacksmith.

Lucy was back, sitting beside Johnny, who was

oblivious of her presence. How could he not notice, when Kerry could feel the tingle from here?

"Pigs," Johnny repeated. "That's all you need to know. They're the most productive crop for your kind of land. Feed's the cheapest, they reproduce like rabbits, and the smell's not all that bad."

"Pigs should suit you very well, you bacon-brain!" Lucy spoke up from Johnny's lap, begad! "Love thy neighbor as thyself."

"What?" Kerry couldn't think. Johnny looked at him slantwise, then started to repeat his pig lecture.

Midway through, an exasperated Lucy shouted, "Hire him, you looby!"

A smile started to break across Lord Stanford's face. "Can you ride, John?"

"Well enough. I won't be doing any steeplechasing the way we used to, but I can get by."

The smile was now a grin, lighting Kerry's whole face. "Tell me, my friend, do you believe in heaven and hell?"

Norris shrugged. "Hell was Waterloo. Heaven is every day I'm alive."

So Kerry had a steward. And a secretary. According to Lucy, that clerk by the fireplace, Jeremiah Sidwell, had been dismissed from his recent position for reporting his superior's errors to their employer, who happened to be the superior's father. He was homeless, friendless, and a financial wizard. Just what a penniless earl needed.

Chapter Thirteen

The Earl of Stanford awoke in a better frame of mind in a too-short bed in a guest chamber, but at least the fireplace there worked. He threatened the butler and two footmen with instant dismissal if the chimney in his own room was not repaired by nightfall, he demanded an interview with his mother for that afternoon, and he sent a frigidly formal note to Goldy Flint via his new secretary, requesting an accounting. And all of this before his kippers and eggs. The earl was ready to greet John's brother Ralph at nine in the morning. In London he'd never be out of bed, sometimes not yet in bed.

He took a deep breath on his way to the stables. Yes, even his head was clear. What a relief it was just knowing Johnny was going to be there to help with decisions, Sidwell to handle the details, and Lucy to . . . well, be Lucy. He was used to her, kept peering around corners and sniffing the air for a hint of her presence.

Ralph Norris was thrilled with the idea of owning Stanford's hunters and was prepared to come down heavy for them. He'd even brought cash. The grooms paraded each of the horses out of the stable block and around the ring, and Ralph turned down only a chestnut gelding that had shown some swelling just that morning.

"Save that one for when you hunt with Westcott," he advised Kerry. "The man's hunt-crazy. That's the way to get to his girl."

"I'm not interested in getting to any—" Kerry began, but Ralph wasn't listening. He was staring at the bays, the perfectly matched, record-setting, bang-up-to-the-bits pair that drew the earl's rig.

"I've got to have them, Stanford. And the curricle. I promised the wife we'd go make a stir in London after the baby's born. We had to cut the honeymoon short. Morning sickness, don't you know," he said proudly, making sure the earl was aware he'd gotten his bride in her current interesting condition on their wedding night.

The bays were just what Ralph needed, he decided. The price he offered was hard for a badly dipped man to refuse, especially when Ralph hinted he mightn't take the hunters if he couldn't have the bays.

Kerry looked at his bays again, and then at all the grooms standing about with long faces as they watched their positions being sold off.

The earl could do some bargaining of his own. If he was going to see his horses go, he may as well see the end of some other mouths to feed. "I'll part with the bays, Ralph, on one condition: you take on the stable staff that I won't be needing. You'll require extra men now, and you'll have to have them bring the horses over anyway."

No amount of bargaining or blackmailing could get Ralph to make the mixed breed Lucky part of the deal. The untrained mutt kept jumping up on the earl, leaving stable-dirt footprints on Kerry's Hessians. The dog barking disturbed the horses and interfered with negotiations, and he chewed up Ralph's gloves when he put them down to write a bank draft for the curricle and pair.

"Take him now or I'll give him to your son as a christening gift," Kerry threatened, to no avail. At least Lucky wasn't as expensive as all those stablehands.

Ralph's check went to Sidwell for the bank; the cash went into Kerry's locked desk, not the vault whose combination was known to the countess.

"We'll decide on expenditures after Johnny and I make a more extensive survey of the estate, and after I hear from Gideon Flint." Kerry wasn't even trying to keep his personal affairs secret. Why should he bother in the house when the county knew? Furthermore, the man was already conversant with the earl's financial embarrassments, having gone halfway through the past five years' estate ledgers before breakfast. Kerry checked; they were indeed the same record books he could barely decipher.

There were still hours to go before luncheon—Kerry had never realized how long the day was when one met it before noon—so he decided to make the tour with Johnny, before taking on Lady Stanford. Leaving Sidwell happily making notations, Lord Stanford returned to the stables, pleased with the day's accomplishments.

Until he realized he'd left himself nothing to ride. Johnny was astride a sturdy, well-mannered gray, and grinning. The old head groom, who was staying on along with Lady Stanford's aged coach driver and two young boys, scratched his head. The gelding had poultices on its leg. The carriage horses were placid, plodding beasts who had never been ridden. And Aunt Clara's old mare was as old as Aunt Clara. If the pony from Cook's cart could bear Kerry's weight, his feet would touch the ground.

"There's a horse fair in Farley today," Johnny offered helpfully, still smiling. Kerry allowed as how it wasn't gentlemanly to knock a one-armed man off his horse.

The cash drawer was unlocked; Sidwell made more notations; Johnny would use the time to move his traps into Wilmott's cottage; and Aunt Clara's mare was saddled.

Lucy didn't even come keep the earl company on the long, slow, bumpy trip to Farley. Of course not. A curricle was exciting, fast, and flashy. A tired old nag was beneath Miss Faire's dignity. Now whose value system was suspect?

He'd be late for the interview with the dowager. Kerry was sure she wouldn't mind. He'd also be late for lunch by a few hours, so he bought himself a meat pasty to eat as he walked from paddock to paddock of the horse fair. In Farley at last, the earl vowed to walk home if he couldn't find a suitable mount. It would be quicker.

He needed a horse, but he needed money for hogs. Therefore he bypassed the front lines of horses on display, those he might have considered at Tattersalls. He also once considered a thousand pounds a reasonable price for a colt with potential. Those days were gone, so he tried not to look at the blooded cattle, the prime bits all curried and braided and prancing through their paces. The next ranks of horses were bound to suit his purse better, if not his taste. Meat pasties and someone's breakdowns, he reflected. How the mighty were fallen. Except he didn't feel diminished in the least; he felt more carefree than in years, almost boyish, dripping juice down his chin and planning to bargain like a rug merchant.

The problem was he couldn't find a horse worth considering. If the price didn't start too high, the horse was too old, too flashy, or too light for his weight. That one might be pretty in the park, but would tire under constant hard riding. This one was too excitable to be trustworthy anywhere outside a ring. One was a cribber, another was weak-chested, a third had a bad hitch.

Kerry did ask several grooms to put their horses through their paces, but none showed well. One rider even confessed his horse couldn't jump, when Kerry asked the lad to set him at a fence. Fine mount that one would be to get around land with fallen trees, streams, and hedges.

One horse did catch his eye, a chestnut mare with a white blaze. She had an intelligent look to her, and a nicely compact but graceful body. She just wasn't big enough for him. The mare would make a fine lady's mount, he judged. Too bad he wasn't in the market for one. Lucy would like how the mare came right over to have her ears scratched.

"Lookin' fer a nice ride fer yer wife, gov?" the eager horse coper asked, noting his interest. "T'mare's trained to sidesaddle, she is."

"Sorry, I'm not married."

"Yer sweetheart, then. Fine gent like you has to have a sweetheart. Yer lady friend would look an angel on this pretty horse."

Kerry answered, "My lady friend already is an angel," and walked on.

"That was lovely," Lucy told him, putting her arm through his.

The earl realized that patting an arm no one else could see must look ridiculous, but he did it anyway, hoping for the warm shiver her touch usually brought. "It was the truth."

"The angel part isn't, and you know it, but I meant how nice that you consider me a friend."

A comrade wasn't at all what the horse dealer had meant by lady friend, but Kerry didn't tell her so. He only repeated that of course they were friends.

Lucinda knew exactly what the trader meant; she simply chose to ignore it and be pleased by the earl's words. Smiling, she told him, "I am so glad. I have never had a friend before."

"What, never? Not in the village or at school?"

"My father did not consider the village children fit company for me, and he believed that too much education is bad for a woman, so I was taught at home. You are my first friend."

"Gads," he said, jaw clenched, "I'd like to give you back what you've missed, show you some of the world."

Lucinda only laughed. "I've seen more of the world in your company these past few days than any gently reared female sees in a lifetime! Gaming hells, bachelor quarters, taverns, bordellos, horse fairs. That's the real world, not balls and Venetian breakfasts." She waved her hand around. "This is the real adventure and, look, there are no other women."

That served only to remind him that she didn't belong in a rough place like this with men shouting who-knew-what back and forth across the aisles between makeshift stalls. Thank heaven none of the louts could see how charming she looked this morning, with a wide-brimmed bonnet trimmed with artificial cherries. There was even a lace overskirt to her gown, which was ridiculously out of place here amid the piles of manure.

The sooner he found a suitable mount, the sooner they could leave. Kerry approached the next row of horses with a less critical eye. He'd have to be blind to buy any of those, however.

Lucy must have wandered off while he studied a dappled gray that appeared passable, for she was back and trying desperately to get his attention over the surrounding noise while a groom led the gray around on a lead.

"Over here. Come on." She urged him on to the corner of the next row, where high fences had been put up around a grassy area. Men were sitting on the fence or leaning against it, yelling encouragement or derision to whatever was going on inside. When they got closer, Kerry could see that a door, brass knob and all, was propped against the fence. Rudely lettered on the door was the legend: STALLION FOR FREE IF YOU RIDE IT. 20S. A TRY.

"You can't mean me to wager on this swindle, Lucy. They find a horse that's unrideable, then make a fortune at these country fairs off the cabbageheads who are vain enough to try. Next day they move on to the next gathering of gullible gapeseeds. Half the fence-sitters are in on the hoax, making side bets about how long the rider stayed aboard, how many bones were broken. They even keep the door handy to carry away the casualties."

"Come closer, he's a real beauty."

The huge black stallion was magnificent except for the mud and blood on his sides, the sweating, heaving flanks, rolling eyes, laid-back ears, and flaring nostrils.

Kerry stepped back from his position along the fence. "Lucy, he looks like the meanest brute in creation. No one is going to ride that bonebreaker. It's a waste of coin to try."

"You could."

He laughed. "I thought we were friends. Thank you for the vote of confidence, but this time I'll pass." Kerry looked around at the crowd of men along the fence. "I see a lot of gamecocks corkbrained enough to try, but not one I'd lay my brass on."

"I don't want you to bet against the horse. I want you to buy him!"

"Perhaps you didn't understand the sign. You pay just to try. No one gets the horse, because no one rides him."

"Stop being so patronizing. Just because I cannot pick up a rock and throw it at you doesn't mean I cannot understand the King's English. *You* can ride the horse, therefore you can own the horse."

"Lucy, that is the most foul-tempered animal I

have ever seen. Why would I want to own him in the first place? I wouldn't wish that widow-maker on Gideon Flint. In the second place, I thought you wanted to keep me around for a few more days."

"He's mean only because the owner beats him. The poor thing is frightened half to death."

"Is that supposed to make me more eager to get in the ring with him? It doesn't."

"But when the owner can't find anyone else to try riding him, he'll kill the poor thing."

Her eyes were shining with unshed tears. He looked away. "That's what they do with man-hating horses, Lucy. It's the only solution."

"But he's one of God's creatures."

"So am I, and I don't want you shedding any tears over me, so I'll just keep looking for a nice horse that doesn't kill people for a living. Besides, this is gambling."

"Not if it's a sure thing, it isn't."

A sure thing, eh? Kerry walked around until he spotted the scurvy cur who seemed to be in charge.

"Had many take your challenge today?"

The man spat off to one side and jerked his head toward a bucket on the other. The bucket was almost filled with coins, most silver, some gold.

"That many fools, eh? And you still own the horse?"

The fellow spat again.

Kerry reached for his purse, then put his hand in his other pocket, the one with his lucky coin. "Do I get this back if I win?"

A tobacco-juice-dribbling nod was his reply.

"Then count in one more fool." Kerry tossed his coin into the bucket and asked, "What's the bastard's name anyway?"

"Hellraker."

"It figures."

When Kerry turned from draping his greatcoat over the fence, Lucy was in the pen with the great hulking beast, stroking his nose and whispering in his ear. The stallion seemed to be soothed somewhat, to his lordship's amazement.

"He can hear you and see you?" Kerry asked without fear of being overheard by the screaming gallery of oddsmakers and wagerers.

"'I told you, he's frightened nearly to death, that's why. Now, go on, get up."

Kerry did, with the stallion's quivering acceptance. "Nice Hellraker, good Hellraker. Listen to Lucy, boy. We all do."

The black let Kerry walk him forward a few paces, Lucy's hand on the bridle.

"You gots to trot 'im twict 'round the ring, they's the rules," someone called from astride the fence.

Lucy started running, her hand still touching the horse. He trotted, at her speed, then faster, until her hand was just touching his rump. They all made one lap of the ring.

By then, however, under Lucy's tender influence, the stallion wasn't quite so scared of Kerry, not nearly frightened to death. So he didn't see Lucy floating along beside, or hear her soft voice whispering kindnesses into his ear.

"Oh, dear," she called as the stallion suddenly reared up on his back legs. "I'm afraid you're on your own."

"God damn you to h—" Kerry yelled as the back of Hellraker's neck collided with his nose at great force. The crowd thought he meant the horse. Lucy knew better. She disappeared. Kerry didn't notice, through the pain and the blood and the necessity to hang on to this monster with every ounce of strength he had. If he fell off, no doubt the beast would trample him and then he wouldn't live long enough to wring Lucy's neck. So what if she were already dead? He'd—

Out of the clear blue sky thunder suddenly rolled, a huge peal that meant a lightning storm was almost upon them. It wasn't as loud as the sound of Kerry's nose breaking, but it was a clap of thunder loud enough to put the fear of God into man . . . or scare a horse half to death.

Chapter Fourteen

The dowager fainted when she saw her son. Kerry was not in prime twig for that confrontation but, oh, if he could get his hands on that harbinger of hell, Miss Lucinda Faire.

After the thunder she calmed the wild stallion enough for Kerry to complete the required circuits, get down, collect his gold piece and his greatcoat, and get back up. If he didn't remount then, Kerry knew, the beast would never let him, and he'd never have his mind so muddled that he'd try again. So he owned an incorrigible, unmanageable mountain of a horse. Now all he had to do was get it home. With Lucy gone, of course.

After tossing some coins to a lad to see the mare got back to the Abbey safely, he gestured to the disgruntled thimble-rigger to open the gate. The poltroon did, with a parting stream of tobacco juice for Kerry's boot and a farewell slash of his whip for the stallion.

Well, the earl didn't have to worry about the black taking fences or leaping fallen trees. The beast jumped gates, carts, and pedestrians, anything that got in his way. All Kerry had to concern himself with was wiping away the blood that still streamed down his face, keeping the horse pointed in the right direction, and staying in the saddle. And ridding his world—and afterworld—of the devil's handmaiden.

" 'Vengeance is mine,' sayeth the Lord," she quoted, for it did not take a mind reader to know his thoughts.

Unfortunately, Kerry was in his bath at the time, in the guest chamber. The butler swore the fireplace in the master chamber was being serviced that very afternoon, but the earl could not wait. He was lying back in the tub, trying to soak the aches and pains away, with a cold towel on his nose. That's what the physician had recommended, after realigning the bones. *That* agony Kerry also laid at Lucy's door.

Unhappily for his resentment's sake, she was looking adorably contrite. Her hair was up in loose curls threaded through with ribbon, and her décolletage was enhanced by a scrap of pink lace that still allowed the shadow of cleavage to show through. Her cheeks were rosy without paint, her eyes downcast.

"Oh" was all she said, for it definitely didn't take a mind reader to know Kerry's thoughts this time either.

"Blast!" He grabbed the iced towel and applied it where it could do the most good. "What in blazes do you mean by coming upon a gentleman in his bath? Get out of here!" he raged, sending the two footmen and their cans of fresh hot water back to the kitchen.

"It's not as if I'm a flesh-and-blood female, you know," she started to say when he interrupted with, "Well, I am. Flesh and blood, that is, and I'll pray you to remember it next time you think of entering my bedchamber or entering my name in the lists for mortal combat." He grabbed up a nearby towel and used it as a shield while he struggled into his dressing gown, then headed barefoot down the hall to his own chamber and wardrobe. "And a real lady would look away," Kerry grumbled, forgetting all about his earlier goal of broadening the misplaced innocent's horizons.

Lucinda had no intention of missing a glimpse of a magnificent male body—heaven knew when she'd get another chance—but she did regret the bruises starting to discolor along his ribs. "I am sorry, you know, about Hellraker. Can you not 'forgive, that ye be forgiven'?"

"Only if you stop spouting chapter and verse at me. Hellraker is a superb animal," the earl added magnanimously, reaching for his brush and comb. "And the thunder was a splendid trick."

"Thunder? What thund—"

Then they heard the moaning. A soft, lowing sound seemed to echo in the room around them. "Ooo, ooo."

"What the—?" Kerry tightened the belt of his robe and picked up the fireplace poker. "My word, it must be Uncle Nigel."

Lucy ran after him as he circled the large chamber, looking for the ghost. "Kerry, Uncle Nigel isn't dead."

The noise seemed to be loudest near the hearth. The earl scraped his knee on the andiron, he spun around so fast. "Isn't dead?"

That's when the ball of soot fell through the chimney and landed on Kerry's bare toes.

When the dust and ashes settled, the ball was revealed as a small boy, blackened, scraped, burned, and bloody. And sobbing loudly.

Having as much experience with crying children as he had with flying carpets, Lord Stanford cursed. "Bloody hell." Then he opened the door to the corridor and shouted for help, loudly.

Three footmen, Cobb the butler, Sidwell, and two other soot-covered individuals, one large, one small, entered the earl's bedroom. The large one doffed his top hat and made a bow. "Sorry, milord. They didn't say as 'ow the room was occupied, just to rush. An' Dickie here, 'e's new. Don't know 'is way 'round a chimbley is all. We be almost done now."

He reached out an ash-encrusted hand for the boy, but Dickie darted away, between the butler's legs and out of the reach of the two footmen. He headed straight for the earl and threw his filthy arms around Lord Stanford's bare knees.

"Here now, none of that," said Cobb, gone pale under his powdered wig at the affront to his employer's dignity. He did not, however, reach to pry the grimy child loose. The master sweep did, but Dickie ran to the earl's other side and latched on there.

He looked up with tear-streaked cheeks and drenched blue eyes, and whimpered, "Help me, please, mister."

Oh, hell, Kerry thought, another one of God's—and Lucy's—creatures. Dickie even smelled like her, right through the earl's swollen nose. Kerry bent down to the child's level. "Help you do what, Dickie?"

"Help me get away from Sniddon, please, sir. I don't want to go back up there. It's hot and dark and scary. I want to go home to my mama." He buried his head in Kerry's robe and started sobbing again.

Sniddon, the sweep, made another grab for the boy, but Lord Stanford stopped him with a raised eyebrow. "The child seems to be burned and bleeding. Why is that?"

"It's 'cause 'e ain't learned 'is trade yet, my lord. I told you 'e was new. You don't see Lem 'ere"—the other cinder-dark bundle of rags—"cryin' for 'is ma."

Lem was shaking his head vehemently.

"Lem seems a bit older, perhaps readier for such work."

"An' perhaps 'e's gettin' too big for the job. We needs the little tykes, we does, if you swells want your chimbleys done right. Now, I'll just be takin' the lad, my lord, an' gettin' on with the work you 'ired me to do."

The butler was nodding, the footmen were nodding, and Lem stared at his bare, scarred feet. The earl made no move to detach the clinging arms.

" 'Ere now, my lord, gimme the boy. You got no call interferin' in my business. I got papers, all right an' tight, to say I bought 'im proper."

"It's illegal to buy children, Sniddon."

" 'Is services, I meant to say. Apprenticeship is legal, ain't it, my lord? Paid ten shillings for 'im, I did, to use 'im till 'e's growed."

"No, he didn't, mister," the little boy wailed. "I was stole by Gypsies and he bought me from them."

"Gammon. 'Is ma sold 'im to buy gin, is what."

"My mama would never do that! You're a liar! I want to go home!"

Kerry believed the child. He did not believe all the bruises on Dickie's bare arms and legs came from climbing chimneys. Even if they were, the boy was little more than a babe, five or six at most. With a deep sigh and the thought that this deed should get Lucy a lot closer to heaven, Kerry reached toward his dresser for a coin. His lucky coin. He tossed it to Sniddon, who bit down to check the gold content. "It's real, and worth twenty-one shillings. Now, take it and get out without another word or I'll call in the magistrate to investigate your so-called papers of apprenticeship."

Sniddon took the money and Lem and departed. The butler exited with a flea in his ear about getting machinery in to clean the chimneys next time, or dangling the multitudinous footmen by their heels with rags on ropes. "Anything but another infernal scene like this one," the earl insisted. Then he demanded a maid or someone to come take charge of the brat. It seemed there was no such creature at Stanford Abbey.

There was Mrs. Cobb, the housekeeper, but she was as starchy as his nibs in the wig, according to the footmen. She didn't consider filthy urchins to be in her province. Lady Stanford's abigail rode an even higher horse. Cook was in the middle of supper preparations, and whatever maids hadn't left on account of the ghosts had left on the earl's arrival.

"Your lordship's reputation, beggin' your pardon, my lord."

Kerry ran a hand through his hair and looked beseechingly in Sidwell's direction. "Sorry, my lord, I know only numbers. I'll, ah, list the guinea under housekeeping expenses, shall I? Or under charity?" And the secretary fled before he could be dragooned into nursemaiding a weeping tot.

Just when Kerry feared he'd have to bathe the child himself—drowning seemed the only way of dislodging the barnacle—his prayers were answered. A female voice filled the air with motherly warmth: "What's the meaning of this outrage, you sap-skulled booby? I have company coming for dinner tonight, so why is the chimney sweep leaving before all the rooms are done? And why are you covered in soot? You'll have to hurry to fix yourself up. You still look like death in a dressing gown."

"Thank you for your concern, Mother, but you'll have to excuse me. I don't think any amount of effort will make me presentable to company this evening."

"That's neither here nor there. The Westcotts are coming and bringing Felicia, apurpose to meet you, so you'd better be there. It would be the height of rudeness to disappoint them. And don't look daggers at me. Since you canceled the ball, someone has to look after your interests and make sure you meet the proper young females."

"And someone has to make sure there is no intimate family dinner where we might discuss the Stanford rubies."

"Fustian. There is nothing to discuss. But what, pray tell, is that piece of offal clinging to your leg? Get rid of it at once."

Kerry ruffled the boy's hair—his hand was already smudged—and asked, "Do you like dogs, Dickie?"

"Oh, yes, sir," Dickie answered, wiping his nose on his filthy shirttails, to the dowager's further disgust, and staring up at the earl with worship in his eyes.

"Then this, Mother, is Master Diccon, my new kenneler. Of course he commands only one dog at the moment, but we are starting small."

"And that way you won't miss me so much when my mama comes for me."

Finding Dickie's mama might be harder than finding the proverbial needle in the haystack, Kerry feared. The needle might want to be found; Dickie's mama might not if she had, indeed, traded the boy for Blue Ruin. Lord Stanford just smiled and said, "I'll share my mama with you until then," which effectively curtailed the dowager's incipient lecture on duty, dignity, and dressing for dinner.

So Lord Stanford took another bath, after scrubbing Diccon through three changes of hot water. The child had started bawling again when Kerry tried to hand him over to a footman, so it was easier to do the job himself. He was already besmirched, and something about the boy's tears caught at emotions he never knew he possessed. Washed, the boy's hair was blond and curly, reminding Kerry of the cherub in the oil painting he had held back from sale. For his sons. Yes, an heir mightn't be a terrible idea after all, especially if he was a trusting, adoring tad who thought you could shake hands with the man in the moon. Of course Kerry might prefer his son to have his own brown hair instead of this pale yellow. Then again, gold-glinting red was nice.

The infant cleaned up better than Kerry did. Soap and kitchen salve might work wonders on the boy's bruises; nothing was going to mend a bulbous scarlet snout in time for public viewing.

Aunt Clara came to the rescue then, having rummaged in the attics for long-outgrown nankeen shorts and jackets while Kerry introduced Dickie to his old tin soldiers and some picture books from the nursery.

Even bubble-headed Aunt Clara noticed what a fine, well-mannered boy he was, no street beggar or city foundling at all. After more questioning they discovered that his name was not Dickie either, it was Richard, Richard Browne. But Diccon was what his father called him, so that was all right. Mr. Browne's name was, of course, Papa. And Diccon knew precisely where he lived: in London, near the park. There were only a few thousand Browne families in London, all near some park or other, but one bit of information seemed hopeful: Diccon's father sometimes took him to work, at a furniture warehouse.

Sidwell was put on the case at once, to contact Stenross in London and Bow Street if necessary. Someone had to be looking for the boy. Diccon was convinced to go along with a footman to view Lucky in the stables. His new charge might be permitted to sleep in the nursery that night, if he promised to be good and release his death grip on the earl's leg.

Aunt Clara started weeping as she watched the boy solemnly take a footman's hand. "Nigel and I wanted a big family, not like your mother, who was relieved to have the heir first thing. We weren't married long enough. Oh, how I wish I could have had a son of his to remind me, even after he was gone." She was sobbing into the handkerchief Kerry hastily handed over.

"Uh, Aunt Clara, they never did find Uncle Nigel's body, did they?"

"No," she sniffled. "I had them bury his fishing gear instead. I insisted on a headstone, you see."

Kerry didn't see at all, but knew he had to wait for Lucy to find out any more. He hurried back to his room to finish his own toilette. She was there waiting, and glowing.

Her gown seemed more rose-colored than red, and her hair, which looked more gold than titian tonight, was held back with a silk rose. Mostly she was smiling a smile that warmed the whole room, just for him.

"What you did was magnificent, and without any prompting."

"Oh, it wasn't so much," he preened. "I couldn't have the nipper blubbering all over the place, could I?"

"You could have handed him back to the sweep. Or had him carted off to the workhouse."

"He's just a baby!"

"Oh, Kerry, you do have a conscience after all!" The kiss she placed on his cheek *almost* felt like a summer breeze. And it *almost* made his nose feel better.

"Don't worry about that, it will heal only a little crooked."

"Crooked? My nose is going to be crooked?"

"Well, I think it will make you better looking, not so intimidatingly perfect. And you know what they say about vanity."

"No, and I don't want to. I do want to know about Uncle Nigel. What do you mean, he's not dead?"

"I checked. He's very much alive and living in France."

"In France? For all these years? Without telling anyone?"

"There was a war on, you know."

"I suppose he could have been captured and been

a prisoner of war," the earl said doubtfully. "But why hasn't he come home now that the war is over?"

"Well, he wasn't exactly a prisoner of war. He was more a spy."

"Then the government should have made a special effort to get one of their own people out earlier than this!"

"That's just it," she said as the dinner gong rang. "He wasn't a spy for England."

Chapter Fifteen

Dinner was not the complete disaster Kerry expected. His attire this evening was not up to Weston's standards in fit or style, but it was acceptable for a country gathering. The deficiencies went unnoticed in light of his battered face, which the Westcotts were too well bred to comment upon. Only John Norris grinned, until Kerry invited him to trade his cob for the black. Then Lord Westcott had to be shown the fearsome beast, so dinner was delayed for a trip to the stable, where Diccon was still playing with Lucky. The marquis was inclined to be suspicious of the boy's presence in a known libertine's household, but he was impressed with the horse despite himself.

"I wouldn't have gotten on his back for anything, not even in my salad days. Tossed salad, I'd be. I daresay a broken nose is a small price to pay for such a noble animal."

And Lord Westcott was off in a rambling, one-sided discourse of all the mean, unbroken horses he'd ever encountered. His monologue lasted through the soup course, the fish, meat, poultry, and sweets, with removes, and was directed to the entire table, not just his partner, the dowager. Lady Stanford kept a smile fixed on her face and pointedly fingered her paste diamonds whenever Kerry looked down the table in her direction. As if he needed a reminder that Westcott was as rich as Golden Ball, and had just the one chick.

Miss Felicia Westcott was a pretty girl, fair-haired, soft-spoken, elegantly dressed in a demure white gown with pearls at her neck and laced through her hair. Kerry thought he might have danced with her at some ball or other but he couldn't be sure; all debutantes tended to look alike. She blushingly denied it when he asked if they'd been introduced, so he gathered she'd been warned off rakes like him. But her duke hadn't come up to scratch, so the Earl of Stanford did not seem quite so reprehensible.

Well, marrying an heiress didn't seem quite so outrageous now either. Kerry vowed to keep an open mind.

Still, he was in no hurry to join the ladies after dinner, even though Lord Westcott's cigar made his hands shake with wanting a cigarillo. He sipped his port instead, and asked Johnny about his day appraising the lands for hog farming.

At the mention of hogs, Lord Westcott set off on a whole new saga of unruly beasts, culminating in the boar that had just trampled poor Tige Welford, one of his tenants. The widow was wanting to up and leave as soon as she could find someone to buy out her herd of pigs. Except for the boar. She'd shot the bastard and was even now making sausages. Westcott thought Kerry could get a deuced good bargain if he hurried. On the pigs, not the sausages.

Johnny was thrilled, even Kerry was excited. Sidwell was more cautious when consulted, citing the other costs involved. They carried the conversation and their glasses into the drawing room, where Miss Westcott was posed gracefully at the pianoforte. The marquis took a seat in the corner and placed a handkerchief over his face for a nap. Aunt Clara was sewing by the fire, and the two other ladies were enjoying shredding reputations on the sofa. Kerry directed John to turn Felicia's pages, so he could continue the discussion with Sidwell of how much of the horse sale money they could afford to pay out, after the secretary's study of the estate's income and expenses. Kerry did notice that Miss Westcott played adequately, more or less in keeping with Herr Beethoven's intentions, and softly enough not to impede conversation around her.

All in all, he congratulated himself after, it was a satisfactory evening. Of course he'd had to accept Lord Westcott's invitation to a hunt two days hence; that was the least he could do in recompense for the tip about Widow Welford's pigs. Lord Westcott declared he wanted to see the black in action. Kerry didn't need Johnny's wink and his mother's satisfied smirk to know the marquis actually wanted to see his prospective son-in-law in action.

"Tell me again about Uncle Nigel, Lucy. I don't know why I'm having such a hard time accepting it. After all, if I can think nothing of having a comfortable coze with a soul in transit, I should not cavil at Uncle Nigel's being a spy."

Kerry was sitting in front of the fireplace in his own room, sipping a cognac. Lucy was sitting across from him with her embroidery, but the mirror over the mantel showed a solitary gentleman in his robe and slippers, talking to an empty chair.

Lucy set aside the altar cloth and smiled. "He never wanted to be, you know."

"I didn't suppose anyone ever wanted to be a spy. I mean, it's not as if some boys are mad to enlist in the army, others hear a calling to join the clergy, and Uncle Nigel grew up itching to be a traitor to his country. All Nigel wanted to do, as far as I ever heard, was go fishing."

"And so he did that day, but his boat capsized. While he was hanging on, waiting for rescue, a fishing ketch came along. Only it wasn't really a fishing boat, and the sailors were not English. They gave him the choice: stay there or come with them back to France. They would not return him to the English shore for fear of the patrols. He might have been rescued, but his arms were getting tired, and the water was getting cold. So he accepted their offer."

"Understandable. He was just saving his own skin."

"Yes, but then the smugglers felt he owed them something for their trouble, so he helped them unload their cargo."

"Which was?"

"Guns."

"Which was treason."

"Exactly. And they said they'd kill him if he didn't tell them everything he knew."

"About what, for pity's sake? Uncle Nigel wasn't with the government or anything. He was just a gentleman of modest means who liked to fish."

"And who knew every current and tide and shoal on the coast of England and half of Scotland."

"Fiend seize it, so he did. And he told them?"

She shrugged. "He did not want to die. After he told them what they wanted, the French let him go to find his own way home. Ashamed of what he'd done, he thought he'd skulk around and discover their plans, to report back to the British."

"To prove his loyalty."

"Precisely. Instead, he got shot."

"But not killed?"

"No, he was taken in and nursed by a family of peasants who made a living fishing. As soon as he was recovered, he intended to pretend to be one of them, to earn passage home on another smuggling boat. Except . . ."

"Except?" Kerry was grinning now. Uncle Nigel's saga was starting to sound like a Minerva Press novel.

"Except that while he was unconscious, the patriarch of the family had him wed to one of the granddaughters. Nicolette was increasing, with decreasing chance of her *chère ami* coming forward."

"The marriage wasn't legal. He was already married, for one, unwilling for another."

"And not Catholic for a third. The family did not care. And Nicolette begged him to stay until the baby was born. What could he do? He had no money, these people had saved his life, and he had no state secrets to bring back to British intelligence anyway. The English would hang him, the French would shoot him. And Nicolette's father would skin him alive if he tried to escape."

"So he stayed all these years?" Kerry finished off his drink and sat up. "What about Aunt Clara?"

"He thought she could never forgive him, so he might as well stay away and let her get on with her life, remarry, have the family they wanted."

"Poor Aunt Clara."

"And poor Uncle Nigel. He wants so badly to come home to her—Nicolette has been dead for years—now that the war is over, but cannot afford to."

"Dash it, I can scrape passage money together. I can pawn my watch again, or Mother's paste diamonds."

"For two thousand pounds?"

Kerry sank back. "What, is he planning on buying a yacht to bring him across the Channel? Won't the packet boat do?"

"He cannot come home without a pardon. Living in France all those years, aiding the enemy . . ."

"With a few tide tables?"

"He also did some interpreting of smuggled papers, to earn extra money for the children."

"The children? No, don't tell me. This pardon thing, one doesn't just petition for it? We can get character witnesses, explain away the whole bumblebroth."

"In a perfect world, yes," she said with a frown. "In this one it requires bribes. Support for the Crown, I believe they call it." She took up her needlework again, angrily stabbing the needle through the fabric.

"Two thousand pounds." Kerry dropped his head back against the cushions. "Where the bloody hell am I going to get two thousand pounds? I already told Johnny we could use most of the horse sale money to buy the hogs, so there'll be an income down the road. And Sidwell thinks that if we chop down the home woods timber, we can earn enough to make the improvements necessary to get the tenants back, hence the rents. But that's years away. I even informed the countess that I couldn't pay a farthing toward her gaming debts. She fainted again, incidentally, when I told her that Flint can wear her diamonds on his next smuggling raid for all I care, but if he tries to sell the Stanford rubies, I'll have the both of them arrested. If I cannot afford to retrieve the engagement ring, I cannot afford to retrieve Uncle Nigel."

"So you liked Miss Westcott?" Lucy asked with feigned indifference.

"She's a pleasant enough chit. But that wasn't what I meant."

"She liked you." Lucinda sucked on the finger she pricked.

"She liked Johnny and Sidwell, too. Did you see the priceless look on Mother's face when I announced I'd invited my secretary and my steward to dinner? That alone was worth all the insipid chit chat. Evened the numbers at table, at any rate, and gave Miss Westcott her choice of gentlemen to flirt with. Of course Johnny stared at her like a mooncalf all night, and Sidwell stammered, but Felicia was happy."

"You didn't stare or stutter, yet she appeared pleased with your company." And why not? Lucinda asked, but kept the thought to herself. "So she might welcome your addresses. Then a match there mightn't be a simple financial arrangement, her money for your title."

"Now you're sounding like Aunt Clara, who looks for April and May everywhere. Everywhere but France, of course. No, I was not struck all aheap by Miss Westcott, and I doubt she is ready to throw her bonnet over the windmill for an earl residing in Queer Street."

"But if you could find pleasure in her company, and she in yours, then love could follow duty." Lucy ripped out the line of stitches she'd just sewn and bundled the cloth away.

"I doubt Miss Westcott has two thoughts to rub together beyond her clothes and her entertainments," he noted, holding his still-full glass of cognac toward the fire, watching the colors change. "Oh, and her horses."

Lucinda tilted her head to one side, studying his face. The only change she could see was the swollen nose and a healthier color. "But that's all you were interested in just a few days ago."

"Was it just this week? I feel I've known you forever." He laughed. "And is this effort to promote a match with Miss Westcott another thread in your fabric of my reformation? I thought we were doing well enough with saving fallen sparrows. Must you aim for leg shackles, too?"

"I wish to see you a better man, yes. But I like you, Kieren Somerfield. I also want to see you happy."

"Thank you. That means more to me than a hundred flirtatious simpers or batted eyelashes from the likes of Felicia Westcott. I like you, too, Miss Lucinda Faire."

They sat in comfortable silence broken only by the hiss of the dying fire, each deep in his or her own thoughts. Then Lord Stanford cleared his throat. "Ah, Lucy, if Uncle Nigel is alive in France, who the devil is Aunt Clara talking to?"

Chapter Sixteen

Dawn was not the best time for exercising horses—unless you wanted to make sure no one saw you make a cake of yourself falling off. Then again, it might be hours before anyone thought to look for his bruised and bloodied body. Kerry rather preferred it that way.

He'd prefer not to face Hellraker at all. His body was not in shape for another explosive battle of wills, and might never be. The horse would only grow more unmanageable left unridden, though, standing in a stall all day. It was better to school him again now, while he remembered yesterday's lessons.

Hellraker remembered, all right. He laid his ears back and ripped off a piece of the earl's jacket. He kicked and bucked and reared, but he got ridden to the point of exhaustion. The stallion learned—for the day at least—that he couldn't loosen Kerry from his back no matter what tricks he used. He also learned he wasn't getting whipped or raked with rowels at every turn. There was no blind obedience yet, but a little respect.

The respect went both ways. Lord Stanford came to appreciate the black's strength and stamina, and his courage, too. There was no hedge so high the stallion wouldn't take it flying, no stream so wide he didn't soar over. With a little more practice, the brute could make a fortune at every steeplechasing event in the county, if Kerry were a betting man, of course. He wasn't, not right now. Those cross-country events took a high toll on horses anyway, he consoled himself. 'Twould be a shame to have such a superior animal lamed.

Or maybe not, Kerry thought as he lost the rest of his sleeve rubbing the beast down. The real shame was that he'd let go all those stablehands. His head groom was too old to dodge the flying hoofs, and the younger lads were far too green. The only one the stallion seemed to tolerate, aside from his lordship, was the fool dog Lucky.

"Just make sure Diccon doesn't get too close," the earl instructed. Lud, what would happen if the boy followed the pup into Hellraker's stall? Had he ordered enough servants to watch out for the boy's welfare? Aunt Clara said she'd have breakfast with Diccon in the nursery, but what then? Gads, a child was a headache. If the Brownes weren't located soon, Kerry supposed he'd have to hire a nursemaid, then a governess, tutors. After that would come a school or a trade. In the meantime were clothes and books and toys and food. Enough food for a growing boy's appetite could bankrupt him. Zeus, when he remembered his own schooldays, he wondered if even the new pigs would be safe.

Which reminded him that he was going to need a boar soon, if he wished to stay in the hog business. All this worrying about money made him feel crass, mercenary. Dash it, things were easier in the old days, when fortunes were won or lost on the turn of a card.

Johnny Norris was back from Welford's farm with good news about the pig deal. They were ready to be fetched as soon as Stanford Abbey was ready for them. Unless they were to be lodged in the east wing, where the roof still leaked, the home woods had to go.

"But not the whole of it," Johnny contended. "I never thought much of that clear-cutting. We could just take what we need in the old growth, let the young trees get more sun. That way you keep the rabbits and quail and deer, and have more timber to cut in a few years' time."

"That sounds too reasonable. Why doesn't everyone else do it that way instead of clearing the whole stand and planting over it?"

"It's harder," Johnny admitted. "Takes more manpower, and you get less yield all at once. But long-range . . ."

So Kerry lined up all those useless footmen, everyone but Simpson, who had a knack with neckcloths, Jeffers, who had Diccon riding on his shoulders, and Derek, who lisped.

"I don't need my silver polished to a fare-thee-well, nor my rugs beaten to a pulp," he told the assembled servants. "I need pens and troughs and sheds, and fields ready to be planted come spring in pig fodder. I need drainage ditches dug, roof tiles replaced, roads graded. I'll understand if you wish to stay as footmen in your warm jobs and clean livery, but you can't stay here. I cannot support you, not with all the additional men I'll need. You'll get references and your pay. If you decide to stay on, there will be a rotating schedule of housework and field jobs, and I promise a return to your usual positions as soon as circumstances permit."

Most of the footmen accepted, knowing how few jobs there were these days, and so did the young grooms, the tenants who were behind in the rents, and whatever out-of-work villagers Johnny could find. With a few experienced lumbermen hired on from Farley, the Earl of Stanford and his crew sallied forth.

In no time at all, fence posts were being cut, and fingers. Shed poles were being raised, and blisters. Shovels, axes, and saws were being employed, and muscles long unused to such hard physical labor. The Earl of Stanford was right there with the men, digging holes and splitting wood or loading fallen trees onto wagons for the lumber mill.

Sweaty and sore, his clothes in muddy tatters, his only pair of boots scored and scraped, the once-fastidious earl was thinking that an heiress mightn't be such a bad thing. Which was a good thing, for Sidwell came out to tell him that Lady Prudlow and her granddaughters had arrived for tea.

He tried, he really did. He made polite conversation, he made insincere compliments. With a Prudlow sister on either arm, he made a tour of the portrait gallery. They giggled and tittered; he shut his ears. For all his attempts to kindle a spark of interest in his own breast, the earl kept wishing he was back in the fields with the men. For all his sipping catlap and nibbling macaroons, he couldn't even tell which Prudlow chit was Priscilla, which Patricia. At least Miss Westcott had a bit of presence.

Just as he was wishing the sisters and their garrulous grandmother to Jericho, Cobb the butler came into the drawing room, his wig askew. It seemed there was a commotion of some sort in the hallway, and without the legions of footmen, he was forced to handle things himself. Could his lordship be so kind as to step outside a moment?

Kerry went, followed by his curious female relatives and their even more rudely inquisitive guests. Derek, the footman who lisped, was trying to deal with box after box being unloaded from a hired carriage that was drawn up at the front door. Diccon was underfoot, for his temporary nanny, Jeffers, was outside doing the unloading, and Lucky was barking. Simpson, the footman elevated to valet just that morning, had taken one look at the names on the boxes—Weston, Stultz, Hobbes—and had gone to join the men in the fields.

"What the—?" Kerry recognized the formal tailcoat he'd ordered before leaving town, but these carefully folded shirts, waistcoats, and breeches couldn't be the clothes Demby was to have cleaned and sent on if the smell of smoke came out. Kerry's whole wardrobe could have been contained in a small trunk, not this mountain of apparel in boxes bearing the names of London's best outfitters.

"There is a letter, my lord." Cobb held out a silver salver.

"Will you excuse me, ladies?" Kerry asked, hinting the women back into the drawing room to continue their tea. "Perhaps Diccon could have a raspberry tart, Aunt Clara?" No one left, and Diccon continued chasing Lucky through the piles of parcels, trying to get a brand-new York tan glove out of the pup's mouth. The Prudlow sisters giggled while their grandmother surveyed the scene through her pince-nez. Aunt Clara was admiring one particularly fancy waistcoat embroidered with forget-me-nots, and Lady Stanford was fuming.

"You can't afford a few piddling gaming debts, eh?" she hissed in his ear, punctuating her remarks with a jab to his midsection. "A ball is too expensive, eh?" Another jab. "You can't finance an adequate household staff, what? But you can rig yourself out like a caper merchant, is that it?"

Kerry stepped aside before she punctured his abdomen. "I swear I had nothing to do with this. If I may be permitted to read the note?"

She didn't give permission; he withdrew to the steps and read anyway.

Demby—for the note was indeed from the earl's former valet, groom, et cetera—wrote about winning the firemen's benevolent raffle lottery, which Kerry already knew. He was sorry, but he would not be returning to the earl's service, which Kerry also knew. Demby was buying a partnership in a small foundry, where he hoped to set up a studio and shop, to work on his sculpture. This was not very surprising, considering the man's revelations on the night of the fire. What was amazing to his lordship was Demby's next line, that he wished to share some of his windfall with his former employer. Not only had Lord Stanford given him the winning ticket, Demby wrote, and saved his life to boot, but the earl had also given him employment where he was free to practice his art. (No mention was made of Demby's feigned tremors, nor the fact that the job was practically a volunteer position in recent times.)

In return, Demby wished to show his appreciation. But how? He knew his lordship's casual attitude toward money, that the earl would lose whatever Demby sent before the ink was dry on the check. He was taking the liberty, therefore, of sending along those recently ordered replacement items for Lord Stanford's wardrobe, and a few additions.

Kerry looked around. Those few additions included enough satin knee breeches to clothe an Almack's gathering, enough lace and linen cravats to strangle the House of Lords, and enough beaver hats to cause extinction of the species. Nightshirts, stockings, dancing slippers, nothing was overlooked—except sturdy boots, woolen shirts, heavy fustian trousers, and a frieze coat for carrying hogmash.

Sitting down on the marble steps amid all that splendor, Kerry threw his head back and laughed. The roof was literally falling down around his head, he hardly had a pot to put his pigs in, debts were piled atop obligations, and he'd be dressed better than Beau Brummell. He laughed even harder when Diccon and Lucky knocked over a box containing a stack of silk drawers. He held one pair aloft, sending all three Prudlow ladies scurrying for the door, and gasped, "And they said you couldn't make a silk purse out of a sow's earl!"

When he finished wiping his eyes, the hallway was empty of everyone but Lucy, who was shaking her finger reprovingly. "That was not well done of your lordship." But her lips twitched. "If there was anyone in the neighborhood who hadn't heard you had a draft in the rafters, they'll be informed by nightfall. And those were nice girls you just chased away!"

"They were ninnyhammers, and you know it. Why, marriage to a peahen like that would send me hieing back to London and one expensive mistress after another, so where would be the benefit? Not in morals, not in the pocketbook. Be content for now, I'll be the best-dressed pig farmer in Wiltshire."

"Just don't go getting puffed up with your own conceit again," she warned. "Your nose hasn't healed yet."

The earl went to bed early that night, throwing out his new valet, lisp and all, before Derek was through the unpacking. Kerry'd been up since dawn at hard physical labor, and had to face Lord Westcott, his hunt, and Hellraker in the morning. Mostly, though, he was hoping Lucy would come again. He was eager to see if his hard day's work met with her approval, if there'd been any change in her appearance to match his blisters and scrapes.

He laughed at himself, inventing excuses to look at Lucy. Why, he hardly took his eyes off her when she was in the room. She fascinated him, he admitted, all innocence and passion combined. He'd never known a woman like her, and not just because she was a specter. If he had to choose a wife, that was the type of woman he wanted, halfway between devil and angel, not some milk-and-water miss like the Prudlow girls. They could never hold a candle to Lucy anyway. A man wouldn't get bored with a female like Lucinda Faire, with her challenging mind and caring nature. And honesty. Why, no woman had ever said she liked him before. There was flattery aplenty, and protestations of undying love, especially outside the jewelry shops, but never simple, honest liking. A man could even trust a female like that, as opposed to a Miss Westcott, whose motives must ever be suspect.

Lucy was a *real* woman. No, blast it, she wasn't a real woman at all. If he tried to touch her, his hands would go right through. If he tried to hold her, call her, keep her, she just danced through his dreams the way she drifted through his life, turning everything upside down.

And he needed a woman, especially after thinking of Lucy, even if he did not need a wife. Celibacy was not Kerry's strong point, nor a virtue he saw much point in pursuing, except that *she* was sure to appear then, and not now, when he wanted her company. Lucy would be steaming mad, singeing him—if not his privates—with her scorn.

The thought did much toward cooling his ardor. Perhaps he could live without a woman's services for a while after all, especially if he had Lucy's lively conversation and luscious form to admire.

She never came.

Kerry rolled over and went to sleep, thinking the hell with her. And dreamed of her anyway.

Chapter Seventeen

If clothes made the man, Kieren Somerfield was the warlord of Wiltshire, the hero of the hunt. His scarlet jacket was a marvel of tailoring, allowing supple movement while defining his broad shoulders and narrow waist. The doeskin breeches fit like a second skin, and the white high-topped boots gleamed with a champagne polish. Demby had outdone himself, with Derek's help. The earl was splendid, except for the vivid colors around his nose that rivaled the scarlet jacket in brilliance.

If the mount made the rider, however, Kieren Somerfield belonged on the wooden rocking horse in the nursery. Hellraker did not appreciate the yowling hounds, the blaring trumpet, or standing around in Westcott Hall's carriage drive, waiting for the rest of the hunt to assemble. In ten minutes Kerry's cravat was disordered, his hair was disheveled, and his hat was missing altogether.

Going on the hunt had not been a good idea. Polite and politic, but not clever. Hellraker was untested, not ready for public exhibition. The men at the Abbey would get less accomplished without the earl, despite Johnny's supervision. Diccon kept crying, sure the Gypsies would come snatch him away while his idol was off riding. And the grapevine had it that Goldy Flint had returned from whatever nefarious mission he'd gone on.

Mostly, however, Kerry's attendance at the hunt was a poor notion because of Lucy. He should have known the fox would be one of those of God's creatures requiring Miss Faire's attentions. He kicked himself for not thinking, saving Hellraker the effort.

By George, chickens were God's creatures, too, and He didn't seem too concerned about losing a few of those to Reynard. And why the deuce couldn't God just save the mangy beast Himself, Kerry wondered, without involving him? A good drenching rain would hide the scent and cancel the hunt. For that matter, why didn't the earth open up and swallow the blasted vermin, saving them all the effort? Most likely, he reasoned, because Lucy wanted him to get the dubious credit. Of course she didn't care what his neighbors thought, as long as he looked good to the Weird Sisters who would seal his fate.

So there was Lucy, two rises over, on hands and knees, trying to unstop the burrow so the fox could go to ground. Tarnation! Kerry was already having enough trouble keeping Hellraker well back from the leading riders so he did not outrun the hounds. Miss Westcott had stayed behind to check his condition, making polite conversation and keen observations on his handling of the obstreperous stallion. He waved her on, indicating a need to check his saddle girth.

When the last rider ambled by, Kerry directed Hellraker toward the hill where Lucy was still trying her best to make dirt move. The flurry of dust indicated her frenzy. She wasn't getting very far very fast.

He got down, holding tightly to Hellraker's bridle. "The hunt is well away in the other direction, Lucy. The fox mightn't come back this way at all."

She gave him a look of scorn. "And Demby's lottery ticket might have lost, too. Now, are you going to help?"

There went his beautiful new riding gloves, and a piece of his breeches—and backside—that Hellraker made a swipe at. And all for naught, for sure enough, Kerry could see the fox come streaking across the field in their direction too soon. The hunt was still out of sight, but the hounds would be on the scent.

"Do something!" Lucy demanded.

"Like what?" he shouted back.

"Pick him up and take him away!"

Pick up a fox? Take him away? She was daft, besides dead. Yet there she was, lifting the small red creature and handing him over, with a beseeching look.

"He has only ten minutes to live, that's how he came to me."

The fox knew damned well that Kerry wasn't any angel or anything, and struggled. "Take him!" Lucy cried, just ahead of the first baying of hounds.

Kerry took the wriggling beast. He opened his lovely scarlet coat and buttoned the fox inside, then remounted. Just as the hunt master came into view, Kerry made Hellraker rear to show he was having trouble with his mount, explaining why he was riding off in the opposite direction. It was an easy enough trick, getting the stallion to act like an unbroken colt, but it also caused the fox to do what many a young, frightened animal will do.

Kerry vowed he'd kill that female if it was the last thing he did. Hell couldn't be worse than this, the dampness seeping right through his waistcoat to his lawn shirt and down his breeches, his neck-or-nothing neighbors laughing at him, and a pack of slavering hounds hot on his heels. Whatever he did, he couldn't stay here.

Thinking quickly, Kerry circled around and raced back toward the end of the field of riders, where the last stragglers, the vicar and a few boys too young to be at the hunt were dawdling along. He figured the hounds would lose the scent with the prey above their heads. He and Hellraker must be carrying so much *eau de* fox, though, that soon the pack was turning, chasing its own tail as it were. So much for that plan.

Kerry left the vicar's company when they reached a stream. The overweight cleric's slug of a horse rightfully refused to exert himself enough to get them both over the water, which Hellraker cleared without a splash. Too bad the hounds wouldn't be confused by the broken trail. They'd pick up the fox on the other side in minutes, the stream being so narrow. The stream was quite long, however.

Unfortunately Hellraker disagreed with the new strategy of wading upstream far enough that the hounds would be thrown off the scent. In addition to being ridden, it appeared, Hellraker also had an aversion to getting his feet wet. There was nothing to do but for Kerry to dismount, still holding the quivering fox against his chest, and lead—drag—Hellraker over the rocks and rivulets.

Leaving the stream when his own toes were turning numb from the cold water getting into his boots, Kerry started to unbutton his coat.

"Don't put him down!" Lucy shrieked. "They decided to end the hunt, so they are going home this way!"

"Blast it, what am I supposed to do? Bad enough they'll think I took a header into the stream, but riding back to nuncheon with a fox in my pocket? Lucy, it's only a—"

"Put him up a tree. They don't have the scent yet. If he's high enough, the dogs won't pick up his smell." She wrinkled her nose. "Likely they'll follow you again anyway."

"Foxes can't climb trees, Lucy!"

"But you can. Please?"

"And how will he get down again after I lead the hunt away, or haven't you thought of that, Mistress Mayhem?"

"Why, you'll come back and put him down later, of course, while they're having lunch."

Climbing a tree with one hand, in wet boots, with a ghostly female shouting encouragement, did nothing for Kerry's temper. Neither did the scrapes along his cheeks from the tree bark, the scratches on his hands from the ungrateful fox, the flapping fabric on his breeches, or the disdainful look on Miss Westcott's face as she rode by him, not a hair out of place, not a speck of mud on her velvet riding habit. Missing luncheon with the arrogant chit was the only ray of sunshine on a gray, gray day.

In a new suit of clothes but the same frame of mind, Lord Stanford set out for Mr. Gideon Flint's house that afternoon. The same starched-up butler informed the earl that he would have passed Mr. Flint on the road if he hadn't come cross-country, a reference to the muddy bite-marks on Kerry's boots and the limpness of his cravat. Hellraker's mood hadn't improved either. Mr. Flint, the butler deigned to disclose, was out paying afternoon calls. Stanford Abbey was certain to be on his itinerary. It usually was.

Curses! Kerry had forgotten to leave instructions barring the door to Mr. Flint. He could be at the Abbey that very moment, chousing the dowager out of the pictures in the portrait gallery, or the sterling silver tea set. Conversely, Kerry still needed to talk to the old makebait to find out his price for the rubies, not that he needed the betrothal ring in any hurry, although Miss Westcott had managed to show some sympathy at the end of the hunt. Everybody had their good days and their bad days, she'd commiserated, and today was the fox's good day. She'd never know. Meanwhile Kerry watched her blue eyes shift over his various stains and spatters, mentally counting to herself how many times he and Hellraker must have parted company. Still, she was polite about his refusal to lunch, poised in the face of his dishabille, and a bruising rider. He could do worse, like one of the Prudlow twits.

Flint had come and gone at the Abbey by the time Kerry checked on the progress of the hog pens. The dowager was resting and had her maid refuse the earl entry—and a chance to relieve his ire. Not till dinner did he get the opportunity to discuss Free-trader Flint, and that in front of Aunt Clara, Johnny Norris, and Sidwell. Therefore, Kerry could not exactly express himself in the terms he might have chosen, terms like *gallows-bait* and *over my dead body*. Instead, he was forced to inquire when Mr. Flint might next honor them with his presence.

"Oh, you'll see him at the assembly two nights hence," the dowager replied. "Over at Farley. Since we will not be holding a ball, I decided we should attend so that you'll meet the neighbors. Miss Westcott and the Prudlows will be expecting you to dance with them."

Kerry attacked his turbot in oyster sauce with unnecessary vigor. "They will be disappointed."

"Don't be churlish, Kieren. Of course you are going. I accepted for all of us." She glared around the table as if daring anyone else to disagree with her. Johnny and Sidwell applied themselves to their meal with renewed diligence. "And Mr. Flint made special mention that he hoped to discuss a certain topic with you," she said with arched brows.

"Oh, it's to be one of those democratic country affairs where they allow in anyone with the price of admission? How quaint. Shall I dance with the butcher's daughter also, Mother? Perhaps I should consider one of the dairy maids for next countess."

"Have I told you recently how much you remind me of your father?"

Kerry swallowed a forkful of veal. "Thank you, ma'am."

"That was no compliment, you clunch. And we shall not be attending a village barn dance, contrary to your priggish comments, but an exclusive gathering of the best of local society."

"With Goldy Flint?"

"Mr. Flint is hosting the affair."

Aunt Clara would not go, she declared with a sneer for her sister-in-law. It wasn't fitting for a widow in mourning.

"After twenty years? Besides, you hypocrite, you've gone to balls and routs and picnics anytime you've been invited. If you had the sense God gave a duck, you'd leave off those wretched weeds and find yourself a new husband instead of living in Kieren's pockets and talking to ghosts."

"Hah! A new husband like that . . . that . . ."

"Excuse me, my lord." Cobb interrupted what promised to be a scene unconducive to digestion. To Kerry's relief, there seemed to be another Situation in the hall. The butler's flaring nostrils eloquently expressed his disapproval of yet another episode beneath the dignity of the noble house he served.

"A Mr. and Mrs. Browne have arrived from London. They regret their advent during the dinner hour, but have been traveling since yesterday afternoon, it seems, in some high state of excitement, and beg your lordship's indulgence," Cobb recited. Then he added, "What shall I do with them?"

"Do with them, you clodpole? Find their son! What did you think, they drove all this way, through the night, too, just to interrupt my supper? How could you make them wait, man?" Kerry demanded to everyone's surprise. "Don't you have a heart?"

They should have let the Brownes hold their reunion in private, but Diccon came tearing down the stairs before Kerry could escort the blond young man and his frail-looking wife to a smaller private parlor. Soon there wasn't a dry eye in the Abbey, including the dowager's, who insisted the fireplace was putting out too much smoke.

Later, after Kerry refused to permit the Brownes to seek an inn for the night, he and Diccon's father shared a brandy in the library. Browne tried again to express his gratitude, and the earl again brushed his thanks aside. "Anyone would have done the same."

"No, my lord, they would not have. That's how such vile practices get perpetuated. There aren't enough men like you who are willing to take action." The younger man cleared his throat. "And I want to show my appreciation. I know better than to offer a gentleman like yourself the reward money, but it was substantial. My family owns one of the largest furniture factories in London. I had heard about the fire in your London home, and your visit to the showrooms of several of my associates. Mr. Stenross senior mentioned you might be bringing a bride home, so with the approval of Mr. Stenross junior, my family and friends have arranged delivery of those items you were considering, and a few additions."

Numbly, Kerry could only consider that the Stenross partners, like Demby, would not trust him with cash either.

A gentleman like himself could not ask the price of the furnishings, but the list Mr. Browne left for his perusal seemed to indicate that the reward money might have retiled the Abbey's leaking roof with gold leaf! If he weren't a grown man, Kerry would have wept.

London was waiting for him. His home and his person outfitted in splendor rivaling Prinny's, he merely had to sell that last painting to live the life he was used to, the life he understood. Who knew, he might even start attending Almack's and find himself a town-bred beauty with a princely portion.

Instead, here he was in Wiltshire, blistered, bilious, and broken-nosed, with his lovely clothes being used as horse fodder.

"Then why don't you leave?" Lucy asked. She appeared soft in the candlelight, and sad.

"Because you gave me a challenge, to bring this place up to snuff, and a Somerfield never backs down from a dare. I won't quit till it's done. As soon as the Abbey is in order, I'll shake the dirt of this place off my feet and be gone, so don't go thinking this is a permanent change in my lifestyle, for it isn't."

"Are you very unhappy here, then?" she wanted to know.

Kerry had to think for a minute, as if happiness had never entered into his considerations before. For all the fuss and bother, he was not unhappy here, no. He had to admit, in fact, that he'd never felt more alive, more purposeful, more in command of his own destiny before. He didn't have to admit that to Lucy, of course. Let her agonize a little after that fiasco with the fox.

"And where the deuce were you last night anyway?" he brusquely demanded. "If I'm stuck here for the nonce, I at least deserve some intelligent conversation."

"Oh, I was trying to answer your question about Aunt Clara's ghost. He's the second earl, poor man. You think you have problems! Why, he—"

The earl held up his hand. "No, don't tell me. I have more than enough difficulties laid in my dish without adding his. The rubies, the roof, Uncle Nigel—it's endless. If the second earl has been haunting the Abbey for the past century or so, I'm sure his situation is beyond my repair."

"I thought a Somerfield never backs down from a challenge."

"That's our motto, all right. A Somerfield never backs down, but he doesn't have to stand up either."

Chapter Eighteen

The direction of the vicar's sermon was that charity begins at home. The direction of the vicar's gaze seemed to indicate that charity ought to begin in the front pew.

And a dashed uncomfortable pew it was, too, Kerry thought, shifting his weight on the hard wooden bench next to his mother. Too bad the Brownes had refused to stay another day; perhaps they would have provided seat cushions in exchange for a few prayers of rejoicing in their son's recovery. Right now Kerry could use a pillow far more than another rug for the Grosvenor Square house.

And too bad the Brownes had refused his offer of that mongrel pup. Not in the City, they told him, with not too much regret. Even Diccon, the little traitor, thought Lucky would be happier in the country with his friend Hellraker. So now Kerry had the mixed breed trailing him and the stallion when they rode out. The earl swore Lucky's lolling tongue was a grin at his efforts to control the ill-humored horse.

The vicar was going on about feeding the hungry. Hades, Kerry thought, if the hefty cleric passed up second helpings, there'd be enough to feed half the village needy, whose eyes were also fixed on the front pew. Kerry couldn't help but be aware of the stares from the back rows of the little church, stares fastened on his superfine coat, biscuit pantaloons, and marcella waistcoat. Many of the parishioners were in ragged homespun, the women with threadbare shawls for warmth. Confound Demby! Kerry noted that neither Flint, the Prudlows, nor the Westcotts went to services here. They chose to attend the grander church in Farley, where their furs and furbelows would not make such a contrast. If Goldy Flint prayed here, he swore, they'd not be sitting on bare benches.

Then the earl's gaze drifted to the choir, where one voice was raised higher than all the others in joyful praise. Lucy was singing with the local members, standing out both in her brightly colored gown amid their white robes, and her slightly off-key rendition. The gown was almost a pinky-coral, far too dashing for church, but her hair was neatly coiled atop her head in a golden-copper halo of braids. And she looked happy as a grig.

That smile of hers shook his heart to its shaky foundations.

She was just a slip of a thing, Kerry reasoned, not a statuesque beauty like Miss Westcott; that was why he had an overwhelming desire to shelter her from sorrow, protect her from the world's evils, keep her smiling radiantly.

Dash it, he reminded himself, Lucy was not some vulnerable little schoolgirl. This she-devil could throw thunderbolts! She needed his looking after as much as he needed another indigent relative.

Still, when he shook the vicar's hand after the service, the earl found himself offering his work crew and some extra lumber to rebuild the church stairs. He also thought the abbey kitchens lost far too much to spoilage. Surely Cook could provide baskets of leftovers for the poor, rather than throw the foodstuffs away.

Of course that meant he'd have to find more slops for the hogs if table scraps were out, but Lucy's singing echoed in his ear the whole carriage ride home, sweet and only a little sour.

"Don't go getting in alt over this," he told her later, after spending all of that afternoon on what the vicar was pleased to call God's work, thus excusing the Sunday labor. Many of the locals, like Charlie the blacksmith and McGivven at the mercantile, had their own jobs to do on Monday, so they worked past dinner completing the stairs. They all supped on food the village women prepared from what Kerry had sent down from the Abbey. The dowager's dinner or not, it tasted better in the common room at Ned's pub.

"Why shouldn't I be pleased?" Lucinda insisted, wishing she could rub his sore shoulders as he groaned from the depths of a comfortable chair in the Abbey's library.

"Because it's not permanent, I told you. This doing good deeds and leading an exemplary life is not natural to me. Besides, it's all in my own self-interest anyway, don't you know."

She smiled. "Can't you confess you are doing something worthwhile just for its own sake?"

"What, like fixing the church steps so I don't break my neck next Sunday?" He put his feet up on a footstool and sighed.

"Like asking the vicar about starting a school."

"What's wrong with trying to lower my poor taxes by getting some of these people off the dole? I am a self-centered, arrogant, overdressed cod's-head, remember?"

"You forgot pigheaded. You are a good man, you just won't admit it. You wouldn't have been given this chance if there were no seed of decency to be nurtured. Know thyself, Kieren Somerfield."

"What about 'to thine own self be true'? I fear you're in for a big disappointment. What if at heart I really am a wastrel and a womanizer?"

"Then at least the church steps got fixed."

Not altogether discontent despite his warnings, Kerry settled back to enjoy a rest of the righteous weary, and the sight of Lucy worrying over her lists. She was tallying virtues versus vices, he supposed, the way Sidwell juggled assets and debits, but Sidwell never bit his tongue in concentration, at least not that Kerry ever noticed or cared. Nor did the earl believe he'd be satisfied to sit watching his secretary for any length of time. Lucy he could watch for hours, even if her hair was no longer trailing down her back in wanton disarray and her gown was no longer as diaphanous as an insect's wing. The grace of her movements, the rise and fall of her breaths, the softness of her cheek—

Well, he wasn't *terribly* discontented with the upright life. He had no urge to wager his watch on the roll of the dice or his last shillings on the speed of a raindrop, for instance. There was no burning ache for a cigarillo or a second, third, or fourth glass of brandy. And he didn't even want a woman, not too badly. Kerry laughed aloud at that thought, and the sound was so cheerful, Lucy laughed, too.

Tap-tap. The library door burst open before the earl could call "Enter." The dowager countess strode into the room, glaring into the shadowy corners. Aunt Clara hung back by the door, looking cautiously around.

"Just as I thought," the earl's mother declared, "there is no one in here with you." She crossed her arms across her chest. "I demand you stop this absurd habit at once."

Kerry had politely if stiffly risen at her entrance. "I always thought it a foolish practice myself, hopping up and down each time a lady stands. Won't you have a seat? You, too, Aunt Clara. Shall I ring for tea?"

Lady Stanford claimed the chair closest to the fireplace, where Lucy had been sitting. "Not that habit, you jackanapes. I mean this deplorable habit of speaking to yourself, as you well know. You already have the servants, what there are left of them, thinking you ready for a restraining device. You cannot wish the Westcotts to hear of this lunatic behavior. Bad enough they think you cannot sit a horse."

Aunt Clara arranged her black skirts and shawls onto the nearby sofa. "Were you speaking with Nigel, dear?" she wanted to know.

"No, it seems there is only one apparition allowed per customer. Have you ever actually seen Uncle Nigel, Aunt Clara?"

"Why, no, dear, I only hear his voice. Does your, ah, friend appear, in person, as it were?"

"Stop it, both of you!" The dowager shrieked, stamping her feet. "Clara might be the village eccentric, and my cross to bear, but I shall not have my son making such a cake of himself, do you hear me?"

"I am surprised Miss Westcott cannot hear you, Mother," Kerry said, getting up to close the door.

"Be sure she'll hear about this aberration of yours soon enough. Then you'll lose the gel for sure."

"Lose her? I hardly know her, Mother."

"What's that to the purpose? I never met your father until we joined hands at the altar."

No one commented on the success of that union. Aunt Clara leaned forward and asked, "But you do like Miss Westcott, don't you, dear?"

"She's a nice enough female, as far as debutantes go. I suppose I shan't mind dancing with her at that assembly tomorrow."

"You'd better do a dashed sight more than dance

with her, my boy," the dowager cautioned. "You'd better fix her interests all right and tight."

"Your mother is correct, dear. For once. Faint heart ne'er won fair lady, and all that."

"What, you, too, Aunt Clara? I said I'd dance with her. I cannot see rushing into anything more permanent for at least another meeting or two," he tried to joke. No one laughed.

Aunt Clara twisted a handkerchief in her hands. "I'm afraid there isn't time, dear. Rumor has it that Lord Westcott refuses to take Felicia back to London. Doesn't want to miss any more hunting, they say. Westcott's butler told Lady Prudlow's head groom that the marquis thinks another season would be a waste, since she turned down all the eligible partis, and that duke did not come up to scratch."

Lady Stanford took up the story: "So that twiddlepoop Westcott will be looking to get the gal fired off right here. If you don't snatch up the chit, he's liable to hitch Felicia to the first respectable beau, someone like Johnny Norris or something."

"So what? There will be other pretty girls, other heiresses."

"Oh, no, you wouldn't want to lose Miss Westcott, dear. So suitable. So dignified and polite. The way a countess should be."

Lady Stanford ignored the jibe. "You skip-brain, you don't have time to find another dowry. Bride, I mean. This is November. Have you forgotten that the next round of mortgage payments is due in January?"

Kerry had. He'd been thinking of what he could accomplish in the next week or so, for Lucy's sake, and in the long range, for income's sake. There was no way he could meet the payment due.

He almost missed his mother's next words: "My annuity is paid out in January, thank goodness, but you cannot expect help from me. I'll have to use my income to redeem my jewels, since you haven't seen fit to show your mother the respect due. So if you don't manage to snabble an heiress this month or next, we'll be living in your confounded pigpens, eating scraps."

"No, I am giving the table scraps to the poor." Kerry got up and started pacing.

"You gossoon, we *are* the poor!"

"I am impoverished, Mother; you do not need to be. You could be living in comfort in the Dower House if you hadn't squandered your annuity."

"You dare criticize me for a few paltry gambling debts? What happened to *your* income all these years?"

"Touché. Very well, I shall try to get to know your Miss Westcott at the assembly, to see if we suit. I am not making any promises, mind."

Aunt Clara came over to pat his hand before ringing for tea. "I'm sure you'll do everything proper, dear."

After Cobb wheeled in the tea cart and Lady Stanford poured, Kerry asked, "Will there be cards at this gathering, Mother?"

Lady Stanford looked as if she'd swallowed a lemon. "Why, do you hope to win a fortune instead of marrying one? That hasn't worked for you yet, Kieren."

"No, Mother, I shall be too busy doing my duty by the young ladies, inspecting their pedigrees, their bank balances, their teeth. Perhaps their hips for breeding."

Aunt Clara giggled into her cup. Lady Stanford returned hers to its saucer with a clatter.

"No," Kerry went on, "I was wondering about the cards for your sake, Mother, since the Stanford flaw seems to be transmitted through the marriage vows as well as through the blood." He swallowed the last of a cherry tart, his favorite, and carefully wiped his fingers on a serviette. "I shouldn't wish to see you sending us deeper into the River Tick while I am struggling to keep us afloat. If I so much as see you with a pasteboard in your hand, I'll tell Lady Westcott that your diamonds are fake."

Aunt Clara chimed in: "And I'll tell your beau Goldy that your bosoms are fake."

"Why, you jealous cat! Just because you never had a real man show any interest in you—"

"Real man, that shady character in corsets? How dare you compare that thatch-gallows to my sainted Nigel?"

"More tea, ladies?" Kerry asked before aspersions flew along with the Spode china. Aunt Clara held out her cup, but the dowager excused herself on account of the late hour.

"Some of us need our beauty sleep if we are to look our best for the assembly. Others wouldn't be helped by a week's rest."

After the door slammed shut, the earl turned to his aunt. "Aunt Clara, what if, hypothetically of course, Uncle Nigel turned out to be not such a paragon? If your hero had feet of clay? Would you still love him?"

"Oh, you are worried that you might discover later that Miss Westcott is pettish in the mornings or that she snores. Of course you would still love her, dear. I didn't know everything about dear Nigel before we were wed. It wouldn't have been at all the thing. But that's what love is, taking the bad with the good." Just when Kerry was about to breathe a sigh of relief, she added, "Naturally, however, I would never love a black-hearted rogue in the first place."

Naturally. "And, ah, you are certain it is Uncle Nigel chatting with you?"

"Quite certain, dear. Who else knows so much about the Abbey? I'm sure if it was your father, he'd be haunting *her*. Then again, he hardy spoke to her when he was alive, so why would he bother now?"

Chapter Nineteen

If anyone had suggested that Kieren Somerfield might someday stand ankle-deep in hog dung, directing inexperienced and incompetent footmen in corraling squealing porkers, Kerry would have laughed and said "When pigs fly."

He wasn't laughing, and they weren't flying. They'd come by slow, smelly, loud wagons, which he and Hellraker had to accompany, for Johnny Norris couldn't grab a piglet or hog-tie a sow.

Getting the stock distributed and settled took most of the morning. Catching escapees and repairing fences took most of the afternoon. Washing off the stench and the muck took two tubfuls of hot water.

At last Kerry felt clean enough to don the outfit Derek had selected from Demby's offerings for formal affairs. As opulent as possible without being ostentatious, the ensemble was more suited to a court presentation. The only thing missing was the ermine cape. Lord Stanford was complete to a shade in a velvet coat of charcoal gray, dove-gray satin knee breeches, sparkling white lace at the collar and cuffs of his shirt, with a waistcoat of burgundy brocade embroidered in silver thread. With his diamond stickpin in the cravat, he'd be bang up to the mark—if he could just tie the blasted neckcloth.

Fingers suddenly more used to handling shovels and saws instead of snuffboxes fumbled with yard after yard of discarded linen, to Derek's growing dismay. It was as if the earl's hands couldn't perform the functions logic demanded but emotion declined. He simply did not want to go to this ball. He did not want to pay court to the local toast.

Miss Westcott would be everything charming, he was sure, dressed to the nines, looking every inch the well-bred daughter of a well-breeched marquis. She would curtsy gracefully and smile demurely, expressing polite interest in whatever topic he chose to pursue. At least she did not chatter or giggle. If one could judge the daughter from the mother, the diamond would be content to stay in the shadows lording it over a small society but deferring in all things to her husband. Like Lady Westcott, Felicia was trained to be an accepting, complacent wife. Give her a full stable and a full closet, a few cicisbei to pay her flowery compliments, and Miss Westcott would be content to stay in Wiltshire while he pursued his own interests in London. Kerry could not begin to imagine Lucy tolerating such an arrangement.

He wondered how she danced. Lucy, not Miss Westcott. The heiress indubitably waltzed well, but not divinely. That would be Lucy's province. He recalled Lucy saying that she'd never been to a ball, but no matter. The way she glided around had to bespeak a grace unmatched by any London deb, no matter how practiced. Oh, how he wished he could be the one to lead her out for her first waltz.

Gads, he amended to himself, finally getting a perfect knot, how he'd like to hold her in his arms, period! "And that's not all I'd like to do," he said aloud, "so if you are reading my mind again, you may as well blush for something worthwhile."

"Oh, la," said Derek, fluttering his eyelashes.

The grandeur of the assembly rooms did not surprise Kerry, not with a pirate paying the shot. After Almack's austerity, this place seemed a veritable Xanadu, with flowers and festoons of ribbons.

The number and caliber of the guests was not surprising either. The well-dressed crowd being assisted from the expensive carriages and waiting on the receiving line could have passed for partygoers at Marlborough House. With little in the way of tonnish society unless one traveled to London, the landed and titled could not afford to be as high-nosed as the *belle monde* in town. A wealthy enough cit could buy his entree here, where he never could among the upper ten thousand.

The only surprise—nay, shock—at the evening's onset was the purple sash across Gideon Flint's ample chest. Atop the sash, which was atop a saffron coat, atop a puce waistcoat with cabbage roses imprinted on it, glittered a markedly recognizable bauble: the Order of the Knights of the Realm. The scapegrace smuggler had bought himself a knighthood! Speak of being more accepting of the lower ranks, everyone knew Prinny even-handedly distributed titles to anyone making a big enough contribution to the royal coffers.

So there the Earl of Stanford waited to shake the dastard's hand, his ancient title not keeping him from point-non-plus, and Gideon Flint, gold tooth flashing in his florid face, was a knight!

Things got worse. Word trickled through the receiving line that the prince had awarded Flint the knighthood for his service to the Crown, not just his pocketbook. The wine dealer's merchant ships—tidesmen, with no bark on them—had been carrying secret documents and couriers between France and Whitehall during the war. Gideon Flint was the espionage agent, and poor befuddled Uncle Nigel wallowed in France. That was beside the point, Kerry acknowledged to himself with no small amount of chagrin; Gideon Flint had done more for the war effort than the Somerfields ever had.

Unable to meet his mother's gloating smile, Kerry swallowed his humiliation and a mouthful of crow. He held out his hand and offered congratulations to Sir Gideon.

"Thankee, thankee, my lord. And that's Goldy to my friends. Sir Goldy. A word with you later, my boy, what?"

Goldy correctly opened the ball with the countess, the highest-ranking lady present. Kerry had the opening cotillion with Miss Westcott and asked her for the supper dance then also, as she was the wealthiest young lady present. The earl reasoned that Felicia's stately beauty saved him from being an arrant fortune hunter. He would have asked the prettiest girl at the assembly to dance even if she was the dustman's daughter, and he did appreciate her serene demeanor. What might be termed hauteur or arrogance or icy aloofness in Miss Westcott, he chose to call dignity. He would not pursue the prattling Prudlow pair if their grandmother left them each as rich as Croesus.

Which didn't mean he didn't dance with both the Prudlow girls, or perhaps the same one twice. His mother saw to that, in her self-conceived function as hostess for the ball, chivvying the bachelors out of their corners and onto the dance floor. The countess partnered the other Prudlow girl with Sidwell, who after meticulous research was deemed well enough connected, although through a cavalier branch, and whose wardrobe had to be augmented with Kerry's castoffs. Sidwell stammered, Priscilla—or was it Patricia? Both girls wore white—filled in the conversational gaps with double-time drivel, and they finished the contradanse well content with each other. The secretary had one of the heiresses on his arm for the supper dance. Kerry wished him well.

Johnny did his part, making sure Aunt Clara was settled amid her shawls and cronies, then staying on the sidelines to chat up the chaperones. He sent a footman for a cold glass of champagne for a flushed Miss Westcott after she returned from a particularly strenuous Scottish reel, then sat out the next dance with her while she recovered her breath. He even good-naturedly offered to try a one-handed waltz with her, which Kerry was pleased to see the beauty was not too proud to accept. That awkward set with Johnny improved Kerry's opinion of the incomparable far more than her graceful movements during the quadrille with him before supper ever could.

The earl purposefully seated Felicia at a small table, away from his family but unavoidably under the watchful eye of hers. He wanted to get to know her better. They spoke of the hunt and horses, mutual friends in London, the last plays they'd seen, and whether country life was preferable to city life. It was the same conversation Kerry'd had with innumerable females; he knew her no better after the raspberry ices than before the lobster patties.

Or perhaps he knew all there was to know? She liked parties but she loved to ride, preferred theater to opera, and did not, naturally, associate with the older, faster crowd he called friends.

No matter. He knew all he needed to know. She was beautiful, not a total widgeon, and rich. She wouldn't curdle his cream at the breakfast table, she wouldn't interfere with his pleasures, and she'd relieve his mind and pocketbook of a great many pressures. He asked for the next waltz, signifying his interest by requesting a third dance together; she accepted, indicating her receptivity to his suit. That was that.

As he rose to escort Miss Westcott back to the ballroom, Kerry felt a heavy hand on his shoulder.

"Care to step outside and blow a cloud, my lord?" Mr. Flint, Sir Goldy, asked, the countess at his side.

"No, thank you, sir. I am sorry, but I no longer smoke."

"Don't be a peagoose," Kerry's fond parent hissed in his ear. "Go on outside."

"I am promised to Miss Westcott for this coming set."

"Don't worry, I'll get young Norris to sit it out with her."

So instead of holding a warm and lovely perfumed woman in his arms, Kerry found himself out on the cold balcony, inhaling the noxious smoke from Goldy Flint's fat cigar. "I daresay the rubies could wait for a more comfortable setting," the earl commented, rubbing his hands together for warmth. "You must know I haven't the blunt for them anyway."

"Who's talking about the rubies?" Goldy asked as he spat out the end of his cigar. "I haven't called in the chits, have I? Mightn't be a gentleman in your sense of the word, but I've never dunned a lady yet." He took a long pull at the cigar and spat out more tobacco. "And I know you ain't got a feather to fly with; I had you investigated while I was in London."

"Why, of all the—"

"Wanted to know what kind of basket-scrambler you were before I took you on as stepson."

"—Presumpt—Stepson?"

"Aye. Didn't want any bailiffs at *my* door, or any jumped-up lordling bleeding me dry with begging his mama for handouts." Before Kerry could protest that outrageous affront, Flint was going on: "I saw as how you got yourself square with the duns, paid off your gambling debts, too, and haven't been back at the tables or the track since. And word is you are trying to make a go of the Abbey. I admire that in a man. Way I see it, you got off to a bad start. Bad influence and all." He held up a pudgy, beringed hand. "Don't mean to speak ill of the dead or any of that. And you're a man growed, not a boy, so it ain't for me to say how you should live your life. But you seem on the right track now, so I am prepared to make your fine mother an offer. With your permission, of course."

"I am, ah . . ." Kerry couldn't put a description to what he was feeling. Flabbergasted? Amused? Insulted? Flint could have knocked him over with a feather, Kerry was in such a swivet. The only other question he had was whether his stiff-rumped mother would accept this diamond in the rough, and on the fingers, pinned through the neckcloth, hanging from watchfobs, at that badge of honor. The rogue was a knight now! That wasn't quite an earl or a baron, but it was a start! And he could certainly keep the countess in the style to which she believed herself entitled.

"I wish you luck, Sir Goldy." Kerry hoped the other man never knew how much. "But you don't need my permission. The countess is her own woman. She will do what she wants." *She always has,* he almost warned.

"Still, I want this done all shipshape and Bristol fashion. Want your blessing on the match at least."

Kerry was able to assure Goldy of his approval. Anyone who'd take that expensive, querulous burden off his hands had the earl's wholehearted support. "And I'll be happy to put in a good word for you."

"Excellent, excellent. I'm prepared to come down heavy with the settlement, too, Stanford, so you don't have to worry about that."

A settlement? For bringing peace and prosperity to his household? "I don't expect any settlement, sir. Mother's annuity stops with her remarriage"—

and blessedly returns to the estate, but he didn't say that—"nor will she have a dowry, of course."

"I ain't asking for one, am I? The woman's prize enough in herself."

"I couldn't agree more. I just don't see that you should have to pay for the privilege, except for making provision in your will, of course, through the solicitors."

"I see what it is, your fine lordship. You're too proud to take Goldy Flint's money, no matter how much you need it."

"That's not it at all." That was it entirely.

Goldy tossed his cigar into the bushes. "Another noble fool gone hungry."

"I am not exactly hungry." And not quite a fool. "But there is one thing you could do for me . . ." He explained about Uncle Nigel.

Goldy slapped his fleshy thigh. "If that don't beat all. I'm surprised you toffs figured out how to put your pants on in the morning."

Kerry grinned. "That's why we have valets."

Goldy laughed and slapped his thigh again. "Well, consider it done. I have the prince's ear right now, and enough brass. I'll send a messenger to London tonight and another over to France. Have that blockhead back in no time to take that old crow Clara off your hands. Me and Margie off on our honeymoon, your decks'll be cleared for the new bride." He waved one hand in the vague direction of the ballroom. "Smart idea, that. Best you've had yet. Fine-looking woman."

"My mother?"

"Westcott's gal, lad. What are you waiting for?"

Kerry clenched his jaw. "I hardly know the lady."

"Cold feet, eh? Well, I'll get you the ruby engagement ring tomorrow. Make the diamonds your wedding present. I prefer to buy Margie her own jewelry anyway, something a little fancier."

The earl wondered what Goldy considered fancier

than diamonds, but he said, "About the jewels, why did you take them from the countess?"

"And let you think I was fleecing her? I know what you thought, Stanford, and I was sorry for it, but there was no other way. She was out of pin money and couldn't pay up. Terrible cardplayer is your mother, boy, but don't let on I said so. I liked the company and didn't want her to quit for lack of funds. It was either take the fripperies on tick or see her in the hands of the cent-per-centers. You wouldn't rather that, would you?"

Kerry held his hand out. "I owe you my thanks, and my apologies. I'll be proud to have you in the family."

"That's big of you, Stanford." Flint shook the earl's hand, almost squashing two fingers between his rings. "And don't worry about me embarrassing you in front of your fancy friends. Margie'll smooth out my rough edges before we come to stay at Grosvenor Square."

Chapter Twenty

"I have to go, you know."

"Yes, you asked Lord Westcott if you could call tomorrow. Today."

They were sitting in his bedroom in front of the fire, Kerry in the soft chair, Lucy on the fur rug not quite leaning against his knees. He could almost reach out and touch the coronet of curls atop her head, now mostly gold with just a tinge of chestnut. He didn't reach out, however, knowing the frustration of trying to capture a mirage. Instead, he tried to tell himself he was satisfied with her understanding, undemanding company.

It was late, or early. The ball had gone on long past the usual time for country gatherings, after Goldy's announcement of his betrothal to Lady Stanford. Kerry's permission must have been taken for granted, because there was no more than a moment's pause between their return to the ballroom and the new knight's public proclamation. Footmen were already pouring fresh champagne before the earl kissed his mother's proffered cheek.

The neighbors did not appear perturbed by the

alliance. Lord Stanford, in fact, was the only one the least surprised by the engagement, everyone else having long been aware which way the wind blew. Even Aunt Clara was *aux anges*, now that Flint was a knight, and promising to take her nemesis on a long bridal journey. She couldn't wait to get home to tell Nigel they'd have the place almost to themselves, but was content to bide at the assembly until nearly dawn, savoring the betrothal as her own emancipation.

The local gentry were not reticent about expressing their approval to Lord Stanford. Goldy was a favorite, it seemed. And his champagne was excellent.

Now there were only a few hours left before Kerry's appointment with Lord Westcott.

"I have to do it, Lucy," he said.

"I know."

"Even with the rubies back, Uncle Nigel's pardon assured, and my own gambling debts paid, hard work just isn't enough. I have to do it," he said again, as if the repetition would make the deed more palatable.

Lucy nodded. "All those people are depending on you for their living."

"And all those lady pigs are depending on me to find them a boar."

"And this wonderful old house is falling apart."

"And the stables are empty, the fields are a disgrace, the cottages are hovels. And you."

"Me?" Lucy looked up so he could see that her eyes were a warm hazel now, not that startling green of when he first encountered her.

"You, Miss Faire. Have you noticed your appearance lately? Your gown is pink. Not rose, not coral, but pink, and with a white gauze overskirt that would be acceptable at Almack's. You appear to have all your unmentionables in place, even gloves, and there's not a trace of paint anywhere. You've even begun to smell like flowers. Lilies-of-the-valley, I think. Can't you see, the odds must have turned to our favor. We're almost there. We cannot quit now."

Lucinda savored the "we" and smiled her most winning smile, dimples and all.

Kerry groaned. "Oh, Lord, I don't want to go out to Westcott's."

Lucy's smile dimmed, but she told him: "Felicia is a lovely girl. Refined, well-educated. She'll make you a good wife."

"An accepting, polite wife. Is that what I want, someone who will accept me for what I have—the title, the Abbey—instead of who I am? Oh, we'll have a marriage like every other in the ton, doing the season with our separate friends, meeting at various dinners and dances. Ever so proper. Then she'll be increasing and staying on in the country, and I'll pursue my own pleasures in town."

"You don't have to return to your former devil-may-care ways, you know."

"Ah, but I will. Marriage to Miss Felicia Westcott will not change the tiger's stripes. I would not have minded so much once." Before I met you, he thought, but did not say. "But now? How can I repeat the marriage vows, knowing I intend to break them? Knowing my wife is likely thinking the same, that as soon as she presents me with an heir she can have her discreet little *affaires*?" He found distraction in winding his watch, but then he listened to its working, and heard his freedom ticking away. "Oh, how I wish things could be different."

"And I," Lucy said softly, aching for what could never be.

Kerry shook himself. "But they aren't. I was born an earl with an earl's duties and responsibilities, even if I am somewhat tardy in coming to them and needed a nudge from the netherworld to accept them. Right?"

She tried for a smile. "Right."

"At least I don't have to go to Westcott with

mounds of debts and Uncle Nigel hanging over my head. And here I thought hell would freeze over before I was grateful to Gideon Flint. But you're not wearing ice skates, are you?" he teased, looking down to where dainty pink satin slippers hid under her skirts. Pink satin *dancing* slippers. "I thought you'd come to the ball, since you'd never been."

"Oh, I was talking to the second earl. He says—"

"Not now, Lucy, please. Westcott is all the duty I can handle in one day." She started to interrupt, but he held up a hand. "No. Right now there is only one thing I want to hear, the strains of a waltz. Do you think it possible for us to have a dance, just this once? Johnny did it with one hand; we ought to be able to manage something, don't you think?"

The earl hummed a popular dance tune and explained the steps. Lucy stepped into his arms, or thereabouts, and hummed along. Yes, lilies-of-the-valley, and yes, the tingly glow he remembered, that warmth, and almost electric shock of desire. And yes, she hummed slightly out of tune. "Do you play the pianoforte like every other well-bred young female?" he asked when he could, hoping she did not hear the quaver in his voice.

"No, my father thought that led to familiarity. You know, young people standing around singing together. I play the harp."

"Gabriel is going to love you, angel." Kerry laughed and twirled her around.

Derek tiptoed into his master's chamber, saw the earl dancing with an invisible partner, and quickly backed out, tears in his eyes.

The rubies arrived early the next morning, along with an emerald ring for the countess. The emerald was as big as a bird's egg and the surrounding diamonds made the Crown Jewels look tawdry.

"And that's nothing," an exuberant Goldy informed them all over breakfast. "The necklace that goes with the ring is so wide, you won't even see Margie's chest under it."

Before Aunt Clara could ruin the old man's breakfast with a remark about the dowager's chest, Kerry thought to start preparing her for Uncle Nigel's return.

"Oh, no, dear, once a person is dead, they stay dead. You must be a little more disturbed than I thought. I mean, ghosts are all well and good, but just think what would happen if your father should decide to return now?" Which ruined everyone's breakfast anyway.

Ruby ring in hand, or pocket, as it were, Kerry set out on a raw, dreary day that matched his mood. Even the angels are weeping, he thought as a cold rain started to fall, but he couldn't see Lucy upstairs in his bed, crying her eyes out.

Rain dripping off the rim of his beaver hat and down his collar, Kerry handed Hellraker's reins to a sturdy-enough-looking groom and started to walk up the steps of Westcott Hall. Now he knew how a condemned man must feel on his way to the gallows. Every step was an eternity, and over all too soon.

A footman showed the earl to the gun room, where Lord Westcott was cleaning a hunting rifle. Marvelous, thought Kerry, looking at the stuffed trophies on the wall, the man was preparing to add an earl to his collection.

"Sit, Stanford, sit," the marquis invited him. "You look like your knees are giving out. Haven't tamed that brute of a horse yet, eh?"

"No, Hellraker and I have come to terms. He hasn't tried to take a piece out of my flesh in days now. I doubt he'll ever be a trustworthy mount, but he'll never be a dull ride either."

Westcott put down his rag and ramrod. "Must be another cause has you green about the gills, then, what?" He laughed, but sobered quickly. "Shouldn't tease about a serious matter. Why, I remember when I had to ask my lady's father's permission. Worst day of my life. Couldn't even decide if I wanted him to say yea or nay."

"Then you do know why I am come?"

"I daresay the whole shire knows why you are come. Can't keep such a thing quiet in the country. Young hellion with debts, mortgages, expensive tastes"—he gave a sharp, assessing look at Kerry's corbeau-colored coat and fawn breeches—"comes asking to speak to an heiress's papa, what do you think?" He sighted down the rifle's barrel.

"I think you insult Miss Westcott, begging your pardon, my lord," Kerry said quickly. "The lady is beautiful, intelligent, and talented, from what I heard of her pianoforte playing. I think any man, no matter his circumstances, would be tempted to offer for your daughter."

"Well spoken, Stanford, well spoken." The marquis put the rifle down and stared at the earl. "But you ain't what I had in mind for a son-in-law."

"I understand completely, my lord, and I am sure I would feel the same way if I had a daughter." Kerry stood to leave.

"Hold on. You didn't let me finish. I was looking higher, not that an earldom is anything to sneeze at, but you said yourself the gel is an incomparable, and my fortune has nowhere to go but to her and her get. But that didn't work out."

Not for the first time, Kerry wondered why the hoped-for duke had cried off before a formal announcement. He did not think it would be politic to ask right now. He cleared his throat instead.

Lord Westcott picked up another rag and some oil. While he caressed the rifle's wooden stock, he went on: "I ain't saying you're not an out and outer, for I made a parcel on you and those bays, but there's no denying you ain't at first oars these days. Penniless knight of the baize table ain't what I wanted for my little girl either."

Kerry started to rise again.

The rifle was aimed at his head. He sat down, wishing the man would just put him out of his misery already, like the other stuffed victims around the room.

"Nor a rakehell, a town beau, or one of those man-milliners neither." He glared again at the shoulder-hugging cut of the earl's jacket. The glass-eyed squirrel on the table next to Kerry seemed friendly by comparison.

"I'm sorry to have taken your time, my lord. I'll just be—"

"But my girl is fussy, and my wife has a yearning to have her close by. Only chick, don't you know. So I gave you a second look. And I liked what I saw. Oh, not at the hunt, but a better-trained animal will show you to advantage next time, I'm sure. No, I mean how you're trying to make something of that ramshackle property you inherited. I said to myself, here looks like a fellow who's tired of sowing his wild oats. Maybe he's ready to settle down now."

"Yes, sir, I believe I am. And I also believe that I can make your daughter a good husband."

Westcott nodded. "A good woman always has a steadying influence, and they say there's no better husband than a reformed rake." He picked up the rifle again. "I'd hate to find out otherwise."

"No, sir, never." And there Kerry'd been worried about forswearing his vows before the Church. Hell, the Church didn't shoot something before breakfast every day. Kerry stopped wondering why the duke had backed off. "Then I take it I have your permission to pay my addresses to Miss Felicia?"

"Her answer is yes, we already discussed it. Our solicitors can settle the rest of the details. Felicia's dowry is substantial, but most of the real money will come when I'm gone. You'll understand, I'm sure, if I insist the bulk of that gets tied up for my grandchildren."

Kerry understood the marquis didn't trust him out of his rifle range. Of all the humiliating, aggravating—no matter, the dowry was enough. He nodded. "Thank you, my lord, for giving me this chance. If I might see Miss Felicia now?"

"I told you, you can arrange for the calling of the banns. Daresay you'll want the wedding as soon as can be."

"Whatever Miss Westcott desires. However, I hope to hear the acceptance to my proposal from her own lips before there is any formal announcement." He wanted to make deuced certain the girl wasn't being coerced into anything, after knowing of Lucy's plight.

Lord Westcott started polishing the rifle butt again, not meeting the earl's eyes. "Well, she ain't here right now. Your man Norris came by earlier on his way to the Widow Welford's place, looking to get the address of that breeder Tige bought his prize boar off of. I told young Norris the boar was the meanest bastard there ever was, but he wanted to check before the widow moved away."

"Yes, Johnny told me he meant to come this way. And Miss Felicia?"

"She was going out for her ride, so went along with him. Nothing wrong in that," the marquis hastened to add. "They've been friends since leading strings, and her groom went, too. Nothing to concern yourself about."

The earl studied the stuffed squirrel. "Of course not."

"Young Norris is a good man," Westcott said in reassurance, although whom he was reassuring was questionable.

"The best," Kerry agreed. "I trust him implicitly. In fact, I don't know how I could get on without him. He's used to commanding from his days in the army, and the men respect him more than they respect me. I still haven't earned their esteem, even after breaking my back alongside them. And Johnny's truly knowledgeable about farming, a wizard at the latest methods after studying all the journals and articles. Most admirable of all to my thinking, he's managed to keep his good humor and open manner despite all the troubles he's seen. A lesser man would have turned bitter under his handicap. Meeting John Norris again was one of the luckiest days of my life, along with the day I met your daughter, of course."

"You make me wish I'd hired him on myself. I always thought a man should manage his own estates. Not get robbed blind that way. But now I'm not so sure. I'm getting too old, my days are too few to waste on all that busy work."

The earl stood to go. "I wish you the best, but I shan't part with Johnny, not even in exchange for your daughter's hand. Good try though, my lord." They shook hands amiably and parted after the earl said, "Please give my respects to Miss Felicia, and tell her that I shall call tomorrow. And better hunting next time."

Chapter Twenty-one

Tomorrow was too busy, so the earl had Johnny bring Miss Westcott some straggling flowers from the rundown conservatory, on his way to meet a delivery of equipment.

The earl, meanwhile, was rebuilding cottages. According to Sidwell, the outlay in materials, with the workmen already on payroll, would be repaid quickly in increased rent revenues and decreased labor costs. Lord Stanford could take a short-term loan, with the pigs as collateral, for whatever was needed to make the abandoned places habitable.

Increasing his indebtedness did not sound wise to Kerry, but Sidwell was persuasive, and so was Lucy, reminding him of those poor families he'd seen at church, some even his own ex-tenants, who would leap at the chance for a workable, livable farmstead. So Kerry and his squad of footmen turned into shinglers and thatchers, whitewashers, and hammer-wielders. Then there were applications at the bank, interviews with prospective tenants, and endless, useless explanations to Goldy Flint why he wouldn't borrow money from his future stepfather or father-in-law. And there were those few hours, late at night, when he sat with Lucy by the fire, talking of the day's accomplishments, his plans for the morrow. With every family he moved in, every roof he made sound, she took on a new radiance. Her gown was the pink of wildflowers, with long sleeves and a neckline almost to her collarbone, with lace and flowing ribbons. She wore a wreath of twined violets in her strawberry-blond hair.

The earl sent Johnny back to Miss Westcott's, begging her apology and making his excuses. "You go, John, you've known her longer; you'll know what to say that won't appear an insult. A note seems cold, and Sidwell would only stutter. Tell her I'll be there tomorrow for sure."

But tomorrow Uncle Nigel came home.

"Never let it be said that Goldy Flint ever does things by half, my lad, no siree."

Lord Stanford wouldn't be saying it, no siree. Not only had the wine merchant fetched Nigel Somerfield home almost overnight, bag and baggage, dressed like a gentleman, but he'd also fetched Nigel's entire French family, in-laws, children, grandchildren. Not only had Goldy seen to Nigel's pardon, he'd also had him made a knight while he was at it.

"Seemed the best to do, quiet down some of the talk, don't you know."

Kerry didn't know how anyone thought to keep an invasion of the Wiltshire countryside by a ménage of French fishermen quiet, but he nodded, inquiring only how Goldy accomplished such a thing.

"That was the easy part. I just said he was my contact on French soil, passing messages to my men about troop strength, planned movements, all that flummery. Said he'd gotten there by accident, which Lud knows was no more than the truth, and stayed on out of service to the country."

"Which country?" Kerry couldn't help asking, watching as the third small child was handed out of the traveling carriage.

"Don't look so worried, nevvy," Uncle Nigel said as he sadly watched Aunt Clara being carried back to the sofa after her third swoon. "I don't mean to stay on and be an embarrassment to anyone. I know there's no way English society can accept this." He waved his hands in a Gallic gesture, encompassing the chattering children and somber adults who were huddled together at the other end of the drawing room, away from the odor of burning feathers.

"I appreciate all you've done, more than I can ever say. You, Kerry, and my new brother-in-law. Oh, I know Goldy ain't any kind of relation to me at all, but he's done more than my own brother ever did. Your father could have searched a little harder, I always felt, Kerry. And I tried to get messages to him. Don't know if any got through, but he never sent any back." Nigel wiped a tear from his eye with a large red handkerchief.

"I never knew, Uncle Nigel, or I would have tried to help."

"I know you would, lad. You were always a good boy. But what could you have done, a little nipper? Besides, that's all water under the bridge. You got Goldy here to lend a hand, and that's all that matters. He's giving us, all of us, passage on one of his ships bound for the West Indies so I can see about that copper mine now that the revolutions there are over. Should be worth a fortune by now. If not, we aim to set up a fishing cartel, Goldy and me. I hear they've got big fish there in the warm waters. Salt 'em and ship 'em, I say."

"But you'll stay awhile? After all these years . . ."

They both looked to where the countess and Goldy were helping Clara back to her feet.

"No, no amount of explaining will make what I did come right, not even with a *sir* before my name.

Clara never cared for things like that, no more than I did. I just wanted to come by to thank you, and to see . . . once more . . . and to beg forgiveness." Tears were streaming down Nigel's weathered face. Kerry had to turn away lest his own watery eyes betray him. "I'll . . . I'll be getting out of your life again."

Aunt Clara had tottered over on Goldy's arm. She reached out a trembling hand and touched Nigel's cheek, brushing away a tear. "But you've never been out of my life, dearest."

Kerry and his mother shepherded everyone out of the room so the reunited pair could have some privacy. The dowager and Goldy led the adults away to the dining room for a hastily prepared luncheon, and the earl gathered his small charges for a foray on the kitchens. These new cousins of his spoke a French like nothing his tutors ever taught, but porridge was a universal language, and so were piglets and a puppy afterward.

Aunt Clara decided to travel with Nigel. She couldn't remember a word of her schoolgirl French beyond *j't'aime*, but that was enough. She adored her new children, was eager for a new adventure, and vowed never to let Nigel out of her sight again, even if she had to take up rod and reel.

She would miss Kerry, of course, and the Abbey where she'd spent the last twenty years, and that kind gentleman who kept her company so many lonely nights. Waving her handkerchief out of the coach window, she made Kerry repeat his vow to offer comfort to the poor fellow.

"Yes, Aunt Clara," he called back, "as soon as I take care of some pressing personal matters myself."

He rode straight off to Westcott Hall, Lucky frisking and barking at Hellraker's heels again now that the children were gone. Kerry kept yelling at the foolish mutt to shut up, the noise was giving him a headache.

Miss Westcott was shopping in Farley. Did he want to wait? No, the earl had too many other matters to attend to, and once a woman started shopping, who knew how long she'd be? He'd call again the next day.

And he whistled all the way home. What headache?

Lord Stanford's headache returned that afternoon when his mother announced they were expected at Lady Prudlow's for a dinner honoring her and Sir Goldy's betrothal. Kieren could not dare refuse, she declared, lest people think he disapproved of her engagement. Besides, the Westcotts would be there, and what in the world was he thinking of, making that poor girl the butt of wagers and cruel jests?

All the neighbors were there at the dinner, along with the vicar, some tonnish houseguests of the younger Prudlows', a few sporting gentlemen up for Westcott's hunt, and a gaggle of ladies of a certain age come to bear old Lady Prudlow company in the country fastness.

They were all waiting, wondering when the rake would retire from the bachelor lists, watching to see when he'd ask Felicia to stroll through the portrait gallery or amble among the potted palms in the conservatory. Tarnation! Kerry felt he was back in the gun room with all those dead creatures staring at him through glassy eyes. Hang it, he was not going to conduct his engagement like a side show at the local fair. Besides, he'd forgotten to bring the deuced ring.

So Kerry stayed on with Ralph Norris long after the gentlemen rejoined the ladies after port, continuing their discussion of winter wheat. Felicia was already at the pianoforte, Johnny turning pages, while the Prudlow girls sang. So the earl chatted with Major Lawrence about the local terrain, with the dowager Duchess of Farnham about her rheumatics, and with the vicar about cushions for the church pews. He even took his turn singing with the others, but he did not take Felicia on a turn about the room.

"I have an appointment to call on her tomorrow, Mother," he said, resting his aching head back on the squabs during the carriage ride home. The countess did not make too many disparaging remarks about his mental capacity or his manhood, just enough that he proposed she and Goldy move up the date for their own wedding.

At home, the earl found that he could not sleep. Lucy hadn't come, so he decided to go exploring and satisfy his vow to Aunt Clara. He wrapped his dressing gown more securely around him, put an extra candle in his pocket, and set out for the east wing and the second earl.

He didn't see the haunt, but he did see stars shining through the ceilings, bird droppings on some of the warped floors, and at least one bat. Devil a bit, this was more than he and a handful of amateur handymen could fix. Such a mess needed architects, engineers, skilled carpenters, and plasterers. Since he didn't require the rooms, especially with Aunt Clara and his mother moving out, and couldn't afford their upkeep, it might be better to tear the east wing down. Then again, the whole blasted thing might fall down of its own accord before he had the wherewithal to make repairs.

Kerry hefted a fireplace poker over his head to check one ceiling for dry rot. It was there, all right, enough so his slight disturbance brought half the plasterwork down on his head.

Now he had a headache for sure. As he lay on the ground, waiting for the dust to clear and the room to stop spinning, he thought he saw a gentleman in doublet and hose step out of the wainscoting. He shook his head, which was a definite mistake, for a black curtain came down over his eyes.

"Thou hast done well, lady. I never bethought myself the varlet could be brought to duty and honor."

"Oh, he only needed a nudge, my lord," Lucy answered. "He's a fine man, truly."

"I doth not contradict a lady. 'Struth, shalt indeed be an heir soon?"

"The good Lord willing. I am sure Lord Kieren is."

"Hmm. He looks a bonny lad, not unlike mine own self in bygone days. Why is he garbed like the veriest hired mourner, forsooth, in those somber hues? Lady Clara had reason and respect for her widow's weeds. What hath this scoundrel?"

"Your many-times-great-grandson is considered a nonpareil, Lord Stanford. Those dark colors are the height of fashion."

"Fie on fashion! The knave depresseth mine eyes. And thou, my lady, with thy gown buttoned chin to toe, might be in a nunnery. Bah! Hast thou told him about me?"

"No, my lord. I tried, but he has been too concerned with other matters."

"He be as thick-headed as ever, but thou art too much the Lady Fair to speak it."

Lucy chuckled. "I believe it would take a miracle to change his stubbornness, not just a tiny push."

"A kick in the noble posterior might do it. Too bad the jobberknoll doth not know what a treasure he possesseth."

Kerry tried to raise his head to say that he did know. He knew without a doubt that Lucy was the best thing that ever happened to him. And he tried to ask the old gentleman if there was aught he could do about it, but his tongue wouldn't find the words and the mist wouldn't clear from his brain.

Chapter Twenty-two

"If you had to choose between love and duty, my lord, which would you select?"

"What is this, Lucy, an oral examination to pass through the Pearly Gates?"

A cold rain falling through the new hole in the east wing's ceiling had woken Kerry. He'd stumbled down the hall, covered in plaster dust, moaning. Cobb the butler lost two years from his life. This morning the earl had awakened much too early when his valet entered to find piles of reddened towels and blood on his sleeping—or murdered—master's head. Derek's shrill cries had the earl off his mattress and lunging for a weapon to defend the household against marauding Huns. Naked.

Derek ran off, his hand over his mouth, before he disgraced himself further. So now Kerry was trying to dress himself for his morning call. Rain was still falling in torrents, his hair would never cover the gash on his forehead, and Miss Westcott was waiting. Kerry was not in the mood for metaphysical word games.

Lucy tried again, although she was distracted by

watching him shave, the way he lifted his chin and turned to the mirror, just so. "Um, well, if two people loved each other very much but you had the power to come between them, and felt it was your duty to do so, would you weigh their happiness against your honor?"

"Cut line, Lucy. All this roundaboutation isn't like you. How can I answer when I don't know the circumstances? Like if I saw a couple eloping, would I cry rope on them? Why should I if they don't mind facing the scandal?"

"But if one of the elopers were your own fiancée?"

He put down the razor and turned to her, his face half covered in lather. "Just what are you saying?"

Lucy studied the buttons at her wrists. "Felicia and Johnny Norris. They love each other and have since they were children playing together."

"And they are eloping?"

"Oh, no, they would never do what I did. Miss Westcott is too aware of the impropriety and Johnny has too much honor to bring her such disgrace."

"But he doesn't have enough honor to offer in form?" Kerry asked angrily.

Lucy shrugged. "He knew he would have been refused. Besides, he cannot provide for her. No man of integrity would offer love in a cottage to the woman he adored."

"Instead, he'll make me a cuckold, is that it?"

"How could you even think that of John Norris? He's your friend! And much too honorable to even consider such a thing as making love to another man's wife, or wife-to-be."

"You're right. I was judging him by myself. Johnny Norris is too fine a man. But what about Felicia?"

"She loves him, but she knows her duty, too. A wealthy marquis's daughter does not marry a land steward or a half-pay officer."

"Instead, she'd marry a half-mad earl and we'll all be miserable," he said in bitter tones.

"No, you are all reasonable adults. You will all try to make the best of things. Felicia would never show her unhappiness; Johnny would never wear his heart on his sleeve; and you would never have known if I hadn't told you."

"Then why did you, dash it? I thought you wanted me to marry a fortune, settle down, try to be generally faithful, beget my heirs."

"I did. I do. But I want your happiness also. I thought you could find it with Miss Westcott. I was wrong, for you cannot be happy considering your own well-being ahead of their chance for love."

"Not even for the Westcott fortune? You had me damned near convinced I could." He furiously wiped his face with a towel, spattering lather at the mirror. "And what about you if I do not fulfill my obligations, marry well, and secure the succession? What happens to your chances if I am not a reformed character?"

Lucy twisted the ribbons of her gown between her hands. "I don't know, but I am willing to take the chance." His happiness was worth any sacrifice to her.

"Well, I am not, damn it! We can all be comfortable, you said it yourself. And there's no guaranteeing that if I don't drop the hanky Johnny will, or will be accepted, so that's a bad gamble against your odds of success. If I gave up Miss Westcott, I'd really only be giving up the money. Even I know money isn't everything; just look at the fortunes that have drifted through my hands these past days. But you, you are talking about eternity!"

"If the money is the only reason for offering, you should never do it! Give her up, Kerry," she begged. "I told you I was wrong. Happiness does not have to be forfeited for duty, and I do not mean just Felicia and Johnny's happiness. You deserve the opportunity to find your own true love someday, too."

Someday seldom came twice. A hard knot formed in Kerry's chest, squeezing down. If he couldn't marry where he wished, what matter whom he wed? What did any of it matter?

"I'll think about it," he told her, turning back to complete his shave. The water was as cold as the chill in his heart.

He should have taken the closed coach in this confounded never-ending rain, but the horses were ancient and the dowager's driver was older than that. In London the earl would not have given a second thought for the hackney driver he'd have hired, sitting out in the teeming downpour. Here, people's feelings had to be considered, their welfare taken into account. Now he was having to be responsible for their blasted happiness!

Felicia and her mother were waiting for him in the parlor, embroidery in their laps. He admired the fancy work, commented on the wretched weather, and gratefully accepted a glass of sherry after his cold, wet ride. A polite interval later, Lady Westcott recalled a message for her housekeeper and excused herself.

How civilized, Kerry thought: the heiress trigged out in style, the chaperone conveniently gone missing, the father likely down the hall cleaning a pistol. He took a deep breath.

"Miss Westcott, do you know why I have asked for an interview this morning?"

"Yes, my lord, I think I do." She seemed uncertain whether to continue with her embroidery or to stuff it away somewhere. Kerry ended her confusion as to the proper mien for entertaining a proposal by lifting the cloth out of her hands and sitting beside her on the couch. He wanted to see her face.

"And do you wish to marry me, Miss Westcott?"

"I am deeply cognizant of the great honor you do

me, my lord," she recited, having that part down pat.

"But that is not what I asked, Miss—blast it, Felicia. I am asking if you would rather I didn't ask, if you would rather marry someone else."

She stared at her hands, the correct, reserved beauty not having a suitable response to such an inquiry. "My lord?"

"Fiend seize it, do you love Johnny Norris?"

Felicia grabbed back her embroidery and started setting fast, furious stitches. "My lord Stanford, you offered for me, and my papa said he accepted for me. That is all that need concern you."

"As I told your father, I prefer to do my own asking. And I do believe it concerns me that my intended might be wishing me to Jericho. Call it vanity if you will—I know that's a great sin of mine; I am working to improve—but my pride does not gracefully accept being a female's second choice."

"Mr. Norris has never sought my hand. We are friends, that's all."

"But do you love him?" he persisted, tipping her chin up so she was forced to meet his penetrating gaze. "Please, I must know the truth. Now is not the time for those social lies, for saying what you think I wish to hear, or what is correct for the situation. I swear no one shall ever know what we discussed here. Do you love Johnny Norris?"

She whispered it. "Yes."

"And would you accept him if he did ask for your hand in marriage? Please be honest, my dear, all our lives depend on it."

"He refuses to ask," she snapped. "He thinks of himself as less of a man, now that he's lost his arm. He cannot ride to the hunt, and swears that was all that commended himself to me in the first place, the gudgeon, since he has neither title nor money. As if I didn't have enough money for both of us, or cared only about foolish titles. He says he is not good enough for me."

"When we both know he's one of the finest, bravest men anywhere."

"He will not listen." She dabbed her eyes with a scrap of lace.

Kerry patted her hand. "It's hard for a man to swallow his pride. We seem to have such a surfeit of it."

"Well, it is hard for a female to wait, dwindling into an old maid, seeing all your friends marry and start their nurseries, listening to your parents despair."

"It would be worse to marry without affection, to live your whole life without love. And you cannot have thought of your pain living so close to him. He'll eventually marry, have children of his own. You'd see him at church, at parties, and you'd always wonder what might have been."

She was biting her lip to keep from crying. Kerry handed her his own handkerchief, more practicable for such a damp day. "I'd hate like hell having my wife wishing I were another man."

"I wouldn't—"

"If you loved him, you couldn't help yourself."

The earl got up and poured a glass of wine for Felicia and another for himself.

She started: "But my father . . ."

"I'll say we decided we wouldn't suit."

"No, he'll never allow that. If you ask, I have to accept."

"I haven't asked, have I? What could be easier? I'll tell him I changed my mind, that I decided I really don't wish for leg shackles at this time. So wearying in the country, don't you know," he drawled in a dandy's affected tones, "away from the tables and the ladies."

Felicia encouraged him with a watery smile, so he went on: "Why, when I'm finished, he'll be thrilled to welcome a steady character like our

Johnny. No reckless past, no unsavory habits, no worries of him gambling away your inheritance. I'll even throw in a hint or two about Uncle Nigel returning to live with me."

"And all those children?"

"Marvelous, ain't it, what a little scandal can do? Your father will be relieved to see a real hero ride up to your door. Besides, he's no fool. Getting such a dab hand as steward for free is no mean feat."

"But will he get him? I mean, this is all very pleasant speculation, but what happens when Johnny does not propose?"

"Oh, he will. First I'll dismiss him. That should send him either here or back to the gin bottle. If he thinks to head for the decanter, I'll tell him you are pining away for him, in a veritable decline. If he still doesn't make the push, I'll break his arm."

"My lord! He has only one arm!"

"So it will be an easier task than I thought. I'll guarantee he shows his handsome phiz at your door, and leave the rest to you. A slightly compromising situation . . . ?" At her gasp he said, "No, I didn't think so. No matter, those tear-filled blue eyes ought to wring his heart, and that trembling lip you showed me a moment ago. And if you'll just swear you won't accept anybody else, but will wither away like the last leaf of autumn, he'll come 'round." He smiled at her, teasing, but then grew serious again. "Uh, there isn't another nobleman waiting in the wings somewhere by any chance, trading taxidermy tips with the marquis or anything? Viscount? Baron? Lowly baronet?"

"No, you were Papa's last hope for a title, my lord."

"Thank goodness, or I'd have to break their arms, too."

Felicia's lips twitched, her polite mask restored. "But what about you, my lord? You are showing gallant selflessness, but you did ask Papa for permission to pay your addresses. Shall you be very disappointed?"

"Shall I mind being the spurned lover?" Kerry brushed a speck of lint off his sleeve. "Shall I drown my sorrows in the fleshpots of London, preying on your conscience? I understand that half the gentlemen in town have thrown themselves at your feet, so naturally you might worry about my wounded sensibilities. Do not, for I have none. I beg your pardon for being blunt, ma'am, but my heart was not involved, no more than yours. And do not attribute any great nobility to me, my dear, for the sacrifice, though great in light of your abundant charms, is mostly mercenary. That, I am assured you will agree, is an unworthy sentiment."

"I don't care what you say, Lord Stanford, I think you have been wondrously noble, a true friend to Johnny and myself. And you must have tender sensibilities whether you admit them or not, else you'd never understand our plight. You'd never place our happiness over your material considerations. Few men would. I think your heart *is* involved, just elsewhere."

The earl's silent study of the tassel on his Hessian boot was confirmation enough.

"You must love her very much."

"Yes, I'm afraid I do."

"But you do not offer for her?"

Kerry just shook his head.

"Then I hope everything comes right for you and your lady whatever the impediments, the way you have made things possible for Johnny and me."

"No, it can never be made right. She is . . . You might say she is from a different world."

Chapter Twenty-three

Kerry and the stallion slogged back home through the continuing downpour. Instead of heading straight for the stables and a hot bath, the earl directed Hellraker toward the south edge of the property, where Johnny and the men were working on the drainage ditch despite the rain.

"Pack it in," Kerry yelled over the raging storm. "The men are all soaked through, and none of you will be any good to me if you all come down with inflammation of the lungs. Besides, this land has been flooded since Englishmen were painting themselves blue. One more storm won't make a ha'penny's difference."

The workers cheered considerably when he told them to go on home, change into dry clothes, and have an afternoon holiday at his expense. He poured a handful of coins into work-roughened hands. "Go warm yourself with Ned's mulled ale at the pub if you wish. Just be ready to work even harder tomorrow."

Johnny took a little more convincing to aim in the right direction.

"Don't let your foolish pride stand in the way, man," Kerry shouted to be heard. "Pride won't keep you warm at nights, or sit by your fireside, or give you children."

"But you want her!" Johnny protested.

"No, I only wanted a rich, well-bred, well-behaved, and beautiful bride. Felicia happened to fill the bill. That doesn't mean I want her, or need her. Not like you, who need her to be your other half. And she needs you, too. She loves you, man!"

Johnny kept arguing about misalliances and unequal matches until Kerry almost did plant him a facer. "It's pouring rain, damn you, and I swear mildew is forming inside my boots! Will you listen to yourself going on how you love her too much to ruin her life? Would you be happy with another woman?"

"No, of course not," Johnny swore, hunched over in his oilskin.

"Then why the hell do you think any less of her love? Would you consign her to a life with a man she hardly knows, bearing his children, barely tolerating his touch? If you love her so much, why don't you want her happiness above all?"

"She won't be happy without a title."

"Gammon, that's Lady Westcott speaking, not Felicia." He tried to snap his fingers, but they were too wet to make a sound. "That," he said anyway, "for Lady Westcott's ambitions. Her daughter's wishes should come first. Besides, titles are not as thick on the ground here in the country, and Lady Westcott says she wants Felicia nearby. Dash it, all they have to do is speak to Goldy Flint on your behalf. He's getting Prinny to hand out knighthoods as if they were ices from Gunther's."

"What about the marquis, then?"

"Westcott's desperate for a trustworthy estate manager, someone he can leave in charge while he rids the countryside of anything that walks, runs, flies, or crawls. He was relieved, I swear to you, to see the back of me. Felicia is a fine girl, much too good for a ne'er-do-well like me, and he knew it. I'd have made her life a misery, Johnny, without even trying. You'll try every minute of your life to see to her care and comfort. That's the way it should be."

Johnny finally rode off, grinning like a May Day fool instead of a sodden ex-soldier. "Kiss the bride for me," Kerry shouted after him. "And stay the night if they'll put you up. The roads were already getting treacherous when I came through."

The dowager had left a message with Cobb. She was going into Farley with Goldy to see the printer about wedding invitations. If she was not back that evening, he was not to worry, as Sir Goldy forecast the storm continuing. They might be forced to stay overnight at the inn there.

How nonsensical for them to set out under such conditions, Kerry thought, and how marvelously wicked. He raised his glass of hot spiced wine in salute. "Good for them!"

"Yes, I think it will be," Lucy agreed. "And I believe Felicia and Johnny will be very well pleased with each other."

"So that just leaves me and my mountain of mortgages. Any other heiresses I should cultivate? Other than the Prudlow girls, by George. I am not desperate enough for that."

"Perhaps now is a good time to speak about the second earl?"

"Is it a sad story?"

"Of course it is. How do you think he came to be a ghost otherwise?"

Kerry sipped from his glass. "Then I don't want to hear it. Not tonight. Tonight is for celebrating."

Lucinda was as relieved as the earl at his narrow escape from marriage to Felicia, so she did not press the topic. Not tonight.

Tonight, with the sound of the rain against the windows and the fire burning brightly, Lord Stanford taught Lucy how to play chess. He laughed uproariously at her efforts to move the pieces, before shifting the ivory men according to her instructions. Then she bested him at Concentration, for he couldn't concentrate on matching pairs at all, not when he was studying her instead of the cards.

Lucy was in near white tonight, with just a tinge of blush. Her gown seemed to be made of layer upon layer of some gossamer stuff that shimmered as she moved, showing baby roses strewn here and there. Another rosebud nestled in spun-gold curls clustered around her face, which was thinner now, more finely drawn. And her eyes that were once a siren's mermaid-green were now spring-soft and gold-flecked, with the innocence of a fawn. She was the most beautiful creature he had ever seen, more beautiful even than the Lucy who'd first appeared to him like a figment of his richest, most sensual imagination. He stared and stared, trying to absorb every facet of her incredible loveliness.

He never knew that, later, Lucy watched him sleep, memorizing him in turn.

A huge crash woke the earl. That and his bed shaking beneath him. The roof of the east wing had finally collapsed under the pressure of the incessant wall of water beating down on it. Kerry and Cobb took lanterns, but the passageways were too dangerous to investigate. Who knew when walls might cave in on them or floors give out? There was nothing to be done about it now, at any rate, and they could just as easily assess the damage in the morning, when the rain must eventually stop.

Unable to get back to sleep and already damp from his excursion to the disaster area, Kerry decided to check on the stable. With the head groom half deaf and the old coach driver half dead and the young grooms likely in the village with the workmen, there was no one left to calm the horses made nervous by the crash. The carriage horses were fast asleep, and the pony and mare were placidly chewing their hay, but Hellraker was kicking his stall's door and pounding against the side walls. The stallion's upset was not helped by the imbecilic pup's frenzied barking.

Those two were never going to settle, Kerry decided, so he may as well go check the pigs. He had no idea what he could do if the sows were agitated over the storm, but he saddled Hellraker, donned an oilskin coat, and took up a lantern.

The trails and paths were much worse, if they were passable at all. It was as if every brook and stream in all of Wiltshire were overflowing its banks, right onto the earl's land. The winter crop was a foot underwater, washed away. The major road was a quagmire, unsafe for man or beast, where it wasn't swept away altogether or blocked with fallen tree limbs. No one would be coming back from the village this night.

Hellraker cleared every obstacle, of course, and leapt muddy rivers as if they were puddles. But the dog got left behind, barking. "Go on home," Kerry shouted. "I'm not fishing you out of any more watery graves." But the dog kept barking and Hellraker balked at the next downed tree, almost sending Kerry flying over his head. "Hell and damnation!" he swore, but went back for the mongrel. He tucked Lucky under the oilskin coat and tightened the belt around him, because he had no free hand, what with the reins and the lantern. "Hang on!" he ordered, and sent the horse forward again.

He could hear the hogs long before he could see them, squealing like banshees even over the storm's din. Nervous, hell, the sows were frightened out of their wits, and rightfully so. Half their enclosures were underwater, and what dry ground was left was shrinking fast.

The earl was too stunned to curse. His collateral, his future, was about to float away. He didn't even know if pigs could swim, but he knew this wasn't the time to find out, not in a raging cyclone of a storm. The water had to be rechanneled away, back to the drainage ditch which, devil take it, was not complete. Or the pigs had to be gotten to higher ground. There was the barn where the fodder was kept, but it was a long, muddy field away. In the dark.

The earl wasn't a praying man. He didn't approve of those folks who petitioned the Almighty for help when it served their purposes, and ignored Him otherwise. So "Lucy!" he cried. "Where are you. I need a miracle!"

Miracles were about as common as hen's teeth that night. Lucy didn't come, and the situation was not improving for the earl's sitting there looking at it. He believed, in fact, that the water had visibly risen in the brief time since his arrival. Surely the pigs' caterwauling was louder as their feet got wetter.

Think, Kerry, think, he told himself. Then he told himself not to waste time on fruitless ventures, just do *something*. Anything. So he rode for the old barn until even Hellraker had trouble lifting his mighty hooves out of the swamp that used to be a productive field. Kerry got down and walked, pulling the horse along after him. Two lanterns hung by the barn's sagging door, so he lit both and surveyed his resources after releasing Lucky and tying Hellraker to the crossbeams. Windfall apples, a corn crib, shovels, bales of hay and straw. Everything he needed to keep his investment warm and fed, could he but get the wretched beasts there. Then he noticed the unused lumber piled near the far wall.

He didn't have time to build a raft, by Jupiter, so he'd better build a bridge. Struggling with planks taller than himself, boards that took two men to maneuver, Kerry proceeded to lay them end to end through the field. They sank nicely into the mud, making a wet but firm surface, except they were not going far enough fast enough. Working frantically, the earl lashed some of the boards together and hitched the line to Hellraker's saddle, calling in his chits.

"You owe me," he yelled at the affronted stallion, "for all the clothes you ruined." At the next trip: "And this is for my broken nose." The black snorted as he slowly picked his way along the laid planks, dragging yet another load behind him, his eyes rolling and ears well back. "And for making me a laughingstock in front of the neighbors," urged the earl.

The last plank was in place, but nowhere near the pigs. Kerry raced back to the barn and grabbed the door off its hinges. In a fury to match the storm's, he used a shovel to pry apart the door's boards, then ran with them back to his makeshift catwalk. Pigwalk.

Almost there. The rear door, a loose-box partition, finally a scattered bale of straw with his oilskin coat thrown on top, and his pigs could hie their little trotters across the mud into the safe and dry barn. He stood gasping for breath, waiting for them to arrive. And waited some more. "Apples," he called. "I've got nice apples for you." Then he cursed. "What, you bastards want stuffed grapes? Or maybe a formal invitation?"

Yelling didn't work, coaxing had no effect whatsoever, and pushing simply succeeded in getting his face flicked with the least appetizing aspect of a hog. Picking up a piglet under each arm and running like a veritable Noah would take Noah's forty days and forty nights, if Kerry could catch the wet, frantic little shoats. And the sows just grunted unhappily. Visions of Tige Welford's trampled body raced through the earl's mind. What an ignominious ending for a peer of the realm, getting ground into the mud by a rasher of ham.

That was when Kerry made an important discovery. Not that the lack of knowledge had bothered him any, but he finally realized what the mongrel hound's other half must have been. One of the mutt's ancestors had to have been the finest sheepdog in all of Britain. If not sheep, then cows or even geese. Kerry didn't care, Lucky could herd pigs!

If every dog had its day, this was Lucky's night. The little dog was running behind the nearest sow, barking and snapping at her heels, getting her moving, keeping her on the wooden pathway. Her babies followed after. Soon there was a line of pigs from the pens to the barn marching single file to the orders of one small yipping cur. Kerry's contribution was in picking up the piglets that slipped off the track into the mire and setting them back on the planks. Between times he ran to the barn to spread more straw, hay, and apples, and settle disputes over which family group claimed which stall or corner of the barn. He was bitten, scratched, and stepped on before Lucky chased the last sow and her brood across the threshold. If there were any stragglers, Kerry could not see them in the darkness, but he'd saved his bacon! He could go home.

He left Lucky guarding his new charges, the dog being too exhausted to complain, and rode out with Hellraker along the planks. And that's when he made another important discovery: the planks were no longer sitting in mud, they were underwater. The floods were still rising, and getting closer and closer to the barn. "No!" Kerry shouted into the stormswept night before his lantern went out.

Chapter Twenty-four

"No!" Kerry raged again when he finally reached the Abbey. The rain hadn't let up and no help had returned. Hermes knew how many porkers he'd already lost, but they'd all be gone by morning at this rate, if they weren't already chilled and sickening.

"It isn't fair!" he ranted, shaking his fist at Lucy, who sat desolate on the window seat in the library, staring at the sheets of rain. "I worked so hard, as hard as I ever could. And for what? I tried, Lucy, you know how dashed hard I tried to do things right, to be a 'good' man. Look what good it has done me!"

He tossed his wineglass into the hearth, only fractionally satisfied by the shattering crystal. "Where's the justice, Lucy? Where's the reward for good behavior? You were so busy looking for a code of conduct, an eternal truth. Well, I'll tell you how life really operates: by the law of the jungle, that's how. Dog eat dog. The strong prey on the weak. Winner takes all. And I lost, Lucy."

"But you didn't, Kerry. You can't know—"

"Oh, I know I'm sounding like a petulant child sent early to bed when his older brother gets to stay up longer, but it's so deuced cruel to have come so close and see it all washed away. And do not, if you have any sympathy for me at all, tell me that nobody promised that life was fair."

"Perhaps this is just a test, you know, like Job?"

"To see how much punishment I can take before I throw in my hand? What's next, locusts? Or was it boils? No matter, I fail. I fold. I quit. As soon as the rain stops, I'll be on my way back to London and my life of indolence. There's a lot to be said for pleasure-seeking, Lucy. You should try it sometime. Parties and plays, races and drunken revels. Elegant clothes that don't get ruined the minute you step out the door. And women. Oh, yes, women. Females I can pay in pound notes and pearls, not with my title and freedom."

"You cannot mean that, Kerry. You were much happier here, with a sense of purpose and accomplishment."

This time he threw his fist at the fireplace, and derived little more satisfaction at the pain. "I mean it, Lucy. All I've accomplished is to give people a false sense of hope. You, too. So after I leave, you can go to your friends and *you* can be the one to complain of the injustice, that they linked your fate with a hopeless libertine. You never had a chance, poor innocent, and for that I am sorry, but I'm getting out of here."

He left, but not for London. He went back out into the storm as soon as he had dry clothes and hot coffee. Wishing the pony cart stood a chance of getting through, the earl had to be content with loading more lanterns, a pistol, and some sacks on Hellraker's still-damp back. He may as well fetch home breakfast before he left, Kerry told himself. And he couldn't leave Lucky out there after the dog's valiant efforts, especially when he knew the mutt couldn't swim.

The ride took even longer this time, the stallion being almost spent. Hellraker still didn't like getting his feet wet though, so they got there, and the old barn was still standing.

And they were not alone. Everyone was there, the laboring footmen, the young grooms, his tenants new and old, Johnny and some men in Westcott's livery, Ned from the pub and Charlie the blacksmith. Even the vicar was filling grain sacks with dirt and handing them down the line to be placed around the old barn's foundation. Some of the men were lifting Kerry's gangplank and carrying the lumber to shore up the drainage ditch; others were busy with shovels, excavating new riverbeds for the water to fill.

Over Lucky's joyful greeting, Kerry swore he heard harp music, slightly out of tune.

And lilacs. The sound of harps and the smell of lilacs. And a wet, cold nose in his ear.

"Get off the bed, damn you." The earl pushed Lucky away. "Just because I said you could sleep upstairs where it was warm didn't mean my bed, you boneheaded mutt. You weren't that much of a hero!"

Lucky wagged his tail and bounded off. Kerry opened his eyes. The sun was in them; Derek must have been in earlier to open the curtains. And put flowers in his room? Not even Derek would go so far. Besides, lilacs in November? He raised his head.

Lucy was at the foot of his bed, bathed in the sun's glow so that he had to squint to get a good look at her. She was all in white, adding to the glare, and she was trailing flowers. She was smiling like the cat in the cream pot, dimples and all.

"All right, so I stayed," he grumbled. "Don't get

your hopes up. I may still leave when the roads dry out."

She shook her head and smiled fondly. "No, I am the one who is leaving. I came to say good-bye."

Kerry sat up, then pulled the covers over his bare chest when he saw her look away. "What do you mean, leaving? You can't go yet. Why—"

"But my time is up, my lord. You knew I was only here for a short time."

"But your job is not done yet! I have no heir, no wife waiting to be fruitful and multiply the Somerfield brood."

"You'll find the perfect girl in time. I've seen how you love children, and how Diccon and the little French cousins idolized you. You'll be a fine father."

"No, I'll have a relapse without you here as my conscience. I'll . . . I'll get foxed and seduce both the Prudlow granddaughters."

Lucinda laughed. "You'd have to be very castaway indeed."

"I'll return to London on the instant, I swear," he tried in desperation.

"No, you love the land and people here now. You'll stay and see them bloom under your care. Then you'll return to London when it's time to take your seat to speak out against poverty and climbing boys and cast-off veterans."

Kerry ran his hands through his uncombed curls. "Lucy, you can't go yet! I'm no paragon of virtue. Goddamn it, I'm not," he shouted as proof.

"No, you are not," she agreed with a little laugh, "but you do have a good heart that will see you through anything. You don't need me anymore."

"Then stay because I want you, not because I need you. Please."

"I would stay if I could, you must know that, Kerry, but I have no choice."

Kerry tried to dredge up more convincing arguments, but he knew he was wasting his time. That glow around her didn't come from the sun; it was still raining. And Lucy's radiant smile wasn't because he was half naked in bed, or because he saved the pigs.

"Oh, Lucy," he sighed.

"It's better that I go now anyway," she said, trying to cheer him. "You know I couldn't have borne the time when the piglets had to go to market."

He did manage a smile at that, the slightest lifting of his lips. "Whatever shall I do without you?"

"You might try talking to the second earl. He really has a fascinating tale about when the east wing was built."

"To hell with the east wing and the second earl! They're both rubble by now."

"Kerry, don't be angry. You'll forget in time."

"Never!" he swore.

"Then remember the best times, that's what I shall do. How you taught me to waltz, and gave me my first curricle ride, and how handsome you looked riding Hellraker the first time."

"With my nose broken? That was a good time? I always said you had some devilish queer notions."

She laughed. "Then what are your best times?"

The earl thought a moment before saying: "Your smile when we waltzed, and your delight when you were up in the curricle, and how beautiful you looked when I first met you." He could not speak past the lump in his throat. He paused, swallowed. "But mostly how you look today. Perfect."

"Because of you and your goodness. You wanted so badly to show me the pleasures of life, and you succeeded. I would have no happy memories to treasure without you."

"Dash it, Lucy, I only wanted to corrupt you, at first. And if you're so happy, why are there tears on your cheeks?"

"Why are there tears on yours?" she answered softly.

He fumbled for a handkerchief on the bedstand and impatiently brushed at his eyes. "Soot from the chimney. We never did get the thing properly cleaned."

She sniffled. "Me, too."

"Oh, God, Lucy, I cannot bear to say good-bye. You are like a part of me, the best part of me."

"I know. You are the song that sings in my heart."

He gave a watery chuckle. "Off-key." Then he reached out, trying to touch her. She stretched her hand out toward him.

"Perhaps we'll meet again," she whispered.

"Do you think so?"

"I'll pray that it be. Farewell, my dearest. I will always love you."

Their fingers almost met. Almost.

Chapter Twenty-five

"What do you mean, barging into Fairview Manor like this? I won't have any havey-cavey doings, even if you brought along a man of the cloth. Our own vicar's already come and gone."

"Gone?" Lord Stanford cried out. "Lucy's not. . . ? She couldn't be, I would have known somehow."

"Lucy?" Sir Malcolm Faire demanded. "Do you mean my daughter Lucinda, sirrah?"

"She lives?" It was all he could do not to take the older man's scrawny neck between his hands and shake him until his teeth rattled. "Tell me she lives!"

Sir Malcolm sneered. "She lives. Though how it concerns a here-and-thereian like yourself is beyond reason." He surveyed his caller's gleaming Hessians, the high shirt collar, and embroidered waistcoat. "What could a London fribble"—he consulted the calling card still in his hand—"like the Earl of Stanford have to do with that miserable wench upstairs who refuses to let go her hold on the thinnest thread of life?"

At the shocked inhalation of the vicar at Kerry's

side, Sir Malcolm ground out: "Oh, I make no bones about it. Why wear the cloak of hypocrisy when everyone in the country knows the girl's a wanton, and a murderess besides? The London papers must have given you every sordid detail of my disgrace, so you'd do better to wonder why I even bother with the trappings of mourning." He waved at the crepe-hung mirrors, the black clothes he wore. "It's so the prying neighbors leave me alone in my supposed grief! People with more courtesy than you stay away." He turned to ring for a footman to show them the door. "I say the sooner the girl is in the ground, the sooner my shame can be put behind me."

"But, sir, she is your daughter!"

"She is no get of mine!" Sir Malcolm thundered.

The urge to murder the man grew even stronger in Kerry's breast. Only the knowledge that time was running out, that it had taken too long to get to Derby, the roads were so bad, made him refrain. He took a deep breath. Nodding toward the card Sir Malcolm had tossed aside, he reiterated: "I am Kieren Somerfield, Earl of Stanford. I have brought a vicar and a special license, and I have come to marry your daughter."

"What?" Sir Malcolm gasped, growing red of face. "That's outrageous! What perversion is this, with the girl at death's door? And you"—he turned to the vicar—"how could you be part of this blasphemy?"

Kerry answered. "There is no blasphemy, Sir Malcolm, no vile motives. My word as a gentleman."

"Your word? Why should I accept your word, my fancy lord? Oh, yes, I know you by reputation. I wouldn't have let a rakehell like you near Lucinda in the best of times."

"But you'd let that old nipcheese Halbersham near her?" Kerry spat out.

"How did you know about that? It wasn't in any of the London scandal sheets."

"I know. I cannot explain how, but I know it all. Do I have your permission?"

"No, blast you! I know your sort, gamesters and wastrels all. Here you are, dressed to the nines, your nose in the air, and run off your feet. You saw your salvation in the gossip columns and you've come to make a deathbed marriage to a poor, unfortunate heiress. Well, you shan't have the wench, nor a shilling of my money!"

Kerry clenched his fists so tightly, his nails cut through his palms. "If you know my sort, you know I am arrogant and overbearing and used to getting my own way. Pigheaded to a fault. And I wish to marry your daughter for reasons I could never explain and you could never understand. But none of them have to do with your blunt."

Sir Malcolm snorted, unconvinced.

"What did your wealth ever give to Lucy when she was alive and well? Did it buy her pretty dresses and gay parties? Friends her own age or lovesick mooncalfs writing odes to her eyebrows? No. You were so afraid of fortune hunters you kept her from having any of the pleasures a young girl deserves!"

Sir Malcolm looked away, but Kerry persisted: "Your money never made her happy, so keep it now, old man. I do not want a groat from you, only Lucy."

"A wager, that's it, isn't it? It's not my brass you want, it's some other scapegrace's fortune you hope to win. That's why a rackety London buck like you is here offering for a dying girl with no reputation." He nodded to himself, like a vulture bobbing over a carcass.

"If there was a wager, it wasn't mine. Can't you believe I have nothing to gain, except Lucy as my wife? If you have any human feeling at all, let me give her my name. Let me restore her honor in the only way I can."

"Honor, what honor? She has none."

Kerry ignored the other's outburst. "I cannot kill that makebait who ran off with her, for he's already got his just desserts. And I shall not call out a man old enough to be my father, although you tempt me, Sir Malcolm, you really do."

Lucy's father took a step closer to the bellpull. The vicar clucked his teeth.

"Stop, Sir Malcolm," Kerry ordered. "Stop and listen. You know marriage to a peer, any peer, even one below the hatches, restores a girl's reputation. Let me give her my name while there is still time. You don't even want her. You've practically disowned her. So let her come with me. She'll lie with my family in Wiltshire; you won't even have a footstone to remind you that you ever had a daughter."

"And you say you won't make any claim on her portion?"

"If she lives, sign it over to our children."

"Lives? My word, the man is madder than I thought! The physician says it's a miracle she's held on so long. He swears she won't last till dawn."

"Let it be on your head if she dies disgraced. I'll worry about her living."

Kerry had another skirmish on his hands, this time with Lucinda's old nanny, whose gaunt frame blocked the door.

"You cannot come in here. This is a sacrilege, wedding with a woman you never even met."

"But I do know her, ma'am, maybe the way one knows a dream or a figure from a novel, or . . . or a vision. I have no explanation to give you, just that I do know her. I know she is the sweetest, most loving person on earth, and she is being killed by unkindness. And the world would be a poorer place without her in it."

"But my lamb is going to die. I did all I could, spooning broth into her despite *his* orders, but she won't wake up." Nanny brought her apron up to wipe her eyes. "The doctor says it's too late now. She never will."

Kerry's eyes were damp, too. "Then at least I shall honor her memory by recalling all the good she has done, and placing flowers on her grave. She loves flowers, did you know?"

They held the wedding as soon as Nanny threaded some ribbon through Lucinda's shorn curls and got a footman to fetch a bouquet from the indoor gardener.

The Earl of Stanford took Miss Lucinda Faire to be his lawful wife, with two servants as witnesses, Sir Malcolm and his lady being otherwise engaged. Kerry stroked Lucy's limp, emaciated hand and Nanny made the bride's responses, until she got to the part about till death do us part. The vicar had to pause and wipe his spectacles while Nanny wept into her apron.

It was done.

Then Kerry sent Nanny off to bring hot soups, lemonade, sweetened tea. He climbed onto the bed beside Lucy's still form, gathered her frail body into his arms, and began the final battle.

"Hello, angel," he murmured into her ear. "Do you remember me? I'm Kerry, the one who loves you. And you love me. You told me so, do you recall? Don't worry, I'll keep reminding you. I never did get the chance to tell you, my darling, because you left just when I was discovering that I had a heart after all.

"You thought I could live without you, didn't you? You said I'd be fine, but you were wrong. I won't be fine at all. Oh, I won't drink myself into oblivion more than two or three times a week, and I won't return to my licentious ways, because you showed me how empty those passing pleasures are. I won't even fall into mercenary habits, for you showed me things of infinite value, which will be as ashes without you. I'll live, Lucy, but I will not be fine, I will not be complete. If you left, I'd have only half a life, for I need you, sweetheart, to show me the good in everything, to show me the rainbows, to fill those aching voids. I cannot be happy without you, Lucy. And you do care about my happiness, I know you do, for it was you who taught me about caring." He paused to kiss her reed-thin fingers.

"And you must love me very much, for you waited until I got here. Did you know I would come after you? I wish you'd done something about the wretched roads, then." He tried to smile, and tried to get some broth into her. He was awkward, especially with her still in his hold, leaning back against his chest, but he would not put her down or let Nanny wield the spoon. He tucked another towel under Lucy's chin and kept speaking softly.

"Do you remember me now? I am Kerry, the one who loves you. Do you recall when we met and you told me you had no reason to live? Let me be the reason, angel. And our children and the life we can have together. We'll fix up the Abbey. It might take decades, but who knows, we might find another Diccon whose parents will help restore the old pile. And I'll show you all the good parts of London when Goldy and my mother aren't staying in Grosvenor Square. You'll make a splash in the ton, love, in your silks and satins, but I won't let that horde of beaus too near you. I mean to be a doting husband. Very well," he said as though she made comment, "you can call it a jealous husband. Oh, did I tell you that we are married? I didn't even forget the ruby this time, but the ring is too big, so it's back in my pocket. We'll have to fatten you up like the piglets, *mon ange*. And we'll keep every one of the little oinkers if you want. I'll never eat bacon again, I swear."

He fed her some more broth, massaging her throat while she swallowed.

"Do you remember now? No matter, you can hear me, I'm positive, so I'll just keep repeating it until you decide to wake up, my sleeping beauty." But first he kissed her as softly as a butterfly on her dry lips, as if she really were a sleeping princess who could be awakened by a broken-nosed earl who needed a shave. Or as if he would share his very breath with her, the kiss of life.

Kerry talked all night until he was hoarse and after, spooning liquid into her when he could, gently rubbing warmth into her wraithlike limbs.

He told her about the devil's wager and the angel's bargain, about his wicked life and her innocence. He spoke of Demby's lottery and Lucky's near drowning, of the hidden paintings and hiding the fox up a tree. Begging her to remember, the earl related how she made him see the good in Goldy Flint, and the importance of love in Johnny and Felicia.

When he was finished he started over, whispering of his great love for her, his desperate need of her. "I am Kerry, the one who loves you. . . ."

Near dawn, Lucinda's eyes fluttered open. "Nanny?" she called in a voice that was raspy from disuse. She sipped from a glass held to her lips. "Nanny, I had the strangest dream about—why, you're not Nanny," she croaked. "You . . . you're Kerry, aren't you?"

With tears streaming down his cheeks, Kerry tried not to hug her delicate body. "Yes, angel. I am Kerry."

"The one who loves me." It was a fact, not a question.

He managed a shaky laugh. "More than life itself. And you love me, wife," he stated just as firmly.

"More than my hope of heaven." Her brows knit. "But I don't remember any wedding."

"You slept through the first one, so we'll have another as soon as you are strong, darling. At the Abbey with all of our friends."

"Yes, I would like that." Her trembling hand was reaching out to touch his beloved face, his only slightly crooked nose. "Ah, I have been waiting a lifetime to do that. But, Kerry, you are not the man in my dreams."

Kerry's arms stiffened and his jaw tightened. "I'm not?"

"No, he was a funny old man dressed for a masquerade in scarlet tights."

The earl relaxed. "Oh, him. I forgot about the second earl. We'll invite him to the wedding, too, angel."

"But he only wants to tell you about your treasure," she insisted drowsily.

"I'm holding the only thing that is precious, dear heart, and I will cherish it forever." He lowered her back to the pillows, but sat on the bed beside her. "You rest now and we'll talk later."

"But you really have to know."

"I do, I swear. I know all about my treasure, Lucy."

"Oh, good, then you won't tear up the east wing until you find that sack of gold."

Signet Regency Romances from

BARBARA METZGER

"Barbara Metzger deliciously mixes love and laughter." —***Romantic Times***

MISS WESTLAKE'S WINDFALL

0-451-20279-1

Miss Ada Westlake has two treasures at her fingertips. One is a cache of coins she discovered in her orchard, and the other is her friend (and sometime suitor), Viscount Ashmead. She has been advised to keep a tight hold on both. But Ada must discover for herself that the greatest gift of all is true love...

THE PAINTED LADY

0-451-20368-2

Stunned when the lovely lady he is painting suddenly comes to life on the canvas and talks to him, the Duke of Caswell can only conclude that his mind has finally snapped. But when his search for help sends him to Sir Osgood Bannister, the noted brain fever expert and doctor to the king, he ends up in the care of the charming, naive Miss Lilyanne Bannister, and his life suddenly takes on a whole new dimension...

To order call: 1-800-788-6262